**Praise for the sultry, su~~~~~
KYRA DA~~~~~

JUST ONE NIGHT

The instant *New York Times* bestseller!

"Frequent explicit erotic encounters and fantasies keep this page-turner crackling with intensity."

—*Publishers Weekly* (starred review)

"Davis's prose is beautiful and her sex scenes both creative and hot."

—*RT Book Reviews*

"Gives *Fifty Shades of Grey* a run for its money. . . . But this novel gives some depth, respect, and sexual tension to the genre."

—*New York Journal of Books*

"Exceptionally well written, and I enjoyed every second I was with this book. It's intensely sensual, and the sex scenes are incredibly HOT."

—*Sinfully Sexy Book Reviews*

"A quick, fun, and sensual read that left me wanting much more!"

—*Romance Book Junkies*

"Tempting, seductive, and purely romantic."

—*Lovey Dovey Books*

"A refreshing, seductive, and highly enjoyable erotic romance."

—*Totally Booked Blog*

"Filled with the salacious, saucy content you'd expect in *Fifty Shades of Grey*. . . . However, beyond the titillating words and visual sexual images, the underlying story is about the choices women make every day."

—*Miss Wordy*

WORKS BY KYRA DAVIS

THE JUST ONE NIGHT SERIES

Just One Night
"Just Once More"
Just One Lie

THE PURE SIN SERIES

Deceptive Innocence
Dangerous Alliance

JUST ONE LIE

KYRA DAVIS

GALLERY BOOKS

NEW YORK   LONDON   TORONTO   SYDNEY   NEW DELHI

Gallery Books
An Imprint of Simon & Schuster, Inc.
1230 Avenue of the Americas
New York, NY 10020

First Gallery Books trade paperback edition July 2015

GALLERY BOOKS and colophon are registered trademarks of Simon & Schuster, Inc.

For information about special discounts for bulk purchases, please contact Simon & Schuster Special Sales at 1-866-506-1949 or business@simonandschuster.com.

The Simon & Schuster Speakers Bureau can bring authors to your live event. For more information or to book an event, contact the Simon & Schuster Speakers Bureau at 1-866-248-3049 or visit our website at www.simonspeakers.com.

Manufactured in the United States of America

10 9 8 7 6 5 4 3 2 1

Library of Congress Cataloging-in-Publication Data

Davis, Kyra.
   Just one lie / Kyra Davis. — First Gallery Books trade paperback edition.
      pages ; cm
   I. Title.
   PS3604.A972J86   2015
   813'.6—dc23

2015017579

ISBN 978-1-4767-5686-8
ISBN 978-1-4767-5688-2 (ebook)

This book is dedicated to my husband, Rod Lurie.

Writing romances has become much easier

now that I'm living one with you.

CHAPTER 1

❀

December 31, 1999

T HERE IS NOTHING more crushing than the ruin of a perfect moment.

They happen so rarely, those fleeting instants when the energy is sparking and the music is penetrating your heart. And how can the music not be right? I'm the one who's creating it. I'm behind the microphone. It's my voice that fills the rooms of Apocalypse, this little piece of heaven and hell tucked away in the corner of Los Angeles's Sunset and Vine. The crowd is made up of actors and writers and musicians, each one a different vessel for their art, each one moving to my songs, my rhythms, my passions. I can hear Tonio's guitar holding up the sound, increasing its intensity as my voice rises higher and louder. Brad is setting the pace with his bold and dexterous beating of the drums. Traci's fingers on the keyboard add gentle melody when my vocals get rougher, stronger, when my song demands that everyone here feel my sexuality, my strength, the force of my will.

In less than thirty minutes the twenty-first century will begin, and no one knows what will happen. Some think that Y2K will propel Western society into chaos; others worry about terrorists and psychopaths; some say it's the beginning of the end of the world.

And I don't care about any of that. I just don't. I care about the *moment*. I care that I now have streaks of pink woven into my dark blond hair and the words *Carpe Diem* tattooed on the back of my shoulder. I care that the bodies on the dance floor are swaying and shaking, their excitement and approval brilliantly clear in this dimly lit space. I care about the walls of the club that look like they're made of stone and the graceful curvature of the ceiling, arched like a Byzantine cathedral. I can feel the eyes of some of these men on me. That gorgeous black man in the corner, the fair-haired muscle boy dancing so close to the stage, the older gentleman at the bar—they all want me. Because right now I have the dynamism, the control. I have the vitality that everyone wants to touch and share.

It is the perfect moment . . . until I spot him standing near the corner of the room. He's almost entirely in the shadows, his features barely visible, but still, I recognize him. There's something about the way that man holds himself. Right now he's leaning against a beam, his arms crossed over his chest, chin up. Like with a lion, it's difficult to tell if he's on the verge of sleeping or attacking. The first time I saw him—when was that, a year ago? No, over thirteen months since we met—I couldn't stop staring. I loved his high, chiseled cheekbones and his lightly tanned skin that hinted at a possible Native American heritage, or maybe Latino. But then his bright green eyes insisted that the story wasn't so straightforward. Oh, and I loved his tribal tattoos and the way his full lips curved into a slow, sensual smile when he saw me for the first time at that club in Seattle. An aspiring musician is how he described himself, but that night, when he sang to me, I could see that his talent was a lot more than aspirational.

His first name is Ash—maybe it's short for Asher or Ashley, I don't know, and at the time I didn't care. I just recall thinking that a man with a name like that had to have a story to tell, one that involved passion and adventure and yeah, okay, maybe a little destruction. We had talked for hours and I had felt like I understood him in a way that I had never understood anyone else. And then, later, I realized I didn't know a thing about him. All our words and intimacies had left us strangers.

Ash is the stranger who took my life.

One night with him, one night of rapture. That's all it took to put an end to Melody Fitzgerald.

And as if killing me wasn't enough, this son of a bitch has re-appeared and he's fucking with my moment!

I pull my eyes away and find Rick, the owner of the club, stand-ing at the edge of the bar. Next to him is a couple. A man with light brown hair and chiseled chin with his arm wrapped around an ironed-straight blonde with the sinuous figure of a runway model. All these beautiful people are here to see *me*! That's what I have to focus on. Not him. Never, ever him.

And yet, even as I refuse to bring my eyes back to Ash, my mind can't seem to leave him.

The music pushes me forward, forcing me to continue even as I feel my chest tighten. There's not enough air in here for this. How could I have not noticed that before? Tonio jumps into his guitar solo and I use the opportunity to take a deep breath, inadvertently inhaling the unmistakable scent of marijuana floating up from somewhere on the dance floor. Doesn't matter, doesn't matter. None of this can matter, nothing but the music and what it can do. With new resolve I fall back into the song, attacking it with even more ferocity than before. The crowd hears it and loves it.

And now it's me that's moving, across the stage and back again, running, screaming, and the crowd screams right back. This is *every-thing*. But then there he is, leaning against that beam, just . . . watch-ing me. Has he followed me? Isn't one death enough for him? The question stirs up some of the rage I've been trying to set aside since our last meeting. Impulsively I knock the microphone stand to the ground with a smack of my open palm. The crowd thinks it's part of the act and so I go on, finding that I can rejoice in anger as much as any other emotion. As we reach the last stanza, Traci's and To-nio's voices join mine, and the sound is an assault on anyone who would ever dream of challenging us. Maybe tomorrow they'll say I'm a cross between Courtney Love and Fiona Apple. Maybe they'll say the whole band is destined for fame and greatness. Yeah, that's what they'll say, those who are sober enough to remember. But right now they just cheer as our song comes to an end.

"Thank you," I whisper into the mic. I look back at Ash. Even from here I can see that he's clapping, but it's a slow, purposeful movement. He puts his hand to his mouth, kisses his palm, and then extends his arm leisurely toward me. It's not so much that he's blowing me a kiss as he is offering it to me. Inviting me to climb down from my pedestal and take it from him. Again I inhale deeply. "So, I gotta ask you guys something," I continue. "It's the end of an era and you're bringing in the new millennium at Apocalypse listening to a band called fucking Resurrection. Is that tripping anyone else out?" There are yells of approval and at least one person cries *hell yes!* "By the way," I add, "it's really just Resurrection, only our parents call us *fucking* Resurrection." General laughter and one woman screams out, "Parents suck!"

Oooh, if these guys only knew how much I agree with that one. "In case you missed it, this stud on the guitar is Tonio." Tonio strums out a few wrenching chords as the crowd cheers. "The hot chick in the leather mini is Traci." Traci plays the opening piano notes of "Sympathy for the Devil." It's doubtful that this crowd recognizes it even as they whistle and scream for her, but *I* do, and the reference makes me laugh. "And allow me to introduce our new drummer! Brad's only been with us for a week and he's *killing* it, am I right?" The crowd roars as Brad launches into a drum solo that is so intense, so aggressive, and so beautiful I turn my back on the audience, momentarily forgetting all of them, even my killer, as I lock eyes with this man who must have sold his soul for this kind of talent. His lips curve into a little half smile as his sticks fly across the stretched membrane surfaces. Physically he doesn't seem to fit with the rest of the group—too athletic, too clean cut, too aristocratic— but his viciously beautiful rhythm is downright sinful.

When he ends with a perfectly executed clash, I realize for the first time that I've been holding my breath. The crowd cries out, solidifying the triumph as I match his smile with my own and slowly pivot back to the room. "And of course, I'm Mercy. I . . ." but I give up on continuing as the crowd erupts again, drowning me out with their cheers, chanting my name.

My new name, a choice I made for myself only months ago, now reverberating through the room: *Mercy, Mercy, Mercy.* It's on the lips and tongues of everyone in this room . . . except for his. Beneath the harmonious hum of voices, like an insidious undercurrent, I can hear his silent accusations: *That is not who you are. You are not Mercy.*

I swallow and look into the spotlight, letting the light assault my vision, temporarily turning the entire club into a murky blur as the crowd quiets enough for me to speak again. "So we got"—I turn and point to the large red numbers projected by a laser clock onto the wall behind my head—"fifteen minutes until the four horsemen arrive. I'm thinking we better stop wasting time and get back into this!"

The crowd cheers again. I spot Rick giving me a thumbs-up as the rugby guy next to him pumps his fist in the air. And again Tonio strums the strings of his guitar. And again my voice rises high then low, elating the crowd and giving me the fortitude to turn my thoughts away from the beast who watches me from the shadows.

And when it's 11:59 we stop midsong. I hold my hands up in the air and point to the numbers. "It's almost Y2K time, people!" I cry and glance back at Rick, who is staring intently at his watch. And then he lifts his hand and begins to tick off the seconds with his fingers as I count them down into the mic, "Ten, nine, eight . . ."

The crowd's counting with me. ". . . seven, six . . ." The pretty blonde has pressed herself against her rugby companion, her lips hovering inches from his. ". . . five, four . . ." The beautiful black man has raised his glass in the air; a young woman behind him scrambles on top of the bar with a small video camera in her hand. ". . . three . . ." The muscle boy is pounding his fist against the stage. ". . . two, one!"

And the room erupts. Confetti flies everywhere and the kind of fragmented light that comes from a disco ball splashes across the celebrants. Tonio pops a bottle of cheap champagne he'd been hiding in the wings and douses everyone in the band with it before passing it around. I let the bubbles tickle my tongue, then turn back to the microphone and launch into a happier, more celebratory tune. The people standing beneath us have woven together like vines against the wall, limbs tangled with limbs, lips against lips. There is no separation, no individual distinctions. They have all become a snarled mass of exhilaration and lust.

Except for Ash. He continues to just stand there, apart from all of it. He's simply watching me. Waiting for me to come to him and claim my kiss.

And I want it. I want the kiss of my killer.

CHAPTER 2

❀

W E PLAY UNTIL one in the morning. That's when Tonio finally lays down his guitar and I throw my arms in the air in surrender. More cheers and catcalls as we leave the stage. An Offspring dance remix pounds through the speakers for those who want to stay here till two.

Traci's on-again, off-again bleached blond and heavily tattooed boy-friend, Ben, known to all of us as Benji, is waiting for us in the wings with Rick. Rick pulls me to him, lifting me in the air. "You were on fire!"

"It was all of us," I say almost absently, "and the crowd was perfect." My mind is still on Ash. Perhaps his name shouldn't appeal to me at all. After all, when people say everything turns to ash, what they mean is that everything is a complete mess.

In that case, Ash should be *my* name. A Complete Mess . . . it could be the title of my autobiography.

Rick releases me and enthusiastically shakes Tonio's hand as Traci pushes past Brad and throws her arms around Benji. "You rocked it, Trace," he says in the few seconds he has before Traci plants her lips on his for a passionate kiss. "I got some really cool shots," he adds, although the disposable camera in his hand casts doubt on his claim.

"Group picture!" Traci squeals and grabs my hand and Tonio's, pulling us to either side of her as Brad comes to my side, leaning in without actually touching me as we all face the camera. Benji takes the picture and then tries to hand the camera to Traci, but she waves it away. "I'm always losing those things, baby. Give it to Mercy."

Without a word I accept the camera, cradling it in both hands as each member of our band drifts back to their previous position.

"You guys are welcome to stay," Rick says, his face pink with drink and adrenaline. "Whatever you want from the bar, it's on me."

"My kind of party!" Traci laughs, now pressing her eager lips to Rick's flushing cheek as Benji makes gestures of mock jealousy.

"Honey, we *are* the motherfucking party!" Tonio exclaims. "This is *our* world, everybody else just lives in it!" I glance over at Tonio and see that he's all smiles, his eyes dancing, his hands restless as he adjusts his shirt, smooths his hair, taps his fingers against the leg of his jeans. Brad takes a small step back from him and averts his eyes. Odd how the natural energy of a crowd is so contagious, while the artificial rush of a stimulant can actually repel. But you don't realize that when you're the one taking the drug. When you're high you see possibility and opportunity where other people see impossibility and total delusion. All those antidrug campaigns would be so much more effective if they'd just admit that long before drugs destroy you, they make you feel *good*. And sometimes that's all you want, to feel *good* when all those people who are supposed to love you are doing their damnedest to make you feel *so* bad.

"Are you all right?"

At the deep baritone vibration of Brad's voice I look up to see that he's studying me. Rick also looks up, his eyes darting from Brad to me even as Traci pulls away from him and slips back into Benji's arms.

I want to say yes, but it's not true. For me, performing really is a drug, blissfully intoxicating, bringing on states of euphoria and confidence. But five feet from the stage is where the withdrawal hits. The memories and thoughts held off by the cheers of the crowd come crashing down, giving me tremors and aches. It's ridiculous, really. But I can't make it stop.

"I'm just tired," I say with what I hope is a sleepy smile. "Tonight was awesome, but I think I'm going to have to cut it short and get some sleep."

"*What?*" Traci gasps as she drops her arms and spins to face me. By the look on her face you'd think I had just announced that I wanted to walk barefoot on a barbed wire tightrope.

"Yeah, I'm calling it a night, too," Brad says, glancing at his watch. Involuntarily my eyes flicker to his T-shirt, which is soaked with sweat and champagne, clinging to his physique. I've never seen another drummer that looks like this guy, all buffed and whatnot. The day he auditioned for us he was wearing a polo shirt. I had almost laughed him out of the room before he even had a chance to take out his sticks. But our last drummer had bailed one week before our gig and we were desperate. And when Brad finally sat down to play . . . well, then the little pony on his chest became a lot less noticeable. All you saw were those sculpted arms and powerful hands pounding out a masterful rhythm.

"I'm going to get my stuff." I gesture to the wooden staircase that leads up to the band's dressing area. "You have anything up there?" I ask Brad.

"Got everything I need here," he says, tapping his hands against his pockets. "I'll just load the drums into Tonio's van and head out."

"I got the drums," Tonio says graciously. "Don't worry about it. Maybe if I lift them enough times I'll get big, purty arms like you!"

Brad laughs and nods. "All right, you get the drums and I'll just see you guys at rehearsal." He begins to turn but then stops, his eyes locking on mine. "You were really something out there tonight."

I raise my eyebrows teasingly. "Brad, I'm always really something."

It's enough to evoke a smile, one that warms me more than I would have anticipated . . . but not enough to put my tremors to rest. And so in unison Brad and I turn away from each other, me toward the stairs and he toward the exit.

"This won't be your last performance here," Rick announces as we start off in our separate directions. Tonio and Traci let loose whoops and cheers in response and probably more kisses as well, but I just nod my appreciation without looking back and keep going up the stairs.

I've barely stepped inside the dressing room when I hear Traci bounding up after me. "Are you really tired, M?" she asks as she catches up with me and reaches for her purse, left by the door.

"Yeah," I say with a fake yawn. "This has got to be the amateur night of all amateur nights. No point in fighting crowds of idiots when last call is less than an hour away."

"Oh come on, don't be like that," Traci chides as I turn away from her to get my own bag, finding space inside for the disposable camera. She gently takes hold of me and rests her head between my shoulder blades. "It's the new millennium," she continues. "We are literally only a year away from HAL going haywire on us. It's time to live for today!"

"Another time," I promise as I pull away.

"You're not going to have one of your Cobain-esque brooding fits, are you?"

She says the words lightly, but I can hear the undercurrent of concern. Traci's the only person I currently know who's seen me during the times when I feel so low I can barely find the motivation to comb my hair.

"No, no brooding." I shrug into the biker jacket I recently picked up at the flea. The stiff leather feels like much-needed armor. "Only sleeping. Promise."

"Got it," she says, eagerly accepting my reassurance. "But if exhaustion's the problem, I've got the solution!" She reaches into her handbag and pulls out a small plastic bag filled with white powder. "Benji hooked us up. We're rock stars, M!" She giggles. "It's time we started acting like it."

For a second I feel my heart accelerate as new memories take hold. That gorgeous feeling, that intensity and clarity that can come from just the lightest sprinkling of white powder. "No," I say quietly. "I really just need a bed."

"Then we'll find you one!" Traci's almost pleading now. "One with an Antonio Banderas look-alike in it, accent and everything."

I give her a playful smack on the arm. "Try not to get into too much trouble."

"*In* trouble? Baby, I *am* trouble! Tonio's the party and Benji's the hookup. That's what you call division of labor," she calls after me with a light laugh.

That used to be me, I think as I walk downstairs, then to the corridor leading to the employee exit, waving good-bye to Tonio, Benji, and Rick as I do. *That carefree girl with a Ziploc full of fun used to be Melody.*

And now? I stop several feet from the door and check to make sure none of my bandmates are watching me before changing direction and heading back into the club. Now things have changed. I stand near the edge of the dance floor, unsuccessfully trying to be inconspicuous. But several people spot me and stop to give me their compliments. "You rocked it!" "You were great!" "Man, you need to let me buy you a drink, girl!" and so on. But I'm not here for that. I'm looking for *him*.

He's not next to the beam anymore. I don't see him on the dance floor or at the bar. My eyes scan the room quickly as another guy asks if he can get me a glass of champagne, but I wave him off with the flick of my hand. Where *is* he?

Not here. The awareness hits me with the force that always comes with extreme disappointment. He's disappeared again. It's what he does.

God, maybe he was never here at all. Maybe it was a hallucination. Like those acid flashbacks I keep hearing about. Maybe I'm finally losing my mind. Considering the hell I've been through, that would hardly be surprising. Of course, Ash doesn't know anything about the avalanche our night together caused, how just his touch had sent everything in my life spiraling out of control. His crime is more of a negligent homicide than a murder. An unintended hit-and-run. Still, blood is blood and mine is on his hands.

Defeated, I head back to the exit and out to the alley behind the club as I search my purse for the two Hershey's Kisses I know are in there. Chocolate is one of those vices that I will never give up.

"Melody."

The word startles me so much I jump, slamming my back against the now-closed door. He's standing not ten feet away.

Ash.

"Bet you didn't expect to see me tonight." He unzips his black biker jacket as he approaches.

I should probably pretend I don't remember who he is. That would be good. But instead I find myself scoffing and shaking my head. "No, I didn't expect you. Coincidence is a bitch, isn't it?"

"Ah, but coincidence is lazy." His stubble is a few days old and forms a very light goatee. It gives him a vaguely devilish appearance. "But us meeting here, in a different state at the beginning of a new century? This feels like the more proactive maneuverings of fate, don't you think?"

I laugh nervously. I had forgotten his eloquence. No, no, that's not right; what I had forgotten is that his poetry can be sweet as well as bitter. I had almost forgotten that he could do more than just make me cry.

"I don't go by Melody anymore," I say, trying to keep it cool. The weak lighting in the alley forces me to strain to see his details. Are his eyes as green as I remember? His hair as black?

"So I've heard."

I reach into my bag and pull out my license. What about that cut on his calf, has it healed? Has it left a scar? "I had my name changed." It's a struggle to keep my voice casual. There's so much I can't see! But I can *feel* him. Even now I can feel the lazy way his fingers ran up and down the back of my neck as we sat on that city bench in Seattle, talking philosophy, music, and dreams. I can feel his lips against mine during that first kiss.

I *hate* that.

"Mercy Raye," he reads as he takes my license from me. "As a singer, don't you think the name you were born with is a better fit?"

"None of us are born with names," I say irritably as I take the license back. "At best a name is just the first gift we're given by our parents. What we're born with is personality."

"And you threw it away, your parents' first gift to you."

"My life, my decision," I mumble as I busy myself replacing my license in my wallet.

"It's that easy?" He's only a few feet away now. "You can change who you are, like that?" He snaps his fingers in the air, bringing my attention to his hands. Those hands had felt rough and capable against the small of my back when he drew me to him.

"No, not just like that." Our second kiss had been in an alley. We were wild and out of control. He had pushed me up against a wall and I had dug my fingers into his flesh as he pressed his mouth against mine. He had tasted like citrus and whiskey. "But I did it," I continue. "Melody Fitzgerald is dead. I'm a new woman now."

"And what brought this on? Did things go further south with your folks?"

"If you were interested in my life you should have kept your word and called me." The words shoot out of my mouth before I can think them through. It would be better if he thought I didn't care, that I barely registered his absence.

"I lost your number," he says quietly.

"You lost my number." Amusement tinged with rage floods through me as I flash him a menacing smile. "How very original of you."

"Melo—Mercy, I know it sounds—"

"Like bullshit?" I ask, cutting him off. "Yeah, it does. And you know, if you're going to bullshit me, it would be better if you at least showed me the respect of putting some effort into it."

"I see." Ash raises his eyebrows questioningly. "And what exactly should I have said?"

"I don't know, be creative," I snap. "Tell me that you were just out of a relationship and you didn't know if you could handle anything serious. Tell me that you were afraid that anything as awesome as our night together couldn't be built to last and you worried that if you called me you'd only end up spoiling a perfect memory. Tell me you have issues, self-doubt, *something* that kept you from picking up the goddamned phone and dialing me up!"

"In other words," he says, leaning back on his heels, "I should tell you it's not you, it's me."

"Oh for God's sake, enough with the fucking clichés!" I shake my head and adjust my purse on my shoulder. "You know what? It doesn't matter. I gotta go. But this has been fun. Really. We should meet up again next millennium."

I start to walk away but he puts a hand on my shoulder and gently pushes me back against the door. "I was just out of a relationship and I wasn't sure if I was ready for anything serious." His voice hovers between a growl and a song. "I was afraid that anything as amazing as our night together couldn't be built to last." I look away. He has *no idea* what kind of chaos he left me to deal with. I can't buy into his game.

But then he takes hold of my chin and guides my face back to him. "I worried that if we continued I would ruin a perfect memory." He runs one finger up and down the length of my neck. I can feel my anemic willpower reaching for the white flag. "I have issues, self-doubt, *and* . . ." He winds his fingers into my hair and brings his lips to my ear. "I lost your number." His breath both tickles and chills. Slowly he pulls back and gives me a smile that makes my heart speed up to an unnatural rhythm, "But I *found* you. That's what's important, don't you agree?"

I don't move. My body is itching for action and yet my mind can't figure out what that action should be. Should I hit him? Throw myself at him? Run away? "I don't know," I whisper, and then, finding my voice, I say just a little louder, "I don't know if that's what's important anymore. A lot of time has passed and things are . . . they're different."

"Yeah." He looks down and nods his head thoughtfully, causing his hair to fall forward in an almost feminine manner. "Last time we talked you told me you wanted to sing onstage. Now here you are."

"I said I wanted a lot of things. You did, too." That night he had whispered his ambitions as I traced the curves of his half-sleeve tattoo with the tip of my tongue, the salt of his skin bringing to mind images of the seashore.

"I did." He reaches forward, taking my hand, and without a word he pulls me away from the club and unhurriedly leads me down the alley toward the street.

"Where are you taking me?" *And why am I letting you lead?* But the thought is lost in a brewing storm of less practical emotions.

"To an adventure, Mercy." He keeps his eyes on mine as he continues to guide me. "Where else?"

When we get to the street there are revelers everywhere. People running down the street with party poppers, metallic foil horns, and silly hats. It's a happy chaos and yet none of it seems real. Like these partiers are nothing but ghosts dancing around Ash and me. Like we are the only ones here tied to the limitations and longings of the flesh. It's not until he leads me to our destination, a parking meter on the corner, that I'm able to look away from him and see what he's showing me. I feel the corners of my lips twitch as I take it in. "You got your motorcycle."

"I did." Again he pulls me to him, his eyes twinkling with mischief as he takes a spare helmet out of a canvas saddlebag. "I think it's time we go for a ride."

✿

CHAPTER 3

I T SHOULDN'T SURPRISE me that he has a sports bike. He had
spoken of it that night, when we had been sharing both our affection and our greed. But he couldn't bankroll a new bike at the
time, so we had found other ways to indulge.

But now? Now we're whipping through the streets of LA, flashing
by the drunken Angelenos spilling out of clubs. All I've had is that
small sip of celebration at midnight. There's nothing in my blood that
will help me turn off my brain. I can't stop thinking about the way my
breasts are crushed against his back as he sits between my legs, the
way it feels to have my arms wrapped around him, literally holding on
for my life. And his leather jacket is so smooth I want to tear this helmet off and rub my face against it like a cat. The bike is a Ninja, faster
and more agile than anything else around us. Everything about Ash
tonight speaks of risk and strength . . . and . . . well, *money*. The man
I met all those months ago couldn't have afforded any of this. So perhaps our time apart has been more prosperous for him than for me.

That feeling is only reinforced when he pulls over to a liquor
store minutes before it's about to close and comes out with a pricey
bottle of champagne and a paper bag filled with other goodies he
promises to show me later. "Where are we going?" I ask again.

He pauses a moment, standing in the middle of the parking lot
as I try to steady myself by holding on to the precariously balanced
bike. There's something in his stare . . . a hunger, a need that I think
I understand.

Slowly he moves closer, opening the saddlebag again, where he places his new purchases. "I knew you'd be there . . . I saw the pro-motions."

"The . . . the promotions for the performance? At Apocalypse?"

"A man handed me a free drink card for Apocalypse a few weeks back, and on it was a picture of a woman I didn't think I'd ever see again," he says with a confirming nod. "But I swore that if I did see you . . ." He takes a deep breath as if steeling himself for a blow. "Let's not do this here."

I look around and note that there are about half a dozen cars in the lot. Two of them have people in them, waiting for their friends. I could ask him where we're going again, but what would be the point? No matter what he says I'm going to go because . . . because I *want* to!

The realization is a little startling. I thought I was less impulsive these days, less led by my moods and whims. But seeing Ash . . . I don't know.

And so I get back on the bike and let him take me away into the night.

And it feels like we drive forever. Past the clubs, the late-night restaurants, the closed stores, the houses, everything, until we're just flying down Highway 1 along the ocean. And when I've totally lost track of where we are he stops, right where the sand meets the pavement. The ocean looks like a giant black shadow, roaring for us as we find a little corner of beach to sit on, the champagne and brown bag held in Ash's hand. He reaches inside and pulls out two plastic flutes and a small bottle of vodka.

"Vodka?" I ask as he pours a shot into each glass.

"Not quite as cold as I'd like," he admits as he expertly loosens the cage around the cork of the champagne and then opens the bottle with only the slightest pop so he doesn't spill a drop. "The champagne will take care of the temperature." In a moment he's filled the rest of our glasses with bubbly. "It's called an Arctic Kiss," he says with a little smile before lifting his flute and handing me mine. "What should we drink to? New beginnings?"

"To new discoveries," I counter.

"To passion!" he rallies, making a game of it.

"Umm . . ." I struggle to come up with something new. And then I look out at the dark sea. How can something be so ominous and so enticing at the same time? My lips curl into a sad little smile as I clink my plastic glass against his. "To the end of the world."

He graces me with a slow, deviant smile as I take a long drink and continue to watch the waves.

"I see you're still captivated by nature." He reaches over, tucks my hair behind my ear. "You don't walk around with blinders on, you notice—"

"I don't know you," I interrupt him with a whisper.

He pauses, studying my profile before offering a reply. "Maybe not." He refills our glasses even though they're still more than half-way full. "But I bet you haven't stopped thinking about me."

I bark out a genuine laugh. "Well, look at the ego on you!"

"I haven't stopped thinking about you, either," he continues. In the distance I can see the flames from a bonfire, but whatever celebrations are going on over there are muted by the sea.

"I've been thinking that I've never met anyone like you before," he continues. "Someone who gets off on both risk and knowledge. I remember listening to you talk about philosophy and music, and you could quote books that you hadn't read in years, rattle off the birth dates of famous composers, name the capitals of every country, and I remember thinking, fuck, this one collects facts like other girls collect shoes."

"It was just trivia, that's all. I'm good at that." I take another sip, my smile fading. "But I mean it, Ash. Hanging out for one night . . . we don't really know each other." *And you don't know what that one night cost me.*

"Alright, if you say so." He digs his fingers into the sand. "Do you do this often, then?"

"Do what?"

"Get on the back of a stranger's motorcycle? Let him take you to remote places where none of your friends can find you?"

"No!" I laugh as I drink a bit more. "But you're . . . I mean it's not like . . . you're not exactly . . ." I stumble and falter as I see the trap.

"I'm not what?" he asks with false surprise. "A stranger? What are you saying, *Mercy*?" He draws my name out teasingly. "That you do know me after all?" He chuckles and tips his glass.

"You're impossible."

"Name one thing you know about me," he presses.

I reach forward and take off my shoes, letting my toes sink into the cold sand. "I know your favorite movie is *Malcolm X*."

"And yours is *Pretty in Pink*," he says. Back on the road I can hear cars passing, momentarily breaking the illusion that we are truly alone in the world. "I know that you think Jimi Hendrix is the best guitarist of all time."

I roll my eyes and lean back on my elbows against the sand, carefully balancing my glass between my fingers. "*Everybody* thinks that. It's not an opinion, it's a fact."

"And you think the second greatest guitarist is Dave Davies," he adds.

I look up, surprised. I had forgotten I had told him that, and I'm shocked that he remembered.

"I know that you didn't go to college," I say quietly. I don't know why I chose that particular bit of info to throw out at him. Maybe I want to hurt him . . . if only just a little.

"You didn't go to college, either," he says. His voice is light, but I can hear the edge of defensiveness.

"I did three semesters at a junior college," I remind him, bringing my eyebrows up and down teasingly. "See? There *are* things you don't know about me."

"No, you told me that," Ash says as he throws back the rest of his drink and then adds more vodka to both of our glasses. "I also think you told me you were kicked out for selling weed on campus."

"Oh please," I snap. "I haven't done that since eighth grade."

He bursts out laughing and I can't help but smile a little, too. "But . . . you did tell me you got kicked out of junior college, right?"

"For selling fake ID's," I mutter. I feel a heat creep up my neck as I look away. "I don't do that anymore . . . Anyway, I had bills. Rent, tuition, it was all on me, and it's not like a part-time job at Urban Outfitters was going to cover me." I sit up a bit so I can drink half of what's in my glass in one swallow. Ash refills it immediately. I'm vaguely aware of feeling intoxicated.

He places a hand on my leg, just a few inches above my knee, not too presumptuous, and yet it feels so intimate. A subtle reminder that I have yet to claim my kiss.

"I remember that," Ash says quietly. Even without looking at him I can feel him studying me. "Your parents kicked you out of the house when you were still in high school."

"You do remember a lot," I say with an uncomfortable laugh. Why had I opened up like that to him? Had I been looking for pity? Probably. Ridiculous that I had ever felt entitled to the comforts of my parents' home. A temperature-controlled bedroom in a picket-fence neighborhood . . . that's not where I belong.

"I remember that you worried your parents didn't love you," he adds softly.

"Yeah." I throw back the rest of my drink, finally managing to drain the glass. "I don't worry about that anymore."

With one hand he reaches out and guides my face toward his, then slips that hand into my hair, cradling my head. "I know that you always make a wish on the first star you see."

"You do, too."

"Yeah," he says with an embarrassed laugh. "Yeah, I do. We know each other pretty well for strangers."

"We talked for a long time that night." I try to look away again, but he holds me in place with just the light but steady pressure of his hand.

"We didn't just talk."

I can feel his breath against my skin. When did he move so close? The world has taken on an appealing fuzzy quality, blurring the stars together into flickering lines of white against a gray-black sky. And it's under that sky that Ash is here, touching me, silently demanding so much while asking so little. He doesn't understand. And slowly, oh so deliciously slowly, he touches his lips to mine. It's not aggressive or overtly sexual, but it's definitely not innocent, either; not as my mouth opens just slightly against his and he reaches around my waist, pulling me just a little bit closer. This is a kiss that dances on the edges of sweetness and sin. It tastes like a promise. When he pulls back, just half an inch, I reach up and touch his beautiful hair. I could lose myself in this man, utterly and completely.

And yet I don't tell him that. I'm tempted to, but part of me just isn't sure if he *deserves* to be told.

"You hurt me," I whisper. His eyes widen in a flash of surprise and then, reluctantly, he drops his hands. "I know I don't have the right to say that," I add quickly, pulling a little farther away. "I know what that night was supposed to be and what it wasn't. Any girl who fucks a guy hours after meeting him and expects him to call is an idiot, no matter what he promises. You don't owe me an explanation. Still"—I shrug and hug my knees to my chest—"you should know that you hurt me."

For at least a full minute he doesn't say anything at all. More cars pass on the highway, the flames from that distant bonfire flicker and die, and the ocean continues its quiet roar. It's odd, because while I'm not sure if Ash deserves my confidence, I *know* I don't deserve his understanding. Melody may be dead, but I still have to deal with the karma of that past life and it's just not pretty.

An all too familiar sense of agitation is beginning to take hold of me. It's like I want to crawl out of my skin and get away from my thoughts. I want to feel something outside of myself, something impersonal, distracting, and wonderful.

"Like I said, you're not like anyone I've ever met before," Ash says quietly.

I don't respond. I just focus on the sounds of the waves. I've surfed those waves before. Some people say that riding a wave makes them feel powerful, but when I paddle out to the horizon it just reminds me of how insignificant I am in the grand scheme of things. I like that. I cherish those moments of virtual invisibility almost as much as I cherish being in the spotlight.

"Have you ever hurt anyone, Mercy?"

I wince involuntarily and then try to cover with a self-deprecating laugh. "Only all the people I've ever really cared about," I say. "My whole past is like one big landfill for broken hearts and misplaced expectations."

"Yeah." From the corner of my eye I see him tap his empty flute against the small vodka bottle. "Okay, so we don't know each other very well. Just a few shared secrets, some trivia . . . But here's the thing. I *feel* like I know you. I felt that way from the moment I spotted you in that club in Seattle, just giving your body to the music while cheering on the band. And yeah, I know that sounds like a line, but I swear I'm keeping it real here. And I'm sorry I hurt you . . ." His voice fades off as he seems to consider what to say next.

"What?" I whisper. "What are you thinking?"

"That I don't believe in love at first sight."

"Seriously?" I snap. "*That's* what you're thinking?"

"Yeah, but . . . I believe that sometimes you can meet someone and almost instantly realize that this is a person you *could* fall in love with. That's possible, right?" When I don't answer he takes a long, shaky breath. "I guess what I'm saying is, let's *get* to know each other because . . . because I want to be one of those people you care about. I'd like to give you the opportunity to hurt me."

I laugh again, although this time the sound isn't coated in derisive sarcasm.

"Seriously!" he insists. "I have this feeling you're worth the pain."

"Well then, you'd be the first person to think so."

"Aw, I'm your first," he says with a suggestive grin.

I groan and rest my head on my knees.

"What about me?" he asks, nudging me with his elbow. "Am I worth it?"

"I'm here, aren't I?" I scrape my nails against the back of my hand, leaving a mark. It hurts, but maybe not enough. The vodka is protecting me from the sting.

"That's a yes."

"Maybe," I counter. "Or maybe I'm just a crazy masochist." This time it's the skin on the inside of my wrist that I scratch. He doesn't see the marks. He just thinks I'm making a gesture, that it's a joke.

"You don't strike me as the masochist type." His teeth are so white they glow in the darkness. I imagine them biting gently on my earlobe, on my neck . . . "And you're not even close to being as crazy as me."

I give him a withering look. "You realize that Crazy was literally my nickname in middle school. Seriously, that's what they called me. Not Crazy Melody, just Crazy. As in *Crazy got detention again,* or *Crazy painted a skull and crossbones on her big toenails.*"

Ash does a quick double take. "Did you really paint a skull and crossbones on your nails? With nail polish?" When I nod, his eyes flash with approval. "That takes serious fine motor skills. You could be one of those Chinese artists who can paint intricate pictures of landscapes on hollowed-out eggshells."

"Okay, so I have no idea what you're talking about right now."

Ash laughs and tilts his head up to the stars. "That's 'cause I'm crazier than you. It'll take more than a middle school nickname to best me. Hell, my stepmom considered institutionalizing me when I was fourteen."

"Oh yeah, that's impressive. My dad *did* institutionalize me at sixteen. And then when the doctors refused to keep me in the nuthouse for more than a couple of days, he kicked me out of the house because he was afraid my craziness would rub off on my little sister."

"Ah, but the doctors kicked you out because you didn't need to be hospitalized in the first place, right?" He rests his forearms on his knees, his drink still clasped in his hand. "So your father locking you up doesn't make you crazy, it just makes him a douche."

I scrunch up my face into a goofy, sardonic expression and tap my finger to my nose.

"Onstage you were a little wild," he admits, "but not out of control. You haven't given in to one crazy impulse all night."

"I got on the back of your bike, didn't I?"

"That was spontaneous, not impulsive. There's a difference." He fakes a yawn. "You're so sane you're almost boring."

I scoff and glance back out at the ocean. "You want me to give in to my impulses?"

"Yes." Ash's lips curl into a sexy little smile. "I'd like to see that."

I get up and the world wobbles under my feet. I'm restless and edgy. I can't stay still. Standing before him, I slide out of my jacket and slowly pull off my shirt. "You have no idea how impulsive I can be." My fingers fumble with the buttons of my jeans, but it doesn't take long before they're in a pile on the sand. Ash's smile grows slowly. I see everything he wants to do to me in the glimmer in his eyes. I see the quiet twitch of his fingers as he plots their course. I take a deep breath and manage to hold myself still as he reaches out and runs his hand up my inner thigh. The warmth of his touch feels utterly incongruous with the cold of the night. "You sure you want me to get a little crazy, Ash?" I ask quietly.

"Yes," he says, his voice hoarse, needing.

"Alright then, just remember"—I lean over and gently kiss his lips—"you asked for it."

And in a flash I've turned from him and I'm running, running as fast as I can toward that dark, roaring abyss before me. I hear Ash calling after me, but the element of surprise is mine and he is now working hard to make up the distance between us. He's yelling warnings about riptides and sharks as if he thinks I'm afraid of those things. But I can't fear something that has no will to hurt me. I've never been scared of anything other than the people I love . . .

oh, and myself. I've always been smart enough to be scared of the dark workings of my own mind.

And so when the cold water touches my toes I keep going until it's splashing around my ankles, then my knees. Ash is cursing, but I only know this because of the tone; his words are swallowed by the sound of the Pacific. I love that.

Swim, I want to swim! I want to be part of this! Once the water is almost to my hips I immerse myself. The cold makes it feel like my lungs are lurching into my throat. It's literally painful.

You have to be alive to feel pain.

I want to swim as far as I can, to Santa Cruz Island, Hawaii if I could! Maybe it's the challenge, or maybe I just need to prove that I can still defeat death no matter how much others may wish I couldn't. Or maybe it's the opposite and it's just time for me to give my life to the sea? Get it over with?

I know it's madness. But . . . it's me.

Then suddenly someone is grabbing my ankle, and I taste the seawater slip down my throat as I struggle to free myself.

And I'm being lifted. His hands on my waist, pulling me from the water, half dragging, half carrying me back to the shore as I shiver and cough and laugh. Yes, I'm alive. The blurry stars shimmer down, twinkling with their own brand of laughter.

"Jesus, Melody, there are riptides out there! And it's fucking freezing!"

For a second I close my eyes and imagine what it would be like to let the water take me. What would it feel like in those first moments after the ocean filled my lungs? Would it just be darkness? Or is there an afterlife? If so, would *she* be there waiting for me?

If I believed that, *really* believed that, would I go to her? Or am I too selfish?

"Melody!" he says again desperately. "We need to get you somewhere warm!"

"M-Mercy," I stutter as the chill sets in. "M-M-Melody's d-dead."

He doesn't answer but instead puts me down on the wet sand and forces me into his leather jacket, which is much longer and warmer than mine. For the first time, I notice he took the time to get out of his jeans and shoes before going in after me, which he hurriedly puts back on over his own wet legs and feet. "You're totally out of your mind," he mutters, and glances up at some houses that line the beach.

Yes, out of my mind. Now you understand.

He points up to one of the homes. "That's where we're going."

"Th-they w-won't l-l-let us in," I stutter. The cold is excruciating, and part of me cherishes it. I find that I'm able to stand although I'm still shivering. His jacket is just long enough to brush against the tops of my thighs. Ash rubs my legs with force, warming them until it feels like a thousand pinpricks are bringing them back to life.

"They don't need to *let us* do anything," he grumbles, and then grabs my hand and runs toward where I abandoned my purse and clothes, scooping them up. He turns to me as if trying to decide if he should dress me, and then he shakes his head impatiently. "Fuck it, I'm just getting you inside." Again he takes hold of my hand as I grab the champagne. He pulls me at a sprinter's pace toward a beautiful house right on the edge of the beach. Even in the state I'm in I know this isn't going to end well.

CHAPTER 4

❦

I COME TO THIS beach all the time," he yells as we run. "Come on, keep moving, you have to keep your legs moving! Anyway, I think the woman who lives here is out of town. I know where she hides the key."

"W-we're b-b-breaking in?"

Ash ignores me, and when we finally get to the house he lets go of my hand and shoves my things into my arms before turning and climbing over the tall fence that surrounds it. In a second he's unlocking the gate and pulling me inside. There's a tree by the front porch with a small birdhouse hanging from it. He reaches up to it, his fingers caressing the miniature awning until he finds what he's looking for. He pulls out a shiny house key that was hidden there.

I half expect an alarm to go off as he slips the key into the front door lock, but there's nothing but silence as he pushes it open. Grabbing my hand again, he pulls me into the dark house and slams the door closed behind us.

"I c-can't believe we're d-doing this!"

"What's wrong, Mercy? Did you really think you were the only crazy one?" He flips on the lights, revealing a pretty little Cape Cod–style interior. And for the first time I can see the lower half of the tattoo hugging his triceps. For a moment the cold seems unimportant as I consider reaching for it, touching it as if this would somehow be the thing that could prove that he's really here, back with me, entering my second life months after he unwittingly destroyed the first. But before I can do anything he's taken hold of me again and is dragging me up the stairs.

"Who is th-this w-woman who l-lives h-here?"

"Am I supposed to know everything?" he says as he leads me through a beautiful bedroom with a steeple ceiling and into a master bathroom. "I think she's in her midthirties, and like I said, she seems to be out of town." He finally releases me so he can start to fill the whirlpool tub, which sits a few feet below a row of windows.

"Oh my G-God!" I don't even know if I'm stuttering from the cold or from shock anymore. I'm going to take a bath in a stranger's house?

"Get in."

I look at him warily and then pull the leather jacket around me a little tighter. It's all I'm wearing other than my bra and panties, which are now both soaked through and sheer. I hadn't thought about it when I was protected by the dark. But now, in the bright lighting of this room, I'm questioning if I'm really ready to bare everything to him, again. I'm also beginning to realize that I just had an "episode." At least that's what my mother used to call them when they happened during my childhood.

Impulse control, hyperactivity, mania . . . I had heard doctor after doctor whisper these words to my father as he glared at the floor. "She needs help," one had said. "She needs self-control," my father retorted. "Discipline. Don't let her fool you, she knows what she's doing!"

"You have to get in," Ash says sternly.

"W-what?" I say, blinking as I pull myself out of the memory.

"Into the bath!" he explains, clearly exasperated now. "You'll get hypothermia, for Christ's sake!"

"The ocean t-temperature doesn't go b-below fifty-f-five degrees at worst here. I'll be f-fine."

"Water isn't like air, genius. Fifty-five-degree water will mess you up. Get in the tub."

"I w-want b-bubbles."

"What?"

I point to the glass bottle of bubble bath by the tub.

He looks at me like I'm an alien from outer space. "Are you kidding?"

Slowly and deliberately, I pull my purse strap over my shoulder and clutch my clothes to my chest, the perfect picture of stubbornness.

"Alright, bubbles." He pours the liquid into the tub, and immediately mounds of bubbles cover the surface of the water like frothy white clouds.

"Now will you get in?" he asks, taking the champagne from my hand.

"Turn around."

"Oh *now* you're modest?"

I just make a turning signal with my hand.

"Jesus." He swivels and covers his eyes as I put down my clothes, careful to leave my purse right by the bath, and then, finally, I get out of the leather jacket and peel out of my bra and panties before lowering myself into the tub. The warm water adds a new pain to my frozen limbs, but then the pain quickly fades as I bend my legs and dip the back of my head in before rising just enough to lean my upper back against the porcelain.

"Okay, you can look now." He turns and stares at me, sort of amused, sort of pissed. "See?" I smile, my teeth finally done with their chattering. "You can't see me." When he doesn't seem to understand, I let out an impatient sigh. "Because of the bubbles, idiot. You can't see my naked parts."

"*I'm* the idiot?" he asks incredulously. He takes a swig of the champagne. I sort of love how he drinks vodka from a flute and champagne from the bottle. "Do you know how dangerous that was? What you just did?"

"Do you know how dangerous it *is* to break in here?"

His lips form a thin, straight line, and for a second I think he's going to curse again. But then he smiles, and eventually, laughs. It's a sound that builds until it's infectious and soon I'm giggling, too. He sits down by the side of the tub, keeping his eyes politely away as he hands the champagne to me. "I know you were trying to make a point, but what would you have done if I hadn't stopped you?"

"You did stop me," I say, tilting the bottle back, taking my fill before placing it beside the tub. I watch as Ash rubs his hands up and down his legs vigorously. He must be cold, too, although he didn't get his hair wet and his upper body has remained reasonably dry. Still, he's cold, and yet it's my comfort that seems to concern him most. I'm almost embarrassed by how much that endears him to me.

"But if I didn't . . ." His voice fades as he looks out at the night sky. "What happened out there, Mel?"

"It's Mercy," I correct as I rub the warm water over one arm, then the other.

"Not to me."

The comment sobers me up. "I told you, Melody's dead."

"I don't understand that."

"She died of . . . of hyperactivity," I say with a forced smile. The bubbles are disappearing; I need a more substantial shield. "Addiction, a hair-trigger temper . . . she suffered from all of it. And that's in addition to poor follow-through, distractibility, lack of impulse control—"

"Right, because you totally have your impulses under control now."

I pick up a small pile of bubbles and blow them at him. "As we just established, I'm the pot, you're the kettle."

"I brought you here because you were freezing. I needed to rescue you," he says wryly.

Oh, if he only knew how true that was.

I let my eyes scan the bathroom, taking in the seashell-shaped soap dispenser and toothbrush holder. Under the sink is a wicker wastebasket with a plastic seashell glued onto it. It's as if the woman who lives here is afraid that the view of the ocean isn't enough to remind people that they're by the sea. The consistency and predictability of it all makes me uneasy.

"I believe in fate, Mel . . . or whoever you are." He reaches forward and touches my hair, twirling a sopping pink strand between his fingers. "I believe in destiny and karma and all that shit. I believe that there's a reason I found you, here in LA, a thousand miles from where we met." He reaches forward and brushes aside some of the suds, making my cover flimsier than ever. "I believe that we have something to explore here. You say I hurt you? Fine. Hurt me back. But . . ." And with this he leans forward, only to stop when he's less than an inch from my face. "Kiss me first."

Again he touches his mouth to mine, but this time the kiss is slow, sensuous. His tongue gently parts my lips. As my eyes close, I hear the gentle splash of the water as he submerges his hand, touching my side, just to the right of my breast, sliding beneath me, lifting me from the warmth of the water and enveloping me in an entirely different kind of heat. My bare breasts touch the thin cotton of his T-shirt. Here in the home of a stranger, I'm exposed to this man who I've trained myself to hate and to love. As he pulls away, I open my eyes slowly and see what he sees, the bubbles clinging to my body. I see the patterns of water I've left on his shirt, evidence of what we've done and what's about to happen.

With one hand he moves the white froth away, exposing me completely before lowering his head, his tongue teasing and hardening my nipples as I reach out, holding him for support. Half submerged, half bared, I'm hovering between two states of mind. Do I hate myself for this? Or is this meant to be? Is fate as real and aggressive as Ash thinks it is? There is so much that connects us, so much more than he knows.

And the idea of all this being out of my control excites me. I pull him closer, pressing myself into him, and run my hands through his jet-black hair. When his teeth graze my skin a little moan escapes me. I want this. I *need* this. And I won't justify it or explain it.

Gently he pulls away and lowers me back into the bath. I don't say a word as his hand moves between my legs. His fingers brush against my clit, sending a jolt through me that makes me twitch and cling to the sides of the tub. The warmth of the water makes every-thing more sensitive.

But then his hand moves away and this time it's a sound of pro-test that slips from my lips. He answers with a teasing smile and reaches behind my head to pick up a small bottle of shampoo. He squeezes the liquid into his palm and then slowly works it through my hair, his fingers pressing against my scalp, making my whole head tingle.

"What if the owner's not out of town?" I whisper as he continues to groom me, as if I'm a doll that he's preparing to play with and display.

"Then she'll see you," he says impassively, only the slightest hint of mischief in his eyes. "If she's a prude she'll think you're a crim-inal and a slut. A whore whose only purpose in life is to spread her shapely legs and receive the touch and attention of her male admirers. A woman who is just depraved enough to enjoy it." He pulls slightly on my hair and then continues his work as he runs the shampoo all the way to the ends. "If she's petty," he continues, "she'll be jealous. She'll look at you and realize that you are a woman who will be desired by everyone who sees you. She'll see me touch you and she'll see how it moves you." He rinses the shampoo off one of his hands and again slides it between my legs, once more drawing forth my moan. "She'll wish she was as sensitive as you are. She'll wish that she could receive so much pleasure with only the slightest touch." His fingers continue to gently toy with me as he watches me begin to writhe and tremble, easily provoking the response that he wants. "And, if she's wise, she'll admire you." He takes his hand away and places it under my knees as his other hand slides from my hair to my back. He bends my knees and lowers me farther down until the back of my head is in the water. I give him my weight, letting him support me completely as he immerses me. Now only my face and ears are above the water. He frees his hand from my knees and uses it to lap water onto the few roots of hair that remain above the surface. The level of trust that is required for this exercise is unearned, but even that risk electrifies me. When he lifts me again I grab his T-shirt with two fists, bringing me close to him.

"She'll admire me?" I ask, my voice low, almost challenging, like I'm daring him to take this to its natural conclusion.

"Of course," he says quietly as he runs his hand over my now clean hair. "She'll look at you and thank whatever god she prays to for bringing this kind of beauty into her home. She'll watch as I touch you." He lets his finger trace a line down my throat to where my breast begins to swell. "She'll be overwhelmed by your passion and sexuality. She'll hold her breath as you rise." He loosens my grip and, taking my open hand, presses it to his mouth as I subtly reach into my purse and palm one small item that I expertly conceal from his view.

He gets to his feet and gently helps me to mine. "And she will watch as you step out of her bathtub," he continues as I stand up straight on the tiled floor, now completely exposed to him. "And she'll watch as I tend to you." He takes a towel that is hanging from the wall and gently removes the drops of water from my skin as I hold my hands behind my back, letting the soft terry fabric linger here, under my breast, and now on the small of my back, then lower, touching the fabric to the trim triangle of curls between my legs. "She'll be humbled by the tenderness I show you," he says, his voice now barely a whisper. "She'll be awed by my desire for you." He takes both my hands, spreading my arms apart enough so that I am completely open for his gaze, and then he pulls me back, out of the bathroom and into the master bedroom. "And when she sees how passionate you are," he continues as he guides me with his hands, laying me down on top of the white comforter, "the way you are overpowered by it"—he's pulling off his shirt, fully exposing his tattoo as well as the muscular definition of his lean body—"the way you lose control"—his pants are now on the bedroom floor, his boxer briefs are next, and now I see the strength of his desire—"she'll want you. Even if she's never wanted another woman before, she'll want you, because you are the essence of eroticism. She'll ask me to show her what I can do to you." And with that he's climbing on top of me, his dark hair falling over his face. "May I show you what I can do to you?"

It's not really a question as much as it is a demand for complicity. There's an aggressive energy to the way he's looking at me, as if he would claim me, devour me, right here at the scene of the crime. I touch my fingers to his throat as he hovers above me and whisper the one word he can't have anticipated.

"No."

His mouth falls open. There's wonder and hurt in his eyes. For the first time tonight I'm reminded of how young he is. Twenty-five, only three years older than me. His eyes only open wider when he hears the rip of the tinfoil and then understanding dawns as he feels my hand slowly, carefully roll the latex over his erection.

As I pull my hand away he lowers himself just a little more until I feel the tip of his cock press against me, waiting for me to open for him. "I don't remember you being this careful, Melody," he says in a low voice.

"Melody's dead."

For a moment he doesn't move, his eyes locked on mine. I reach out to him, but in one sudden move he grabs my wrists, slamming my arms against the bed. It's almost painful, and I can feel my pulse beating against his grip.

"Whoever you are," he growls, "you are most definitely alive."

And then it comes: he thrusts inside me with so much power I cry out. He releases my arms and immediately I wrap them around him, clawing at his back as he continues to move inside me. It's been so long since I've enjoyed this kind of intimacy, since I've given in to these kinds of cravings. I bite down on his shoulder, tasting the salt of his skin. It's so familiar and so foreign and so incredibly perfect. We roll together on the bed, and now on top I immediately rise above him, never losing our connection. And yet he's still in control. He grabs hold of my hips and pulls me to him, forcing my clit against the hardness of his body. I'm shaking as I drag my nails over his chest like an animal fighting for release. I can feel the power of my orgasm coming and I hear myself whimper.

But then he stops and turns us over again, holding me down once more. "Not yet, *Mercy*," he says, whispering the words into my ear. "You're not allowed to come just yet."

Slowly, torturously, he rotates his hips against me. I can see the glistening of sweat over his tanned skin, giving him a primal, savage quality that I can't resist. It's as if he's been training for this moment, plotting new ways to humble me.

He places one leg between mine, his cock still caressing my walls, and then he lowers more of his weight on me. I feel the strength of his thigh pressed between mine as he pushes himself into me again. I feel like I'm surrounded by him, lost in him. Perhaps I am.

"Would you like to come now, *Mercy*?"

"Oh yes and yes and yes . . ."

And suddenly he pulls away, only to flip me onto my stomach, this time with a pillow pressed against my pelvis lifting my hips toward him. He pulls my legs apart and enters me again in the same circular motion, but now the sensation is even stronger as I feel his teeth on the back of my neck. Desperately I move my hips in time with his, matching his rhythm. His hands are moving up and down my back, brushing the sides of my breasts, reaching under me. When he touches my clit as he continues to move, it comes, an orgasm so strong I'm sure it must be shaking the whole room. This feeling is bigger than me, bigger than everything. I hear myself cry out here, in this stranger's house, as if begging to be discovered. The danger of it is intense, delicious, strengthening the wave of my pleasure.

"I'm not done with you, *Mercy*."

His voice seems so far away and so close and his hands feel like they're everywhere. My mind can't make sense of it or of anything. I know the weight of him is lightening until it's nonexistent, our connection gone. I feel an overwhelming sense of loss. But now here are his hands again, gripping my waist, guiding me up until I'm on my feet, standing on the soft fabric covering the firm mattress, facing the wall as the man behind me stands on the floor. He caresses my back once again until his hands find the curvature of my butt. He presses into my soft flesh with his thumbs, finding erogenous zones I didn't know existed, causing me to shake. And then he's cupping me, and his hair tickles my back as he murmurs, "Bend your knees."

Slowly I do, keeping my back straight, once again putting all my trust in the strength of his arms. It's only when my knees are parallel to the bed, as if I'm sitting on an invisible chair balanced only by the strength of his hands, that he stops me. His chest presses against my back, his breath in my hair as his erection finds my sex again, wet and throbbing as he enters me, thrusting up inside of me, grinding against me. I feel completely supported as he continues to balance me while he pushes deeper than ever before. He steps back and then forward again, finding new angles, sucking gently on my neck, kissing my shoulders, exploding my fears with his tenderness. This man can't be the instrument of the pain I've felt for so many months, not this man who holds me, cares for me, and lifts me to previously unknown planes of ecstasy, highs that no drug has ever been able to bring me to before. This man can't be my killer. He must, he absolutely must be my savior.

And as he increases his pace, as I feel him fill me, devour me, hold me, I hear him moan against my skin, crying out words I can't understand and don't need to interpret. I know by the slight tremor in his arms that he has satiated his hunger and released his power and passion inside me.

"Mercy," he whispers as he rests his forehead against the back of my head.

I don't know if he's speaking to me or to God . . .

And I don't care.

CHAPTER 5

✤

A LITTLE AFTER 3 a.m. I'm still lying naked on the bed of a stranger. By my side is Ash, breathing steadily in his sleep, spent from our passion. *La petite mort.* A former lover, born in Paris, shared that expression with me. "The little death," the sense of exhaustion and even unconsciousness that follows an orgasm. But it can mean so much more than that if you think about it. The transcendent feeling that sex can bring, the way it lifts you away from all your earthly worries, an escape . . . it can even mean the spilling of a life source. That first night I was with Ash, I remember coveting that feeling of otherworldliness. I just didn't know I'd have to die for it.

The little death. I've thought about that phrase a lot lately. It's haunted me. But then again, I am haunted by so many ghosts. In the silence of this room those phantoms are more real to me than Ash, whose arms I lost myself in less than an hour ago.

I sigh and stare up at the darkened light fixture above us, thinking about the nature of time and how odd and baffling it is. A thousand of Einstein's theories couldn't explain it. Energy, yes, I see how energy works, how it emanates from us, through us all with an invisible force, uncontrollable and pervasive. But time? How can the painful events from months and years ago seem so close, while the memories of yesterday seem so far away? For the life of me I can't remember what I drank with my breakfast yesterday morning. If the police came to me and asked about my whereabouts three weeks ago, I'd have to make something up, relying on my patterns and habits rather than on any kind of recall. But I remember the last day I talked to my father like it happened seconds ago. No, that's not right, I don't remember it, I *relive* it. I *taste* the stale cereal I ate for breakfast that morning, I *smell* the peppermint in the tea that accompanied it. I see the little moth hole I found at the bottom of my white cotton dress hours after putting it on. I can feel the chill of the air on my face as I stand in the parking lot watching as he sits by the window of that diner, calmly sipping from a brown cup, waiting for the child he wished he could forget. Everything that happened that day is happening now and it will happen again tomorrow.

Studying the silhouette of Ash's darkened profile, I wonder what's going to happen now. Will he disappear again? Will I ever tell him about the destruction he caused even if he does stay? I close my eyes against the darkness of the room. How do I feel? Am I sad? Scared? Anxious? Content? Satisfied? How can I not know? And what if this indiscretion leads to another end? *La petite mort.*

I can only survive so much.

Deep breaths, one after another. Funny that I could be more concerned with all these existential questions than I am about being arrested. Here we are, just hanging in the house we broke into. It's reckless, to say the least. But the law and the possibility of injury or even death don't scare me. When someone threatens my heart, though, when they hurt my *soul*, only then will you find me cowering in a corner.

"But I need you, Daddy!"

La petite mort. It can be applied to so much more than sex.

"Save me, Ash." I whisper the words, hoping they'll be light enough to float into his dreams and strong enough to linger in his subconscious. "I'll break into a thousand houses and make love to you in a million beds if you just stay and help me live."

And in his sleep, Ash turns his head away, giving me a different kind of invisibility—and it's much colder than the Pacific.

So I get up and tiptoe down to the clean and sparse kitchen, sort through the cabinets until I find a half-empty bottle of gin. I pour some into a large water goblet, hoping that if I drink enough it'll help me fall asleep, or if not, perhaps it will at least bring me unconsciousness.

The little death . . . it can mean so many things.

CHAPTER 6

❁

T HE LIGHT OF the morning wasn't nearly enough to jar me from my induced sleep. In a state that was just short of wakefulness, I think I heard Ash rise. Perhaps I mumbled something about nausea and he hushed me, a finger against my lips. Then the sound of a match, a different scent in the air, and finally his mouth against mine, opening my lips with the gentlest of pressure, the sensation of smoke pouring into me, burning my throat, filling my lungs as the taste of burnt grass lingered on my tongue, the quieting of my stomach, and then sleep and sleep and sleep. Yes, I believe that was real, that it happened . . . then again, maybe it was all a delusion.

And now the room is thoroughly warmed by the afternoon sun and I'm still curled up against Ash. But I hear something disturbing the stillness. The distant slamming of a door, the shuffling of objects, the soft sound of footsteps coming up the stairs. All an illusion, all woven into the pattern of a dream.

And then the door to the bedroom flies open, crashing against the wall, there's a sharp cry of protest, and immediately I'm awake, shrinking under the gaze of a woman with dark eyebrows and platinum blond hair wearing pink velour pants and a hoodie. She's like an apparition from a fluorescent Juicy Couture nightmare. Perhaps that's why I match her scream with one of my own, or maybe it's that I suddenly realize I am lying on top of the covers completely naked.

Or maybe it's that I know we're caught.

I jump up and try to grab the comforter to cover myself, but my efforts are undermined by Ash, who is lying on top of it as well. He's also awake, but his reaction is less of alarm and more of annoyance. Leisurely, he gets off the comforter and covers himself under the sheets, his eyes slightly red under his half-mast lids. "Everybody chill."

We're about to be hauled off to prison and he wants everybody to chill. I pull the comforter around me tightly as the woman in pink carries on. "What the fuck are you doing here? This is my bedroom. Oh my God you're in my *bed*! What are you doing?"

"We were sleeping," mumbles Ash.

"In what *universe* is this anything but completely fucked-up?" pink lady demands.

"I . . . I'm really sorry—" I begin, but she stops me with a talk-to-the-hand gesture.

"Whoever you are," she seethes, "you need to shut up."

"There's no need to be rude," Ash says, yawning. He's casually propped himself up on several pillows and is looking for all the world like a dissolute seducer from the cover of a Harlequin romance.

"No need to be . . ." she repeats, her voice fading off as she tries to harness her rage. "This is *my* bedroom. You could have slept in any of the guest rooms. You did not have to sleep here! We've been over this!"

"Wait—" I say, raising my hand like a timid schoolgirl. My head is pounding but even in my punished state, I'm beginning to put the pieces together. "You guys know each other? Is Ash a guest here?"

"Oh no, you're not guests, you are trespassing *in my bedroom*!" the woman snaps before turning back to Ash. "My cousin is sleeping naked in my bed! It's like we're in some kind of redneck, hillbilly hell!"

Ash looks at me impassively. "Did I tell you that my cousin Eva Castillo is the owner of this place?"

I shake my head, unable to find my voice.

"Hmm." He sighs and relaxes more of his weight against the pillows. "Oh what a tangled web we weave."

LESS THAN FIVE minutes later I'm scurrying into a guest room, once again clutching my clothes to my chest, but this time wrapped up in a towel his cousin reluctantly let me borrow after Ash promised we'd wash it. Ash is in Eva's bathroom changing. Eva is ripping the sheets off her bed in a frenzied state of disgust and rage as she waits to continue her argument with my lover. The guest room has sky-blue walls and white wicker furniture. The bedding is covered in illustrations of blue seashells, and the prints on the walls are of fuzzy otters and leaping dolphins. And here I am, naked, shamed, completely violating the aesthetic.

We hadn't broken in. He had a standing invitation to stay here whenever he needed a place to crash. I am not an outlaw. It was all a fantasy.

Or was it all a lie? Is there a difference?

I sit down on the edge of the bed and pull on my clothes. My undergarments are in a state of ruin, so I toss them aside and opt for a commando approach. The denim of my jeans chafes, and the way my shirt clings to my bare breasts makes me vaguely self-conscious. It should probably make me severely self-conscious, but everyone in this house has already seen me wearing less. I try to run my fingers through my hair, but they get caught in the tangles. That's what happens when you have sex with wet hair.

But was it worth it?

Visions of Ash bathing me, touching me, the way he felt when he was inside of me . . . Yes, yes I suppose it was. Down the hall I can hear Eva berating him again.

In another minute Ash is here, opening the door, looking rumpled, tired, and absolutely beautiful.

"You lied to me," I say as the door closes softly behind him.

"I misled you," he corrects. Each step he takes in my direction is predatory and beautiful. "I never actually lied . . . at least not that I can recall . . ."

"Why?"

And now he's standing over me, pushing my tangled hair behind my ears, letting his fingers dance along the line of my jaw. "You wanted danger and risk. You craved adrenaline. So I gave it to you. Without ever putting you in harm's way I created a scenario that provided you with the thrill you required." He's touching my shoulder, his legs on either side of mine. "It was my gift to you." And then his hand moves under my hair, sliding against the back of my neck. "I wanted you happy."

"You think you made me happy?" I ask, almost challenging him.

"I know it."

Neither of us moves, each hoping to extract something different from this moment. How do I balance the romance of his charade with the dishonesty of the setup? "Ash," I begin, but I'm interrupted by a shriek coming from the master bedroom.

"Dear lord, there's a used condom in here! Ew, ew, ew, *ewwww*!"

I bite down on my lower lip. "That's pretty bad."

"In my defense, I did put it in the wastebasket . . . but yeah, I probably should have wrapped it in tissue."

I start giggling. I don't know why, but suddenly the whole thing seems hilariously absurd. Ash just smiles, the tips of his fingers moving up and down the back of my neck now as he waits for me to catch my breath.

"I have to smooth things over," he says. "Eva's a little tightly wound. But she's family, and I don't want her to be angry with me for long. You get that, don't you?"

No. I don't get it. I have no idea what the word family *is supposed to mean.*

But I like that it means something to Ash, and it would be nice if he could help me understand. "Can I help?" I ask. "Maybe if I apologize, or say it was all my idea . . ."

I see the glint of approval in his eyes and it immediately soothes me. "Couldn't hurt," he admits. "In about ten minutes she'll be at her kitchen table, drinking her tea. You can tell her all that then, before I get you a car."

"A . . . a car? You're not driving me back?"

"I really have to stay and talk things out with Eva. It'll take a little time."

"Oh." Outside I can hear the rumblings of a truck pass, then nothing but the whispered roar of the Pacific. "This isn't New York. I won't just be able to hail a cab."

The edge in my voice has scraped the approval away from his expression and there's a big part of me that wants it back. But there's another part of me that wants to scratch those dark, unsympathetic eyes right out of his head.

"There's a hotel just down the beach. I'll walk you there and . . . you know what? Fuck the cab. You're too good for that. I'll call and get you a town car to meet you there, my treat. One with little bottles of water and leg room."

"A town car," I say slowly. He is still standing over me, straddling my legs. Slowly I lower my back against the mattress as he watches, everything about him anticipatory. And then I curl my knees to my chest and kick them out to the right of him and get up without so much as grazing his jeans. "Fine, I'll take a town car and you can take a shower," I say coolly. "You need it."

CHAPTER 7

THE SUN'S ALREADY preparing to set by the time I get to talk to Eva. Just as Ash predicted, I find her sitting at her breakfast table, glaring into a big yellow cup with a smiley face on it as if the contents are some kind of grim prophecy rather than herbal tea. I'm hit with a pretty powerful sense of guilt. Somehow having sex in a stranger's bed seemed less offensive than having sex in the bed of a family member. If my parents had ever had sex in my bed, I would have slept on the floor until they bought me a new one.

I take a seat cautiously across from her. "Mercy," I say, pointing to myself by way of introduction. It's an awkward start, but what do you say to the woman whose house you sort of, kind of broke into?

She glances up from her cup and for the first time I note the dark circles and the red blood vessels shooting across her eyes like spider webs. "Mercy," she repeats, and then lets out a low laugh. "Mercy me. Tell me, did you meet Ash last night? Did he impress you by telling you this was his house?"

I sense the underlying accusation in the question: *Did you spread your legs for him because you thought he had money?* I let it slide for no other reason than it's the least offensive thing anyone's accused me of in a long time. "No, he didn't tell me that," I say truthfully. "But he didn't tell me it was your house, either." I shrug, tap the toe of my shoe against her floor. I'm too pissed to cover for Ash. I *always* have to live with the consequences of my actions, and this last year I had to live with the consequences of his, too! My soul, my heart, they're both riddled with all the bullets I was unable to dodge. That Ash should have it easier *again* . . . it's not fair, it's not right, and I'm tired of it.

Still, I'm hardly blameless. "I'm sorry we were in your bed," I say quietly.

"I have a thing about germs," she said through gritted teeth.

"If you like, Ash and I can wash the sheets." When she doesn't seem appeased, I add, "In bleach . . . after we sterilize them by putting them in boiling water. And you can toss that wastebasket you found the condom in. I'll get you a brand-new one with, like, twenty seashells on it. And then I'll scrub the bathroom down with *more* bleach. I'll clean until the disinfectant fumes are strong enough to burn membranes right off your nostrils."

She shakes her head. "Thank you, but sheet boiling might be a step too far."

I suppress a smile and offer her my hand. "Peace?"

She stares at me for a moment before reaching forward, turning my hand upward, and then, before I have a chance to ask what she's up to, she pulls a small bottle of Purell out of her pocket and squeezes a dollop of it into my palm. I immediately burst out laughing, and after a moment's pause she joins in, lifting her smiley cup and shaking her head. "Leave it to Ash to start my year off with a curveball."

"Are you two close?" I ask, beginning to feel relaxed.

"We're family," she says with a shrug.

I shift uncomfortably in my chair.

"So you did just meet last night, right?" Eva prods.

"No, we've met before . . . once," I hedge. "A long time ago."

Eva's dark, meticulously waxed brows drop into a furrow. "You two dated?"

"We were never dating." Outside the kitchen window I can see colors slowly materialize across the sky in preparation for the night.

"I figured," she says triumphantly. "Ash doesn't reunite with

exes . . . or to be more accurate, none of his exes are willing to reunite with him."

"Why not?"

"He's a fuckup, that's why not."

My shoulders stiffen involuntarily. I had been thinking something similar just seconds ago, but hearing it from her . . . hearing
it phrased like *that* . . . it doesn't sit well. "He seems to be doing
alright."

"Please." She laughs. "His grandmother died and left him some
money. And what does he do? Party, buy a Ninja, spend it on loose
women . . . oh, I didn't mean . . ."

I wave the insult off with the flick of my hand, my eyes still on
the window.

"I just mean he's irresponsible," she continues, "and selfish . . . a
bit of a womanizer . . . and honesty's not his strong suit." She laughs
again and sips her tea, never noticing that my breathing has become shallower. "He'd kill me if he heard me saying all this, but be
warned. Ash is fun to party with and he can be a fairly good friend,
but when it comes to relationships? Do *not* tie yourself down to this
one."

"Do you want him to end up alone?" I whisper.

"Excuse me?"

I turn my gaze back to her and grace her with a slow, cold smile.
"Ash, your cousin, your *family*. If you don't think he's worthy of
being in a relationship, would you prefer for him to spend his life
alone? That is the alternative, isn't it?"

"Well I . . ." Eva puts her cup down and crosses and uncrosses her
legs. "At least until he grows up a little bit more . . ."

"But what if he doesn't? I mean, once a bad apple, always a bad
apple, right?" I ask. Eva recoils, her eyes confused, maybe a little
scared. "I'm surprised you bother with him at all," I continue. "But
maybe you'll get lucky and he'll drive that Ninja off a cliff."

"Now just hold on a minute—"

"Hey." Ash enters the room, clean and fresh from the shower, wearing different clothes that I assume he must have left here last time he stayed. He stops suddenly as he notes the tension spread out across the table. "Everything cool?"

"Absolutely, baby." I rise and kiss him deeply while lowering my hand to his ass, a show for Eva's benefit. "I was just thinking about how fun it was to get it on in Eva's bed . . . oh, and in her bathtub. But I think it's time we change it up a bit, find someplace nicer to hang." I pull away, walk back to the breakfast table, pull Eva's tea bag out of her cup, plop it into my open mouth, and literally suck out the rest of the flavor before dropping it back into her half-empty cup. "You can bleach your own damn sheets."

BY THE TIME Ash catches up with me I'm already out the door. "Wait, Melo—Mercy, wait!" he calls as I storm out the gate.

I slow my steps, allowing him to catch up. "What was that all about?"

"She's an unholy bitch!" I snap.

"Ah, she's just a little crazy. A germaphobe."

"Yeah, I don't really give a shit about her phobias." Our feet hit the sand, softening our steps, relaxing our pace. "The things she was saying—"

He stops, forcing me to stop with him. "What was she saying?"

I look up into his face and see genuine bewilderment and . . . and innocence. "She . . ." I falter as a seagull lands a few feet from us before lifting up in the air again.

"*She*," Ash repeats, dragging the word out, encouraging me to continue.

I should still be angry with him. I *should* be. But . . . but not so angry that I want to see him hurt by the disapproval and judgments of those who are supposed to love him. I can't be party to that. "She was just kind of judgmental," I offer lamely.

He hesitates, tilting his head to the side. "That's it? She was judgmental?"

I shrug, not wanting to go into detail.

"Well, we made love in her bed," he says with a smile, putting his hands on my waist. "It might not be unreasonable to allow her to be a *little* judgmental, right?"

"Yeah, I guess, I mean of course, of course you're right." I stare down at my hands, pretending to examine my fingernails. "Look, I'm just hungover, that's all."

He smiles, his hand slipping just under the hem of my shirt. "Tell you what, the town car won't be here for another hour and a half, so let's walk to that restaurant together, get a little breakfast before you go. Okay?"

"'Kay." I swallow, sticking my hands into my pockets.

"Hey." He leans into me a little more. "I'm going to see you again, soon."

"Really?" I ask. My voice sounds so small, so pathetically hopeful.

"Wednesday night?" he suggests. "Are you free?"

"The band's rehearsing in the late afternoon, but I should be home by seven."

"Perfect. I'll take you to this awesome steak place. You like steak?"

Not particularly, but I just smile and let him take that as a yes.

"Come on, let's walk," he says, gesturing toward the restaurant.

And so we do. I think I did the right thing by not sharing my conversation with Eva, but . . . but now I'm weighed down with another damned secret. If I collect too many more of these they'll crush me.

I glance out at the ocean one more time. What I wouldn't do to be enveloped in its cloak of invisibility now.

CHAPTER 8

❁

I CAN'T STOP THINKING about him.

On the second I went hiking in Griffith Park, all the way up to Amir's Garden, where the sycamores' arced branches shaded the green metal benches, and I thought of him. On the third when I pulled on my wetsuit and paddled out into the waves of Hermosa Beach, the power of the ocean lifting me instead of defeating me, I thought of Ash. On the fourth I rented a bunch of DVDs and waited by the phone. *I waited by the phone!* I *am* a cliché! And the son of a bitch didn't call.

And now it's Wednesday and I'm driving up the 101 to Calabasas to rehearse with the band and still not so much as an e-mail. After the way he seduced me in the alley, after I made myself vulnerable to him on the beach, after the way he touched me, kissed me, the way his hands dipped into the water of that bath, gently pushing away the bubbles that clung to my skin, after all of that he didn't call.

I suck in a sharp breath and put a little more pressure on the gas pedal, causing my twenty-year-old Volvo to sputter and shake as I force it past the speed limit. Perhaps I could chalk it up as just one more humiliation in the string of humiliations that has been my life, but the thing is that *isn't* my life anymore! I've had my reincarnation, and the life that Ash was a part of is a life that he *ended*. It's like when people insist they used to be Cleopatra in a past life. Those people really believe they used to rule Egypt and fuck Julius Caesar.

Some of them "know" it. But it doesn't really matter if it's true or not, because in *this* life no one is driving them around in a chariot.

So yeah, I used to be Melody, but that's over and nothing about her life applies to me. *Nothing.* I don't associate with Melody's friends, I don't have her addictions—and I *refuse* to have her pain!

The only problem is someone forgot to tell that to Julius Caesar.

I roll down the windows with the archaic handle and let the wind lift my hair and pound against my skin. For just a moment there I had believed Ash when he told me that our meeting was fate. For a minute, an hour, a night, I had believed that the connection that Ash and I shared was stronger than loss. Stronger than death.

Suppressing tears I veer onto the Wendy Street exit, slamming down on the squeaky brakes in time to stop for the light. My greatest friend and my worst enemy has always been Hope. I suppose that's one truth that really is stronger than death.

I don't pull into Traci's driveway until about twenty minutes after we were supposed to start, which experience tells me will be fifteen minutes before Tonio will arrive. There are two other cars in the driveway, parked tandem style, and several run-down clunkers parked on the street right in front. I can never figure out how many roommates Traci has. Sometimes it seems like four, other times I'm sure it's ten.

I shiver a little as I step outside and don't bother to knock on the door as I enter. I'm immediately greeted with grunts and waves by four guys, all in various states of recline. On the TV is the most recent Austin Powers movie, bright colors flashing against a scuffed gray screen. The place isn't dirty—Traci always makes sure of that—but it's cluttered and it reeks of weed. "They're in the kitchen," one of the guys on the couch, who looks disturbingly like Shaggy, informs me. I give a curt nod as I walk past them, although it's doubtful he notices the gesture since his eyes never leave the TV.

The kitchen is a brighter, happier scene. Traci painted the walls a brilliant white and furnished it with the hippest things she could find at garage sales. And sitting at the triangle-shaped dining table is Brad, in a blue cotton button-down, sleeves rolled up to the elbows, sipping coffee, his leather messenger bag in the chair next to him. Across from him with a blue floral teacup and saucer is Traci, a vision in a pink and turquoise tie-dyed Lycra dress and high pigtails that look like drooping alien antennas. Suddenly my black fitted T-shirt with the white hearts and skull pattern running up and down the long sleeves feels conservative. But one glance at Brad reminds me it's not.

"You showed!" Traci says, jumping to her feet and giving me a hug.

Brad gives her a funny look. "Of course she showed. She wouldn't simply not show up for a rehearsal."

I don't say anything and take a seat by Brad's side. The truth is, I have ditched rehearsal a few times. Those were the rare days when I hid under the covers, unable to find the motivation or courage to get out of bed and face the world. It doesn't happen often, but it happens.

"Is traffic bad?" Brad asks as Traci pours me a cup of black tea, using the service she recently found at the flea market. I stiffen slightly, irritated by his passive-aggressive way of reminding me that I'm late, but when I meet his gaze I see nothing but curiosity.

"Um, no . . . I mean not by LA standards. Took me about forty-five minutes."

Brad processes this and checks his watch. "Should we call Tonio? See what's holding him up?"

"Big boy here's eager to start so he doesn't have to listen to me whine about Benji," Traci says with a light laugh as she reclaims her seat. "I caught him chatting up another girl last night. Totally messed with my head. I've been crying on Brad's shoulder for the last twenty minutes," she says, kicking Brad lightly with her blue platforms.

"It's not that," Brad insists. "But it's important that I'm back in

LA by seven thirty, and with rush hour . . ." He shrugs, checks his watch again. "I just want to be sure we get in some good—"

"What is this? High tea? Aren't we missing the queen and her corgis?"

I swivel in my chair at the sound of Tonio's voice. He's smiling from the doorway, a thin layer of perspiration covering his forehead and his hand firmly on his hip. "Sorry I'm late. I had a little sleepover with a gorgeous blondie, but getting her to leave was almost impossible! Girlfriend just did *not* want to go!"

Traci and I exchange glances as Brad studies his coffee. Tonio has not come out of the closet yet, which makes for an uncomfortable situation for everybody, seeing that his closet has a glass door and is lit up with a strobe light. A few weeks back, Traci, Tonio, and I had watched some old *Saturday Night Live* episodes after rehearsal, and when Dana Carvey came on as Lyle, the effeminate heterosexual, the whole room fell into an incredibly awkward silence.

"Right," Traci finally says, slapping both hands on the table. "We're all here now. Let's do this!"

Five minutes later we're in the garage, pounding out harmonies that make the very ground beneath us vibrate. I try a few variations on our tried-and-true songs, going high where I used to go low. We allow Tonio a few more guitar solos, and it all works, but without the crowd, the stage, the lights, it always feels a little flat to me. Screaming out angry lyrics at nothing but air and half-empty paint cans, it's almost depressing.

It's not until Brad stops us about an hour in that things get interesting. "I was hoping we could try something," he says as he reaches into his messenger bag and pulls out a manila folder. Carefully he extracts several photocopies of sheet music.

"What the fuck is this?" Tonio asks as Brad hands one to him.

"Just something I wrote." Brad gives me my sheet and then hands one to Traci.

I stare at the notes covering the page—all handwritten in pencil. "Um, we usually just jam it out," I explain. "Traci will play around on the keyboard until she finds a good tune, or Tonio will just pluck one out, and then I'll, you know, make up some words."

Brad leans back on his heels, totally relaxed and unfazed. "If you don't like the words, feel free to switch them up. After all, you're the one who has to sing them."

I stare at him blankly for a moment, holding the music to my chest. The guy has been in this band for less than two weeks. Where does he find the confidence?

Traci tentatively plays a few notes. They're discordant, but not in a bad way. Just . . . different. Hesitantly, I hold the music out in front of me and look at the lyrics.

Who are you
To tell me not to fear
To tell me that
The night's all safe and clear
You don't know
The demons I see
You've never met
The monster in me

Tonio's guitar whines to life as he joins in with Traci, who has now picked up the tempo. It's a steady, haunting melody . . . even chilling.

Don't say you know me
Every smile can lie
Don't say you know me
Every monster can cry
Don't say you know me
Don't say you know me

My heart speeds up as I hear Brad join in with the drums. The beat gives the whole thing a rock 'n' roll feel . . . but this isn't an in-your-face song. Instead it has a . . . a stealthy quality to it. More

Nine Inch Nails than Alanis Morissette, but maybe more melodic than either.

If I'm scared it's because
I'm something to fear
If I'm angry it's because
Of the one in the mirror
Don't say you know me

The music is building; there's an urgency now, an unmistakable warning built into this new rhythm. It's ominous and important and exciting and just straight-up amazing.

Look, Luv, every heart
Is bloody and dark
When you learn that
The truth becomes stark

Don't say you know me
I'm the monster who cries
Don't say you know me
Don't say you know me

The instruments fall silent. In fact, it seems that the world has fallen silent. I can see actual goose bumps on my arms. That's never happened to me during a rehearsal before. Not once.

I pivot, staring at the man behind the drum set. His brown hair is cut short, his clothes neat, his smile bright . . .

Every smile can lie.

Who is this guy?

CHAPTER 9

❀

WALKING OUT INTO the rapidly diminishing light I can't
help but feel a little disoriented. That last hour of rehearsal
had been . . . different. Despite the angsty nature of our songs, our
group's unofficial motto has always been *Don't take anything too
seriously.* Sometimes we get decent-paying gigs, sometimes we
don't. We all find other ways to scrape by. As long as we're having
fun, everything's groovy.

And today *was* fun, but it was also . . . work. We had never
started with sheet music before. That would require one of us sitting at home, alone, working out a melody and then writing it down
so we could teach it to the others. I had done that occasionally, but
I had always been too embarrassed to bring those sheets of music
to rehearsal. It felt like it would somehow screw up the dynamic
of the band. Instead I had pretended to think up the songs and
melodies during jam sessions, allowing the group to change what
they wanted so it fit our vaguely socialist sensibilities. But Brad has
woven in a thread of discipline. We went over and over that song,
allowing this newbie to correct us and guide us. Tonio's jaw was
clenched tight by the time we were done, Traci looked a little bored.
But I had sort of . . . loved it.

And here's the kicker: at some point in the rehearsal I stopped
thinking about Ash.

I get into my car, leaving the door open a moment to air it out as
I warm up the engine. Brad walks out, the strap of his leather mes-

senger bag crossing his chest diagonally. The look should be wimpy, but all it does is further emphasize his broad chest and muscular build.

"Your left headlight's out," he says, pointing to the dead light.

"Yeah, I know. It's an electrical issue. Sometimes if I just . . ." I switch the headlights on and off a few times to see if it'll kick in.

Brad is now standing right in front of the car, his head tilted slightly to the side, a vague expression of amusement on his face. "Now both of them are out."

"Fuck." I slam the base of my palm against the wheel before getting up and walking to Brad's side so I can see the problem. "I guess I'll just have to choose well-lit streets on the way home."

Brad gives me a sharp look. "You can't drive forty-plus miles on the 101 *at night* without headlights."

"I'm in North Hollywood, so it's more like thirty-eight, thirty-nine miles." I look up at the layers of gray clouds that cover the sky. Rain is a distinct possibility. "I better get going."

"I'm taking you back to LA."

"Really," I say dryly. "And are you driving me back here to Calabasas tomorrow so I can get my car?"

"There's got to be a bus or something," he muses.

"How long have you lived in LA, Brad? Public transportation isn't really our thing."

Sighing, he shuts his eyes and puts his finger to the bridge of his nose as if trying to work out a difficult equation. "Okay," he says, his eyes still closed. "I'll find a way to get you back here tomorrow, assuming you can't get back yourself. We'll make it work."

I study him, taking in his appearance and his obstinacy. There's something soothing about hearing him say the things that someone who looks like him is supposed to say. Men who wear button-down shirts and messenger bags are supposed to offer damsels in distress rides when they need them. What they're *not* supposed to be are drummers in rock bands. I glance back at my car with its useless headlights. "I have an idea, wait here a sec." Without waiting for him to answer, I rush back inside the house. Two minutes later I'm back to find Brad standing right where I left him, looking mildly bewildered and moderately annoyed. "Traci works at a clinic in NoHo on Thursday mornings, so I'll just hitch a ride with her when she drives back here."

"She works at a medical clinic?" Brad asks, surprised.

"Mm-hmm, she's a part-time office manager of a medical marijuana clinic. Great pay, better perks. You ready to go or what?"

TEN MINUTES INTO the ride we've still barely said a word. I fidget nervously with my car keys, occasionally glancing back at the crumbs in the backseat or the *Wall Street Journal* and *New York Times* that lie by my feet. "This is a nice ride," I finally say, desperate for some way into a conversation. "It's a Saab turbo?"

"I just got it last October from a private dealership," he says with a nod. "Seven years old."

"And in good shape." I stare pointedly at the radio. "That's one of those stereo systems you can take with you, right?" I ask. "You can remove it from the car so no one steals it?"

"Yep."

"It works?"

"It does."

"You wanna turn it on?" I ask, frustrated that I have to spell this out for him.

"Not really in the mood for background music right now."

"Okay, really?" I rest my head against my window. "You are one weird cat."

He laughs at that, and I'm surprised at what an appealing sound it is. Deep, rich . . . It's weird, but his laugh is actually sexy. I shift slightly in my seat, adjusting the strap of my seat belt. "Can I ask you something?"

"You want to know about that song I wrote."

I smile, charmed by his intuitiveness. "What inspired it?"

He doesn't say anything for a moment, his eyes on the road as he changes lanes in an attempt to get around a truck. "Can I answer your question with a question?"

"I really wish you wouldn't."

Again he laughs, but he proceeds anyway. "What was your first impression of me when I walked in for the audition?"

"Um, yeah, let's not go down that road."

"Come on, I won't be offended."

"Well . . ." I gather my thoughts as the cars in front of us force us to slow. "You know that movie *Weird Science*? Where they turn that Barbie doll into a living woman? I thought you were kind of like a tame, male version of that."

Brad's forehead creases as he takes that in. "I'm not sure I'm following."

"You know, you sort of seemed like a walking, talking Ken doll."

"A Ken doll."

"But with darker hair," I say quickly. "And obviously I assume you're anatomically correct and everything—"

"Are you serious?" He glances over at me, checking for signs of jest.

"Hey, a lot of little girls love Ken," I point out, rushing to reassure him. "I mean, *I* didn't, but there's got to be a reason why Mattel has kept him around all these years."

"Jesus."

I throw my hands up in the air. "You asked the question."

Brad is now scowling at the road as our speed continues to drop. "I have to admit I haven't heard that one before. But I do know that people see me as a straight arrow, Ivy League type. A nice boy." He says the last words with such contempt that I turn to him now with genuine curiosity. "People take one look at me and they think they know what I'm about."

"But they don't," I say quietly.

"They don't have a clue."

"And the monster?" Outside someone is yelling curses through their open window, while someone else has just started blasting their music loud enough to vibrate half the highway with their bass. And beside me, brooding quietly, sits this beautiful anomaly. "The person who is afraid because he's something to fear?" I press. "Is that you?"

"Music is interpretive." He gives me a sidelong glance as little raindrops begin to pelt the windshield. "It *could* be me. It could also be you."

My lips part, but no words come out. There's something happening here, a bizarre and disturbing bit of magic. For a few minutes we don't talk, just drive with no sound other than the increasingly rapid pounding of the rain.

"Damn," he mutters, breaking the silence. "You know, I don't think I'm going to be able to take you home."

"But . . . you *insisted* on taking me home!" I sputter.

"I realize that," he mutters. "But traffic's a mess and I have dinner plans that I absolutely cannot be late for." He narrows his eyes as he considers the situation, then gives me a curt nod. "You'll have to join us."

"Wait—"

"You'll join us for dinner and then I'll take you home," he says definitively.

"But . . . you . . . you . . ." I have to struggle to get the words past the indignation clogging my throat. "I don't know what your dinner plans are, but what if I don't *want* to be your little tagalong? Or am I supposed to just go along with this because you say so? I suppose you think I should be happy to pony up pizza money just for the privilege of—"

"First of all," he interrupts, "we're not having pizza. Secondly, you don't have to pony up *anything*. I have dinner taken care of."

"Wait, now you're paying for my dinner?"

"Yes, it seems I am."

I hesitate as I consider my all-Top-Ramen-all-the-time food supply. "Well . . ." I breathe, relaxing back into my seat. "Alright, then."

And we fall quiet once more, staring at a road illuminated by brake lights and listening to the quiet music of the rain.

CHAPTER 10

❀

I T TAKES WELL over an hour to get into Los Angeles, another thirty minutes before he pulls off the highway and into the Silver Lake neighborhood. As soon as I realize where we are, I feel a little lighter, a little giddy. I lean forward, peering eagerly through the water-streaked glass, taking in the shops and cafés, all a little gritty but none of them dirty. This is a place for the young and hopeful.

"You have a beautiful smile," he says quietly. "You should wear it all the time."

My hand flutters to my mouth as if confirming that the smile is still there. How can this guy get me so flustered? What's going on with me?

The view changes as he pulls onto the residential streets. They're mostly comprised of small homes with meager front yards, yet there is a sprinkle of wealth mixed in. A sleek two-story house stands between two 1970s homes, and on the corner there's an extravagant Spanish-style minimansion. Things are changing.

A few minutes later he maneuvers his car into a curbside parking spot. "This is where I live," he says, gesturing to a little complex of apartments. There's a gate, and from the street you can see that it leads to a narrow courtyard made up of cobblestones surrounding a small fountain.

He gets out of the car, but I continue to sit there, unsure if I'm supposed to wait for him while he grabs whatever he needs before

we go to the restaurant. But in a moment, Brad is at my door opening it for me. "Shall we?"

Tentatively I step outside. "We're eating at your house?"

"We are. Come on, I'll introduce you to everyone."

"Okay." I try to imagine what Brad's roommates will be like.
Rockers? Frat boys? Fellow aliens from whatever planet he's
from?

As he opens the gate I check out the adobe walls of the building. The place looks pretty old, maybe a little run down, but it's
charming all the same.

He leads me to a place with a curved dark wood door and I follow
him inside. There's no real foyer, just a nice-size living room with
hardwood floors. The walls are adorned with M. C. Escher prints
along with a few posters of New York: the Empire State Building at
night; the Brooklyn Bridge at sunrise; a black-and-white image of a
man walking a tightrope between the Twin Towers. And on a cushy
couch covered with a dark red slipcover is a woman in her fifties
with dyed blond hair and a little girl, around five or six, with frizzy
brown curls, a bright blue dress, and almond-shaped eyes that are
trained on Brad.

"Daddy!"

I gasp as she jumps off the couch and throws herself at him just
before he lifts her into the air.

"I told you he would be here for dinner," the girl says, twisting
in Brad's arms so she can see the blonde. Looking at this woman
now, I note that she has the same angular face as Brad, the same
thick eyebrows and Roman nose. She gets up from the couch, her
beige cotton pants and silk knit top now wrinkled and her cardigan
slightly askew. "She was insistent that you would make it."

He has a little girl. I stare down at the floor and lay my hand
against my stomach as I try to steady my breathing.

"She knows I don't break my promises," Brad says simply.
"Mercy, this is my mother, Sharon Witmer, and this is my daughter,

Miss June Witmer. Mom, June, this is Mercy Raye, the lead singer of the band."

"Hello, Mercy." Sharon offers me her hand and I take it almost mechanically as June giggles and presses her cheek to her father's shoulder.

"Mercy isn't a name!" she says.

"Neither is June," I reply, keeping my eyes low. "It's a month."

"It's *my* month!" she says, pounding her chest with her little fist.

I bite my lip and then slowly force myself to meet her eyes. They're glittering with spirit and humor. How is it that children can find so much joy in the most trivial moments? "You *own* the month of June?" I hear myself asking with exaggerated awe.

"Weellll . . . I don't *own* it . . . but it's my birthday month, but other people get to use it, too."

"That's crazy generous of you," I say with a solemn nod. "And thoughtful. They really should call you Empress June."

June's delicate little eyebrows knit together as she considers this. "Are empresses like princesses?"

"Sorta, but you know how princesses are always getting rescued?"

"Uh-huh."

"Well, no one has to rescue an empress because nobody would dare mess with one. Empresses are da bomb."

June breaks into a fit of giggles. Brad's mother puts her hand on my shoulder. "Well, Mercy," she says, "it looks like you have a new fan."

MINUTES LATER, SHARON'S taken off, and not long after that, Brad has us all sitting down to a Trader Joe's stir-fry, freshly defrosted and sautéed in olive oil. I listen to Brad ask June about her day with Grandma, and I ask June about her school. I quickly learn that she's in pre-K and her teacher, Miss Jenny, is *the best*! Just as her dad's cooking is *the best* (I'm not on board with that one) and her grandmother is the *most wonderful grandma on earth*! And this afternoon they watched the *most fantastic movie, ever*! She's a girl of superlatives and I'm totally charmed. It's odd, because I generally try to avoid little kids, but now that I'm here, well, it's not so bad.

And Brad . . . he just kinda blows my mind. He shows June so much respect! Patiently correcting her grammar and table manners here and there, but mostly letting her talk, laughing at her knock-knock jokes and considering her theories about *A Rugrats Vacation*. We end up hanging out at the table long after we're done eating, laughing and chatting even as the leftover morsels start to crust onto our plates and our water goes from cold to room temperature. When I was a kid I had been told that while at the dinner table the talking should be left to the adults. My little sister, Kasie, was a master at the whole no-speaking-until-being-spoken-to thing. I was not. Inevitably my father would try to shut me up and I'd push back, challenging him until we were both so mad that we were speaking without thinking, spewing insults and anger all over our meal.

"Are you going to stay the night, Mercy?" June asks, bringing me back to the here and now.

"I'm going to have Maria come over when she gets back from her late shift," Brad says, jumping in. "She'll stay here with you while I take Mercy home. Maria's a neighbor," Brad adds for my benefit.

"But she won't be back from the late shift for a long, long time, right?" June asks hopefully. "After my bedtime?"

"After your bedtime," Brad agrees, and then checks his watch. "Which is in twenty minutes."

"Uh-oh!" June is immediately on her feet and rushing from the room. I give Brad a questioning look.

"She gets all-alone time before bed," he explains. "Time she can play by herself with her dolls and picture books. I invented that to give myself a little break in the evening," he admits, "but it's become important to her."

"Oh, so we won't see her again until she goes to bed?" Am I relieved? Disappointed? I have no read on myself.

"Probably not." Brad gets up and starts to collect the plates. "Anyway, that's my daughter."

"And she's the best daughter *ever*!" I say, imitating the sweet lyrical chime of June's voice. Brad gives me a look, but I just laugh and shake my head. "Seriously, she's adorable. Can I ask—"

"Where her mom is?" Brad finishes for me as he reaches for his daughter's empty cup. "She's—"

"That's not what I was going to ask," I say shortly.

"No?" He pauses and tilts his head to the side. "That's what everybody asks after meeting her."

"Yeah, well I'm not everybody and it's not what I want to know," I say, finishing what's left of my water.

"All right," Brad says, drawing out the words as he tries to figure me out. "What would you like to know?"

I look around the apartment. It's not a Beverly Hills estate, but it's still better than the hole-in-the-wall I live in. "What's your day job?"

He hesitates a moment. "I usually work nights; it's better for June that way." He takes my empty glass and heads to the kitchen. "I can get her to and from school, go on field trips, that kind of thing," he says over his shoulder.

"Okay." I follow him in and grab a dish towel that's hanging from the handle of a drawer as he puts the dishes in the sink. "What's your night job?"

"Sometimes it's drumming," he says with a little smile. He turns on the water and waits for it to steam. "I don't really have a career at this point. I simply do what I need to do to pay the bills. What about you? Are you aiming to be a rock star?"

"Oh, I don't know." I pull myself up onto the counter and take a dish he's just cleaned from his hands. "I just like making music and being onstage, so I guess I'll do it until it's not fun anymore. But I don't anticipate ever making any real money from it."

He gives me a sidelong glance and hands me another plate. "So then what *do* you want to do when you grow up?"

I smile and lean toward him, almost conspiratorially, and whisper, "Everything."

He laughs, but then the sound dies on his lips as he studies me. "You're serious."

"About experiencing as many aspects of life as possible? Yeah, I'm serious. Why should I limit myself to one career when I can try twenty or thirty or a hundred?"

"Because you have a calling. Traci told me that most of Resurrection's songs are yours. That you just came up with them during jam sessions without ever writing down a single note."

I chew on my lower lip, thinking about the drawer full of my secret sheet music.

"You can be great," he continues. "All you have to do is really commit to it and you could be a . . . an icon."

The comment startles me so much I almost drop the wet plate.

"I mean it, Mercy."

"Yeah, well." I can feel my cheeks heating up as I return my attention to my task. "You know what they say the secret to happiness is, right?"

"No," he says, giving me a funny look. "What is it?"

"Low expectations!" I chirp.

"Jesus." He shakes his head. "Who says that?"

"I don't know, maybe just me." I dry another dish he hands me. "I will say that fronting for a band is a lot better than the other jobs I've tried so far. I tried retail, that was not fun. I had a brief stint as a telemarketer, that was just hell. But from a paycheck perspective they were all more reliable than singing."

"So how do you support yourself now?"

"Oh you know, I pick up odd jobs. I'm working at that club Envy tomorrow night . . . wait a minute, why am I telling you this?" I put down the dish towel. "You never actually told me what *you* do and I asked first. So give it up, what's the deal?"

Brad sighs. "All right—"

"I'm done with all-alone time and I've washed my face and brushed my teeth!" We both turn to see June in the doorway wearing a lavender nightgown covered in smiling ponies. "Can Mercy put me to bed tonight, Daddy?"

I glance up at Brad and the expression on his face stops me. Something about that request got to him and he looks almost overwhelmed. "You'll have to ask her," he says quietly and I swear I detect a little quiver in his voice.

I turn back to June and am once again swallowed by a whirlpool of mixed emotions. And the way she's looking at me like she thinks I'm *good*. Like I'm innocent.

"Sure," I whisper and slide off the counter. "I'll tuck you in, Empress June."

June beams up at me and places her tiny hand in mine. I have the sudden urge to scoop her up, feel what it's like to have her pudgy little arms around my neck, smell her hair . . .

But instead I let her lead me to her bedroom and I listen intently as she guides me through her small collection of treasures here. *Here in the corner is my Lite-Brite, here are my Barbies, the drawings on the wall are my drawings . . .*

She's turned the whole bedroom into her own little Utopia, I can see that. But I can't shake the feeling that I'm an illegal alien. I don't belong here.

"Before you tuck me in, you have to read me a short story and sing me a song."

I take the story she has in her hand, something about an owl and a fish becoming friends. The premise seems far-fetched but I'm willing to go with it.

Once we're done with that she climbs under the covers that are piled on top of her purple plastic Minnie Mouse bed.

"What does your dad sing you?" I ask as I sit on the edge of the child-size mattress.

"It changes," she explains. "Sometimes he plays something for me on the stereo." She points to a portable CD player attached to two little speakers sitting on top of her dresser. "He plays your song a lot."

"My song?" I ask.

"'Mercy Street'! That's how I knew your name wasn't really a name. It's a street! Does that mean you're empress of the whole street?"

My mouth goes slack and then I quickly get up from the bed and cross to the other side of the room, my back to her as I stare down at the silent speakers.

"Are you okay?" June asks, her perpetually effusive voice registering concern.

"Yeah, I just wanted to look at your stereo system here," I lie, forcing myself to keep my voice even and light.

"Mercy Street," the song that had been playing on the radio when I had gone to meet my father that night.

Dreaming of mercy
In her daddy's arms again

How could a child guess the origins of my name?

I place my fingers against the silent speakers.

I had sung along with Peter Gabriel as I pulled into the parking lot of the diner. The timing of it was just unreal. What were the odds of that fourteen-year-old song being played on the radio at that moment? It simply had to be a sign!

"I have speakers kind of like this at home," I say aloud, still keeping my back to June.

It's a long song. Even the radio version goes on for over four minutes, but I refused to turn off the engine until it was over. And as the sensual, haunting notes surrounded me, I found that I was flooded with the strongest sense of hope. Hope that I could fix things between my dad and me. I thought that maybe, just maybe, he would take me in his arms. Maybe I had a home. Maybe just this once he would grant me mercy.

It had been such a nice four minutes.

"Are you *suuuurrre* you're all right?" June presses.

"Yep." I finally turn back to her, making my face a mask. *Show her happiness, ease, don't let her see all that ugly that lives inside of you.* "How about a lullaby?" She beams at me and then snuggles up in the blankets again, closing her eyes, prepared to be lulled to sleep. I start singing Concrete Blonde's "Lullaby," which is the only lullaby I know. But the song is gentle in its own way and the imagery is sweet. I try to let the song soothe me, too. I need that. And as I sing about her breathing being the wind and her tears being the rain, I imagine myself disappearing into the elements, becoming part of everything while simultaneously becoming nothing. Is that what death is? If so, how beautiful.

I close my eyes as I continue to sing and hold my hands out in front of me, feeling the air, trying to sense what else is in it. The souls of the dead? If not, perhaps their molecules, their energy, all of it surrounding me, entering my mouth, filling my lungs. Ashes to ashes, dust to dust, that's how the saying goes. But we are all so much more and so much less than that. We're stardust.

As the last lyrics of the song leave my mouth, I open my eyes and see that June is fast asleep. And leaning against the doorframe is Brad.

"That was stunning," he says quietly as I adjust her blanket and pull myself to my feet.

I walk past him out of the room and whisper, "I want to go home."

BRAD'S NEIGHBOR MARIA, a frazzled-looking woman in her late forties, is home from her shift at the grocery store within ten minutes, and as soon as she agrees to hang out with the sleeping June we're in his car, heading back to my studio in North Hollywood. For some time we don't speak. I know he can sense that I'm in some kind of funk, but he doesn't ask and I don't volunteer an explanation. It's not until we're closing in on the 134 that he breaks the silence.

"This is how you look when you're deep in thought."

"Excuse me?" I don't even bother to turn my face from my window.

"Almost every time I've caught you deep in thought you look just like you do now . . . sad."

I press my lips into a thin line and keep my eyes on the blurred and shadowy landscape.

"Except earlier, when I was taking you back to my place, right when I pulled off the highway . . . you were thinking about something, I could see that . . . but you were all light and sunshine. That was the exception. That's when I complimented your smile."

I finally turn my eyes away from the glass as I try to figure out where he's going with this.

"What were you thinking about that made you happy?"

"Oh." I hesitate, retracing the night to the moment he must be referring to. "I was thinking that Silver Lake was where Resurrection played our first professional gig."

"Oh yeah?"

I nod, watching the slick road as he maneuvers around some of the slower-moving cars. "We were an opening act for another indie band. That was about . . . I guess six months ago now? It was also the first time I had ever performed in front of a paying audience."

"How'd it go?"

"A lot of people came after we were done, you know, people who just wanted to see the headliner. But still, we got a decent-sized crowd, better than we expected, and . . . I was singing *our* songs, not just covers. It was *wild*." I shake my head, still a little in awe of that experience. "I could feel the . . . the approval and the *love* of that audience. It was actually tangible. I mean . . . okay, you don't always know when you're breathing in smog, right?"

"I guess not," he says, clearly thrown by the seeming non sequitur.

"Trust me, you don't—otherwise everyone in LA would be gagging every five minutes. But when you breathe in the air at the beach, it just feels cleaner and you *do* notice that. It's like all of a sudden you realize, *Oh, this is what it's supposed to feel like to breathe.*"

He takes a moment to let that soak in. "Wow," he finally whispers.

"Exactly! And that's what it was like. There were all these people, most of them strangers, coming together in this celebration of music, and I was giving them that music. And I was up on that stage just inhaling that experience and . . . and it felt *clean.*"

"It felt clean?" he repeats. "Not empowering or sexual or rebellious?"

"Oh, it was definitely empowering and sexual." I laugh. "But being empowered and turned on by other people's happiness? Knowing that there were men in that crowd who wanted me because they were watching me do something I love?" I shrug. "To me, that's clean . . . in fact I would go further than that, I'd say it's pure."

"I never thought about it that way." He says the words so quietly I almost don't hear him. "What about rebellious?"

"Yeah, well you gotta have people who care about what you do in order to rebel," I reply with a bitter laugh. "But again, that's the thing. Those people in the crowd, they cared. And somehow I think I actually surpassed their expectations, which is *not* the norm for me. Trust me, my middle *name* is disappointment. But not this time. This. Was. *Awesome!*"

"Ah, there it is."

"What?" I glance around the car, trying to spot what I'm missing.

"Your beautiful smile."

I roll my eyes, making a show of how cheesy I think he's being.

But the thing is . . . he's right. I'm smiling. A few minutes ago I was Miss Morbidity, and now I'm smiling.

"This is my exit," I say quietly. From that moment on our conversation is dominated by directions on what turns to take, but the smile doesn't fully go away. When he drops me off in front of my apartment building, I'm not in a bad place.

"Rehearsal on Saturday?" he asks as I get out of the car.

"Yep," I chirp. It's not until I've trotted up the path to the front door of my building that I realize he's still there, double parked, waiting to make sure I get in okay. I'm not sure if anyone has ever done that for me before, at least not since I was eight. I unlock the door and wave at him as I step inside the entryway.

What a very interesting night.

And it takes a full forty minutes before I remember to be depressed about Ash standing me up. Forty minutes . . . not bad.

CHAPTER 11

❁

UNFORTUNATELY, MY LATENT depression doesn't pass so easily. It's Thursday now, a day after Ash and I were supposed to meet again, and still no word. I know I should call him, but the humiliation is too acute, the history too loaded.

If only that night with Ash hadn't been so . . . so off-the-charts amazing. If only he hadn't kissed me so gently and then so very passionately, his hands roving over every curve, finding the most sensitive spots on my body, all this before tossing me aside, *again*! And why did he have to look at me like that? Like his hunger for me could never be satiated?

Why did he have to tell me I was worth his pain?

All this is going through my mind as I walk through the employee entrance and into the dark back rooms and offices of Envy, LA's hottest nightclub. I can hear the muted pounding of the music coming from the floor. I can picture the blue lights that I know everyone is bathed in, the artfully structured martini glasses. I can practically smell the designer fragrances of the patrons. But back here everything is brown and completely unembellished. One wall is lined with metal lockers, the kind you might find in a second-rate gym or high school. It's like Oz behind the curtain back here.

I kind of like it.

"Right on time." I look up to see the owner, Matt, coming out of his office, a sub sandwich in his hand. Matt's in his late forties, but I only know that because I happened to get a peek at his driver's license once when he left it on his desk. Botox, fillers, weekly facial—he's done it all. And we won't even get into the hair transplant. In the end he looks ageless but weird. Still, he owns the three most successful nightclubs in LA, so there are always women trying to get his attention. Envy is where the rich and famous come; they're the only ones who can afford the drinks.

"Have I ever been late for this?" I ask as I remove my three-quarter-length, shaggy black faux fur coat to reveal black leather hot pants and a white metal-studded bra top.

His eyes scan my outfit dispassionately. "Hot."

I smile and give him a quick curtsy. "I aim to please."

"I'll make sure everything's ready for you."

I shake my head as he walks away. If only he could find a med spa that could inject him with a little personality.

I find the locker Matt lets me use and start working the combination. I only work here the first and last Thursday of every month, and boy, am I glad this is one of those Thursdays. I desperately need to distract myself. Moreover, I need to be reminded that I'm still desirable. That this is *Ash's* problem, not mine.

But then, what if that's not true? What if the new Mercy is just as problematic as the old Melody? The very thought makes me want to hyperventilate.

No, no, I'm not gonna go there. Not right now. Right now I'm just gonna dance.

I go to the door that leads to the floor and peek outside. I think I see Winona Ryder at the bar. And I'm absolutely sure that's The Rock on the other side of the room. Love me some WWF. And then I see Preston and Aaron coming toward me, both of them dressed in the prerequisite black. Their main job is to work the door, keep track of the "list," VIPs and whatnot. But right now they have a different task, and knowing that, they have both assumed a stoic, almost threatening expression. If they were wearing black suits rather than black tees they could be Secret Service. They file into the back room, one getting on either side of me, both taking a wrist. Aaron leans close enough to my ear so I can hear him over the increasing volume of the club. "Looking good, girl."

"Matt said I looked hot."

Preston looks down at me, surprised. "No! I have never heard him use that word, have you?" he asks, looking over my head to Aaron.

"Only when he's talking about chili peppers."

This gets all three of us giggling, but then the music changes. It's our cue. Immediately Preston's and Aaron's faces grow hard and determined as I go with a full-on sex-kitten pout. As we step onto the floor the spotlight finds us immediately and the crowd parts. One step, two, three, four . . . This is where we pause for a beat. They hold my arms up as I move the rest of my body to the music, slowly, sensuously, but making sure that it's just playful enough that this little display can't be taken too seriously. Then they pull me forward again; this time we take a full eight steps before we stop. I pretend to struggle a little more, and just when it looks like I won't be able to get away, I pull myself from their grasp, sending them stumbling back. And then, in my stilettos, I run straight to a small platform in the middle of the floor, leap, pull myself up to the elevated surface, and get right into the gilded cage that waits for me there.

Literally. It's a cage. For $175 a night I dance in a cage twice a month. I'm fairly sure that Matt has added the part about my locking *myself* in the cage to make it seem less sexist, but even so, I'm pretty sure that Gloria Steinem would not approve. Personally, I don't see the problem with it. I like to dance, I like to be the center of attention, and really, there are only so many acceptable ways a girl can be an exhibitionist. At least this one's legal.

I grab the bars, my body rigid and strong, and then as Destiny's Child's "Jumpin', Jumpin'" begins to play I relax into moves that a man might expect from someone in my position. I use the bars both as props and for support as I arch myself backward. The people on the floor have begun to dance again, but I can feel the eyes that are still on me. How many men will dream about me tonight? I smile at the sandy-blond movie star looking down from the balcony before turning my eyes to a Latino pop star at the bar. Almost everyone here is in the business. Everyone here has the opportunity to see the perfectly maintained bodies of the Hollywood starlets at work and at play. And still, right now, they're looking at *me*. I am not perfect, unlike the women of their world. I don't have a plastic surgeon on call. But when you know how to move, when you can turn your dance into a siren's song, then flaws become assets. I don't hide the scar under my collarbone, I leave the mole on my lower back exposed, I'm not bothered by my thighs touching when I stand. When these men look at me they don't see a fantasy or a manufactured image. They see a woman who is touchable. Someone who will be soft where a woman should be soft, who will be sensitive where a woman should be sensitive. A woman whose lipstick will smear and whose hair will tousle. A woman strong enough to embrace imperfections and passionate enough to make her lover feel like a man.

That's the woman they see dancing in the cage. That's *me*.

I dance for forty-five minutes straight, take a fifteen-minute break, and then I'm back, locked away behind golden bars, dancing right into the witching hour. For every shift I arrive at ten, leave at one. A hundred and eighty minutes of being wanted and desired by the city's rich and powerful.

And in the second hour, when Santana's "Smooth" comes on, I know exactly how to personify the song. I give my dance a Latin flair, blending salsa with my own unique style. The Hollywood agent puts down his drink as he eyes me, the director in Armani takes a step closer. There's just something about this song. Everyone feels it. Suddenly people are dancing alone without care, while couples are pressed so close only the thin layer of their clothes is keeping them from consummating this rising euphoria. My heels tap lightly against the floor of my pretty prison, my hips sway in time, I drop my head, letting my hair fall forward before tossing it back with a flourish as I look straight into the eyes of the first man who comes into focus . . .

Brad.

I almost stumble, the surprise is so great. How did he get in? *Here* in this gathering of agents and stars? No one I know has ever come in here!

Suddenly I'm struck with terrible self-consciousness. And for me to be self-conscious while on a stage is unheard of! But oh, the way I must look! Elevated in the middle of the room, half naked in a cage. The strangers here have never given me a moment's pause, but to be seen like this by someone I hang out with, play in a *band* with, knowing he'll conjure up this image every time he sees me! Someone who will undoubtedly mock me and laugh at me! Even in the unreliable lighting of the club I can see the shock on his face. He could *not* have been expecting this!

I struggle to think of words to mouth to him, some way to turn this into an innocent joke, but as I try to cook up a strategy I notice something. Something in his expression. The shock is fading and . . . and it's being replaced by . . . something else. Something very familiar.

Ooh.

And then, almost of their own volition, my lips spread into a slow, delicious smile. Reaching forward, I wrap my fingers around one of the bars as I once again move my hips to this unique rhythm.

My eyes never leave Brad's. Releasing the bar, I raise my arms above my head, my body moving faster. The music is affecting me in a whole new way now. It's caressing me, penetrating me, turning me into a seductress . . .

. . . not just of the room, but of this one man.

The crowd is now in a complete frenzy. They're dancing, drinking, laughing, and Brad . . . Brad is staring. And just by the way he tilts his head, the way he's hooked his thumbs into the front pockets of his jeans, I can tell that he knows this dance belongs to him.

I run my hands over my skin, my chest, my stomach, the length of my thigh. Santana's guitar is building in intensity, melodic, lustful, hot with passion and life. I lift my hair up, exposing the nape of my neck, and the whole time my body never stops moving.

Brad is the drummer in my band. I have to play with him, work with him, and part of me knows this is a bad idea.

But a bigger part of me simply doesn't care.

Again I grab the bars, this time bending my legs, letting the metal just barely brush the inside of each knee as I get lower and then lower still, inviting him to imagine me lowering myself in front of him, practically forcing him to think of all the things I could do to him at this level.

To broadcast that image across a crowded club is almost enough to scandalize *me*. But the thing is, the people here only see a woman dancing the way a woman in a cage is expected to dance. Only Brad knows that this is more than an obligatory performance. Only he suspects that this just might be foreplay.

When I rise, I allow myself a spin, whipping myself around; the music is getting faster, Santana is on *fire*. There's no point even feigning control anymore—the music, the lust, these are the things that have the power now, they'll do with me what they will.

And maybe, just maybe, Brad will, too.

Oh, the things you discover while dancing in a cage.

Even after the music changes to an Everclear remix, our game continues. It stays like this for ten, twenty, thirty minutes. Each song bringing forth a new seduction, a different way to tempt and taunt. And Brad barely moves, his stillness offering an odd allurement of its own. His eyes never leave me, our connection is never broken.

And when it's finally time for my break, I step out and into the room. I'm supposed to go right into the employee area. I am not to fraternize with the guests.

But this is not a night for rules. As I walk past Brad, I make a small gesture with my hand, looking at him and then pointedly toward where I want him to meet me. When I step into the back area, I leave the door a little more ajar than usual. Matt isn't around; no one is. I'm here alone.

And now, ten seconds later, I'm here with Brad. He's walked into this space with the confidence of a man who belongs here, even though we both know that he absolutely does not. I curl my finger, beckoning him. My back is pressed against the bare wall. And when he steps closer, I see the strength in him in a way I didn't before when I was trying to reconcile his chiseled form with his mild temperament and conservative clothes. Now his strength and his power doesn't just fit him, it *is* him. He's standing less than four inches away, not touching me, but everything about the way he stands, the way his eyes slowly move up and down my body, tells me that everything he *can* do to me he *wants* to do to me. He can lift me up like a feather, carry me like a princess, have me right here, right now, up against this wall.

"I don't understand," I say, a little breathless, a little awed. "If you're not on the list it's almost impossible. People wait in line for hours—"

"I know the doorman." His gaze moves slowly up my waist, across my chest.

"Preston? Aaron?"

"Oscar."

Oscar? Oscar isn't the doorman, he's the bouncer, a bookie and gambler during the day, and he does not seem like the kind of guy Brad or anyone who gravitates toward legal activities would hang with.

He reaches forward and places his left palm against my waist, his fingers spreading to the curvature of my hip. His touch practically burns through the leather I'm encased in as he adds just a little pressure, just enough to arch my back toward him, so now there's not much space between us at all. "I like the way you move."

I swallow hard, realizing for the first time just how big his hands are. I have a small waist, but still, I gasp when he puts his right hand on the other side of me and I find that they almost wrap around me completely. They're not calloused, but they're not soft, either, and as I tremble in his grip I imagine those hands crushing me to him, holding me as close as possible as he lowers his mouth to mine. I let my lips part, just a little, inviting him to do just that.

But wait, *there*—a flash of doubt in his eyes. A hesitation. And then, to my screaming disappointment, he pulls his hands away, his thumbs go back into his pockets, his eyes drop to the floor as he seems to consider something before taking a rather significant step back.

It's enough to make a girl cry.

"You're too talented for this," he says, his voice low, maybe a little hard.

I look at him, bewildered. "What? What are you talking about?"

"To be dancing in a cage," he says, finally looking up at me again. "Too talented to be a living, breathing adornment of the parties of the rich."

"I'm not an *adornment*," I hiss, indignation edging out some of my desire. "I'm a performer."

"You're a singer, a musician," he corrects. "You shouldn't be doing this. You should be in front of a microphone. You should be recording an album. You should be doing *something* that will advance you, because, trust me, this won't."

My mouth goes slack for a moment, and then suddenly, just like that, my indignation is gone. It's been completely replaced by straight-up rage.

"You don't get it," I say, my voice shaking with barely restrained emotion. "I'm not trying to be better anymore. I'm just trying to be *me*!"

"This is you? The girl who dances in a cage while—"

"Excuse me, but I don't have to live up to your standards of success!" I interrupt. "I don't have to live up to *anyone's* standards. I own my life now, got it? I *own* it!" With those last three words I reach forward and smack my hands against his chest, shoving him, although he doesn't budge. "I choose what I do, and you know what else? I choose who I want to spend my time with, and I don't choose to spend my time with privileged assholes who like to stand in judgment of me!"

"Privileged?" he says incredulously.

"Yeah, privileged." I'm shaking now, my hands that were so ready to run over his back balled up into fists. "Tell me something, Brad, how do you support yourself and your kid? Oh wait, let me guess, Mommy and Daddy help. Isn't that right? You're living off love and inheritance, and that's great, but some of us don't have any of that! Some of us have to work for a living. I had to *waste* money on a cab to get here because I can't afford to *invest* in headlights until I'm paid out for tonight's gig!"

"Mercy—"

"*I'm not finished!* Because you should know I don't live in the future. And I refuse to live in the past. With me it's all about the now, and right now I *like* this attention. I like this little job that you think is so beneath me. And so you know what I'm going to do?"

"What." It's not so much a question as it is a statement of resignation.

"I'm going to go back out there and I'm going to Dance. My. *Ass off!* And if guys stare at my ass while I'm doing it, then it's a job well fucking done!"

I push past him, not waiting for Preston or Aaron to escort me. The hell with them, the hell with all of them! As I close myself into the cage Len's "Steal My Sunshine" comes on.

Yeah, that's right! I think as I start to dance. No one is going to steal my sunshine!

The silliness of that thought mixed with the buoyancy of the song actually makes me giggle a little. Did that really just happen? Did I say those things? Who knew I could become so righteous about cage dancing?

But the giggle dies on my lips as I see Brad again, working his way through the room, heading toward the exit.

And then, just like that, he's gone.

He's gone and I'm left here . . .

. . . dancing in my prison.

CHAPTER 12

❀

I DON'T GET HOME until almost 1:45 a.m. The money I have to spend on taxis does nothing to improve my foul mood. It seems like a pretty cruel irony that I have to pony up money for what is normally a luxury because I can't afford the necessity of fixing my friggin' car.

When I get out it's cold and drizzling. I dig my keys out of my bag and start up the walkway. When I'm about ten feet away from the door to my building I spot Ash. He's just standing there, under the awning, beside the door, in his leather jacket and jeans, arms crossed over his chest, waiting for me.

I stop abruptly. "You have got to be kidding me."

He responds with his Cheshire cat grin, white teeth glittering in the gloom.

"It's late, Ash, I don't want to talk," I say, quickly getting ahold of myself as I walk past him, jamming my keys into the front entrance.

"Ah, come now, Mercy, I've been waiting out here in the rain for some time, just for you."

"Have you?" I glare up at the sky, wishing the drizzle would turn into a downpour and really give him something to complain about. "That's funny, because I've been waiting for you to call for five fucking days."

I finally manage to get the door open, but he puts his hand out against it to stop me from slamming it in his face. "Hear me out, just this once."

"This would make twice, and for a pretty similar offense." I put my hand on my hip. "How did you know where I live, anyway?"

"You showed me your license, remember?"

I pause for a moment as I take that in. "You memorized the address?"

His smile is just as compelling as it's ever been. "There is very little about you that I will ever forget."

Well *damn*! I chew on the bottom of my lip for a moment and then somewhat reluctantly step aside. "You get ten minutes."

He steps inside, walking past me. "Make it fifteen."

UPSTAIRS HE MAKES himself comfortable, throwing off his jacket and relaxing into the cream-colored sofa in my studio apartment. He's slowly taking it all in. The tiny, freestanding flat-screen TV on my black metal Ikea entertainment stand; the turntable on a small side table and the collection of records I have stacked below it; the surfboard leaning against the wall. My bed is in a small alcove and the kitchen is separated from the dining area by a tiled counter. The walls are papered with B-movie posters, one large Rolling Stones poster, a smaller photo of Little Richard, and a giant print of the Roman Colosseum lit up at night. "I like your place."

"You're wasting your minutes," I retort. "In fact, I don't know why I let you in here at all."

"I have a good excuse," he says, giving me a doe-eyed look.

"Maybe I don't want a man who needs excuses."

I take off my coat and Ash's eyes get significantly bigger. "Whoa, I like *that*!"

I give him a withering look. "I was working tonight."

"Singing?" he asks, clearly confused as to why I'd change my look so dramatically from gig to gig.

"No." I throw open my closet and find a hanger. "I dance at Envy twice a month, in a cage."

"Are you serious? Well then I *really* like that!"

I smile a little. Maybe his reaction should mildly insult or annoy me, but after my argument with Brad, Ash's enthusiasm is welcome. "What's your excuse?" I ask as I cross to him, perching myself on the arm of the couch farthest from him. My purse is still clutched in my hand just in case I need to swing it at him.

"Something came up. Something unexpected and . . . and big."

"What could have possibly come up that would invalidate promises you made less than a week ago?"

He drapes his arm over the back cushions, looks me in the eye. "My future."

I look away. I'm getting tired of futures. Still, I might as well hear this. "Tell me."

And so he begins his story of the last week. It seems that in addition to music, Ash has a love of acting. It's why he moved to LA. His parents told him his pursuit was hopeless, that he was wasting both his time and his inheritance. And for a while there it looked like they might have been right. But now something has happened: on Tuesday he found out he had scored a principal role in a TV pilot. And unlike so many pilots, this one was guaranteed to be green-lit. Everyone at the studio is completely in love with the script, the show's creator, the choice in director, and yes, the casting. And the names attached to this thing! The producers are movie stars! The other actors have devoted followings and credentials. The female lead just finished up a run on Broadway! This role is going to change his life in the most spectacular ways imaginable. "This is it," he says, his smile now charged with excitement. "This is everything I've been waiting for."

"That's it?" I say flatly. I toss my purse onto the coffee table. "You didn't call me because you were . . . happy?"

"Well, no"—his smile falters, then vanishes—"it's not like that." He stares down at his hands as if he blames them for their idleness. Perhaps he wishes he was holding me. Or maybe he just wishes he was holding a drink.

"No, I'm sure it wasn't," I agree. "I'm sure you were very busy, too. I mean, there must have been contracts to sign, agents to talk to, oh, and there must have been other girls to call, right? I mean I should probably consider myself lucky for making the list."

"I went to tell my parents." The words shoot out of his mouth with almost a venomous intensity. Taking a deep breath, he rests his forearms on his knees and trains his eyes on the floor. "I got a last-minute flight to Oregon and I went to tell them the news."

I don't say anything. As far as I'm concerned there's not a lot to say. So he went to see Mom and Dad. Last I checked, the phones in Oregon worked pretty damn well.

"I knew that if I told them about my success they'd realize they had been wrong to doubt me," he continues. "It sounds ridiculous, doesn't it?" he asks with a bitter laugh. "That a grown man would crave the approval of his parents."

I feel the edge of understanding poking against my rib cage, trying to get to my heart.

"Clearly I don't *need* it," he explains, still keeping his eyes on the floor. "But they're my family. It would be nice to feel connected to the people who brought me here." He makes a vague gesture, indicating that he's talking about being brought into the world in general.

"So if they didn't give you approval, what *did* they give you?" I ask quietly. "Trepidation? Advice?"

"It was more along the lines of disappointment." He finally lifts his head and looks toward the window as a siren goes by. "I should have called you," he adds. "What can I say? I screwed up. I just let this whole thing get to me and I, I don't know . . ."

I wave his regret aside with a flick of my hand. I'm no longer thinking about myself or my bruised pride. "What could they be disappointed in? You got the part. You're gonna be big-time, right?"

"It's not what they wanted for me. Not stable. My father thought I'd be more sensible. Find a job that had a predictable trajectory and stay away from the 'Hollywood lifestyle.'" He uses his fingers to make air quotes around the last two words. "Anyway, my dad's extraordinarily good at being disappointed in me," he says with a bitter laugh. "He has a lifetime of practice."

I scoot off the arm of the sofa, sitting now on the cushions of the couch. Not close to him, but not quite as far, either. "What about your mother?"

"Mom's a little less passive-aggressive than Dad. Given the choice between disappointment and anger, she'll go with the anger every time. It suits her." He angles his body toward me. "It pinkens her cheeks."

"Maybelline offers an easier fix for that," I note, "and it lasts longer."

Ash raises his eyebrows. "You'd be surprised at how long my mother can stay angry. She can stay pink for years."

I laugh and shake my head. "They just need time. When they actually see you on television it'll feel more real for them. Then they'll be calling all the neighbors, their coworkers, the gardener, the works, all to brag about their son the celebrity." I reach over and give him a friendly swat on the arm. "They'll come around, Ash."

"Not so sure about that, Mercy." He says my name carefully, as if forcing himself to remember the change. "I'll still never be the man they wanted me to be. But hey, once I've got the money and the fame, I'll be above their bullshit. I'll have fuck-you money!" Even his laugh is laced with pain.

I pull my feet onto the couch, hug my knees to my chest. I don't mind that he's covering. Stiff upper lip and all that. I've played that part before. I don't have to see his pain to know exactly what it is. I've *lived* it.

"I'm your eldest daughter, and I'm sitting here and telling you that we need you!"

"You are not my daughter. My daughter Melody is dead."

I wince and look away, not wanting Ash to know that my thoughts have wandered back to my own heartbreak. Still, I can't stop myself from reliving that moment. Hearing those words, seeing him walk away from me, leaving me.

I had a fresh cup of coffee in front of me, but when I wrapped my hand around the mug it didn't feel warm. I scratched my fingernails against the back of my hand but it didn't hurt. And I thought, yes, perhaps he's right. I must be dead. Because I have no one in this world and I feel . . . nothing.

So Ash's parents are like Melody's. But he won't be alone in the world. Not if I have something to say about it. "Maybe," I say in a low voice, "maybe you're the man *I* want you to be."

He gives me an incredulous look. "Twenty minutes ago you were ready to scratch my eyes out."

I let out an exaggerated sigh. "I'm not some kind of hysterical drama queen, Ash. I wasn't going to scratch your eyes out."

"Right hook to the face?"

"Bingo."

He laughs and another siren goes by, rushing off to put out one more fire, imprison one more person, or revive one more heart.

"Seriously," I say, keeping my hands in my lap. "I think you were right, about fate that is. I think we're supposed to be here, together, just like this."

"So we can help each other?" Ash asks. He reaches forward, takes my hand, weaves his fingers between mine.

"So we can heal each other."

For a moment he doesn't move, and when I look into his eyes I see innocence there, and ignorance, and pain. And then he leans forward, slowly, oh so slowly, and places his lips right up against mine. I can taste the faint remnants of vices he indulged in earlier on his tongue. Bourbon and herb, little escapes to elevate him above the pain of rejection. But there is no rejection here. Not now. Not anymore. Just escape. And I will take in his pain so I can drown out my own. It's a seductive and beautiful melancholy, and as I lower my lips to his neck he raises his mouth to my ear and whispers, "I really do like your outfit."

I burst into giggles, resting my head in the crook of his neck. "I'm glad," I finally manage. "But I'm not so fond of yours."

"No?"

"Too many layers."

He pulls back a little, cups my face in his hands. "I'm only wearing one layer."

"Like I said, too many. But don't worry." I reach for the bottom of his shirt and pull it up, revealing his abs. "I have a remedy."

I remove the shirt from him, tossing it aside. I give myself a few seconds to take him in. Here in the light of the room, without the disadvantage of a screaming cousin to distract me.

His tattoos cover his upper arm, crawl over his shoulder, and lick the gentle swell of his pec. His chest is smooth and hairless and I can see the subtle outlines of his abdominals accentuating his flat stomach. He's beautiful. So very masculine, but with a unique feline quality. I can imagine him prowling through the night looking for pretty little things to play with or devour. Of course I want him. And I understand him. And maybe, just maybe, he understands me.

I lean forward and gently kiss a bird that is woven into the bold strokes of black and gray ink on his bicep. "Tell me what this is."

"It's the phoenix." He reaches up, pets my hair. "The thunderbird. The Native Americans believed he brought the storms."

A mythical bird that brings the reverberating warnings of thunder. I like that. "And this?" I ask as I lower my face just enough to kiss the drawing of a geometric sun that's above the inside of his elbow. "Does it have a story?"

"It's the sun, the bringer of growth and power. The highest deity of the natives."

"Hmm." I let my tongue dart out and taste it one last time as I pull away. "I want to see the back."

His eyes twinkle with his signature sense of mischief and he stands, turning his back to me. I stand, too, and press myself against his back as I reach around his waist to undo the button of his jeans. I bend my knees so I can let my tongue dance over two arrows facing different directions directly below his shoulder blade, just like I did on the first night we met. "And these?"

"The arrow pointing to the left symbolizes protection, the one to the right is to ward off evil."

I straighten, raise myself up on my tiptoes, placing my lips by his ear once more. "Have you been tempted by evil, Ash?"

"Tempted?" He turns and uses his finger to slowly outline the contours of what there is of my top. "Yes. I've been tempted." He reaches around, and with impressive speed and force, he manages to unhook and then almost violently yank off my top. Then, gently, he brushes his hands against my breasts, toys with them until my nipples are erect and tender. "But not by evil," he says quietly. "There is no evil here."

"No?" I ask innocently. I put my fingers on either side of his waistband and then I pull away just enough and drop down, pulling his jeans down with me. He steps out of them without a word and suddenly I realize, he really was wearing only one layer.

Again I feel his fingers in my hair. "Tell me, how many naked men have you had in this room?"

"Ash," I breathe, kissing the area right above his knee, then a little higher, "you're my . . ." But then I hesitate, flushing slightly.

"I'm your what, Mercy?" he asks, his voice a seductive growl.

"Shh! I'm trying to count."

"For fuck's sake . . ." But now it's his voice that fades as I move higher up his leg. The truth is, Ash *is* the first man I've had here in this particular studio. He's the only man I've been with since he and I lit up the night that one time in Seattle. But he doesn't need to know that. He doesn't need to know about the emotional pain he caused that led to my temporary celibacy. All he really needs to know is what's happening right now, and right now, I want to taste him.

I lift my fingers to the trim groom of the curls from which his erection grows, straining against the very air, ready for me, waiting . . .

I let my tongue dart out again, this time against the tip. Exploring him gently, learning his body through sight and touch and taste. Slowly I take in more of him, hearing him groan. My hand reaches between his legs, cupping him, toying with him, playing with that thin stretch of skin loaded with nerve endings, listening to the hum of his pleasure, feeling him shake against me. Quickly I take him fully into my mouth, running my lips up and down, driving him to the point where I know he's within seconds of losing control. I reach over to my purse on the coffee table and pull out a condom. Ripping the foil, I remove the condom and put it in my mouth, using my lips, my tongue, my precarious control to roll it over his erection.

He leans down and grabs my shoulders, pulling me up and then pushing me backward until I'm up against the wall, and then he's on me. His mouth is on my throat, his teeth grazing my skin as his hands move over my breasts, pinch my nipples, and then one hand lowers between my legs. We're only a few yards from my bed now and he closes that distance in seconds as he pulls me away from the wall and drags me to the mattress, on which I fall back, my knees slightly apart as he pulls off my hot pants and throws them aside. Whatever reluctance I harbored when I saw him at my door is now overridden by a more appealing ache and wanting. Slowly, so slowly he climbs on top of me, his eyes studying every inch of my body as he makes his journey. "What is it you want, Mercy?" he asks, his voice gruff, demanding.

"You," I whisper, "inside of me . . . *now!*"

And in one swift, ferocious movement he flips me over onto my stomach and then I feel him between my legs, and then that insane sensation of him pressing inside me with a rapturous force. I gasp in pleasure, my cheek against the soft sheets, my back against his hard body. His thrust is so strong, so deep it feels as if he's asserting his authority, declaring me his as he claims me. It only takes a moment until that ache inside me strengthens, bringing me to the brink. "This is what you want, isn't it?" he asks, his voice both teasing and authoritative.

Yes is what I mean to say, but it comes out as a primitive groan. His hands are squeezed between my flesh and the mattress, toying with my breasts; his lips are on my ear, growling more words that I'm now too delirious to understand. He turns me on my side, his chest still pressing into my back. I gasp again as he changes to a half-kneeling position, lifting my top leg up into the air to give him the full access he wants. I feel cradled against him, and yet the ferocity of his movements is utterly irresistible. "Go ahead," he says, his voice louder now, firm, insistent, "come for me. Right here, right now."

And in less than a minute I do. The orgasm rocks through me, sending me into a crazed state of bliss. I bite down hard on my lower lip to keep from crying out and alerting my neighbors through these paper-thin walls. A moment later I hear him call out to me, his member pulsing inside me as he comes.

Carefully he lays my leg back down, his hand stroking my back before he collapses against my mattress, lying flat on his back while his sweat remains on my skin and mine on his. We just lie there, breathing. It's so good in so many ways.

And yes, this man does know how to make me happy. And I . . . I *almost* feel safe.

It's just that when he called out to me, he didn't call me Mercy. He called me Melody.

CHAPTER 13

❀

I T'S A FEW minutes before ten in the morning when my phone rings. Ash is in the shower and I'm only now getting out of bed, tired and pleasantly sore, wearing nothing but my favorite oversized Red Hot Chili Peppers tee. "Hello," I yawn into the receiver.

"Hi."

I stiffen at the sound of Brad's voice and I'm suddenly feeling very awake. "What do you want?" I ask.

I hear his sigh, and for a second I imagine I can feel it, too, that it's tickling my ear and he's right here, next to me. "Look," he says, "I was hoping for a chance to talk to you before our rehearsal tomorrow afternoon. Can I take you to lunch? We could meet up at one?"

"No thank you," I chirp and hang up the phone. Two seconds later the phone rings again. "Hello?"

"Mercy," Brad says, a little exasperated now. "I really think it's a good idea that we talk."

"Yeah," I say, glancing toward the closed bathroom door. "I know you do. Otherwise you wouldn't have asked me to lunch. But as with so many other things, you and I disagree on this point."

"We have to play together. It won't be good for the dynamics of the band if there's tension between us."

"Hmm." I walk over to the kitchen and pull some ground coffee out of the refrigerator. "We don't actually *have* to play together. I mean, I'm the lead singer of the band. You're the drummer. So maybe we just need a new drummer."

"You're not going to find another drummer with my talent in time for our next gig."

"We might," I counter as I select two cups and a coffee cone. I'm out of coffee filters so I use a paper towel. "There are lots of drummers in LA. And you're not *that* good." From the bathroom I can hear that the water's been turned off.

"Mmm, I'm pretty good."

I laugh. I can't help myself. At that moment Ash opens the door and steps inside the common space wearing nothing but a bath towel secured around his waist. Drops of water glisten against his light brown skin, somehow making him look both dangerous and vulnerable at the same time.

"Look," I say, tearing my eyes away from him. "Why don't we just forget the whole thing? We'll just pretend it never happened and move on."

"Sweeping things under the rug, leaving things unsaid, those are never good plans," he replies. "Let's be adults about this."

"Are you saying I'm childish?" From the corner of my eye I see Ash walking over to the couch to retrieve his clothes.

"I'm saying that your plan to pretend that something that happened *didn't* happen isn't . . . mature."

"Fuck. You."

I hang up the phone and slam it down on the counter.

"Who was that?"

I look up to see that Ash has his pants on; his shirt hangs in his hand.

"It was just my drummer," I grumble.

Ash hesitates a moment. "The big guy?"

"He's not that big," I snap. "I mean, I guess he's probably six three-ish and he's got kind of a muscular build, but he's not Hulk Hogan or anything. He—" I'm interrupted by the ringing of the phone. "Oh for God's sake!" I snap up the receiver. "*What?*"

"I was out of line," Brad says.

"Aren't you always?" I note dryly.

"Look, I just want to clear the air. If you don't want to have lunch, let's have coffee."

"I don't want coffee. I don't want lunch. What I want is for you to learn to take no for an answer. You want to see me? Show up for rehearsal. I'll let you stare at my back while I perform . . . Oh that's right, you think that's uncouth."

I hang up again.

"So," Ash says, turning his back to me as he puts on his shirt. "I take it the two of you have some sort of thing going."

"What? No!" I turn back to the mugs; for a split second I can't even figure out why they're there. I'm that pissed and that flustered. "We just had a disagreement, that's all."

"It didn't sound like a disagreement between two people who are only friends."

"That's because it wasn't. It was a disagreement between two coworkers . . . or band members, or whatever. I was going to make coffee, do you want some?"

"Sure. So if you two don't have a thing then why was he asking you out?"

I turn and give Ash a blank look.

"The coffee?" Ash reminds me. "The lunch? The learning to take no for an answer?"

"Oh, he wasn't asking me out. He just wanted to talk through some stuff before rehearsal."

"Uh-huh."

"Really, that's all it was." I turn on the kettle. And reach for the coffee grinds. "Do you take cream? I mean, I sort of hope you don't because I don't have any. But I have 2% milk and—"

"If it *was* a date, and I didn't want you to go," Ash interrupts, "would you?"

I pause in the middle of scooping coffee into the makeshift filter. "I just told you, he wasn't asking me out on a date."

"But if he had been, and if you hadn't just been in an argument . . ." His voice fades off for a moment as he tries to regroup. "What I'm asking is, if I told you that . . . that I don't want you going on dates with other guys, would you be cool with that?"

I turn to face him, tablespoon still in my hand. "*Is* that what you're telling me?" I ask in almost a whisper.

He takes a deep breath and then gives me a curt little nod. "Yeah. Yeah, that's what I'm telling you."

I lean back against the counter. I'm twenty-two years old and no one has ever asked that of me before. I mean, okay, lots and lots of guys have wanted to party with me, sleep with me, and quite a few have done both. But not one of them has ever wanted anything that even resembled a commitment. At least not with *me*. Not with Crazy.

"Mercy?" he says. I can hear the note of anxiety in his voice.

"What? Oh . . ." I meet his eyes and carefully put the tablespoon down behind me. "Yeah, I mean . . . yes. I'm okay with that. I won't date anyone else . . . no one but you."

Even as the words leave my mouth I can feel the accelerating pace of my pulse. Excitement mingled with just a splash of panic. But Ash's smile is just what the doctor ordered. He steps up to me, and weaving his fingers into my hair he pulls me to him, kissing me deeply. "You know what?" he says as he pulls away. "Forget the coffee. Let's go out. We have celebrating to do."

"Yeah?" I ask, now beaming at him, my heart going a mile a minute. "What are we celebrating?"

"My pilot!" he exclaims. "Your new boyfriend is going to be a superstar! Now put on something hot. I know this great place that serves caviar omelets and mimosas."

"I don't know if I'm in a mimosa mood."

"Neither am I." He laughs. "But they also make a kick-ass Bloody Mary."

As the kettle starts to boil he steps away to find his shoes. I turn off the burner and put the cups back into the cupboard. So I'm dating a man who is going be a superstar.

But as odd as it might seem, the word in that sentence that I find amazing is not *superstar*.

It's *dating*. I'm not just hooking up, I'm *dating*.

A huge grin spreads across my face. I'm dating Ash. The man I'm fated to love.

❈

CHAPTER 14

Saturday's rehearsal is hell. Pure and utter hell. And it's partly my fault. I spent all yesterday and today fluctuating between giddiness (thanks to Ash) and anger (thanks to Brad). And when I see Brad I'm . . . well, I'm not nice. I'm short with him, sometimes dismissive. I nitpick at his performance, which is hard because he really is pretty good, and I cut him off when he tries to offer new ideas. To his credit he does not nitpick back. But he is clearly aggravated with me and has very little patience. Poor Tonio and Traci have no idea what's going on. We get through a few songs but it's tough, and by the time we get to the fourth one we find that we can't go more than a minute without sniping at one another. Traci finally puts an end to it by throwing up her hands and signaling for all of us to stop.

"That's it!" she says at the top of her lungs. "We're all going to take a ten-minute bong break!"

"I don't smoke," Brad says from behind his drum set.

"Well, you might want to consider starting," Traci retorts, "because you seriously need to mellow out. You, too!" she says, turning to me when I start to snicker. "I'll have you all know that I ended things with Benji last night," she chokes out. "And yet here I am, keeping it together, doing what I'm supposed to do even though this breakup may be the hardest thing I've ever had to deal with!"

Tonio and I exchange quick glances. We both know that this is the fifth time Benji and Traci have broken up, and it's always the hardest thing she has ever had to deal with.

"Well I'm not saying no to a bong break," Tonio says helpfully as he frees himself from his guitar.

"Great, are you two coming? Or are you guys just going to hang here for some cathartic hate sex or something?"

"Oh come on, Traci," I begin, but she already has her back to me.

"Suit yourself, both options are open, but do *something*, because what's going on here is *not cool*."

Tonio and Traci disappear into the house, leaving Brad and me in an empty garage, staring at the silent instruments.

"I knew this was going to happen," Brad mutters. "This is why I wanted to deal with this before rehearsal. If you could have just been reasonable—"

"Oh my God, would you stop being such a little bitch?" I snap.

"I'm being a bitch?" He throws his sticks on the ground. "All I wanted to do was talk to you, clear the air over coffee or lunch. Why is that such an outlandish proposition?"

I turn my back on him, glaring at the wall. The truth is, I don't know why it's outlandish, other than that having lunch or coffee with Brad somehow hints at . . . at intimacy. And for some reason that scares the hell out of me. Brad has never been a possibility, even before Ash showed back up. And Ash *did* show up! And we're dating exclusively, which means I actually have my very first boyfriend. Brad's presence shouldn't be so much as a blip on my internal Richter scale.

And yet.

"Look," he says, breaking into my silence. "We're alone now."

"I noticed." I cross my arms in front of me. It's cold in here. I didn't notice it when I was singing and biting Brad's head off, but now that it's quiet and it's just the two of us, the chills running through me are a little more pronounced.

"So," Brad continues, "will you allow me to take this opportunity to apologize?"

I turn back to him, a little reluctant, a little curious. "You want to apologize?"

"Yeah." He sighs and rubs his eyes. "Yeah I do. I'm sorry, Mercy. I didn't mean to insult you the other night."

"And yet you did," I point out. "You know, I don't need your approval, and I sure as hell don't need your scorn."

"Trust me." He gets up and crosses the garage to where I stand. "I have no scorn for you. If anything I'm in awe of you."

"Yeah, right." I let out an awkward laugh and lower my eyes.

"Hey," he says softly, his voice low, soothing, even seductive. "Look at me."

Slowly I look up to find his dark brown eyes looking back down at me. Ash was right, he's a big guy. His chest, his shoulders . . . he makes me feel positively tiny. But then he has a nice, narrow waist to offset it all. I've never been with anyone like Brad.

As soon as the thought crosses my mind I feel myself blush. These kinds of thoughts are dumb and completely irrelevant to anything going on in my life.

"If you only knew how amazing you are onstage." The man has such a beautiful baritone. Even when he's speaking gently, like now, it feels . . . powerful. "I'm not simply talking about getting the approval of an audience; there's so much more to it than that . . . or at least there is for you. You're better than everyone else here."

"Better than you?" I ask with a little smirk, using the opening to goad him.

"Yes," he says simply. I blink in surprise. I hadn't expected that. I'm not even sure if it's true.

"When you walk on the stage," he continues, "it's like you absorb all the light in the room and then . . . then you *become* the light. You glow and you're brilliant and you . . . you shine. For you to be a background dancer in a club, a place where everyone is so absorbed in their own self-importance and networking that they won't *allow* themselves to give you the attention that your presence deserves . . ." He shakes his head. "Mercy, you shouldn't be in the background of anything, anywhere. You're the light. You're the *star*."

"I . . ." I stop. There's no way to respond to such breathtaking praise. There's no way to even fully process it.

"One of these days I hope you realize that," he continues. "I hope you see who you are and what you can be."

"I want to be me," I whisper. "I've told you that, and maybe that sounds trivial. Maybe it sounds weak or unambitious, but if you only knew . . ." Again I stop myself. What on earth am I thinking? I'm going to confide in this man? About things I don't even want to acknowledge to myself? Really?

I force a little laugh and shake my head. "Okay, I think we're wading into the deep end of the pool here."

"I'm a strong swimmer."

I press my lips together and walk past him to his drum set, letting my fingers slide over the surface. "What got you into drumming?" I ask, carefully maneuvering the conversation away from me.

"Emotional reasons," he says, a note of amusement in his voice. "Unspent aggression, angst, rebellion, anger . . ."

"Sounds like rock 'n' roll to me." I look back at him over my shoulder. "And your daughter? How's she doing?"

I see the spark of understanding in Brad's expression. He knows I'm trying to avoid a certain kind of conversation. "She's good," he says, walking over to my side, picking up his drumsticks, gently tapping the cymbal to add just the lightest chime to our conversation. "She's been asking about you."

"She has?" I ask, genuinely taken aback.

"You made an impression on her." He hesitates a moment before taking the conversation on another turn. "So aside from dancing at Envy, do you have any other jobs that might raise eyebrows? I'd like to be prepared so I don't say something stupid while in a state of shock like I did last time."

I take the sticks from him, sit down behind the drums, and tap out a light beat. "Sometimes I walk dogs. There are a lot of people in my neighborhood who have irregular schedules. They'll be home for weeks and then all of a sudden they'll be working three twelve-hour days in a row. So some of those people will call me to be their temp dog walker."

"Do you like dogs?"

"Love 'em. If my landlord would allow it I'd have one. Hell, I'd have five."

He chuckles, shifts his weight back on his heels. "Anything else?"

"Um." I pick up the beat a bit. I'm far from being a skilled drummer, but I know how to create a rhythm. "Three days a week I do phone sex."

There's about thirty seconds of silence. I keep my eyes on the drums. Finally he asks, "Are you serious?"

"1-900-555-SEXX. If you watch late-night TV you may have seen our ads. The agency forwards the calls to my house, and for a few hours I just, you know, talk dirty on the phone. It's no big deal."

"Do you . . ." Brad takes a moment as he tries to pull together his thoughts. "Do you have a porn name?"

"Cherry Pop. I usually make a little heart out of the O in Pop . . ."

"Cherry . . ." He shakes his head, this time as if to clear it. "Do you pretend to be having sex on the phone? Is that how it works?"

"Sometimes," I admit. "But I get a lot of fetishists. I've learned to really eroticize my feet. I like to say I give good foot."

"Jesus."

I glance up, ready to see the judgment, but all I see is amusement. "Like I said, it's not a big deal," I say again. "Some of these guys just want to talk. It ends up being, like, a miniature therapy session. They'll even ask for advice on how to pick up girls."

"But none of these guys want you to talk dirty about . . . normal sex?"

"First of all, I'm not really sure I believe there is such a thing as *normal sex*. I'm not even sure I believe in the word *normal* at all, but yeah, okay," I say, momentarily distracted by a spider slowly making its descent from the ceiling. "I do have a few clients who just want the straight-up dirty talk. The thing is, all these guys, regardless of their preferences, all really want the same thing, and once you figure out what that is, well the whole thing stops feeling so weird."

Brad cocks his head to the side, and for a second I imagine putting my lips right there, where the tendons of his neck are pulled taut, tasting his skin. "What's the thing they're looking for?" he asks, his voice so low and so quiet I feel the vibrations of his words more than I hear them.

I blush again and turn my attention back to the drums. "They want to feel wanted." I silently roll the wooden stick over the taut membrane of the instrument. "Every single one of us wants to feel wanted. But some of us . . . I mean some of them . . . well, they're just not. They're the unwanted." I lift the stick to the cymbal, careful now to avoid Brad's eyes. "So these guys, they pay a few bucks to some 900 number, and for the space of a phone call they can pretend that there *is* someone out there who is . . . you know . . . excited about them, who is *passionate* about them, someone who wants them." I sigh and get up from the stool. "I don't mind facilitating that fantasy." There's so much more I could say. I could tell Brad how very familiar I am with different versions of that fantasy. I could tell him how much I relate to the longings of my invisible clients. But I won't. I don't want to admit that at twenty-two I'm totally floored that I've finally found someone who wants to be my boyfriend. No, I don't want to tell him how much I have in common with the men who ask me to lisp false praise and passion into the phone. No need to let him know that I'm quite that pathetic.

Brad's quiet for a moment, then wraps his hand around the other end of one of the drumsticks I'm holding but doesn't pull it away from me. He's so close to me now, if I move even a little my arm will brush against his and . . . and it's like he's holding my hand without even touching me, like we're connected through the tools of his music. "You see the world differently than anyone else I've ever met," he says softly.

When you're an outsider you have to. But again, I refrain from articulating the thought.

The door connecting the garage to the house flies open and Traci steps into the rehearsal area, followed by Tonio. "Are we good?" she asks. "Can we get on with this?"

"Yeah." I let go of the drumstick and hand the other one over. "We're cool." I feel Brad's eyes on me as I walk back up to the microphone. I have to take a second to steady my breathing, which has become inexplicably shallow and quick. "Let's raise the roof," I say softly into the mic.

Tonio starts us off with the slow strumming of his guitar and I hold on to the mic with both hands, like it's a raft. Like we're all in the deep end of the pool, and I'm the one who doesn't know how to swim.

❀

CHAPTER 15

Brad and I aren't at one another's throats anymore, but within minutes Tonio and Traci realize that rehearsal has gained a new kind of tension, most of it stemming from Brad. He quietly, politely suggests we might want to tighten this one stanza in one song and then add another hook to another song that sounds to him like a potential single. We go over and over things in a way we've never done before. Traci and Tonio are not loving it, and they'd give Brad the same attitude I was giving him earlier if I didn't so clearly have his back. And why wouldn't I? Every time we apply this new kind of focus to one of our songs, it improves. We change a note here, leave room for a little more vocal improvisation there, and all of a sudden we're playing at a different level. His style is a little contagious, or at least I find it so, because I, too, start pushing for improvements and changes. I start expressing my vision in a way I haven't before. I'm pulling away from this idea that making music is just about having fun. I keep thinking about how Brad said I'm this light, this *star*, and I find myself wanting to live up to that outlandish assessment. I sort of want to try to be as good as he thinks I am.

When we're done, Brad and I walk out together, leaving a sulking Traci to pacify Tonio's frustrations with a gin and lime.

"They hate me," Brad mutters, his hands in his pockets.

"Yeah," I agree, "but try not to take it personally."

He laughs and shakes his head.

"I like what you add to the group," I say as a car speeds past us on this residential street. "I think . . . I think maybe I needed you . . . I mean we," I say, correcting myself quickly. "We need you."

Brad hesitates a moment before saying quietly, "It's mutual."

Even at this early evening hour the birds are singing, adding a little bit of nature to this concrete city. Keeping my eyes on the ground, I walk with him to the sidewalk, where we stop. My car is to the left, Brad's to the right, but it's me he turns to. "Would you like to have dinner?"

I feel a spasm in my chest that I try desperately to ignore. "You mean with you and June? I—"

"No," Brad says, cutting me off. "June is having dinner at her friend's house so it would just be us."

Oh God, is he asking me out on a date? I turn my gaze upward as if looking for divine guidance. But no, I'm being silly. Guys like Brad are not interested in girls like me, not to have dinner with anyway. I'm projecting, that's all. And even that's bad because, really, I shouldn't have anything to project.

"I would love to but I have plans with . . . um, my boyfriend."

"Ah." Is there a note of sadness there? I try to get a read on him, but now he's looking past me, his expression close to blank. "Guess it's just me, then." Nodding to my car, he asks, "You got your headlights fixed?"

"Yesterday afternoon."

"Good, then drive safe." And then he puts a hand on each of my shoulders and gently pulls me forward. It's not exactly a hug—his arms aren't around me—but . . . it's something. He's too tall for my head to go over his shoulder, so I find myself resting my cheek against his chest, hearing the rhythm of his heart. "Enjoy your evening, Mercy," he murmurs, his breath in my hair as he places a single kiss on the top of my head and then releases me and turns to leave.

"Brad?"

He stops, waits without pivoting back to me, turning his head slightly so I can only make out a sliver of his profile. "I just . . ." I swallow hard and take a deep breath. "You know I don't share Traci and Tonio's opinions, right? I mean I . . . don't hate you."

He turns his head a little more, and now I can see the wry smile on his lips. "I'll try not to take it personally."

And then he turns and walks away.

THE NEXT THREE weeks are . . . interesting. I'm seeing Ash once or twice a week, which I guess is normal for an exclusive couple. Oh, and I've become incredibly fond of using the word *exclusive*. Rehearsals are great . . . for me. I can sense a confrontation brewing within the band and I *really* don't want a confrontation. My feelings about Tonio are fairly neutral, but Traci's different. She sort of unwittingly saved my life not too long ago. She's also the only person other than Ash who I knew in my last life . . . well, *knew* is an exaggeration. We attended the same junior college and occasionally went to the same parties. We almost never talked, but I noticed her playing the piano at a house party one night. She was good. A few weeks later we ended up in the same small group, all of us leaving a party together on some dude's suggestion that we go on a nighttime hike up to some remote little spot he knew, do some shrooms, and find our higher selves. At the time it seemed like an excellent plan.

Traci ended up having a vision. She said she saw musical notes floating around both of us, she said she heard people clapping for us. She explained that we were to be in a band, we would make people happy and inspire them to dance, and we would keep toads for pets.

I remember the part about the toads specifically. Maybe it's not as elegant as "Riders on the Storm" or as whimsical as "Lucy in the Sky with Diamonds," but it seemed pretty cool at the time.

Anyway, she gave me her number—whether that was before or after we left the party I don't remember. But I do know that I found it years afterward, just eight months ago now. It was at a time when

I was completely and utterly lost. A few months earlier my father had actually published my obituary in the local paper of the little Arizona town my family was currently residing in.

By the time I read it . . . well so much had been lost. I *felt* dead. And there it was in print on a newspaper clipping that was balanced on the palm of my cold, still hand. The horror was real. Melody was gone. I didn't exist.

You need a death certificate to publish an obituary, and the fact that he was able to get anyone to publish this thing without it suggests that he paid someone off. And *that* means my father had put more value on my death than on my life.

It's a detail I've never been able to push aside.

And what exactly do you do when your father pronounces you dead? When all your hopes have been shredded and burned? What do you do when you find that every time you look in the mirror all you see is ugliness?

Or, as Brad would say, a monster. I looked in the mirror and I saw a monster.

Taking a new name, a new identity, that was the easy part. It did help me put some distance between me and the shredded remains of my former life. But still, I was hollow. A girl with no family, no origin, no history. I desperately needed . . . *something*. Something other than the silence that seemed to follow me everywhere.

And so when I stumbled across that crumpled-up paper at the bottom of the purse I no longer used and saw Traci's number, I remembered that night on the hill. I remembered her vision, but now I saw it differently. Her hallucination took on the form of a life raft. If I could at least find a way to integrate music into my life in a more tactile way, it would give me my touchstone. It would give me the endurance to breathe.

And Traci remembered so much. She remembered the parties we had been to. She remembered talking to me. She remembered the hike and her visions. She just didn't remember my name.

When she asked me to repeat it, apologizing for not quite catching it at the beginning of our conversation . . . well, I took that to be the biggest sign of all. I told her my name was Mercy and I wanted to play music with her. She said yes.

With one word she saved my life.

So no, I don't want to piss Traci off. I don't want this band to become something she doesn't recognize.

But I'm beginning to realize, I don't want to be stagnant, either.

Right after our next gig I try a different approach. I take her hand as we leave the stage and pull her aside, putting distance between us and the men. The wings of the stage are dark and a little musty, but the fading cheers of the crowd out front have given the space a hint of vitality. "Did you see that?"

She looks at me with somewhat impassive eyes. "See what?"

"They loved us!"

"They always love us," she retorts before yawning loudly.

"This was different. Those rehearsals paid off. This is the best we've ever been, and they *felt* that! It wasn't just that they were cheering us . . . Some of them, they, like, closed their eyes and really listened. They were . . . they were in awe," I say, using Brad's word. I glance over in his direction. He's trying to talk to Tonio, who seems utterly disinterested.

Traci laughs. "They weren't in *awe*. They were high. You remember what that's like, right?"

"Oh what the hell are you talking about?" I ask, exasperated. "I still get high."

"Really? When?" She uses both hands to toss her hair back, her go-to gesture when she's feeling defiant. "It used to be you'd hang out after rehearsal and you'd smoke a doobie with us. Not every time, but most."

"I just haven't been in the mood lately." The sound of the cheering is gone, replaced by the music of a DJ. Brad and Tonio have started moving our instruments and equipment off the stage.

"You haven't been in the mood since Captain America over there crashed our party." She shoots Brad a poisonous glare as he carries some of his drums out to his car. "Tell me, are you going to start wearing polo shirts, too? Maybe change your name to Babs or Bethany or something?"

"No, I . . ." I falter as I try to think back. Has it really been that long since I took a hit? When I started my new life, all I swore off was anything that was physically addictive. My coke days are *over*, and never again will I be chasing the dragon. That's a definite. But pot? It's the only easily accessible drug that helps ease my mind when I get that I-want-to-jump-out-of-my-skin feeling. But I guess . . . I guess I just haven't had that feeling after rehearsals lately. So maybe it has been that long, but . . . oh, wait . . . the smoke-filled kiss.

"I took a hit on New Year's Eve after our gig." Tonio has packed up Traci's keyboard and gestures to us that he's going to be loading it into the car as he heads out.

"You went home after our gig," Traci snaps. Then she looks at me again, noting my expression. "You *didn't* go home after our gig!" she says slowly. "What did you do?"

"Well, there's this guy—"

"Wait . . . oh my God." She grabs my arm. "You found the Antonio Banderas look-alike? You are so *good*!"

"I did not find a Banderas look-alike," I say, irritated. Then, looking down at my hands, I add sheepishly, "He's more of a Johnny Depp type."

"*Better!*" she squeals, attracting Brad's attention as he carries out the rest of his drum set. Traci flashes him an innocent smile. "Just girl talk," she calls over to him, then turning back to me she adds, "Did you know that Depp has a movie coming out this year? *Chocolat*. It's based on some book. He's playing a hot Gypsy. I would so fuck a hot-Gypsy Johnny."

"Well, New Year's Eve guy, Ash, is not a Gypsy, he's an actor."

"Ew."

"Johnny Depp's an actor!" I protest.

"Johnny Depp's a star, totally different."

I laugh and shake my head. "This guy's also a great singer and he rides a motorcycle."

"Wait . . ." Traci leans back on her heels. "Are you still seeing him?"

"Yeah." The music changes to the Chili Peppers' "California-tion." "He's kind of my boyfriend."

"Shut up!" This time she smacks me on the shoulder. It's a playful slap, but it still kinda hurts. "Is he here?"

"No." I swallow and look away. "He wasn't able to make it, but he says that if I invite him again he'll make sure to be here."

"Definitely invite him." She links her arm with mine and starts leading me off the wings of the stage. Without even asking I know she's taking me to the bar. I glance back just as Brad steps back in-side. An image spontaneously pops into my mind—Brad reaching out to me, drawing me to him, kissing my hair one more time, tak-ing my hand, leading me somewhere else to something . . . better. But instead he lifts his hand in a quiet motion of farewell. As Traci pulls me into the bar, I see him step through a door, the word *Exit* lit up above it in glaring red neon.

But then of course he's not going to stay here. He has someone to go home to. Someone who loves him. What must that be like?

"When I meet this guy," Traci says, bringing my focus back to her as we burst through the employee door into the club, "if I think he looks like Johnny, too, can we talk about the possibility of a threeway?"

"You know, I'm not that into threeways," I admit. Several of the people here approach us with congratulations and praise, but both Traci and I manage to disentangle ourselves from them quickly.

"You only say that because you've never tried it," she says once it's just us again.

"Oh, I've done it a few times."

Traci does a quick double take. "You have?"

"Yeah, but—" I'm interrupted by some guy asking if we're selling CDs. We direct him to the other side of the club, where one of Traci's roommates is peddling them for five bucks a pop. "This is what I've learned about threeways," I say, picking up the thread. "If a guy you're hooking up with asks if another guy can join in, your hookup guy is most likely gay; you're just there so he can pretend he's not. And if it's two women and one guy . . . well that's a little better, but only because when the guy turns his attention to the other woman you can just take a break and use the time to read a book or something."

Traci stops, five feet from the bar. "You didn't pause to read a book in the middle of a threeway."

"Have you read Neil Gaiman's *Sandman*? It's, like, impossible to put down."

Traci blinks and then throws her arms around me. "I fucking love you."

"I fucking love you, too, Traci," I reply, keeping my voice light. But the truth is, I'm not entirely comfortable with this conversation. Not because we're talking about sex, but because I'm talking about Melody's life as if it was my own, and I don't *want* it to be my own. If I claim these experiences, don't I have to claim the others?

Traci pulls me up to the bar and bangs her hand against it to get the bartender's attention. If anyone else had done that they'd be ignored at best and thrown out at worst, but Traci—with her tousled auburn hair and bright blue heavily mascaraed eyes and skull-and-crossbones necklace—is one of those people who can make obnoxious look cute.

"Best whiskey on the rocks." She looks at me for confirmation, then adds, "Make it two. It's on Danny," she says, referring to the owner.

"He said he's buying us drinks?"

"Of course he did. When has one of these guys ever *not* covered our drinks?" When the whiskeys arrive she puts down a three-dollar tip and then turns back to me. "So your boyfriend, he lives in LA?"

"He rents a small house in Santa Monica."

"Okay, so a small house in Santa Monica equals a small fortune. Are you sure this guy isn't the *real* Johnny Depp?"

"I doubt Johnny rents." I laugh.

"He might," she counters, "if it was a nice enough place." The guy behind Traci offers her his bar stool and she hops up, flashing him her sweetest smile as she does. I have a feeling I would have hated Traci in high school. "*Is* it nice?"

"Yeah, he says it's fairly new construction, and it's on a bit of a hill, so apparently it has a decent view of the ocean and—"

"*He says?*" Traci asks, stopping me. "*Apparently?* You've never seen your boyfriend's house?"

Just then the whiskeys arrive and I take mine eagerly. This interrogation is getting to me. All I wanted was for her to acknowledge that the rehearsals had improved our performance, and now we've veered off into threeways and houses.

"Can I tell you something?" she asks.

I grimace involuntarily. When someone asks if they can tell you something it's never something good. She presses on without waiting for a response.

"Your boyfriend's cheating on you."

A genuine laugh escapes my lips. "No way."

"Why couldn't he come tonight?"

"He was cast in a pilot and, I don't know, they were working on some pilot stuff tonight," I say, taking another sip. I'm not loving this whiskey, but it's better than the conversation.

"Are they in the middle of filming?"

I shake my head no. "Not for another month."

"Then he's not working," Traci says flatly. She crosses her legs, pushing her short skirt dangerously high. "It's not like they do table readings at night, and if he was meeting with his agent or something that would have been an earlier dinner."

"How do you know so much? You don't even date actors."

"Yeah, that's because I *know* actors. Once you really get to know a few you don't date them anymore. Not unless damaged and needy gets you hot."

Another man stops by the bar to tell us how great we were. Traci smiles, exchanges a few words with him, and then manages to get rid of him with little fuss. "You don't get it," I explain. "Ash was the one who *wanted* to be exclusive. It was his idea."

"He wants *you* to be exclusive," Traci corrects. "Maybe he wants to fuck around while you hang around. I believe that's the traditional way of doing things."

"He wouldn't do that," I say quietly, lifting my glass again.

"He's a man," Traci says with a laugh. "Trust me, they all do that."

"This guy's different."

"Oh come on, Mercy—"

"I said he's different!" I slam my glass back down on the bar so hard the whiskey goes splashing over the side. Traci's jaw drops. The guy to my left, who has *not* offered me his seat, casts an amused glance in our direction.

"I—" Traci begins, but she's immediately interrupted by Tonio, who seems to come out of nowhere to throw an arm over each of us. He smells like cigarette smoke and radiates with artificial adrenaline.

"My bitches!" he says with a laugh. "You two drinking without me?"

I shrug him off and step away from the bar. "Take my place," I suggest. "I'm outta here."

"Oh come on, Mercy," Traci groans, "don't be so touchy. I was just speculating."

"Yeah, well I'm done speculating for tonight, I want to go home." I turn around and walk through the club and out the door into the cool night air. The streets are pretty quiet right now. It's too early for last call, but too late for people to bar hop over to another location. A lonely street vendor is selling hot sausages to stragglers. I find myself suddenly disgusted with my familiarity with this scene. I don't want to be this intimately aware of what the streets always look like this far after midnight. I don't want to be the girl who can speak with experience about threeways, the girl guys want to fuck but won't give up their bar stool for or be *loyal* to! I mean other than the conspicuous lack of cocaine, *which I miss*, how is Mercy's life so different from Melody's?

I close my eyes and count to ten, trying to remind myself that I'm overreacting. I'm letting Traci get inside my head. My life is fine . . . or at least it's not horrible. I love that high I get when I'm on-stage, in front of a crowd, singing my songs. Maybe if I had started doing that at a younger age I wouldn't have gone so overboard with the drugs. And Ash *is* being loyal. I didn't ask him to commit, he offered. So the idea of his cheating is just silly. Things are going great for us. They really are. We're having the kind of fun I haven't had in ages. He may not have been able to come tonight, but it's not like he's been avoiding me. We've been going to clubs and dive bars, pool halls, all places I enjoyed in my last life, but it's totally different now because this time I'm going to those places as part of a couple. *I'm part of a couple!* Every night I'm with Ash feels like a celebration of that.

The only problem is, when he leaves, I don't feel so celebratory anymore, and it's not just because he's reintroduced me to hang-overs. When he leaves . . . I don't know, there's this weird sense of emptiness that I can't quite explain.

I glance back at the bar I just stormed out of. Typical that neither Traci nor Tonio came after me.

If Brad were here, would he have come after me?

I push the question aside and start heading to where I parked my car. Even if I chose to pursue Brad, the best I could hope for is a one-nighter. No way is a guy like that hitching his wagon to someone like me. So then once we were done sweating it out in the sheets, all I'd have to show for it would be one lousy memory. Plus, the obligatory awkwardness that follows those kinds of encounters would probably cost me one kick-ass drummer.

I spot my car, which I purposely parked under a streetlight. Ash is the one who matters here. I do love the way that man touches me, the way he's learning my body, the way I'm learning his. And it's right that after everything we should be together.

But as I slide behind the wheel I'm reminded that I haven't told Ash what *everything* is. He certainly doesn't know how he brought about Melody's death. I wish I could pretend that I don't know why I haven't opened up to him, but the truth is, I know.

I haven't told him because, while I've trusted Ash with my heart, I don't trust him with my soul.

I'm not sure if I ever will.

CHAPTER 16

❀

I T'S EARLY ON a Sunday morning and my phone is ringing. Two weeks have passed since my confrontation with Traci and not much has changed. In two more weeks Ash will be filming his scenes for the pilot and his elation has been growing exponentially. Last night we were out until almost four. There had been drinks, dancing, greasy late-night breakfasts, and all sorts of sinful fun. It was all great . . . except now my phone is ringing and I am in no way, shape, or form ready to face the day.

"Ash, get that for me?" I ask, saying the words into my pillow. When he doesn't answer, the memory of how last night ended comes back more clearly. He didn't spend the night. He wanted to sleep in his own bed so when he woke up he could start studying his lines right away. Well bully for him, but now *I* have to get the friggin' phone.

I roll over on my mattress, eyes still shut tight, and flap my hand around until I find something that feels like a receiver. "Hello," I croak.

"I need a favor."

"Brad?" I open one eye and peek at the digital clock on the nightstand. "It's nine fifteen in the morning."

"Yes, I wanted to call earlier, but decided I should wait for a more reasonable hour just in case you were sleeping in."

"Nine fifteen on a *Sunday* morning. It's not reasonable."

"Mercy, my mom is back East. Her flight was supposed to land at LAX at one o'clock, but there's a snowstorm over there. She doesn't think she'll be able to get in until well into the evening, if she's able to make it here today at all."

"Oh, that's a shame. Can we talk about this at ten?" I glance at my window, see the sun peeking out from behind the blinds, and immediately scrunch my eyes closed again.

"She was going to watch June tonight, but now she obviously can't. I was hoping you could fill in for her."

I immediately sit up. "Wait a minute, are you asking me to babysit?"

"I'll pay you," he says, his voice tinged with urgency and worry. "I don't expect you to do this for free."

"Brad, it's me, Mercy. The girl who dances in a cage and constructs toe-sucking fantasies for needy fetishists."

"Don't dance in a cage while you're with June and try to keep feet out of the bedtime stories and you'll be fine."

"Wow," I say lightly as I drop my aching head into my hands. "This is really not your finest parenting hour."

He chuckles, and I smile despite myself. I try to visualize what Brad looks like right now, still dressed for sleep, his normally neat hair a little mussed, the strains of worry creasing his forehead.

"So you'll do it?" he asks.

"Oh come on, are you really telling me you can't find someone a little more suitable?" I ask. "Like, I don't know, one of the homeless schizophrenics that hang out on the Promenade? Or maybe a nice cross-dressing hooker with cultivated maternal instincts?"

"She likes you, Mercy."

"Yeah, I like her, too, but—"

"Just this one time," he says. "I swear I'll make it worth your while."

"What exactly does that mean?" I push myself to my feet and cross to the window, happy to discover that I'm not nauseous.

"We'll talk about it when you get here . . . say six forty-five?"

I open the shades and discover a pigeon sitting on the ledge. There's something sort of surreal about the way it's looking at me, with its head cocked to the side, like it was eavesdropping on the conversation. I can still feel grains of sleep in the corners of my eyes . . . maybe this entire phone call is a dream. Isn't that more likely than the possibility that Brad looked at me and thought, *Oh yeah, that's a caregiver*. "How long would you want me to stay?"

"I'll need you for the whole evening, until late if you can manage it. You know my address, right? You can get here on your own?"

"Yeah, but—"

"Great, I really can't tell you how much I appreciate this." And just like that he hangs up.

I put the receiver back in the cradle and stare at it for a few minutes, waiting for him to call back and tell me he's joking. But it doesn't ring.

I'm going to take care of a child. A little girl. Tonight.

I fall back down onto the mattress and stare up at the amoeba-shaped water stain on the ceiling.

How can I take care of a little girl?

I can't. That's the answer, I can't. After all, June is the only child I've even exchanged three words with since . . . well.

I put one hand over my eyes and try to take a deep breath, but it gets trapped in my chest, doing nothing more than adding pressure to my heart. Slowly I get up and, as if of their own volition, my eyes travel to my turntable. Without giving it too much thought I cross over to the records stacked below it and pull out Peter Gabriel. Carefully, with miraculously steady hands, I put it on, place the needle into the groove, and step back as the room fills with the eerily elongated notes of the synthesizer, starting low and then layered with something higher. Soon the sound is complemented with those light chimes and that odd whistle and finally the slow rhythm and the melancholy, seductive voice of Gabriel as he sings about empty streets and dreams . . . I back up, my eyes still on the turntable, listening, just listening. And, oh, there's that chorus, all those quiet notes of longing and hope. I feel just the faintest smile on my lips. When this song came on the radio that night, I had decided immediately that it was *my* song. *This* is what I thought would be my touchstone. It was supposed to be symbolic of the renewed faith I was going to have in family, my renewed faith in love.

And now? I sigh and lower myself onto the sofa. The song still has meaning for me. It's just that now it symbolizes the *hope* for love rather than the realization of it, and while I suppose that's better than nothing, it's not much.

With a flick of my hand I wipe away a tear that has escaped. It is a song about dreams after all. How had I expected any more from it than that?

But did those dreams have to be the precursor to so many nightmares?

Another tear slithers down my cheek and I shake my head, laughing at my own stupidity. God, I'm ridiculous. Why must I overthink everything? Brad didn't ask me to take this child under my wing. He just asked me to watch her for a few hours. I *can* do that. Of course I can. It's really not that big a deal.

And I sure as hell shouldn't be crying over the past.

After all, I have no past to grieve.

WHEN BRAD OPENS the door and finds me there, the look of relief on his face is so intense it actually amuses me.

"You're five minutes early," he says gratefully.

"*You* thought I wasn't gonna show at all," I say, shaking an admonishing finger while stepping past him into the living room.

June is standing on the couch, her hair in one huge, bushy ponytail, and the moment she sees me she starts jumping up and down, happily hollering, "She came, she came, she came!"

Brad calmly crosses over, lifts her off the couch, and places her on the floor. "No jumping on the furniture." Turning back to me, he points toward the kitchen. "There's a Trader Joe's pizza in the freezer."

"It's yummy!" June chimes in.

"And cranberry juice in the refrigerator. I'll have my cell phone on me, but I can't have it out while I'm working—"

"Wait a minute, you *work*?" I ask incredulously.

"Of course I work. How did you think I support . . ." His voice fades off. "Wait," he says slowly, "you weren't serious about that stuff you said at Envy."

"No?" I ask meekly, "I wasn't?"

"I work," he says impatiently. "And tonight's a . . . it will be lucrative. So if there's a real emergency, then call and obviously I'll come. But if it's not an emergency . . ." He makes a small gesture with his hand indicating that I should refrain from contacting him for anything short of a house fire.

He pulls out a wrinkled yellow Post-it from his pocket and hands it to me. On it the word *Commerce* is written in Brad's hurried cursive, and under it is a phone number. "Commerce?"

"It's the name of the place where I'll be," he explains. "Only call there if you have no other option and you can't reach my phone."

"Tell her the latitude and longitude, Daddy!" June suggests.

I give her, then Brad a quizzical look.

"It's a game we play," he says with a little smile at his daughter. "I give her the latitude and longitude of a place and a map and then she pinpoints the place."

"Ah, very educational. So what's the latitude and longitude of Commerce?"

His eyes dart away from his daughter. "It's a little ways outside of the city lines."

I study him for a moment and then fold the note in half and carefully put it into my wallet. "June," I ask, "would you give me a minute alone with your dad?"

"You guys going to talk 'bout grown-up stuff?"

I do a quick double take. I don't know that anyone has ever referred to me as a grown-up before.

"Yes, June," Brad says, answering the question for me. "Just go play in your room; one of us will get you in a few minutes."

She points at him threateningly. "Don't leave without saying good-bye!"

"Do I ever?"

"So don't start!" And with that she turns on her heel and half stomps, half prances to her bedroom, closing the door with a gleeful slam.

"She's so great," I whisper.

"Yes, a bit of a handful at times, but great. I can't tell you how much this—"

"Are you a drug dealer?"

"What?"

"Commerce?" I repeat again. "It's going to be a lucrative night? Whatever it is you're doing, it's not . . . normal."

"First of all, I thought you didn't believe in normal," Brad says as he crosses his arms over his chest. A black-and-white New York looms behind him. "Secondly, look who's talking."

"I don't have a kid," I snap. He raises his eyebrows at my sudden change in tone. "You are that child's world. If you're doing something that will put yourself at risk, I'm not helping."

"I'm not putting myself at risk."

"Then tell me how you make your money."

He hesitates for a moment and then gives a quick nod as if he's come to some sort of decision. "I play poker."

"What do you mean you play poker?" I ask, seating myself on the armrest of the sofa. "You mean you, like, have a poker night with your pals?"

"No, I mean that's what I do. It's how I earn a living."

I sigh and wait for him to laugh at his own joke and tell me what he really does. But Brad remains quiet. And after about a minute my eyes begin to widen. "Wait a minute . . . you're serious? You gamble for a living?"

"Poker isn't really like gambling, not if you do it right."

"Oh." I turn that over in my head for a moment. "Kind of like how dropping acid isn't really like taking drugs if you do it for enlightenment?"

"No." He takes a seat on the couch right next to me so that now I'm looking down at him . . . but not by much; the man really is very tall. "Gambling is playing games of chance for money," Brad explains. "Poker isn't about chance. If you're good you'll win much more than you lose."

"But—" I pause, tucking my hair behind my ears as I formulate my thoughts into an intelligent question. "If you lose, do you lose money?"

"Of course." Outside I hear some of the other tenants of the complex walking past us, their voices light with laughter.

"And if you win?"

"You win money."

"That's not gambling?" I ask.

"No."

I chew on my lower lip and turn my eyes to the upside-down people in the M. C. Escher print. "Is there a dictionary to back you up? Because to me the fact that you're using the word *win* rather than *earn* means you're kinda feeding me a line of bullshit."

He laughs and shakes his head. "You're just going to have to trust me on this." He puts his hand on my knee. The move almost makes me jump. "Can you stay past midnight?"

"You're going to play poker for more than five hours?"

"It might be a little longer, but not much. It takes a while to get to the Commerce Casino and back," he explains. "I wouldn't ask, but I can't afford to miss tonight."

"Yeah, sure, of course," I say, looking down at his hand again. "I can stay."

"Thank you, Mercy." Has my name ever sounded so seductive? "Sixty-five dollars? Will that be enough?"

I pull my leg away and get up, crossing to the poster of the tight-rope walker making the journey from one World Trade Center building to the other. "It's not exactly cage dancing money, is it?"

I hear Brad sigh. "How much do you need?"

"I want you to teach me how to play poker. I want you to pay me in lessons."

"Instead of money?" he asks incredulously.

"If you can support two people on the money you're making, then, yeah, I want the lessons more than I want the sixty-five dollars." I turn away from the poster. "Deal?"

He gets up, crosses to me. I catch the scent of his cologne, notice the way his muscles tighten and relax as he walks. He offers me his hand and I place my palm against his. "Deal."

Why do you trust me? Why do you think I have what it takes to care for a child? What do you see when you look at me that I can't see in the mirror?

"I'm just going to say good night to my daughter," he says, releasing my hand.

"Wait," I say, feeling a sudden stab of panic. "Is there anything she *can't* eat? I mean, I know she can have pizza and cranberry juice, but does she have any allergies or anything?"

"No, no food allergies."

"And what if she wants a snack? Is all the food here safe for her?"

"As long as it's not alcoholic, yes, it's safe," Brad says with a be-mused smile.

"Right, okay, just checking . . . Does she have any *other* kind of allergies? Asthma? Any medical conditions I should know about?"

"She occasionally gets ear infections."

"Oh." I lean my weight up against the wall. "What do I do if she gets one while I'm here?"

"If she gets an ear infection in the next five hours just wait it out and I'll deal with it when I get back."

"Okay, makes sense." I clasp my hands in front of me, staring down at the floor. "I don't want to make any mistakes."

Without even looking up I can tell Brad is studying me. His gaze reaches out and tickles my skin.

"You won't make a mistake," he says in that gentle, rumbling voice, and then I hear his footsteps go down the hall, to his daughter.

"DO YOU LIKE to draw?" June and I have been playing Candy Land for about twenty minutes and we're both getting a bit bored.

I smile and sit back. "Yeah. I'm not any good at it, but I always enjoy it."

"You have fun doing things you're bad at?" June asks, tilting her head to the side.

"*Especially* if I'm bad at it." I take the pieces off the board and fold it, sensing that we're done. "When you're bad at something you know you can get better. Maybe you won't get to be the best, but no one expects that since you started off so bad. If you have paper I'll show you." June jumps up and runs off to her room, immediately coming back with several blank sheets of paper, and then runs to where the phone is perched on the counter between the kitchen and dining area and grabs a few black and blue ink pens that she hands over to me. I accept it all graciously and draw a woman, a big smile on her face. She looks a little like the drawing of a woman you would find on any ladies' restroom. "See, all I have to do is progress past stick figures and people will be impressed. No one is impressed when an Olympian comes in fifth place, but everyone's impressed when the pudgy, flat-footed kid makes it around the track."

"Who's the pudgy kid with flat feet?" June asks.

"No one, I was . . . making something up in order to be clear." When she gives me a skeptical look I laugh. "I guess I failed at that."

She smiles uncertainly and looks down at the pens. "Daddy always thinks I should draw with pencils."

"Would you prefer a pencil?"

"No, I like pens." She takes the paper from me and starts to make her own inky additions to the drawing. "I don't want people to be able to erase what I've done."

"And what about when *you* want to erase what you've done? Like when you make a mistake?" I challenge. "How do you feel about pens then?"

"Good!" she says, shouting the word like a playful challenge. "*You* said the most important thing is to improve! If I erase my mistakes how will people know I got better?"

I sit back in my chair, unnerved by this child's casual wisdom. But her hands and mind are too busy with her drawing to notice my silence. Her tongue is between her teeth and her pen is moving with steady, deliberate movements as she creates an image next to mine. After a few minutes her eyes light up, her smile making little apples out of her cheeks. She jumps to her feet and holds the picture in front of her. "Ta-da!"

I hesitate a moment, then reach forward and touch the drawing, looking at the image of a little girl with frizzy brown pigtails holding the hand of the much less detailed woman I had drawn. When I don't say anything right away she taps the picture impatiently. "That's you and that's me!"

I run my fingers over the image. "It's beautiful," I say quietly. "It's perfect."

June cocks her head to the side, a gesture that is the perfect imitation of her father. "Did my picture make you sad?" she asks, a note of hurt in her voice.

"No," I reply. "It's just . . . well . . . it's that your picture makes me *feel*. And that's what all great art should do."

"Feel what?"

I laugh and shake my head. "I don't know, June. I'm not always great at figuring out my feelings. I guess . . . I guess it makes me feel alive. How 'bout that?"

"But you *are* alive! So of course you feel like that!" She shakes her head and lets out a surprisingly world-weary sigh. "You're silly."

Again I laugh, this time reaching out to take her hand. "True. You know what else I am?"

"What?"

"Hungry. You ready for pizza?"

She nods her head enthusiastically and off we go, hand in hand, into the kitchen. It's uplifting and . . . and it hurts a little . . . and I totally feel alive.

CHAPTER 17

❀

J UNE'S BEDTIME IS at eight thirty. If Brad isn't coming home until after midnight . . . well, that's a lot of snooping time. It starts innocently enough. Going through his spice rack takes about thirty seconds. Then I peek in each of the kitchen drawers and cabinets, where I find a mishmash of neglected kitchen tools and a fair number of spiders that scurry around when their home is disturbed for what may be the first time in over a year. The cupboard is packed with different kinds of nuts, unsalted brown rice cakes, steel-cut oatmeal, and protein bars ready to be taken to the gym. So he's not a junk foodie, but he's not exactly Martha Stewart, either.

The living area comes next. His mail is in a pile on a table by the entryway. Cable bill, health insurance bill, day-care bill all tucked neatly into standard white envelopes as if the unobtrusive packaging will hide their nefarious nature.

Nothing at all of interest in the bathroom. All the drugs are over-the-counter stuff. Children's cough and cold remedy, Ibuprofen, gummy vitamins. A hairbrush for her, a comb for him, toothbrushes for both of them. Totally normal.

I hesitate when I get to the closed door of his bedroom. I have no right to go in here. I really, *really* shouldn't.

But if I did, who would know?

I place my hand on the doorknob, count to three, and then throw the door open while jumping three steps back as if I expect the space to be guarded by pit bulls and ninjas.

But the only things in the room are a carelessly made bed, a dresser, a bookshelf, a desk with a keyboard on it, and a drum set.

He has a drum set in his room.

I step inside to get a better look. It's actually better than the set he's been keeping at Traci's. He's been holding out on us. And the keyboard. I walk over to examine it . . . It's pretty standard, but I didn't even know he could play this. And then, in addition to the filled bookcase, he has stacks of books everywhere, mostly on history and politics. Huh.

So this is probably when I should turn around and leave. That would be the respectable thing to do.

But what if he's started to compose more music for the band? If he is and I find out about it first, then I could sort of discreetly prep Traci and Tonio, make sure they don't use their budding hostility to dismiss the song before playing it. So then looking through these drawers, just for the music . . . well, it's sort of a good deed, right?

The top desk drawer is a bit of a mess. Pens without lids, envelopes, more bills. I don't see any sheet music, not even in the open envelopes (and I look in each one), and it's probably not going to be in this large, fat envelope at the bottom of the drawer from . . . I look at the return address that's peeking out from the chaos a little more carefully. Harvard? Does that say Harvard?

I push everything aside, pick it up, and check out the contents.

It's not just from Harvard, it's packets of information accompanying an acceptance letter from their law school.

He's going to Harvard? But when I check out the date on the letter, I see it's from five years ago. So my drummer *went* to Harvard law school . . . and now he plays poker for a living.

So maybe he won't make the alumni newsletter.

Who is this guy?

I start going through the drawers in earnest. I know I'm breaking every rule of common decency, but come on, what else is new? After searching every desk drawer and the first three drawers of his dresser, I finally find another thing of interest in his sweater drawer . . . a photograph in an envelope. Not of June, but of a woman who has her almond-shaped eyes and full pink lips. It was taken at a beach.

I study the photo. I have no idea what her ethnicity is, but she is drop-dead gorgeous. Brown skin, wild, wavy brown hair, and a smile that could light up a football stadium. And her figure is . . . perfect. I look down at myself. I've always liked my body. Surfing, running on the beach, hiking, dancing—all of it has worked to keep my waist tiny and my legs and arms strong. But I'm not built like *this* bitch. She's got some full-on Claudia Schiffer shit going on.

I replace the photo, suddenly feeling tired. I drop down on the bed and stare up at the ceiling. Why am I here? In this house, in this room? It would have been so easy to say no to Brad this morning. Easy not to come in here, *really* easy not to look through his drawers.

My phone rings and I pull it out of my pocket, pressing it to my ear. "Hello?"

"Hey," Ash replies. "Just calling to say I had fun last night. Sorry I had to dash."

"Happens." I turn on my side, run my hand over Brad's comforter.

"You want to do it again tomorrow? I got us on the VIP list for Graffiti."

"I've never been to Graffiti. Hear it's hot, though."

"Baby, I got you hooked up," he says teasingly. But then his tone shifts to something more sincere when he adds, "I won't leave you this time. I missed having you next to me when I woke up this morning. I missed the smell of your hair."

I close my eyes, imagine being wrapped up in his arms. The funny thing is, he never really *has* held me, has he? Come to think of it, I don't know if anyone has *ever* held me. Brad came close with that almost-hug he gave me outside Traci's, but that's it.

Of course my mother must have held me, but that was a very long time ago, if it ever happened at all.

"Mercy?"

"Yes," I sigh, "I'd like it . . . if we could wake up together, that is."

"Yeah," he says quietly. "Tell you what, be ready for me at . . . say, nine-ish? Actually, let's just plan on my being at your place at nine thirty. Is it weird that we've only been apart for, I don't know, maybe eighteen hours and I already miss you?"

I smile as his words wrap around me, giving me an invisible version of the hug I'm craving. "I'll be ready at nine thirty," I promise. "And I miss you, too, Ash."

I hang up the phone, my eyes still closed. Somebody misses me. What a lovely first.

IN MY DREAM I'm on a surfboard, past the breakers of Manhattan Beach, and the ocean is raging. Water pours from the sky, and differentiating between rain and the spray of the turbulent sea is impossible. I can't stand so I lie on my stomach, clinging to the board as I'm tossed to the left and then to the right. I'm not meant to have control. I'm nothing, absolutely nothing compared to all this. And I can't manage this and I can't survive, not with the tools I have.

Give up. That's what I'm meant to do. Let go of the struggle, surrender to the waves, breathe in the water, and wait to see what this death will bring.

But then the air changes, a breeze caresses my skin, brushes my sopping hair from my face. It's gentle, and loving and kind. There are beautiful messages tucked inside the howl of this storm, insights and guidance that I can't quite understand.

And the sky grows darker and darker until I can't see the sea at all. Everything grows completely still . . .

It takes a moment for me to realize that I'm really on Brad's bed, that I fell asleep here, that the dream is over. With my eyes still closed I move my body, stretching my limbs, adjusting my position. And when I finally do open my eyes I see Brad, sitting on the edge of the mattress, watching me.

"Oh my God, I'm—"

But he puts his finger against my lips, stopping my apology before it starts.

"You were tired," he says, moving a lock of hair away from my face.

I prop myself up on my forearm, looking up at him while he looks down at me. The door to the bedroom is closed. How long has he been here? Watching me sleep?

He gets up and walks to his desk. "You found my acceptance letter."

"Oh shit." I squeeze my eyes closed. "I'm so sorry, I know I shouldn't have—"

"I didn't go," he says, stopping me again. "I wanted to. I had planned my whole life around it. But then, sometimes things don't work out the way you plan them. Sometimes you get careless, if only for a day, an hour, and then your whole trajectory changes."

"June?" I ask as the pieces fall into place for me.

"Yes," he says, his voice thick with both love and pain. "Her mother, she just didn't want her, and once I saw her . . . when I actually held her in my arms, I simply couldn't give her up. Maybe I should have. The unselfish thing would have been to give her up. We had an adoptive family lined up and everything." He grows quiet for a moment, and as I watch him I still feel like I'm in my dream, like this moment is just a little removed from reality. And then he turns his head slightly, glancing back at me as I lie in his bed. "You should know, I am *not* unselfish. If I want something I won't let it go once it . . . or she, is within my grasp."

I bite down on my lip, forcing myself to remember that we're talking about June. "You think you're selfish," I whisper, "and yet it sounds like you've sacrificed a lot."

"Yeah, yeah I have. It's worth it, but it's not the life I imagined for myself. And there are days, many, many days, when I wonder if I've done the best thing for her. It's a real possibility that I didn't."

He drops the acceptance packet back down on the desk and moves over to the drums, running his fingers over the surface.

"You play in here?" I ask.

"It's why I chose this place," he says with a sigh. "The man here before me was a musician and the nephew of the owner. They invested a lot in getting this room soundproofed for him . . . Well, not perfectly soundproofed but close. As long as I don't play in the dead of night I can get away with it without disturbing the neighbors."

I sit up, scoot to the edge of the bed, dangle my legs. "Tell me again what got you into drumming and, you know, feel free to throw in a few specifics this time."

His shoulders move as he lets out a small chuckle. "All right, well let's see. I was a kid and my father . . . he had his issues. A very domineering, abusive guy."

I'm hit with a moment of queasiness, something that frequently happens to me when I hear about messed-up fathers. "He hit you?" I ask.

"Me?" he asks. His back is still turned to me so I can't see his face, but the rigid line of his shoulders speaks volumes. "I got whacked a lot when I was small, nothing too bad. He would *threaten* to hit my mother and me all the time. He'd break furniture, occasionally put a hole in a wall, and then he'd pull back his arm, fist clenched, as if he was about to throw a punch, as if he was about to break my mother's nose, jaw, whatever. But he never did throw that punch. It was all about intimidation. He wanted us to flinch and cower, beg for forgiveness, acquiesce to his demands. He was giving her something to fear without ever giving her something to report."

"How clever of him," I say dryly.

"No one ever accused him of being stupid." He sighs. "He was a highly educated man. A respected member of society. And I was his angry kid, determined to best him in every way. I wanted to defend my mother, but I was too small. I needed an outlet."

"Oh," I say with the dawning of understanding, "that's where the drums came in."

"That's where the drums came in," he repeats with a nod of confirmation. "My father hated the drums, which made me love them all the more. At the time my mother was a music teacher at an all-girls Catholic school, and when I started playing . . . it was the only time she ever stood up to my dad. She insisted I be allowed to play and so I did. He would start yelling, she would start crying, and I would go down into the garage and beat the hell out of those drums. And since I've never been able to do anything halfway, I made sure I was the best damn drummer around." Finally he turns toward me, and the expression on his face is startling. Pain, anger, guilt—it's all there, mixed up in his all-American features, making him look dangerous and vulnerable and absolutely beautiful. "The day he ran off with his mistress was the best day of my life," he continues. "I will never understand why my mother didn't feel the same way."

"Oh, Brad, really?" I whisper, genuinely surprised by this rare flash of ignorance. "Haven't you figured it out by now?" When he creases his brow I explain, "Those of us who are self-destructive will always love the ones who hurt us most."

His eyes widen with a startled understanding. "Jesus," he murmurs, and I quickly avert my gaze as I struggle to contain my own emotions. "But didn't you have an outlet, Mercy?" he asks quietly. "A way to escape and cope?"

"Drugs," I say simply. "My outlet was drugs. Maybe if my mom was a music teacher I would have thought to find comfort in my voice; then again, maybe not," I say with a self-deprecating laugh. "Drugs were just easier . . . more efficient. I popped my first pill when I was twelve."

"So young?" Brad asks.

I nod, bringing my eyes to the overflowing bookcase. "I was at my friend Gina's house and I started feeling . . . I don't know, antsy I guess. Like I needed to go on a twenty-mile run up the steepest mountain around, or jump rope for an hour while yelling out gibberish at the top of my lungs, like I needed to crawl out of my skin. I get like that sometimes," I say with a shrug. "I told Gina how I was feeling and she led me into the bathroom, took out this very official-looking bottle of prescription pills from the medicine cabinet. She told me that it's what her mom took when she got a case of the nerves. I remember that's what she called it. *A case of the nerves.* Anyway, the meds had been prescribed by a doctor, so I figured they must be safe. So I took one."

"And what happened?" Brad asks gently.

"It helped!" I say with a laugh. "Nothing had ever helped before, but this thing did. It was some generic label with a name I couldn't pronounce, but I figured my dad would find out what it was and where to get it. I mean, why *wouldn't* he? He had been complaining about how hyper and weird I could get all my life, and here I had found an actual chill pill! I couldn't wait to get home and tell him about it."

Brad doesn't say anything, but without even looking at him I can tell he's listening. Listening with a brain that can understand books about free trade and the roles race and class play in our society, and listening with a heart that has been exposed to all those primitive cruelties that can never be explained in a textbook. "When I told him about the pill?" I say quietly. "It was the first time he ever hit me. Gave me a huge shiner. Told my sister I got it by riding my bike without wearing a helmet. So you see, he was able to use me as a punching bag *and* a cautionary tale. A twofer!" I laugh and shake my head. "She was only five at the time. The next time he hit me he told her my face was swollen because I had been chewing gum with my mouth open and a bee flew in there and stung the inside of my cheek!"

"You've got to be kidding me."

"Totally serious!" I insist, still giggling. "Poor Kasie, by the time they threw me out they had her convinced that if she so much as put her elbows on the dinner table it would somehow lead to certain self-destruction. Still," I say, my laughter finally fading out, "I think it's better to be hit than to have someone always threatening to hit you. Anticipation of pain is usually more intense than the pain itself."

"I'm not so sure about that," Brad murmurs.

I lower my gaze to the floor. "You may not have planned to be a dad so young, but you're a great one. June will never be able to fully relate to our stories. And that's the way it should be."

"I hope you're right," he says. For at least a minute or two, neither one of us says anything. He must be right about the soundproofing, because I can't hear the traffic on the street or the water flowing through the courtyard fountain. I can only hear my own thoughts, which are just loud enough to cause physical pain. "Did your parents plan for you?" he asks, his baritone adding warmth to the cold silence.

I consider not answering, but then I hear myself say, "Once upon a time I would've told you that yes, they planned for a child, but no, they did not plan for *me*."

I sense him shifting his position, perhaps taking a step closer to me. "And now?"

"Now?" I focus on the orderly woven rows of beige fabric that make up the thin carpet beneath our feet, both flawless and dull. "Now I would tell you that I have no parents." I pause as I consider what it's like to say the words aloud. "I'd say that I am a product of my own invention, that I am free from the burdens of family and expectations. And I would tell you," I add, taking in a long, shaky breath, "I'd tell you that I am utterly and *completely* alone."

I can feel him studying me, but still, I can't meet his eyes. I should never have opened my mouth. I should never have come here. I should never, ever pretend that there is anyone in this world who might understand.

I hold my breath as I feel him approaching, one slow step at a time, only stopping when he's just a few inches from me. I bite down hard on my lip and wait for his judgment, or for him to make light of it, or find a way to get us out of this uncomfortable exchange. But instead he reaches forward, and I feel the brush of his hand against my hair. "You deserve more."

I blink several times as his fingers continue to wind their way into my blond and pink locks. Slowly I raise my head just as he is lowering his. The kiss is slow, needing, beautiful. I lift my arms and wrap them around his neck, and then I'm being raised, onto my feet, my body against his, wrapped up in his arms. His large hands move up and down my back. I've never been surrounded by this kind of strength, this power. He picks me up, and it's as if I weigh no more than a daisy that he's picked for a bouquet. He's cradling me in his arms and his mouth is still on mine, parting my lips with the tip of his tongue, tasting me as he gently lowers me onto the firm mattress, his body on top of mine. I can feel him react to me, feel his heart accelerate with mine, feel his desire pressing against me.

I pull off his shirt, and for the first time I really see what he has been doing such a poor job of concealing. This body, this carefully structured work of art . . . he overwhelms me.

And then he's removing my top. His hand goes to the small of my back and he's crushing me against him as his lips find the edges of my bra, one hand brushing gently over my hardening nipples, straining against the layered black lace, needing him. He pulls on the fabric, just enough to expose me, just enough so he can brush his lips over the delicate pink flesh as his hand moves lower, unbuttoning my jeans easily with one hand, slipping that hand inside the denim, inside the silk of my panties, his finger brushing against my clit, bringing forth a moan of pleasure from my lips. I know he can feel how wet I am, how much I want him. And yet, for all his intensity, I know he is being careful with me. He is so much stronger than me, yet I don't feel intimidated. Delicate, yes, but also so cared for. And the slow, deliberate movement of his fingers—dear God, it doesn't seem possible, but here I am, already dangerously close to an explosion.

His kisses move from my breast to my shoulder, to my neck,

finding that secret spot that always drives me wild. And against my skin he whispers, "You are not one of the unwanted."

He knew. He heard the words I didn't say. I dig my fingers into his back, wanting to draw him even closer, wanting him inside me, and oh, oh God . . . this is too consuming, too wonderful, too intense. I'm shaking now, so very close. Everything about this man is so intoxicating, so male, my grip around him grows tighter. There is nothing predatory here, nothing feline, not like Ash . . .

Ash.

Ash is the reason I'm not unwanted.

"Brad," I say, pronouncing his name as a warning. But his kisses are on my jaw, he's touching me, toying with me, my entire body aches for him. In another few seconds I will come, I won't be able to stop it.

I can't let this happen.

"No . . . no!" I push with all my might against his shoulder. I'm nowhere near strong enough to move him, but he releases me immediately. I quickly roll off the bed, grabbing my shirt as I stand up.

"I'm . . . I'm so sorry," I say. I'm shaking, my legs are weak even as I back away. "I . . . I don't know . . . I just . . ." There are no words. I have never wanted someone this badly, never deprived myself of so much.

I pull on my shirt. "I'm really sorry about snooping in your stuff. That was totally not cool."

"Mercy . . ."

"Tell you what? You don't have to pay me anything. No money, no lessons, 'kay? I'll just head out." I'm trying to button my jeans but my fingers are clumsy, I can't get anything right.

"Mercy . . ."

"Don't forget, we have a gig in two days, so, you know, practice, practice, practice, right?" Finally, I'm able to fasten my jeans. I almost cry in both disappointment and relief. "Of course you probably practice every day, right?" *My purse, where did I leave my purse?* "I wish I had a sound-insulated room at my place. I'd be caterwauling at all hours of the night." *I left it in the living room, I remember now.* "Actually, you know what? It's totally none of my business. Just be ready for the gig. I am really sorry, um, I gotta go." I turn away from him and start to open the door, but he comes up behind me and pushes it closed again.

I stare at the closed door, feeling the warmth of his body as he stands so close behind me, his arm to my right, holding the door closed, his breath in my hair.

"I have to go," I whisper.

"Not before we talk."

"I have a boyfriend."

"One who doesn't even care enough to come to your performances."

"He did see me perform!" I whirl around and immediately regret it. He's so close. And yet I have just enough distance to really see him. The man must *live* in the gym. And I'm here, pressed up against the door, quivering like a child.

I close my eyes tight and take a deep breath, which turns out to be yet another bad decision, because now I'm simply breathing in his scent, knowing that it's on my skin as well. "You may not think that Ash does all the things that a boyfriend should do," I say, my voice quivering uncontrollably, "but we have a connection. Against all odds he cares for me, and for my entire life I have been disappointing the people who are supposed to care for me . . . *every time.*" Finally I find the strength to open my eyes, to meet his gaze. "You need to get this," I whisper. "I'm not just asking you to let me out of this room. I'm asking you to save me . . . from *me.*"

Brad doesn't look away, doesn't move, and for a moment I think that there truly is no mercy in this world. That I will once again find myself giving in to an enticement that is put before me. That I will lose myself in the moment, and in doing so lose the future entirely.

And then, slowly, he pulls his arm away from the door and takes a deliberate step back.

Without turning I put my hand back on the doorknob, open the door, and back away, slowly at first, and then, my legs still unsteady, I stumble into the living room, find my purse, and run. Out of that home, out of the courtyard that leads to it, down the street to where my car waits for me, and then I am off as fast as I can go. Running away from temptation, running away from Brad.

Running away from Melody.

CHAPTER 18

✿

I AM ALMOST NEVER early for anything, but a full half hour before Ash is scheduled to show up I am completely ready for him. I have spent extra time on everything. I deep-conditioned my hair, meticulously applied my makeup, wore my best, purposely torn jeans and a new crop top, showing off the results of the eighty sit-ups I did earlier in the evening. All I'm missing is the belly-button piercing that I've been meaning to get, and if he wants to get it tonight I'm totally game.

And when he calls me to let me know he's running late I don't complain. On the contrary, I tell him I'll take a cab to Graffiti. I know that makes his life easier, considering he's coming from Santa Monica, I'm coming from North Hollywood, and the club is in between the two (as is pretty much the entire city of LA).

I make a call, and within ten minutes a black-and-yellow pulls up. Last night was an anomaly, I think as I slide into the back. I just screwed up, it happens . . . a lot in my case. But not anymore. Tonight everything is back to the way it's supposed to be. From now on everything will be better than before. I have *decided*.

"Graffiti, please," I say to the cabbie, only to then have to give him the address because, really, how often do these guys get to go clubbing?

We're there in no time. Like most clubs there is no sign outside . . . well, no sign other than the valet that is conspicuously out front and the line of people trying to get in.

And there's Ash, pacing the sidewalk, to the right of the hopeful

partiers who are waiting to be let in. He looks wild, agitated. "Ash?"
I ask as I approach. He turns to me, steps into my space, weaves his
hands into my hair as he pulls me to him, kissing me with an urgency I hadn't expected. Some of the people in line hoot and whistle
their approval, and as the kiss goes on, his hands move to the small
of my back, then lower. I find myself wondering if he plans to make
love to me here, right on the sidewalk with all these people cheering us on.

When he finally pulls away it's not by much. "It's happening," he
whispers. "Everything I've ever dreamed of, it's all happening."

I search his face, trying to understand, but what I see confuses me
even more. His eyes look almost black, his pupils dilated from the
lack of light, and . . . and there's anger there, determination in the set
of his mouth, and there's an energy radiating from him, an invisible
need, a longing that crackles around him like static electricity.

"Ash—"

"Hush now." He covers my mouth with his hand. "No need for us
to be standing around on the sidewalk, talking in the cold."

He runs his hands over my arms, but I don't mind the night's
chill. What unnerves me is this unknown element that has given
Ash his crazed glow. Without another word he pulls me up to the
bouncer, who waves us in immediately. "How'd you get on the list?"
I ask as I trail behind into the club. The chill from outside is replaced by an almost muggy heat brought on by a crush of people
moving to the rhythm of Jay-Z's "Big Pimpin'."

"Because I'm me," Ash says over the din. "Because things are
changing." He's pulling me toward a staircase, toward another
bouncer who checks Ash's name and waves us up. Ash is taking the
steps two at a time now, as if running toward a new kind of salvation.
The space we enter is illuminated with red-tinged lighting; the walls
are lined in a brocade-textured fabric of gold and rouge, elements
of purposely worn luxury from a different era. People are seated on
the black tufted leather of love seats placed strategically around low
wooden tables with leather trim. I recognize the man sitting with

those women there, but I can't say if I've seen him on a small or big screen. The room is filled with people like that, actors and actresses who have had just enough exposure to make you look twice, but not enough that you would know their name. There's a small crowded bar here, and this is where Ash leads me first, maneuvering us through the horde. Pushing my back against the counter, he takes a wide stance, so when he leans in to kiss my neck he's straddling my body, making it clear to the world that I'm his. He looks up, above my head to the pretty bartender in a skintight tank. He orders us drinks, but even though he's right next to me, the pounding of the music and the confusion in my head make it impossible for me to understand what he's telling her. And yet I hear him so clearly when he brings his lips to my ear and whispers, "You're going to like this."

"Ash, what—?"

But he quiets me again, this time by placing a hand on each of my shoulders, at the base of my neck, holding my gaze. "When you look at me, what do you see?"

"I see . . . I see . . ." I hesitate; what does he need from me? "I see my man," I say lamely. "I see the one I'm fated to be with."

"Do you see greatness?" he asks, a tinge of insecurity in his voice now. "Or do you see failure?"

Really, these are the choices? "Greatness," I say meekly. "Ash . . ."

Two shots are delivered by the bartender, tinged pink in color, a wedge of lime split by the edge of each tiny glass. Ash drops money onto the bar and lifts his drink. "To greatness then."

I smile uncertainly and accept the toast, throwing back the drink before I can think better of it. I can easily identify the mingled flavors: cranberry, vodka, triple sec, a variation of a Cosmo in a shot. But stronger, definitely stronger.

"This project, this show, it's better than *The Sopranos*," he continues. "We're bringing something new to America, to the world. We're changing everything, and by being part of it I'm changing my life."

I study him for a moment, taking in the words and expressions of extreme confidence. I place my hand on his chest, feel his heart beating against my palm. Its pace is fast, demanding, needing. "Are you happy?" I ask, my voice only just loud enough to be heard over the music. There are people who have begun to dance, little pockets of revelry by each bottle service table. "Do you like the life you're about to claim?"

He gives me an odd look. "I don't think you'd ask me that if you really understood the man that I am," he says simply.

I flush; the words sting more than I believe he intended them to. "I know who you are," I say, defensive.

"Oh?" He raises his eyebrows; he's taunting me, the glimmer of mischief in a subtle form of provocation. "Tell me then, who am I?"

I open my mouth to speak, but then close it. The things I want to say reveal too much. I look out at the crowd; more and more women are finding little patches of floor to claim as their own, dancing in place, seducing their partners. "You're a man who has strong passions," I say, a light laugh in my voice making it clear that all the implications one could draw from that are intended. "A man who likes risk, a man who likes *life*."

"Go on," he says as he leans closer into me, so that there's almost no space between us now. With every breath my breasts brush his shirt, and from the way his eyes are traveling over me, I can tell that he's noticed, that everything he's doing is intentional.

"There are things you want to do," I continue. "Things you want to try." I pause as he looks past me to the bartender, wait as he orders us another round. "Others have tried to hold you back, but they can't. You're too determined for that. Too wild."

"Hmm." He brings his lips to my ear once more. "You know what else I am?" he asks.

I give a tiny shake of my head. I sense the bartender behind me, placing a drink on either side of me, too close, too intimate.

"I'm the man who is going to be inside you tonight," he says.

I flush as I hear the giggle of the bartender, know that she heard. And yet as he gives her his money, as she steps away, I find that my entire body is tingling from the suggestion. Ash lifts one of the shots, presses the glass against my bottom lip. "You want that," he says, his voice smooth, maybe a little amused. "Don't you, Mercy?" Before I can answer, he tilts my chin back with the firm force of his hand, opens my lips with the pressure of the glass, lets the drink trickle over my tongue until all of it is gone. When he pulls it away he replaces it with his, so that now he's fed me two shots in succession, bringing me to the level of intoxication that he wants for me. "I asked you a question, didn't I?" He pulls the now-empty glass away, beckons the bartender to come back with yet another drink, this time for him. "Answer, please."

"Yes," I say as he receives his cocktail. "It's what I want."

He smiles, throws back his drink. "You're with a celebrity now."

I laugh, although I don't know why. The music morphs from Puff Daddy's "Satisfy You" to Eminem's "Real Slim Shady." "Oh I love this one," I say, bunching his shirt up in both my fists before giving him a little shove, pushing him back as I move past him, and, while always facing him, backing into the center of the room, each step in perfect time with the deviant notes of the synthesizer and the thrum of the bass. My hips loosen as the room takes on that lovely fuzzy quality that comes with a perfect buzz. The crowd around me parts, clearing a path, bowing to my presence, my energy.

I place my hand flat against my exposed stomach as the rap begins, moving my body with quiet aggression and tantalizing persuasion, absorbing the essence of the music, enhancing it with my own desire, making it part of me. I bring my arms above my head before moving to lift my hair, piling it on top of my head, revealing the nape of my neck. The men in the room are turning from their friends, from their dates, from the strangers they were flirting with. Some of the women are shooting daggers in my direction, but most look on with grudging admiration as my moves prove to be as fluid and skillful as they are alluring. Ash's wayward grin gives him a tantalizingly dangerous quality, bringing to mind images of the Big Bad Wolf from childhood fairy tales.

He moves toward me as I continue to dance, and now he's right here, his body two inches from mine. Without so much as a touch, he joins me, maintaining those inches of space as he matches my movements with precision, simultaneously complementing and mocking me as he claims them as his own. We move like this from side to side, keeping with the rhythm. When he advances, I step back, but never so far as to extend the space between us. We move along the floor, not touching, but completely connected. And now *everybody* is watching. No one can say I'm a background dancer here.

We *own* this.

He breaks the invisible barrier with his hand, moving it to the small of my back, and I respond with a new kind of enthusiasm. My body jerks and writhes with the music, with him, all with an atypical grace that defies the traditional disciplines of dance. With his free hand he explores my body—his palm is on my hip, then the side of my breast, my stomach, my leg. He can touch me anywhere; I won't resist, because when I'm dancing the rules don't matter. Or maybe it's that when I'm dancing I realize that they never really do. The music is irreverent, rebellious, combative, and for so many, discomforting. These are states of mind I'm intimately familiar with. Music and dancing as a form of anarchy; it's irresistible.

I lower myself in front of him, letting the beat dictate my pace. My fingers hook into the waistband of his pants suggestively, playful as I look up at him, biting my lip. And then slowly I rise, allowing my body to move against his. There's no shame, this is Ash after all. This is the man who will be inside me tonight.

He whips me around, pressing my back into him as we keep moving. "They all want you," he says.

And I answer, "*Yes.*"

This is power, this is everything.

This is what Ash and I can be.

CHAPTER 19

❀

THE NIGHT IS out of control, and I love every second of it. Ash
and I get the party started. After that one dance the floor fills
with couples as well as with several groups of women tearing it up
on what serves as the VIP dance floor. But none of them outshine
Ash and me. Halfway through the night he throws down for bottle
service and we share Absolut with strangers as Ash regales them
with stories of his upcoming pilot. At one point I actually get up *on*
the bar and move to Snoop Dogg and Dr. Dre. I can't remember the
last time I let loose like this. There is no order, no conventions that
need to be adhered to. No thoughts of the future or the past. As the
VIP room fills up, the small crowd becomes increasingly diverse.
Black, Latino, Asian, white, gay, straight—the only commonality is
youth. We are all here to live and be young.

When last call finally brings things to a close, Ash and I stumble
out onto the street, an almost half-full bottle of vodka clutched in
my hand. We get hot dogs from a street vendor and find a curb to
sit on as we devour them, knowing that there is no way in hell that
Ash is sober enough to get us home on his bike.

"This," Ash says between bites, "is our town."

I laugh and place the vodka between us. "You really going to be
a star?"

"Damn right. You gonna cheer me on when I get the Emmy?"

"Depends. Do I get to walk the red carpet, stand by your side
as the flashbulbs are going off and the paparazzi are shouting your
name?"

"Abso-fucking-lutely." He pushes his hair from his face and glances in both directions, scanning for cops before bringing the vodka to his lips.

"Then yes, I'll cheer you on!" I declare before biting down on my dog. I take a moment to chew before asking, "What about your music?"

A small scowl crosses his face. "What about it?"

"The first night we met you told me that music was the thing that fed your soul."

"Yeah," he agrees with a laugh, "and you told me that was a cliché. Some things don't change."

"Yeah, but the sentiment was true, I could see it. And I heard you sing. Remember that? Singing in the streets of Seattle? Or what about when we were in your motel room and you got out your guitar and sang Green Day's 'Time of Your Life'?"

"It's called 'Good Riddance,'" he mutters, his eyes now on the traffic moving down the street, the girls blasting tunes from their convertibles while guys in clunkers honk their horns for no apparent reason.

"I think the name depends on what kind of mood you're in," I say, laughing. "But you were seriously connected to that music. It was, like, part of you. You're not just going to toss that for acting, right?"

For what seems like an eternity he doesn't say a word, just stares straight ahead. I sense that I've said something wrong, but I have no idea what that could be. "You sound like Eva," he says.

"Eva," I repeat. Visions of pink velour pop up in my head before I can stop them.

"I spoke to her today," he continues. "She doesn't believe in me."

I give my head a little shake. "Wait, how's my asking about music equal not believin' in you?" I ask, keeping my voice light. I know the mood has changed, but . . . God, how much have I had to drink? Everything around me is off-kilter and warped, albeit pleasantly so. Maybe he is making sense and I'm just missing it.

"Maybe you think like her," he says coolly. "You think I'm wasting time trying to get my acting career going. You think I should be making my living operating cranes or pouring concrete, maybe even go back to school and get a contractor's license since we all know I'm too dumb to graduate from anything more complicated than a trade school."

I reel back to get a better look at him. Is he joking? "You're really comin' outta left field with all this . . . or is it right field?" I hesitate, and then rest my head against my knees. "Why does random shit always come out of fields?"

"No, no, I know what you think of me. I know what my parents think, what Eva thinks, I know what everybody thinks!" For the first time I catch the slight slur in his words, but then it's entirely possible that I don't sound much better. "And," he continues, "I know how everything is gonna play out and how you all are gonna be proven wrong." He grabs the depleted bottle of vodka and takes another swig.

"Whoa." I grab the bottle from him and put it down on the pavement with a definitive thump. "Slow down there, Nostradamus. We might need your mental powers to predict where the next cab's comin' from."

"You think I should be like you, right?" he asks. His scowl has now turned into a full-on glare and it's directed at me. "I should do a bunch of conventional day jobs and then use music as a time-sucking hobby?"

"*Conventional* jobs?" I repeat. "You mean the dog-walking thing? They're mixed breeds, Ash. *Mixed breeds!* Nothin' conventional about my pooches."

"Maybe you think that I should play at dive bars and the second-rate clubs you play at," he continues. "Belt out a few original tunes and a ton of covers. Maybe make some extra pennies from selling CDs to drunks? Let me tell you somethin', I'm not gonna live as a starving artist. I'm better than that. People are going to know me!"

I lift my head from my knees. "Did you really just say that?"

He lets the words hang there for several seconds as he continues to stare out at nothing. "Okay," he finally says. "Maybe went a lil' far with the truth telling—"

"Fuck. You." I take the remainder of my hot dog and slam it against his shirt, mustard and all, then jump to my feet.

He reaches up, grabs my hand. "Melody, I'm sorry, really—"

"It's Mercy, asshole," I snap, yanking my hand away before storming down the sidewalk.

"Mel . . . Mercy, come on!" he calls after me as I turn the corner, walking past another closing club, squeezing through the crowd of people waiting for rides. "What's going on?" I turn to the chick who asked the question, the woman I just bumped into, a model type with caramel skin and carefully constructed microbraids. I touch my cheek, feel that there are tears there. "My boyfriend called me by the wrong fucking name!" I yell.

A series of *oooooh*s rise up from the crowd as Ash appears around the corner in his attempt to get to me. As well as a few *busted*s. Three other girls burst out in the chorus of Destiny's Child's "Say My Name." Ash looks around, clearly bewildered by the response. I use the moment to grab the arm of the woman who initially addressed me as a cab pulls up. "Are you taking this? Can I share your ride? I gotta get out of here."

"Course, honey, get in."

In a matter of seconds I'm in the cab with her and two of her friends. Ash stands by numbly as we pull away. I look out the window and see him watching us as we leave.

As it turns out, the women live in West Hollywood, which, not surprisingly, is in a totally different part of the city from North Hollywood. We go to their drop-off spot first, spending most of that part of the ride talking about Ash and me and that ridiculous argument. Everyone agrees I'm in the right. Once my new friends are gone, I pay a fortune to be taken back to my studio on the opposite side of town. The silence of this part of the drive is infinitely worse than the bitch session during the first half. I just don't understand what happened. Yes, I'm drunk; yes, he's drunk; but that doesn't mean that he didn't mean the things he said. If anything, it means he's been thinking them and *not* saying them for some time.

And that means that Ash thinks I'm pathetic. That my music, my band, all of it is beneath him. And if that's true, then he must think that I'm beneath him, too.

And maybe, just maybe, he's right. Obviously I'm not dead, no matter how much my father may wish otherwise. But maybe . . . maybe it's worse than that.

Maybe I'm nothing.

When I get home I don't go to sleep. Instead I take out a cheap bottle of white from the refrigerator and turn on the TV. I'm definitely not as drunk as I was when I made the scene in front of the club over an hour ago, but this wine will help with that. And the TV will help, too. I need the voices of other people, even if those people are trapped on a screen, completely unaware of my existence.

I settle on some *X-Files* reruns, but I don't sit down. I stand there, pacing in front of the sofa, amped and angry, drinking from the bottle like a hobo with a habit. You know, for all the craziness that goes on in the *X-Files,* at least Mulder and Scully know what their purpose is. They know why they're here, to fight shapeshifting criminal masterminds and find aliens. The world *needs* Mulder and Scully.

No one needs me.

I take another swig of wine. Why *am* I here? I mean, does anyone really want me to be? It was easy to dismiss Brad's suggestion that rock 'n' roll was some kind of rebellion for me. It's not. But maybe living is. Maybe staying alive is literally the only way I have left to say fuck you to my parents.

But . . . is that really a good reason to live? Is that enough?

I stand still for a moment and stare at the TV. I'm just drunk enough to see the existential dilemma of the *X-Files*. Mulder and Scully's search for answers has yielded nothing but questions. We still don't know what the Smoking Man's deal is, or why the aliens chose Earth, or why this secret, überpowerful shadow government that's protecting the aliens hasn't just killed Mulder off by now. I mean, just take a shotgun and blow the dude's head off! This should not be hard! But they never do. So Mulder lives on, as does his quest for truth, even though the only things he seems to find are secrets and lies. He may act smart, but his real "truth" is that he's as clueless as the rest of us.

And that's the one part of the show that's realistic. It's why I love it. It's a reminder that it's not just me. We're *all* clueless.

After all, the world is filled with scientists, theologians, and philosophers, who have clocked not just hours but years, collectively *thousands* of years of trying to figure out why we're here, and yet not one of them can prove that their hypotheses are correct. People, animals, insects of the past, trillions of dead things fill the ground, cover the trees, float in the ocean. Every time we move, we are stepping on a grave. And still, no one can prove that they know what happens to us after we die. Is there really an afterlife? When I die, will I still be *me*?

I start pacing again, now covering the entire expanse of the studio as I consider the question. God, what if the answer is yes? My parents couldn't even handle me for the length of my childhood, and now some God is supposed to put up with me for all of eternity? That's just not gonna work.

But then, what I'm doing now isn't working, either. Nothing is fucking working! I take the bottle of wine and slam it, hard, against the counter dividing the kitchen from the so-called dining area.

The bottle breaks. White wine and shattered glass rain onto the floor. For the most part I remain unscathed, except for one cut, a small one, from a flying piece of glass that scratched the skin on the inside of the wrist that's not holding the bottle. I crouch down and study the mess, lifting up one particularly large and pointy-edged shard. Then I look at my wrist. It's bleeding, but not profusely. I didn't hit the main vein. I look back at the shard and then gently place the flat surface of the glass against the inside of my wrist. If

I turn this on its edge, if I press it hard against the skin, well, that could be it, couldn't it? How is it possible that a life's worth of blood can be contained within two blue veins? How can it be that all I have to do is make two little slashes and that's it, I die. I get to leave. The ease of it seems positively mystical. I mean, *that's* an *X-Files* episode.

I pull the glass away so I can see the scratch again. It doesn't even hurt, not at all. How odd that I could cut myself so close to that life-or-death vein and feel no pain. As usual it's all about figuring out where the line is. You can push *just* this hard and suffer very minimal consequences, but push a little harder and everything you ever knew and ever loved is gone.

Can I feel pain? Physical pain? I wonder as I go to the sink and wash the blood and alcohol off the shard of glass. Surely I'm not too drunk for pain, am I? Because if I can't feel pain . . . then I'm not alive. You have to feel things to live. Almost without thinking about it I find a spot on my thigh where my jeans are ripped and use the glass to make a small cut into the skin. It's really barely a surface wound, and yet I can see that thin line of blood bubbling up, becoming more pronounced with every second.

And I feel pain.

I look up at the TV and see that an alien worm is infecting human hosts, making them homicidal. Wouldn't that be nice, if we could so clearly identify what gets under our skin and makes us do the stupid shit we do?

I look down at my wrist and make another cut, this time just a little to the left of the vein. More blood, more pain, and yet I'm still here. Gently I put the glass down on the countertop. And then I break down and cry.

❀

CHAPTER 20

WE'RE PLAYING AT 1960 tonight, a reference to the street address, not the year—although they have clearly tried to integrate a beatnik sensibility into the place, with the cocktail waitresses dressed in all black and sporting ridiculous-looking berets. Everything about this nightclub feels like it's trying just a little too hard, and although the location is good, this place just hasn't caught on. As we move to set up I can see that tonight's crowd is sparse, one of the worst we've had in a while. Undoubtedly this is one of the second-rate clubs that Ash thinks are beneath him.

"Hey," Brad whispers as I start to walk past him setting up his drums. Traci has already hooked up her keyboard, Tonio's guitar is ready to go. Both are outside, getting a smoke in before we begin.

"Hey," I reply, sticking my hands into my pockets. It's almost 10 p.m. and I got out of bed just four hours ago.

"New look?" He gestures to my hands. I'm wearing what I affectionately call my dominatrix gloves. Long leather gloves that go all the way up past my elbows.

"Had them for a while and figured it was time to bust 'em out." I adjust the one on my right arm. They're not going to be the most comfortable things to wear while performing under the stage lights, but they look hot and they cover up the angry red scratches on my left wrist. Maybe if we went full-on Marilyn Manson the marks might be a plus, but I'm not ready to go there just yet.

I glance meaningfully out at the floor. The stage is dark, and being back by the drums makes us inconspicuous, but still, it's not really good form to be hanging out on the stage before a performance.

He gets up, examines the drums, and then steps off into the wings with me.

"Do we need to talk?"

"Nope." I glance around at my surroundings. This place is pristine. It's almost as if someone has taken out their anxiety and aggression on the dust mites.

"Are you sure?"

"Yep . . . well, okay, I do have one thing to say. Thank you for hearing me and stepping aside." I shrug. "That's it. Now there really is nothing more to talk about."

He raises his eyebrows. "Do I get to say one thing, too?"

"Nope, we're done." I look over to the door and expect Tonio and Traci to come through any moment. "We can go straight to pretending nothing happened."

Brad lets out a low laugh. "That seems to be your go-to strategy."

"Yep." I stretch each arm in front of me, limbering up before the performance. "I am exceptionally good at pretending that things are other than what they are. Been doing it since I was four."

Brad studies me, taking in my expression, my body language. "Are you okay?"

Just then Tonio and Traci come through the door and I gesture to them to hurry. We're supposed to be on in a minute. Under my breath I say to Brad, "I'm okay enough."

We all walk out together, finding our places onstage. Within seconds the lights go up and we dive in. Always better to introduce yourself after the first few tunes, after the crowd has learned to love you.

I stand front and center, pouring my anger and angst right into the mic. It's a risky way to start. Angry women aren't really in right now. Even Alanis Morissette has gone Zen. But I don't know that I have any gentleness to share at the moment. Right now I want to dig my fingernails into the world and just rip it up. And so that's what

I do, song after song. The audience doesn't resist, but I'm not sure they're entirely with me, either. I sense their trepidation, I can hear the conversations they'll have when they leave. They'll say I'm bitter, mean-spirited, a man hater. If I were a man singing about women like this—say, Eminem—I'd be a revolutionary.

The injustice of it all just pisses me off more. I can hear the spite dripping from my tone, from the way I enunciate certain lyrics and scream others. I see the problem. Even Eminem balances his rage with humor, and I'm not balancing mine with anything. I don't *feel* balanced. I just feel frustrated, and angry, and . . .

. . . and there he is. It's Ash, standing in the back, just like he was that first night he reentered my life at Apocalypse. But now he's holding a bouquet of red roses and wearing a hangdog expression that makes it clear he's here to express regrets.

And I stop singing. Just like that, in the middle of the song, I stop singing. It takes Tonio and Traci a few chords to figure out that they should stop, too. Brad on the other hand stopped with me, so the last bit of this song the crowd heard was an instrumental melody, unmolested by my angry ramblings or the beating of the drums.

And now we've all stopped, the rest of the band members looking at each other nervously, the crowd murmuring, unsure if this is part of the show or some kind of epic fuckup they'll be able to tell people about later. And I'm just standing there, looking at Ash, who's looking at me.

Just as things go from weird to extremely uncomfortable, I bring the mic to my lips again. "I want to do something different," I say in an amplified whisper. "We haven't performed this next one in a while, but now seems like a good time for a revisit."

I turn to Traci and mouth the word *"Want."*

Traci arches one eyebrow. We haven't done this one in ages and it's questionable whether everyone in the band has it memorized well enough to execute it well. But nonetheless, she runs her fingers over the keys, produces the first few chords of the song, cluing Tonio and Brad in to what we're doing, and slowly I pivot back to the room. After two full counts of eight I start to sing:

I don't want to hate
the man that you are
I want to feel the laughter

I don't want the wound
that's hurting my heart
Give me something lighter

That night that we had, I want it again
I don't understand this future
Let's go back, let's do it again
but make it last forever
make it last forever

I don't want this loss
this stab to my soul
Give me something better

It was a dream
Then the nightmare unfolds
Can't you give me your forever?

That night that we had, I want it again
I don't understand this future
Let's go back, let's do it again
but make it last forever
make it last forever

I want it to last forever

The crowd loves it. It's the first thing I've sung tonight that gets the hoots and hollers I've been wanting. And both Tonio and Traci are totally on their game. They remembered the notes and the rhythm perfectly. But Brad's dragging a bit, which isn't like him. Of course he's not as familiar with the piece, so perhaps it's to be expected.

And Ash? Ash gets it. Or at least he thinks he does. It's funny how different this is from the last time I saw him at a performance. That had been confusing, but it had felt like, like somehow he was a manifestation of all my dreams and nightmares, an apparition from the past, a prediction for the future, a god, a demon.

Now . . . now he looks very human. He lifts the flowers in the air, silently broadcasting his apology. The cheers of the room have softened me and I'm charmed by the gesture. "*Now* we can tear it up," I say into the mic. And off we go, to another, more upbeat tune. The room is finally warm; they like us, and perhaps more important, they're rooting for us. Ash is digging it, too. His body is moving ever so slightly to my music. For once *I* am moving Ash rather than the other way around. I draw a unique sense of empowerment from that. Perhaps that's reflected in my performance, because the crowd is just getting more and more enthusiastic. It doesn't mean anything's forgiven, and it certainly doesn't mean anything's been fixed, but it does mean that this time onstage is giving me the therapeutic relief I've come to rely on. The beat of Brad's drum is lifting me, the whine of Tonio's guitar is drowning out the perpetual chorus of self-doubt, Traci's keyboard has given my life a sense of harmony. And my voice, my voice is my true savior. I lift and lower it, giving it a rough edge here and then a smooth gentleness there. These little touches grant me the illusion of self-control and personal strength. When I'm here, onstage, the world has meaning and I get to decide what that meaning is. The only reminder that it's ever otherwise is these stupid gloves, and half the time during this performance I don't even notice them, and when I do, well, I push the reason for them aside. I can do that when I'm onstage.

When we finally wrap, our little crowd goes wild. We've redeemed ourselves. They love us. In this moment everything really is okay.

And then the spotlight disappears. We're in the dark and there's nothing to do but walk away from the love.

What is the opposite of stage fright? What do you call it when you are terrified of the moment you must step away from the spotlight? With every step into the club's back room my anxiety builds. The owner is here, standing to the side, nodding his approval, an envelope full of money in his hand. This is a job after all, more an act of prostitution than passion. I accept his congratulations as I take the payment, try to pretend that my hands aren't shaking. The owner doesn't linger. He goes off into the club to survey the scene. Tonio and Traci are already collecting their instruments. There's a rave on the other end of town and they want to get there as quickly as possible. I could go, too, drop some X for a few hours of artificial bliss. Maybe I should. I mean, Jesus, who am I being good for? What's the point?

A hand is placed on my back. "You still *okay enough*?"

I look up to see Brad, those beautiful deep-set eyes looking down at me, and for just a second I consider falling against his chest, asking him if he would wrap those big strong arms around me again, see if they can protect me from . . . everything.

"I—" But before I can even finish the thought, Ash steps into the space. For a moment he just stands there, about fifteen feet away, looking at me, then Brad, then me again, the roses taking on a rather Goth-like appearance in the dim lighting. My heart is pounding so hard it actually hurts. When he finally does walk toward us it feels like his pace is particularly languid.

"Hey there, Luv," he says quietly, and then he cups my chin and places his lips against mine, right there, with Brad's hand still on my back. It takes me aback, not just because of Brad but because of how we left things last night. Part of me wants to smack him upside the head, hard. But to do that here . . . in front of Brad, knowing Tonio and Traci will be by my side in a moment, I just feel like I've hit my week's quota for drama.

And so I let him kiss me, and Brad removes his hand.

When Ash finally pulls away his eyes immediately turn to Brad. "So," he says, "you're the new drummer. Awesome beat." He lifts his hand for a fist bump.

Brad reciprocates the gesture with a wry smile. "And you're the new boyfriend."

"Not so new," Ash corrects, pulling me to him, away from Brad, draping his arm over my shoulder. "She and I go way back." He then turns back to me, his expression softening as he leans in to give me another kiss, this time on the cheek. "You were amazing tonight. And I know you wrote that song for me."

I flush and look away.

"Hey." He turns my face back to him, looks me in the eye. "I've never been so honored." Again he switches his focus to Brad. "That song was about our first night together."

"Yeah?" Brad asks, crossing his arms over his chest. "To me it sounded like it was about disappointment."

I feel Ash tense, his grip on my shoulder involuntarily tightening. "Um," I say awkwardly, "it's about different things at different times I guess . . . Sort of depends on my mood when I sing it."

Ash doesn't even seem to hear me. He's in a staring match with Brad. "You know what they say, the road of love is never smooth," he finally replies. For once I let the cliché lie. "But Mercy and I always find our way back to one another," he continues. "That's what's important. We've got an unbreakable connection. What you see before you?" He uses his free hand to gesture to the two of us. "This is fate."

"I don't believe in fate," Brad says simply. "I believe in choices."

"Oh my God, are you Johnny Depp guy?"

I turn to see Traci clutching her keyboard lengthwise against her body. Tonio is right behind her with his guitar. I don't know why they were onstage for so long after we finished, but at this point I'm just grateful they're here now to interrupt this weirdness.

"Johnny Depp?" Ash asks, a huge grin spreading across his face. "That's how you describe me?"

"Not only that," Traci adds as she walks up to us. "She's refusing to share you. I asked for a threeway and she totally shot me down. You must be pretty special."

And now we've entered into a whole different *kind* of weirdness. I wrinkle my nose. I don't know what's worse, that Traci thinks that not offering your boyfriend up for a threeway makes him special or that she just implied that I've had threeways with all my previous nonspecial boyfriends. Probably the latter.

"I'm game for a threeway," Tonio offers, and then casts his eyes on Brad. "What do ya say?" He gestures to Traci. "Should we hook her up?"

Traci and I exchange looks. We just got a peek inside Tonio's closet.

"Okay," Ash says with a laugh. "We'll leave you guys to it." He gives Brad a wink. "Mercy and I need a little alone time." And then softer, a little more vulnerable, he turns to me. "We do, right?"

I give a small nod. He places the roses in my hand, which I accept without comment. And then, just like that, I let him lead me out. As we walk out the back exit I feel Brad's eyes on me. I don't even turn around to say good-bye.

Maybe leaving like this with Ash, the flowers he's given me held against the crook of my leather-covered arm like I'm some sort of MTV beauty queen . . . maybe this is romantic.

Or maybe, just maybe, this is good-bye.

CHAPTER 21

❀

W HEN WE STEP outside he turns to me. The streetlight
above us makes his black hair shine and highlights the
chiseled cut of his cheekbones. He's so beautiful. But then, devils
always are. He walks me up to his bike. "Here," he says softly, "I
got you something else, too." He reaches into his saddlebag and
pulls out a flat, square box. Without a word I take it and open
it. It's a Betsey Johnson necklace. Clunky and cute and fun and
very me.

"Thank you," I say simply and close the box.

"Least I could do," he says with a sheepish smile that disappears
quickly when I don't smile back. "Where do you want to go?" he
asks. "There's a Denny's a few blocks over, or you could hop on the
back of my bike and we could be at Lori's Diner in less than five. Or
maybe your place? We could go there if you want privacy."

I stare down at the red petals, almost black in this lighting. "I
want you to take me to your home."

He blinks, his body still. For the longest time he doesn't say anything at all.

"Did you hear me?" I ask. My voice sounds unnaturally loud in
the stillness.

"It's all the way in Santa Monica," he finally says, his lips curling
into a practiced smile.

"I don't care."

"It's not exactly looking great right now. I, um, wasn't expecting
company."

I swallow and look down at the sidewalk, which is covered in cracks and stains of unknown origins. "Either you take me to your place or we don't talk. And I don't mean we don't talk tonight. I mean that there will be nothing left to say." Finally I find the courage to look up and meet his gaze directly, and I can see both understanding and discomfort in his stare. "If we're gonna do this, if we're going to have any chance at all, you have to let me into your life. You have to at least care about me enough . . . you have to *trust* me enough to show me where you sleep at night. I . . . I don't think I'm being unreasonable."

Ash's smile is gone. "I've . . . I've told you about my house in Santa Monica."

"You have."

"Yeah." He glances down the street. "I . . . I may have made it sound a little nicer than it is."

I laugh. Not a giggle, or a chuckle, a full-blown laugh. "Oh my God, Ash, if all you're doing is trying to keep me from finding out that your place is a dump, we'll have no problems. Really, I don't care. I just need you to let me in."

He continues to look off into the distance; the wind plays with his hair, reminding me of all the times I've done the same. We've shared so much intimacy while maintaining so much distance.

"Yeah," he says again after almost a minute of silence. "Okay. You can follow me." He sucks in a sharp breath of air and lets it out in a low whistle. "Get ready, you're about to see my life."

EVEN WITH THE light late-night traffic, it takes a while to get to Santa Monica. But tonight the distance doesn't bother me. As I follow Ash's bike I find myself bouncing between eagerness and apprehension. It's not that I'm scared about what I'm going to see when I check out his digs, it's that I've committed myself to talking to him about everything else once we're there and to be honest, I'm not sure how that's going to go. It could be that after driving all this way, I'll be turning around and driving all the way home in less than twenty minutes.

The thought terrifies me. If I can't make this work, what do I have? Nothing but a perfect track record of failure.

He leads me to a residential street on the very outskirts of Santa Monica . . . in fact I'm not entirely sure we're not technically still in LA. It's borderline.

He parks on the street in front of a spot just big enough for my car. Great; as if I wasn't jittery enough, now I have to parallel park behind a motorcycle. It takes me several minutes, but somehow I manage it without knocking over the Ninja or having a breakdown. He waits for me curbside, and as soon as I grab my flowers and lock the door he points to the parking sign. "I don't have an extra permit, so just know if you decide to stay over you'll have to move this by ten a.m." He says the words so fast that it takes me a second to work them out. He shoves his hands inside his leather jacket and gestures with his chin. "This way."

I walk half a step behind him, my roses held in front of me. It feels like an odd procession, like a piece of performance art or something. But I don't point it out. I sense that Ash isn't in a joking mood.

When he finally stops it's in front of a relatively modest but perfectly decent house. It seems crazy that this would be worth the fuss of hiding. I'm about to say something along those lines when he speaks up.

"I live in a guesthouse behind this." His hands are still in his pockets and he's staring hard at the ground. "We just need to walk down the driveway on the side there and then go through the backyard."

"Oh." I try to catch his eye, but he won't look at me. "Lead the way."

He takes me down the driveway, but before he opens the gate to the backyard he whispers, "Just be sure to be as quiet as possible. The woman in the main house is elderly, but her hearing is confoundingly good. Even closing the gate too hard will wake her."

I make a gesture of a zipper over my lips. He smiles gratefully and lets us in. We walk through a small patch of green grass and then, finally, get to his door. The way the house is situated, I can't really get much of a sense of it from the outside, but as soon as he opens the door I begin to understand.

On the plus side, it's not a studio. Unlike me he actually has a bedroom, a kitchen, and a living room. On the other hand, it is the smallest one-bedroom I've ever seen in my life. The living room is large enough for the impressively sized, and probably very expensive, flat-screen TV mounted to the wall, plus a love seat and coffee table, but that's about it. When he leads me to the kitchen I'm shocked to see he actually has less counter space than I do, and that's *bad*. There is barely enough space to fully open the refrigerator door. There is a little breakfast area where he has put a small square table and two plastic chairs. If he wanted to host more than one person for dinner he might be able to fit in a third chair, probably not a fourth. He takes the roses from me and gently lays them on the table, then pours two small glasses of sipping tequila and gives me one to hold. Drink in hand, he leads me to the bedroom, which is barely big enough to accommodate his double bed, very small dresser, and medium-size desk. And the bathroom? If I were to stretch my arms out to either side I would *almost* be able to touch two walls. The counter space situation in here is even worse than in the kitchen. The only place to put anything is either in the medicine cabinet, the shower rack he probably bought at Ikea, or the top of the toilet. The shower curtain has seen better days.

This is not new construction. There is no hill, no ocean view. It's basically a pool house converted into a microscopic guesthouse . . . except there's no pool. He stands in the four-foot area that constitutes a hallway and puts his hands into his back pockets. "So, not exactly Buckingham Palace, huh?"

I smile and use my head to gesture to the front door. "Who's the elderly lady with the superhuman hearing? Did you know her before?"

A quick wince and again he averts his eyes. "She's my great-aunt. I do pay her rent, and I sort of feel like I'm doing her a favor because I'll go grocery shopping for her, get up on the stepladder and change the lightbulbs, change the batteries in her remote controls. She has arthritis so those little things are hard for her."

"So you're staying to help her out," I clarify.

"Yes . . . well, sort of . . . When I move I'll still come here and help out. My good deeds aren't really dependent on my living in a rathole." He takes a long drink and then falls silent for a moment before continuing. "I really *should* be able to afford something better. Everyone who knows me would tell you that. Eva, my parents, my friends, everyone. If I was just better with my money I could live better, but . . . I have a hard time with it. What can I say, I'd make a lousy accountant." He lifts his glass to his lips again as his eyes dart back to me. I can see the fear there. He's afraid I'll reject him.

Or worse, he's afraid I'll judge him.

"I'm not great with money, either," I say with a little smile, gently placing my glass on the center of the coffee table, next to a small and disorderly pile of magazines. "I mean, I don't think I am. I've never had any to test the theory with."

A spark of hope in his eyes, a smile that hints at relief. "I guess I exaggerated when I told you about this place. Thing is, I *am* going to have a fantastic place pretty soon. I'm making bank for this pilot. So I figured I'd just wait until the checks started rolling in, find a new condo, and then show you *that*. I . . . never wanted you to see this."

I flinch at that. I mean, yes, part of me is actually charmed by his sheepish vulnerability, but there's something about this that's just a tad . . . off-key, and . . . and it's not the place. It's his effort to keep it from me. It's that he thought he needed to lie. "How could you think I would care about this?" I ask, trying to keep the hurt out of my voice. I let my eyes move to the television, which I now realize is just ridiculously large for this room. "It's not like this is, like, a crack house or something," I reason. "It's just . . . intimate."

Ash allows himself an amused smile. "I think the Realtor's term is 'cozy.'"

"Yes!" I agree. "A cozy opportunity."

"Yeah." He walks over to the coffee table and picks up one of the magazines, a *National Geographic* with a cover photo of a space shuttle. "You know those pods the astronauts use when they land in the ocean? The ones they always show in movies?"

"Yeah?"

He smiles and throws back the rest of his drink. "My place *is* bigger than that."

I start giggling. I can't help myself. Ash puts his finger to his lips. "Shh, you'll wake up my great-aunt."

And that just makes me laugh harder. Ash looks irritated at first, and then he smiles, and finally he's laughing, too. We're both giggling like idiots. It's not like there's anything that funny going on. But it's nice, sharing this moment, and when we both finally settle down I don't feel that apprehension anymore.

He sits down on the love seat and gestures for me to do the same. I hesitate a moment, but then accept the silent invitation. It's not a big piece of furniture.

"You were good tonight," he says quietly. "You were happy."

"I was happy?" I repeat, not clear about where he's going with this.

"Yeah, you were having fun."

"Oh, I get it." I pick my drink up and then fall back against the cushion, try to find a way to put another quarter of an inch of space between us. "You're moving up in the world and I'm just having a good time. Right? That's how you see it?"

"Fuck, Mercy, since when is telling someone they look happy an insult?"

"It's not, but—"

"I was wasted last night," he says, cutting me off. "I didn't mean the things I said."

"Alcohol doesn't turn people into liars. It lowers their inhibitions." I lift my glass as if using it as a visual aid before tossing some back. "It gives you the audacity to say the things you would otherwise keep to yourself."

"Yeah, but . . ." He throws his hands up in the air. "Will you at least agree that when you're drunk you're not always at your most articulate? That sometimes things come out wrong? Can we agree on that?"

I take another sip and press my lips together as I stare at the dark screen.

"Hey." He angles his body toward me, puts his hand over mine. "You *should* be having fun. It's a *compliment.* You've dealt with too much bullshit for too long. People trying to force you to behave in ways that have nothing to do with who you are."

"And who exactly am I?" I ask, my eyes still on the screen.

"The girl who burns the candle at both ends. You're the beautiful, sexy, edgy girl who gets up on a stage and sings into the early morning hours just because she can. And that makes you better than me."

Finally I meet his eyes. "I don't get it."

"We, all of us, should be able to celebrate our lives as they are today. But most of us can't do that, *I* can't do that. I'm living in the future, thinking about what's coming rather than what is, and then I see you and, you know, you're all about the moment."

"Yeah," I say uncertainly, "that's me." I finish the rest of the tequila and put my empty glass next to his. What he's saying isn't all that different from the things I told Brad in the back room of Envy. But it's still not comforting to hear and I don't exactly know why.

"I want to learn from you. I want to absorb just a little of that vitality. I want . . . I want you to show me how to be happy with my life." He takes a sharp breath. "Will you do that, Mercy? Will you teach me how to just *be*?"

I study his expression and then turn away. I know the ocean isn't that far, but I can't hear it. All I can hear is the traffic a few blocks

over on Santa Monica Boulevard, and all I can see is this claustro-
phobic little space and Ash, looking at me with all that hope and
need, asking me to give him something I don't have and something
that he may only want in theory. Because sometimes when we're not
clear about what we need we'll just ask for anything. At least I do,
and Ash and I are so very much alike. I hang on to my silence for
some time, maybe a minute, maybe two. It's only when I feel Ash's
mood shift, when I know he senses something is off, that I speak up.
"Last night, after I got home, I broke a bottle and I cut myself. I cut
myself on purpose."

"What?" he asks, confused.

"The girl you see onstage," I continue, "that's not me, at least it's
not me all the time." I pull my feet up on the couch, sit cross-legged,
resting my forearms on my thighs. "Sometimes I'm not this life
force or this . . . this source of light. Sometimes I'm just . . . numb. I
don't want to be numb. I want to *feel*. And sometimes the only thing
to feel is pain. That's all that's available, and what's weird is the pain
sort of helps, because when you hurt you're not numb. When you
feel that pain you know you're alive."

Again the room grows quiet. I wait for Ash to lecture me. To
throw me out. To tell me how disgusted he is with me.

"Did you cut yourself badly?" he asks, sounding somewhat bewildered.

"No. It's just . . . more like a scratch, I guess."

"Oh." He studies the ceiling for a moment. Perhaps he's silently
asking for advice from God. Or maybe he's just trying to think up a
way to politely get rid of me. "Well," he finally says, "my last room-
mate was into branding. He had this big branded eagle across his
upper back. And I had this girlfriend who had her tongue pierced."
He shakes his head. "That *had* to hurt, but it was her choice and she
got what she wanted out of it. So as long as you're not doing any real
damage . . . You're not, right?"

"No," I say softly. *Not yet.*

"And it makes you feel better?"

I nod.

"Well then," he says with a sigh, "who am I to give you a hard time about it?"

My mouth drops open. In a million years it never occurred to me that he, that *anyone,* would react like that. "Are you actually telling me that you're cool with me cutting myself?"

"It doesn't exactly sound like you're describing a habit, Mercy," he points out. "It was a one-off. All I'm saying is that you should live your life the way you want to live it. I'm just hoping you'll still let me be part of it." He runs his hands over my unkempt hair. "I'm never going to judge you. I like you the way you are."

My heart leaps to my throat. I feel tears stinging my eyes.

"Can you forgive me for last night?" he asks.

I lunge forward, placing my mouth against his, holding his jacket in my hands as I pull him to me. He seems surprised at first, but soon yields to my desire. He grips my shoulders and adds his weight to our kiss, pushing me back even as he moves forward, making it his own. His mouth moves to my shoulder as one of his hands moves back up to my hair, and the other one pulls the fabric of my shirt aside so he can graze my skin with his teeth. There's a new kind of urgency now. A new kind of need. This man who wants me *as I am*, he needs me. And just knowing that makes touching him more intense and more erotic than ever before. Gently I pull his jacket from one arm and then the other before slipping my hands under his shirt. I'm caressing him, learning him, caring for him.

"I want to be inside of you," he whispers, his hands moving to the bottom of my tee, pulling it from me, his hands rough against the softness of my skin. I feel him fumble with my bra before freeing me, removing all the impediments that separate us. And now his hands are woven into my hair, on either side of my head. He's holding me still as he moves in for another passionate kiss.

I linger a moment, then pull away from his grasp, lowering myself as my fingers quietly unfasten his belt buckle, then pulling the leather strap away and dropping it to the floor. My hand moves under him and pulls his wallet from his back pocket, holding it up for him to see before looking inside and pulling out what I want. "You're learning," I say sweetly as I hold up the little packet. "And," I whisper as my hands go to the waist of his pants, "you've won." I pull the denim fabric from him with a jerk of my hands, throwing it behind me with little care or consideration. "In a matter of weeks you'll have the future you've always wanted. You'll have your new home, your new celebrity, the success you've been craving. This should be the best year of your life."

"Yes." He sits up and I watch as he removes his shirt, then close my eyes as he cups my breasts. "I've won. And you're my prize." He leans forward and his teeth pull gently on my earlobe. His hands are now unbuttoning my own jeans, reaching inside them, inside my panties. "You're wet," he notes.

"Yeah." My voice has a different cadence now, more needing. "I am, for you." I feel the pressure of his hand, his fingers, and then the scrape of the fabric against my skin as he peels it off me—jeans, panties, it all has to go.

"Prepare me for you, Mercy."

Ah, I do love hearing that name on his lips. It has the ring of victory. I get down on the floor as he turns to me, allowing me to once again unroll the condom with my tongue, covering him, preparing him for his conquest.

And that's me. He's conquered me, overwhelmed me, and it's what I want. I straddle him slowly, holding myself above him as he strains for me, curling my back into a comma as my mouth finds his shoulder, as my teeth gently graze his skin. "I'm ready to take you, Ash," I whisper, and then I lower myself onto him, feeling him enter me, his strength, his pain, his accomplishment—I want it all. He's holding me with his hands and then he lowers me, my arms slip down to my sides, then even farther back until my back is flat against his lap, my arms dangling down so my hands are pressed into the floor. I let my head fall back as I use the strength of my arms to move me, thrusting myself against him, seeing nothing but the cream-colored ceiling above me. And what does he see? My body, stretched out and on display for him as I take him in over and over again. Me, his prize, his fate.

But then in a moment he's pulling me up again, pressing my chest against his, and with a series of swift movements he has us on the floor, turning us until we're on our sides, my back pressed against his chest. I slide my legs forward, under the coffee table, stretch them out in front of me, pressing myself into him, and I feel him enter me from behind as he places his arm in front of my breasts and uses the floor to lift himself, giving himself a deeper and more satisfying angle. My legs are pressed together, making me even tighter than before as he penetrates me. He's controlling our rhythm now, and my position allows him to fill me and touch me in ways he hadn't before. I stretch my arm above my head, steadying myself against each thrust; it looks and feels like the whole world is shaking.

And then suddenly I'm repositioned onto my stomach. The change comes so fast I barely know how it happens. But the welcome burden of his weight is on me now, his legs on either side of me, and our connection has not been broken. I cross my legs at the ankles, once again tightening my embrace. I hear him moan as I scratch my fingernails against the frayed carpet, as if clawing it away, destroying its flaws.

But it's only when he pulls me up onto all fours that I find that I am about to completely lose control. Now at our most primal, feeling him claim me like this, one hand on my hips as the other reaches around to toy with my clit—it's too much. "Ash!" The name bursts from my lips with such force I'm sure his aunt must have heard it; the whole *neighborhood* could have heard and I still don't care. His energy is savage; I feel his passion, his desire, sense his anger and his pride, and when I climax I am overcome with pure and all-embracing pleasure, a beautiful and complete release. And then it's his voice that fills the room, his volume lower than mine, but his tone no less insistent. His release comes before I've had a chance to even think of recovering from my own, and the sensation of him pulsating inside me is just . . . fucking awesome.

For a moment neither of us moves. And then slowly, with the gorgeous exhaustion of spent passion, he frees me from his grip and falls back as I fall forward. And as I lie there, my cheek to the ground, trying to stabilize my breathing, I think, this is our connection, this is our fate.

This is us.

CHAPTER 22

❀

T HE PILOT IS going to be shot in New Mexico, and the two days before Ash leaves to shoot his scenes are just sort of . . . perfect. He takes me to this awesome restaurant where we dine on crème fraîche and caviar and drink spectacular specialty cocktails with sophisticated and unique names. Afterward he gets us into Skybar at the Mondrian hotel. There are even more stars here than at Envy. I even spot Mulder! And the view; we can see the lights of the entire city beneath us, looking like scattered diamonds.

When that metaphor popped into my head . . . well, it was the only time in the evening that I felt a pang of sadness. Once, when I was a kid, I told my little sister I was going to be a jewel thief. I was going to steal diamonds, but instead of selling them I would keep them in my attic and they would all glow, and when I walked on them it would be like walking on stars.

The expression on her face when I told her that, I remember it so clearly. She was delighted, and so I kept spinning the tale until it took us into late afternoon, almost to dinnertime. It was always so nice to see Kasie light up like that, so rare. She was such a serious kid, but when she laughed . . .

The memory of that laughter hurts my heart. But then Ash puts his arms around my waist and whispers something mildly obscene in my ear, and I laugh and find a way to push the memories aside.

Ash just keeps buying me drinks—at eighteen dollars a pop. We cap off our perfect night with a stay in a suite at the Mondrian. We stand out on the balcony, smoke a little weed, and gaze out at the City of Angels as we talk and talk about how all of his dreams are coming true.

And I am part of those dreams. I am here, sharing it all with him. He wants me. He cares for me. He might even love me . . . eventually. He hasn't said the words yet, but, well, he can't fight fate, can he?

I am hungover but happy when I finally see him off for his month-long excursion. Everything is perfect, perfect, perfect.

Except for the band. Rehearsals become less perfect by the second. Brad is constantly trying to turn us into more serious musicians, and by serious I mean good. And I back him up, but perhaps not with the ferocity that I did before. It's just that I'm nervous about Traci and Tonio seeing Brad and me as a team. I don't want anyone to be confused about which man is my partner. Particularly me.

When we walk out together I keep the conversation light and casual, pretending that we are nothing but acquaintances who play music together. I don't even ask about his daughter.

That last part is hard. I've been thinking about June a lot. There's just something about her . . . She just, just worms her way into your heart without even trying. I keep flashing back to that first night I met her. The way she threw herself into her father's arms . . . What must that be like? To be loved like that? What must it be like for Brad to know that he brought something so marvelous into the world?

But the only things I ask him about are related to our music or the weather. Do you think Tonio's guitar solo should be longer? Will it rain tomorrow? Do you think we should cut the instrumental intro to the new song?

And every time we talk he seems . . . sad . . . or disappointed or dissatisfied. I can see that there are things he'd like to say that he won't, and I am so profoundly grateful for his restraint. Still, it makes me feel awful. And it occurs to me that if he feels hated by Traci and Tonio and shut out by me . . . what's left to keep him in the band?

He can't leave. I just . . . he just . . . he *can't*.

And so when we're booked for a rare early evening private party in Silver Lake I insist that everyone in the group make themselves available for dinner and drinks afterward. I give them five days' notice only because I want to make sure Brad can come. I even give him the latitude and longitude of the location as a goodwill gesture.

The amount of thought and time I put into picking the perfect restaurant is a little silly, but this is just so important to me. I know that if I can get all three of them in a social environment where they *have* to talk to one another, Tonio and Traci will come to realize that Brad isn't the Ken doll that he appears to be. Everything will be better and he'll stay.

He has to stay.

I select a new Mexican/Californian fusion restaurant in the neighborhood that's been praised for its margaritas and reasonable prices. It's a five-minute drive to Brad's, so he won't have to factor commute time into how long he can hang. And as soon as we all walk in I know I've made the right choice. It's a sprawling place with a warehouse feel to it. The bar is separated out enough from the restaurant that it doesn't disturb diners, but not so far away that you can't sense the festive atmosphere. We all scoot into a U-shaped booth next to a group of about seven women of various ages, all laughing and drinking together. Traci immediately orders up a pitcher of blended, frothy sin.

"That party was whack," Tonio complains, referring to the gig as he scans the menu. "How lame is it to have your mom throw you your twenty-first birthday party?"

"I didn't find it so odd that she threw her daughter the party," Brad counters, "but I did find the male stripper a little disconcerting."

Traci giggles as she puts aside her menu. Behind me I hear the group of women toasting with their shots of tequila. "Did you see the way the mom was *looking* at that guy?" Traci asks. "I mean, coo, coo, ca-choo, Mrs. Robinson!"

That makes us all burst into laughter. And we haven't even had drinks yet. This is going rather well, thank you very much!

But when the pitcher does arrive the women at the next table break into their own set of giggles and, I don't know, the laugh of one of those women . . . it's familiar, and although I can't place it, it puts me a little on edge.

"Do you think we should just say no private parties going forward?" Tonio asks after the waitress has left with our orders.

"We can be discriminating, but we don't want to have any blanket rules," Brad reasons.

"Yeah." Tonio nods slowly, as if Brad has just said something uncommonly wise. "Flexibility. We gotta have that."

A woman at the other table lets some expletive fly, and again their group bursts into laughter, and *again* there's that one familiar voice.

"Are you okay, Mercy?" Brad asks. Both Traci and Tonio look over at me to see what the source of Brad's concern is.

"I'm fine," I say lightly and lift my glass. "We should toast."

"Right!" Traci lifts her glass high above her head so it looks more like she's lifting a lighter at a concert than preparing to say cheers. "To Resurrection!"

We repeat the words, clink our glasses as the chips and salsa arrive. But Brad is watching me, and he's not the only one. One of the women from that table is looking at me, too . . . I can *feel* it.

And for reasons I can't even begin to explain, I suddenly feel the urge to run.

I sip the margarita and try to angle myself so that only a sliver of my profile can be seen by the people at that table. "You know what's going to be a good gig," I begin, reaching for a chip. "The—"

"Melody?" a woman's voice asks.

For a second I freeze, red salsa dripping from my freshly dipped tortilla chip.

"Melody, is that you?"

And now I can place the voice.

Over nine and a half million people in LA County. Over three million in Orange County, which is where I would know this woman from. Over eighty thousand restaurants when you combine the two neighboring counties together. So no, I must be wrong about the voice. This meeting, it simply *can't* be happening. "I'm sorry," I say, recovering slightly. "You have the wrong person."

"You're not Melody?" she asks, confused. If I turn around, look at her, if I shoot her my most intimidating glare, maybe she'll go away. But I desperately do not want to turn around.

"Her name's Mercy," Tonio corrects, but now from the corner of my eye I can see Traci. She has a little frown on her face, her brow creased as she stares down into her drink, deep in thought. The name Melody is clicking with her.

"Oh . . . my bad." The woman laughs and I immediately hear the intoxication in her voice. She's not falling-down drunk, but she's not sober enough to pick up on the subtle or not-so-subtle clues of my protective body language. "I'm so sorry, I don't know why I was so sure it was Melody! But we do know each other." She places a hand on my shoulder and I wince. "It's me!" she says, giving me a gentle shake. "Jessica Garcia! Jessy! We had the same OB-GYN at that clinic! You know, for our prenatal visits?"

I can feel all of their eyes on me. Traci, Tonio, Brad. They're all watching me, every single one of them picking up on different clues, but all coming to the same conclusion that this woman isn't mistaken.

Don't turn around. But my mind and body aren't really connected anymore. And I feel myself twisting, turning my head, finding the instinct too strong to resist . . .

. . . like a lemming running off a cliff.

And when I see her . . . oh God, it's like no time has passed at all. I'm in the clinic in Fullerton. There are Latin instrumental ballads playing over the speakers. The magazines are months, sometimes years, old. The place smells like antiseptic, and every expectant mother in there seems like a child herself. There in the corner I can see the blond fifteen-year-old pregnant girl, gripping the hand of her mom like her life depends on it. And there, there's the Mexican girl with smooth dark skin and scared eyes, clutching her belly as if she has a stomachache rather than a baby. And then there's Jess. Jess with her flower tattoos and bright red lipstick, sitting by my side, laughing with me about the shoddy decor and the lack of decent reading material. Distracting me and helping me cope as I wait for my appointment with my doctor. *Our* doctor. I had seen her there three out of the nine times I went. I was there eight times in my first four months of pregnancy. But of course she didn't know that part. She just knew that I was about her age, which made us the oldest two women in there. She knew that I had blue-green hair at the time and five piercings in each ear. She knew that I was someone she could hang with. And she knew that our doctor was always running behind, sometimes by over an hour, and that she was scared and I was scared and that maybe if we talked together, laughed together, we could help each other cope with that fear.

But what she didn't know is that I had so much more to fear than she ever did.

"You look great!" Jessy is saying, completely oblivious to the shroud of silence that now covers our table. "You've totally regained your figure! Are you breast-feeding? I am. I thought I would love having boobs, but once you go dairy farm they stop being sexy, am I right? I swear, this is the first time I've been able to go out for a girls' night since Jax was born! I had to pump for days just to pull it off. And now of course I'm going to have to pump and toss when I get home 'cause of the booze. Oh my God, I'm being so rude!" She laughs. "Peeps, this is Mercy," she says, turning back to her table. "She and I were preggers at the same time in the OC. Mercy"—she turns back to me—"these chicks are from my moms' group. We meet at—"

But before I can hear one more word I am out of my seat and running as fast as I can to the door. A waiter balancing a tray tries to dodge me but fails, and a bunch of plates go crashing to the floor.

But I don't stop to help. I don't even acknowledge him as he yells after me. I just have to get out of there, *now*.

And when I'm outside and the night air is cool against my skin I just keep running. I don't know where I'm going and I really don't care. I must get away from that place, from that woman, from this devastating feeling of humiliation and shame and self-loathing, but most of all from this encroaching coldness that seems to be filling my gut.

So I keep running and running, crashing into pedestrians as I do, almost tripping over a small dog, never answering the curses that are thrown at me by these strangers who have been subjected to my carelessness.

And as I see a busy street up ahead I suddenly realize what I'm going to do.

I'm going to run into the traffic.

The very thought makes me pick up the pace. I didn't even know I could run this fast. People are just getting out of the way now. I hear the alarmed voice of a stranger loudly question if I've stolen someone's purse. But of course it's so much worse than that. What I've stolen is someone's life.

And there's the Don't Walk sign, glowing bright red. And there are the cars and the trucks, all moving along at speeds that can kill. And I'm so very close.

I widen my stride, my hair whipping behind me. I'm close enough now that people are beginning to realize that I'm not stopping. And they're not yelling curses anymore. They're just yelling.

And I don't care.

Twenty feet from the curb.

I see the Corvette turn onto the street a little too fast.

Fifteen feet from the curb.

The timing is perfect. It will reach the curb at about the same time I will. It won't be able to slow down.

Ten feet.

Will it be able to swerve in time? Will it hit me? Will I die?

Seven feet . . .

There are no cars in the lane left of the Corvette now and it's not slowing down. It'll be the last one to make the light. If it swerves it won't hit anyone else. I'm the only one in danger and the danger is right there, within reach, mere seconds away . . .

Five feet from the curb.

I'm so close, it's right *there*!

Three feet, two feet . . .

An arm wraps around my waist, yanking me off the ground, pulling me away from the curb at the very last second and pressing me up against my assailant even as I kick and scream.

And I know who it is.

It's Brad. He's saved me.

And immediately all that adrenaline that was coursing through me, making me feel completely awake and alive . . . it's gone. Just like that.

He's saved me. I'm safe now.

And being safe like this, it's just enough to remind me that as far as most of the world is concerned, I'm dead.

❀

CHAPTER 23

During the short drive to Brad's house neither one of us says a word. I rest my head against the window, staring blankly at the street, practically catatonic.

He parks less than half a block away from his building, gets out, goes to my door, and leans over to unlatch my seat belt. "Do you want me to carry you?" he asks.

I consider not answering but eventually shake my head no.

"Good, you can walk then." He pulls me out of the car, maybe a little rougher than I had expected. I keep my gaze straight ahead, my eyes unfocused as he pulls me through the entrance gate, through the courtyard, to his front door.

When he lets us in there's Maria sitting on the couch, reading *Details* magazine.

"Everything go okay tonight?" he asks her.

She nods, gives her report of good behavior as Brad thanks her, gives her a few bucks, and escorts her to the door. I don't say a word and I keep my eyes on the wall. If Maria greeted me I didn't notice it. I sit down on the upholstered chair by the coffee table as Brad goes to peek in on June. When he comes back he stands opposite me, leaning against the wall. I know I need to look at him eventually, although I'm not sure I see the point of it. I know what I'm going to see. Unease, fear, pity, disgust—these are the universal reactions to my behavior. When I was sixteen and my father took me to the loony bin, the nurse who admitted me directed all her attention to my father, making him feel comfortable, letting him know she was going to do everything she could to make the process of getting rid of me as easy and stress free as possible. She was very sympathetic . . . to him. But she never looked at me.

You'd think the whole thing would have made me feel invisible. But oddly enough, that kind of extreme and purposeful avoidance doesn't make you feel invisible at all. It makes you feel like you are the most conspicuous person in the world. You're the side-show freak. You're the dead body on the side of the road after a car crash, the one that decent people won't look at and low-class rubberneckers will gape at.

When you're normal, people whisper about you when you leave the room. When you're a freak, people whisper about you when you're five feet away.

"Mercy."

I hear myself sigh in response to my name, but it's odd because I don't actually feel myself breathe.

"Mercy," he says again, a little sterner this time. Slowly, re-luctantly, I direct my eyes to him, and the jolt of surprise breaks through my anesthetized state. There's no fear there, or pity, or dis-gust . . . Maybe a little confusion, a little concern, a lot of frustration. "What the hell?" he snaps.

The question feels both general and specific. "What do you want to know?"

"Were you trying to kill yourself?"

"No. I just . . ." I look over at the tightrope walker between the two buildings of the World Trade Center. "I wanted to see if I would die."

Brad takes a second to let that sink in. "I'm not sure that's better."

"No," I admit, a humorless smile on my lips. "But ya gotta admit, it's different." I get up, walk to the poster, and put my hand on the tiny tightrope walker. "You remember the first night you brought me here? You started to tell me about June's mom, but I wouldn't let you."

Brad takes a seat on the couch, leaning forward as he listens. "I remember."

"I knew you were going to say bad things about her. That's what people do. They talk shit about their ex . . . particularly when kids are involved. But whatever June's mom did or didn't do, she is still better than me."

"How do you figure?"

"She gave her daughter life," I explain, my voice cracking just a little as I turn back to him. "She gave her a father who loves her and a grandmother. She left her daughter in a loving home." I shake my head, my eyes darting around, taking in the warmth of the room. "I wanted to do that. I wanted to give my little girl something like this."

I'm trembling a bit now, and I grab the backs of my arms to still myself. "I was on X the night my daughter was conceived. I took cocaine the afternoon after that."

"Why?" he asks simply.

"*Why?*" I repeat incredulously. The question is so ridiculous that it actually brings me back to earth a bit. "I don't know, to punish my parents? But . . ." I run my hands through my hair. "Okay, here's the weird thing about me and drugs. Yes, there were days when the drugs were just for fun or to enhance an experience. I mean, have you ever really listened to house music? That annoyingly repetitive techno beat?"

"Yes, of course."

"Okay, well that music makes a hell of a lot more sense when you're on acid."

Brad grants me an amused smile. "Tell me about the other days."

"The other days?" I study the smooth, almost pristine surface of the ceiling. "On those days the drugs helped me feel normal. That's what's weird. What made other people feel crazy helped me feel normal. And really, what was the point in stopping? What's the worst that could've happened? That I would die? Who cares?" My eyes shoot back to Brad and I feel a flash of defiance. "Really, who *cares*? My parents had already kicked me out. I was never going to be the person they needed me to be. I mean, I couldn't even do that when

I was *sober*. My little sister had stopped responding to my e-mails. I didn't have a boyfriend, so why *not* just live my life the way I wanted to live it, and if that meant checking out early then so fucking be it. At least I could have a little fun and comfort while here."

"But you got pregnant," Brad says, his voice low, steady, completely unfazed by my rambling.

The words stop me, and for a moment I just look at him. "Yeah," I finally say, choking the word out. "I did. And I know . . . I *know* that when you've taken the kind of drugs I did during that first month, the smart choice is to get your ass to an abortion clinic. And I'm *totally* pro-choice. But . . ." I shake my head, trying desperately to keep the tears back. "It was my one chance, you know? I could bring a life into this world. I could give her the things I didn't have: love, patience, understanding. I could make her smile and laugh. And maybe . . . maybe she would like me." I take a long breath. "Maybe, maybe I wouldn't be alone anymore. Maybe I could be . . . like, *good*. I could do something good. I could . . . I could not be alone. And I could hold someone wh-who wanted me to h-hold them." I shake my head and look toward the window. My voice is so meek I barely recognize it. "No one ever wants me to hold them," I whisper, determined to stop the tremor. "Fuck them, yes. Lots of guys want me to fuck them. But I don't remember anyone ever wanting me to just give them a hug. Not the guys I date, not my parents, not even when I was a kid. People . . . they just don't want that from me. I'm not that girl."

"So what did you do?" he asks softly.

"After I found out I was pregnant?" I shrug. "I called my dad." A little laugh bubbles up as I'm reminded of what a completely absurd decision that was. "See, I knew I was going to have to stop the drugs," I try to explain, "but some of the stuff I was taking was physically addictive. I did lines, smoked . . . well, I smoked pretty much anything that was handed to me. I needed to find a way to sober up fast and make the withdrawal safe for both me and the baby. I didn't think I could do it on my own, but I figured if I could get into a decent rehab center, then, you know, maybe. I just needed the money for it."

"So you called your dad for a loan."

"Yeah . . . I mean he didn't even have to give the money to me. He just had to hand it over to the rehab center. I had found, like, ten that I thought might work for me and I had gathered all the information together for him so he could pick the one he was most comfortable with. I did serious research. I walked into that meeting *prepared*."

"And what did he do?" Brad asks, his voice so gentle now that part of me just wants to curl up in his arms, beg him to change my history, just find a way to give me a different past.

"Mercy?" he asks, when I don't answer. "What did he do?"

"My name isn't Mercy," I say quietly. "Or at least it wasn't. It was Melody. And what he did was he murdered me . . . Now, the guy who knocked me up, when he did that he killed Melody, although God knows he didn't mean to and it took a while. I guess you could say that guy put me in hospice. But my father? What he did to the woman I was, to *Melody*? That was premeditated. He just looked me in the eye and told me he was done with me. He told me that I was dead. He said that my mother wanted nothing to do with me, that my sister was being trained to forget me." I take a very deep breath and put my hand against the wall to help stabilize myself. "He told me he couldn't help me or my baby because *we didn't exist*."

"Jesus," Brad whispers.

My lips curl into a hideous smile. "I was still determined, though! Yeah, it was going to be harder, but I . . . I just had to try, you know? I had to get myself clean and I had to give this kid a chance. And I decided that if I had a girl, I would name her Mercy. Like the Peter Gabriel song and like . . . well, like *mercy*, the thing my dad just couldn't give me. Just a little fucking mercy!"

"What happened to the baby?"

Again I'm tempted not to answer, but finally I say, "It was *total hell*, but I got clean and I got us through the first trimester. Maybe I wasn't as hooked as I thought, I honestly don't know. The ultrasound re-vealed that she was indeed a girl. And you know, I was feeling pretty damn good about myself." I laugh. "I'd won. I had beat the odds and I was going to have the family my dad was so desperate to deny me. I *won*! But then, a little more than four months in, I lost." I shrug and shake my head. "It was probably all those drugs I took early on that did it. Or maybe the process of the withdrawal was too much for her, maybe I didn't do it right." Again I pause. My vision has gone out of focus again; I'm staring at nothing. "I had one shot at happiness and I literally killed it. I killed her. I killed my last chance at mercy."

Brad gets to his feet, still facing me. I'd back away from him, give him more space, try to keep him from contaminating himself, but I'm already up against the wall. As usual, there's nowhere to retreat. "They said the fetus was in distress," I say dully. "Even when she was inside me, even then she was in distress. I wasn't able to give her any comfort at all! I wasn't . . . I wasn't able to give her *anything*. So, you know . . . I took Mercy's name, tried to give her life, because I figured she had a lot more right to live than Melody, and well, like Daddy said . . . Melody was already dead."

Brad takes a step forward, but I turn away from him, bringing my focus back to the tightrope walker.

"Do you think this guy had a death wish?" I ask.

"Philippe Petit?" he asks.

"Is that his name?" I ask, looking over my shoulder at Brad be-fore turning back to the picture. "I bet lots of people thought he did. Walking around up there, no net, one itsy-bitsy misstep away from a horrifying death. But . . . I kinda have my doubts. What people don't get is that sometimes you have to play chicken with death in order to be reminded that you're *not* dead. Death is the thing that you can face, and tempt and toy with, but the only way to do that is if, like, death is *outside* of you. It's separate, it's the other. You can only face death if you are totally and completely alive."

"There are other ways to feel alive," he says, wrapping me up in that wonderful baritone.

"Like being onstage," I say with a quick nod. "But you can only stay up there for so long. Maybe there are other ways, too, but I don't know of them."

He takes a long, deep breath. "Try this." He puts his hand on my shoulder, gently but firmly turns me around, and steps closer to me, so there is no space between us at all. For a moment I think he's going to kiss me. But instead he just wraps his arms around me. He holds me. And there I am, just standing there, my head against his chest, so unfamiliar with this feeling that I honestly don't know what I'm supposed to do.

And then, slowly, ever so slowly, I raise my arms and wrap them around him. I suck in a sharp breath and hold it for ten seconds, twenty, thirty . . .

And then everything comes out and I'm sobbing. I feel my chest heaving against him as he strokes my back, kisses my hair. And I squeeze him tighter and he just doesn't let go. For the first time that I can remember I am just holding someone. And Brad, he's not asking anything of me, not right now. And he's not expecting anything. It just is what it is, and as that continues to sink in the sobs continue as well. His shirt is soaked with my tears and it's pressing against my cheek and it . . . it feels so . . . *wonderful*.

And he's right. This tenderness, this hug, it doesn't seem possible, but it actually makes me feel alive.

CHAPTER 24

❀

I SPEND THE NIGHT at Brad's, in his bed. He sleeps on the couch.
To be honest, I didn't think I'd be able to sleep at all. But in the
end I'm just exhausted and spent and it's staying awake long enough
to get my shoes off that's the challenge, let alone getting into the
men's T-shirt Brad's lent me.

And now, blinking at the morning light, still curled up under
the covers, I find I can't exactly quantify what happened last night. I
don't know what Traci or Tonio think. I don't really know what Brad
thinks. Part of me wishes that he had spent the night in this bed, next
to me, holding me the way he held me in his living room. But the
more pragmatic part of me knows it would never have stopped there.
Not just because of him, but because of me. Last night I wouldn't have
cared about what was wrong and what was right. I wasn't thinking in
those terms. Last night, after I had told my story in its entirety for the
first time ever, I wasn't really thinking at all. I was feeling. I was feeling fear and pain and loss and *so much need*. Brad had fulfilled a lot
of that need. If he had lain beside me in this bed I would have insisted
he fulfill the rest.

And now? I shift positions and survey my surroundings. Is the
acceptance letter to Harvard still in the desk? Is the picture of June's
mom still in his sweater drawer? In my gut I know the answer to
both questions is yes. I feel a pang of jealousy over that picture. I bet
no one has a picture of me tucked away *anywhere*.

But then, is my jealousy so broad? Or is it the fact that *Brad*
doesn't have a picture of me tucked away that bothers me? I turn

over on my stomach and put a pillow over my head. I feel like I'm hungover except I didn't drink last night.

I hear the bedroom door open and there's a moment's pause before I hear him say, "Mercy."

I pull off the pillow and turn my head to the side so I can see Brad standing in the doorway. He looks . . . edible. Seriously. His hair is all mussed, he's wearing loose navy sweats and a Hanes gray tank that emphasizes his physique. As spent as I am I could push it all aside and just devour this guy.

"Sorry, did I wake you?" he asks as he gently closes the door behind him.

"No," I say truthfully. I prop myself up on my forearms, arching my back just a little. I wonder if I look sexy, lying here wearing his tee. The thing is, the tee is just *huge,* maybe even too big to really pull off the oh-aren't-I-cute-wearing-my-guy's-clothes thing. I'm drowning in this.

And he's not my guy.

I look away and shift my position to sitting up, pulling the covers firmly around my waist.

"I just don't want June waking up and seeing me on the couch," he explains.

"Makes sense," I agree.

He nods and moves to sit on the edge of the bed, then seems to think better of it and leans up against the wall. "I'd also prefer it if she didn't see you coming out of my room this morning."

"Oh." I pull the covers up a little higher as I study the gray striped pattern on the comforter. "I, um, I get it. I know I'm not exactly the kind of role model people want hanging around their kid."

"I wouldn't want June seeing *any* woman coming out of my bedroom in the morning," Brad clarifies. "It's difficult to explain and she's four."

"*Oh.*" I don't even try to hide the relief in my voice. "Well that's cool, do you want me to bail now? Or is she up already? I could climb out the window. Trust me, I'm a pro at climbing out of guys' windows in the morning."

Brad drops his head and laughs. "I don't want you to climb out the window. In fact, would you stay? I have to take June to school, but it's only a ten-minute drive. I could come back with bagels."

I look down at my hands, pick at the remnants of my electric blue nail polish. "It'd probably be best if I headed out."

"Stay anyway," Brad says, locking me in his gaze. My pulse starts to pound a little harder as I continue to clutch the sheets. After a moment he walks across the room, pulls a book from the shelf, and tosses it over to me. "Here's reading material. It'll take me a half hour to get her off, ten to school, twenty to get bagels. You can entertain yourself here for an hour and then we'll talk."

"Brad—"

"All right, I'll just come out and say it. You owe me and now I'm calling in a favor. The favor of your presence." He takes a step toward me and now my pulse is just out of control. "Only for a few hours," he continues. "Only to talk. Will you do that for me?"

"Yeah," I croak, and then clear my throat and let my mouth move into a self-deprecating grin, amused by my own awkwardness. "I'll stay, for a bit."

"Good," he says with a smile. "I'll . . ." He looks down at his attire and then casts a despairing glance at the digital clock on the bedside table. "I'll shower later." He goes to his dresser and pulls out a pair of jeans, boxer briefs, and a pair of black socks, then goes to the closet and grabs a button-down and a pair of loafers. "Stay here," he says again. "I'll change in the bathroom, then get her up."

"Okay," I say as he walks out, clothes tucked under his arm. When the door closes I lean back against the headboard and shut my eyes. "I'm lusting after a man who wears loafers," I say to myself. "What is happening to me?" I open one eye and look down at the book. Some nonfiction thing about the history of American political campaigns. Very respectable and probably very academic and structured. It's like I was caught up in a tornado, blown out of Oz, and dumped into a black-and-white Kansas.

It's kinda cool.

The only problem is, if the analogy really fits, I don't belong on this side of the rainbow. In fact, if I stay here I will cause all sorts of problems. I'll have hearts and brains and courage splattered all over the floor. No, I'll have to click my penny loafers together and get back to Oz.

And I'd better do it quickly, before I fall head over heels in love with Kansas.

❁

CHAPTER 25

WHEN HE GETS back an hour later he has a bag of Noah's bagels and two coffees that smell a little like heaven. I've taken the time to shower and dress. His comb doesn't really work for my hair, so I just pulled it back into a wet ponytail and now I'm on the couch, legs crossed underneath me, fully immersed in the history of American campaigns.

"This book is warped!" I exclaim as he places my coffee on the side table. "Everyone in here is a puffed-up, power-hungry opportunist."

"It's entertaining." He puts the bag of bagels down and pulls out plastic containers of maple-raisin-walnut and sun-dried tomato shmear.

"Yeah, but these *people*! I mean, okay, I've heard of Watergate, but I didn't really know what went down. Those break-ins? That's hard-core! Oh, and this 1828 election between Jackson and Adams? Where they're all talkin' smack? Adams accused Jackson of straight-up murder and whoring around on his first wife, and Jackson's peeps were callin' Adams out for being a pimp!" I laugh. "Course these days that would sort of be a compliment, but *still*! This is crazy! Do they teach this in school?"

"Some of it, certainly the part about Watergate," he says before disappearing into the kitchen.

"*Damn*," I mutter as I flip to the next page to finish the chapter. "I should have gone to class more often."

When he comes back it's with two plates and a butter knife. I place the book down on the corner of the coffee table as he puts everything in front of me. "How are you feeling?"

"I wasn't sick," I say a little defensively as I peek inside the Noah's bag.

"All right." His tone implies he's not buying it.

I look up sharply. I sense a confrontation coming. But instead Brad just sits beside me on the sofa and crosses his ankle over his knee as he leans back, happy to let me pick my bagel first. "I'm a political junkie," he says, gesturing to the book.

"Oh?" I select a blueberry bagel and hand over the bag as I use the knife to cut mine in half. Figures he'd give me a butter knife to do this with. He's such a guy. "How long have you been into that?"

"Since I was a kid," he says, pulling out an everything bagel. "Back when I decided I wanted to be president of the United States."

I drop my bagel. "You wanted to be president?"

"Yeah, I did."

"*Why?* Do you have any idea how much that job would suck?"

"This from the girl who wants to do everything," he says with a laugh.

"Not *that*! I'm crazy, but I'm not a complete moron! When you're president there are people trying to kill you all the time and you can't so much as walk down the hall without being surrounded by the men in black. Plus, if you trip over your shoelaces, drop an F-bomb, sneeze into your soup, or commit any other human error you're going to be on the cover of the *New York Post* with some kind of headline like, 'Sneezy the Foul-Mouth Prez Falls on His Face.' I mean, really, this is *not* a good job."

"But dancing in a cage—"

"Rocks," I say definitively. "Dancing in a cage rocks."

He lets out a rich laugh and it's so . . . wonderful. Like his daughter is wonderful, and the rhythms he creates with his drums are wonderful. I'm sitting here in the middle of a world of wonderful.

And again, I absolutely don't belong. I pick up my bagel from where I dropped it on the table and start to cover it with the sweet cream cheese. "What made you want to be the leader of the free world?"

"I think I could have made a difference," he says as he opens the sun-dried tomato cream cheese. "The most important thing a president can do is surround himself with the best people. The best economists, the best military strategists, the best minds for education, agriculture, and so on. I am extremely good at recognizing the talents of others. I would have had the most impressive, efficient, and effective cabinet in history, and we would have helped shape this country's legacy for the twenty-first century in ways we could all really feel proud of."

I wipe my fingers off on a paper napkin, lean over, place my hands on his scalp, and proceed to move them around his head.

"What are you doing?" he asks.

"Checking for swelling."

He chuckles and takes my hands in his with the intent of moving them away. But then something happens and he just . . . holds them. The backs of my hands are against his palms, and my own hands are supported and open. His eyes move over my lifeline, then up the length of my fingers, caressing my calluses with this invisible touch.

My teasing smile is gone.

Pull away, pull away . . .

But I don't. I can't. And when his thumb moves over my palm there's a little chill. It starts at my shoulder blade and spreads across my back, down my spine. My lips part just a little, and when he looks up my heart just . . . stops.

You don't belong here, you don't belong here.

I press my lips back together, force myself to smile, and then, reaching deep inside myself, I find the discipline to remove my hands from his, bring them back to my plate, my eyes now turned away.

"So you think you could build a good team," I say, careful to keep my voice completely casual, refusing to acknowledge that anything happened. Because it didn't . . . not really. "Tell me about the motivations that you *couldn't* put in a campaign speech."

I don't have to look up to know that Brad is still looking at me. I take a large bite of my bagel and reach for my coffee.

"When you were a kid," he says, finally relaxing back into the sofa, "did people tell you that if you worked hard enough you could be president one day?"

I nearly spit out my bagel. "No," I say, my mouth still partially full. "They told me that if I shut up and did what I was told I could *marry* a *politician* one day. You know, a successful one, just maybe not the most powerful man on earth. Then as I got older they altered the message and told me that if I shut up I might avoid expulsion."

"Did you?"

"No."

Brad laughs. "Well, they told me I could be president, but when people say that they don't mean it. It's one of those things patronizing adults say to kids to fool them into believing the world is a more equitable place than it is. But as a kid of five or six, all I got was the patronizing part. And I remember thinking, I'll show these condescending SOBs, I *will* become president!"

I tuck a strand of pink hair behind my ear, take a sip of coffee. "That's what you thought . . . at five or six?"

"Yes." He shrugs, a small admission that he knows he's weird.

"Huh." I chew on that for a second. "So I take it you were not a just-playin'-with-my-Hot-Wheels-and-watching-*Barney* kind of kid."

"I was more into Legos and the Discovery Channel."

"Discovery? Racy," I say as I take another bite. "Lots of crocodile-on-crocodile action. So did you tell people about your presidential ambitions?"

"Sure, why not? When I was a kid I believed I could do the things I put my mind to. I just needed to be disciplined, thoughtful, creative. I assumed that if I could master those talents the world would open up for me."

"And now?"

"Now I know it's not that simple."

I hesitate, staring down at my half-eaten bagel. I lift my eyes to the side table, where June's picture is prominently displayed. "Do you want to tell me about her mom?"

"Do you want to hear about her?" he asks, a note of surprise in his voice.

"Oh, I don't know." I shrug. Then after a few seconds I shake my head. "I take it back. I *do* know. I'd really like to know about June's mom."

He checks my expression, making sure that I mean it. And then slowly, he proceeds. "I met June's mom at a party in San Francisco in the last weeks of summer before my senior year at Stanford," he continues in a slightly more conversational tone. "She was about to enter Berkeley as a junior after studying at UCSB for two years, that's where her family lived. At the time I thought she was the most gorgeous thing I had ever seen."

I flash back to the photo in the sweater drawer. Suddenly I'm not so sure I want to hear about her, but I can't think of a way to tell him I've changed my mind without sounding petty.

"So there I was, plotting my approach," he says, looking up as a small bird thumps against the window and then departs. "But before I had it figured out she approached me and said, 'You look like you have good genes.'"

"Excuse me?"

He laughs and shakes his head, as if still mystified by the encounter. "Do you know how many times I've replayed that scene in my mind? Particularly in light of what happened? But I don't *think* she had any plans to get herself knocked up; in fact I'm sure of it. She was a genetics major and she was trying to be funny."

"Right," I say with a nod, "she just wanted to let you know that you looked like a master-race kinda guy. Funny."

"I don't think she meant it like that, either," he says with a pacifying smile. "Whatever the case may be, it started us off. We began talking and I told her that I wanted to go to law school because, well, it's important that the future president of the United States know the law, and she told *me* that she was going to cure cancer. I proposed marriage right then and there."

"Did you."

"She understandably didn't take it seriously, but yes. I simply couldn't see how anyone could vote against the guy who was married to the woman who cured cancer. With those kinds of bragging rights I figured they'd have to just hand over the keys to the Oval Office on my thirty-fifth birthday."

I smile but keep my gaze on the bagel. He's right, of course. Having a cancer-curing wife would be an asset to any politician. Having a cage-dancing wife would not.

"The point is, we clicked. I took her back to my dorm that very night. We dated for almost three months."

"And then what? You just decided she wasn't so great after all?"

"No, she's the one who broke up with me. I was heartbroken," he admits. "I was convinced I was in love."

Fuck! I am so not liking this story!

"Why did she break up with you?" I ask, trying really, really hard not to sound bitter.

"She wasn't ready to commit." He shifts his position as if trying to get comfortable and takes a long sip of his coffee. "She wanted to get her PhD from Cambridge. Work in the best labs in Switzerland. Being tied down to a man at such a young age . . . she thought it would hold her back."

"Yeah, you know what else can do that? Pregnancy."

God, I'm such a bitch.

He doesn't respond. His silence makes me feel worse. "I'm sorry," I mutter. "I didn't mean . . . Sometimes I just say stupid shit. I . . ." I throw up my hands, not sure how to redeem myself.

"It's okay," he says quietly. "I've said worse. When she asked to see me less than a month after our breakup, I assumed she was coming back to me and I let it be known that I was more than ready for that. But that's not what she wanted. And when she told me the real reason why she was there . . . I got angry. And I got scared. And my pride was hurt. I said things to her that I may never forgive myself for."

I put my coffee down, finally lifting my eyes to him. "It was a bad situation," I remind him. "She took you off guard and she was kinda telling you that you were going to have to trash every one of the plans you had made for yourself. I don't know if anyone would have handled that well."

"She wasn't asking me to change my plans," he corrects. "She calmly told me she should have been stronger and said no when I *pressured* her to have sex without a condom."

The way he says the word *pressured* makes it clear that he doesn't think there was any pressuring involved.

"She suggested that I lacked a certain self-awareness." His jaw is positively rigid. "She said I needed to understand that I could be manipulative, and that the extensive amount of time I spent strength training was indicative of a latent misogynistic aggression. She said that while I probably wasn't fully conscious of it, I could be physically intimidating, particularly during intimate encounters."

"Are . . ." I sit back, shake my head. "I'm sorry, *but are you fucking kidding me?*"

"No," he says with a humorless smile. "And then she told me that all my issues were simply an inevitable result of my upbringing as well as being raised in a patriarchal society that was obsessed with social Darwinism. But she was certain I could get it all worked out in therapy—oh, and by the way, would this be a good time for me to write her a check to cover half the cost of next week's abortion, or would it be easier for me to just pay her back next month."

"Wow." I shake my head. "That's . . . I . . . *wow.*"

"She was twenty years old, on her own for the first time and pregnant," he says quietly, his demeanor morphing into something more brooding. "She was embarrassed, she was angry, and most of all she was scared. If I had been able to put aside my hurt feelings and pride, if I had reached out to her at all, everything might have ended up differently."

"But you didn't," I fill in.

"No. Instead I told her to go find the real father and have him pay for the fucking abortion. I called her a whore and a liar. I called her . . ." He hesitates and scratches at his light stubble. It's a nervous gesture that seems totally incongruous to his normal state of cool confidence. "I used words that I have never used before or since about a woman. I kicked her out of my place and then I trashed it. Almost a thousand dollars in damages, all caused by me."

He's looking at me now like he assumes I must be appalled. I actually check behind me to see if there's some sort of church lady over my shoulder to give him the reaction he expects. "Oh," I finally reply, "are you waiting for my judgment? When I was sixteen my married, drug-dealing fuck buddy stopped returning my calls and I reacted by beating the shit out of his Corvette with a baseball bat. So it sucks that you broke a few light fixtures and called your pseudointellectual ex a whoring cunt, but if you're trying to freak me out you're gonna have to do a little better than that."

He laughs. "I have never met anyone like you."

I reach forward and squeeze his hand and say in a hushed voice, "That's a *good* thing."

He glances down at my hand and now I immediately move to take it away, but he stops me, sandwiching my hand between his. "Let's go somewhere."

"What?" I say with a slightly shocked laugh. "You mean, like, for breakfast? We just got bagels."

"No. June's going home with a friend from school today. Let's *go* somewhere."

"I . . . I don't understand."

"Have you ever been to the LACMA?" he asks.

"No."

"It's the best art museum in LA County. It has some really interesting multicultural exhibits and—"

"You are avoiding telling me the rest of this story," I interrupt as the realization hits me. It actually surprises me. Brad doesn't avoid things. He doesn't have to because he's so insanely together . . . right?

His grip tightens on my hand, and for several seconds he doesn't say anything at all. "Stanford made me go to counseling."

"Um, okay. Been there, done that. Did it help?" I ask skeptically.

"Oddly enough it did." He finally lets go of my hand, scratches at his stubble again. "And I took responsibility for my part in things. I called her at least a dozen times trying to apologize, but she wouldn't take my calls. I sent her a check. She sent it back. Months went by, I applied to Harvard, dated a few other people, but, still, I knew I had unfinished business. People told me to let it go but I needed some kind of closure. I needed to prove to her that I wasn't the Neanderthal she had made me out to be."

"How were you going to do that?" I ask warily.

"I don't know, but I knew it started with a face-to-face apology. Maybe it ended there, too. So I drove up to Berkeley and I went to her favorite coffee shop." Outside there's the sound of small children laughing in the courtyard. Brad glances in that direction, but I get the feeling that whatever he's seeing happened a long time ago. "I was about to call and ask her to meet me, and swear that if she gave me three minutes I would never bother her again. But then she walked in."

"And she hadn't gotten the abortion," I say, wincing just a little.

"She was very pregnant, and she had already found a family to give my child to."

"Wait," I say, putting my hand over my heart, "can she do that?"

"She told the adoption agency that she had gotten drunk at a house party and passed out. She told them that at least one man, maybe more, had taken advantage of the situation. Since she couldn't identify anyone she decided not to go through the trauma of reporting it. It was the perfect catch-22. If I didn't come forward I would never see my child. If I did I would have to prove that I wasn't a rapist."

"Wait," I say again as I'm hit with the image of Brad sitting across from this woman who was using all the things that make Brad *Brad* against him. His strength, his honor, his plans for his future, all carved up into a weapon that she aimed at his heart. "What was this woman's name again?" I ask tensely. "Satan? Was it Satan?"

"Her name's Nalla, and the truth was I didn't want to be a parent at twenty-one. I wanted to go to Harvard. I wanted to run for office. But I also didn't want to live my entire life knowing that someone else was raising my child and that the child might be led to believe that her father was a rapist. That"—he takes a deep breath—"that would have destroyed me. I wasn't capable of enabling that lie. I came forward."

I shake my head. "So . . . what did *she* do?"

"It was touch and go for a few days there. She didn't want to admit she lied, but in the end that's what she did. Deep down she didn't want to slander me. But when she initially told me she was pregnant I had not acted like a man who had any interest in being a father. I think she thought she was protecting me."

Bullshit. But I keep the thought to myself.

"She wanted to bring this little girl into the world," he continues, "and to give her to people who could love and care for her."

"And she was cool with you being that person?"

"No," he says with a laugh. "She did all she could to talk me out of it. She even sent the couple she had selected to adopt our daughter to Stanford to prove to me that they were the better option. And you know what? For a while I thought they might be."

"But *why?* Why was she so intent on keeping you away from your kid?"

"She didn't think I would be able to give June everything she deserved," he says simply. "But she also thought that being a parent at such a young age would ruin my life. She thought I was giving up too much and I thought . . . I thought she was giving up everything. But I . . . I wanted to be willing to give up everything, too, *if* it was the right thing to do. I visited the home of this couple, I saw the nursery they had already set up. They wanted this child, they had *planned* for this child. They were in their thirties, lived in a great school district, financially secure, had lots of family support all lined up. It was everything a kid could want or need. I"—he clears his throat—"I told them they could have her." He looks away abruptly and it occurs to me that he's hiding a tear. "I told them they could have my daughter."

"But . . . but you *didn't* give her up," I say, as if he needs to be reminded.

He takes a deep, shaky breath. "Nalla asked that I be in the delivery room with her. She needed a partner she knew and trusted and she . . . we had grown a little closer. Not dating, but we were sharing this . . . this *loss*. And so I saw the birth of my daughter. I held her in my arms and then . . ." He pauses for a moment before adding in a voice just above a whisper, "The world changed. I held my infant daughter in my arms and it triggered some kind of explosion that blasted me into a completely different reality than the one I'd been living in only seconds before. And I couldn't do it." His shoulders slump under the weight of the memory. "I couldn't just give her away. I could barely stand to put her *down*. Out in the lobby were two people, *good* people, thinking they were about to become parents based on promises I had made, and I couldn't keep my word!"

I put my hand over my heart. The scene is too brutal, too unfair to *everyone* . . . well everyone except the bitch giving birth. The whole thing makes me feel ill. I reach out my hands to hold him, but with his head still turned away, I withdraw them, unsure if my touch would be welcome.

"What I did," he continues, his voice even lower than normal, "it was reprehensible. I devastated those people. If you could have seen them when I broke the news . . . The woman didn't just cry. It was . . . it was almost a howl of grief and . . . you know, it's entirely possible that they'll never get over it. And I didn't do it for June, because I do believe they would have been good parents; they were certainly more prepared for the job than I was. It was a completely selfish act on my part. I destroyed those people because *I* wanted June, not because I thought she needed me."

"You did it because you became a parent," I say, trying to reassure him. But when he doesn't answer I sigh and rest back against the cushions. "So was that it then? No legal fight or anything?"

"No," he says with a shake of his head. "Nalla, she backed me up. She's the one who acted unselfishly. She gave me our daughter even though it wasn't what she planned, but she trusted me. She believed in me. And when the birth mother backs you up, that's it. It's all I needed to get my way and get it immediately. June was mine." He takes in a deep breath. "I was a father and I was a monster and the life I had thought I was going to have was simply gone."

I rub my hand back and forth against my jeans where my healing cut is beginning to itch. He gave up Harvard, he gave up his dreams, and when he told that couple that they couldn't have what they had come to think of as their child . . . he must have felt like he had given up his honor and decency, too.

You could say that the losses cut even deeper than that, since he had expected so much more out of life than I ever did. But he had also gained more, and as perverse as it is, I'm still incredibly jealous of him. He has a *family*! A mother, a daughter, a *life*! I'd give up everything I have to be in his shoes!

But maybe that's because I don't have anything to give up.

For a very long time we both just sit in silence pondering our different heartbreaks and losses both past and future. I can hear the distant sound of traffic and the fountain in the courtyard. But in this room it's just our breathing.

Brad shifts his position so now I can see his face again. He's not crying, but his eyes have a red hue. I don't know that I've ever seen him look lost before. I want to help him, distract him, take his mind off the past and the hurting.

I lean forward, take his hand, and say softly, "So . . . are you ready to go to the LACMA?"

He blinks in surprise, maybe even shock, and then . . . then he starts chuckling, and then laughing. "Only you," he chokes out.

"What?" I ask teasingly. "You wanted to go. You remember how to get there, right? You have the latitude and longitude?"

It's enough to make him laugh even harder. He lifts both my hands and kisses them.

It's like having my hand kissed by a prince.

CHAPTER 26

✥

W̲e̲'̲r̲e̲ ̲a̲t̲ ̲t̲h̲e̲ LACMA in less than an hour, without the
benefit of the precise coordinates. We park by the Page Museum next door and walk into the adjoining park at the La Brea Tar
Pits. On the southern side there is a large pool of tar with a sculpture
of a stressed-out mammoth floating about in it. I have passed it in
my car at least a hundred times and always found it a little disturbing. I knew they have found fossils in that tar, and I assumed they
were from mammoths—hence the statue—but still, it was unsettling
to think that this poor fiberglass creature will be sinking forever as a
demonstration of the demise of his predecessors.

But now that I'm here, actually walking in the park, I immediately decide that this place is a lot more cheerful than I gave it credit
for. It's a weekday afternoon, so there are only a few picnickers
lounging on blankets in the grass under sculptures of giant sloths
and other totally bizarre things. Brad grabs my shoulder and points
to the grass. "See that?"

I stare down at the spot in question. There's black stuff bubbling
out of the ground fifteen feet away from a woman who's idly reading
her book. "That's tar?" I blink and then look up at Brad.

"It's right under the surface," he explains. "All over this entire
area. Millions of years ago, this was an ocean. The plankton that
died here eventually turned to tar, and now it just keeps coming up
whenever it finds a porous sedimentary rock to move through. It's
been doing that for at least fifty thousand years, and it goes on for
several blocks. They've found it in sewers, streets, even under build-

ings. You just never know when or where it'll come up, and when it does, you never know what they'll find in it. So far they've excavated millions of fossils."

"Millions?" That number can't be right.

"Millions, from over two hundred different species. They pull them out from there." He places his hand on my other shoulder and turns me to the right, pointing to a big corded-off area that is nonetheless completely visible to the public. "And then they clean them up and display them over there." He turns me to the left, where the extremely modest-looking Page Museum is. "It's the only consistently active excavation site in the world; they just keep finding things."

I kneel down and stare at the bubbling black goo. People hate this stuff. It smells, it's impossible to get off, and I suppose some people think it's ugly.

"It's magical," I say aloud.

"The tar?" Brad asks, surprised, but I can sense he's also pleased.

"It's the purest black I've ever seen. It's glowing. And . . . and it can't be suppressed." I glance up over my shoulder at Brad. "Look at everything we've built here. The concrete streets, the commercial buildings, the grass that would never grow here naturally. We've tried to make this city exactly the way we think it should be, right down to the imported palm trees, but the tar"—I look back at the onyxlike substance—"that's real. The things that we find in it are real." I pause for a moment as I consider that. "Someone should write a song about it."

"You should," he says quietly, and then offers me his hand, helps me up. "Come on, I have more to show you."

We start at the Page Museum. It's completely run down. They show an illustrated movie about the origins of the place that has the production value of a 1960s educational reel. Amid the fossils there's an animatronic mammoth that is so shaky and creaky you expect it to crumble at your feet every time it moves its trembling trunk. In a room with glass walls, people in white lab coats clean each tiny fossil. They don't even bother looking up at the guests peering in on them; they're too busy doing their thing, cleaning the molars of a sabertooth.

And I love it all. I love that something so frayed and used up can still teach people about amazing things and make children happy. I love that this place doesn't seem to care about silly things like ugly flooring or its outdated aesthetics. It only cares about the things that make it unique. It's basically the best place ever.

Brad and I go to one of the few interactive exhibits, a place where you can pull a big metal rod thing out of the tar. It's supposed to show you how difficult it would be for an animal to pull out its leg should it stumble in there, and it *is* hard. I have to seriously struggle with it to get it out of the pit. Brad has it out in two seconds. So now I know, if he ever steps knee-deep into a pool of tar he'll be fine.

The whole thing makes me feel like a kid. And as if to enhance that feeling, Brad buys me a little stuffed baby mammoth from the gift store. This is the first stuffed animal I've ever owned that I like. When I was a kid my parents would occasionally give me *high-quality* stuffed animals. I remember having a big white tiger stuffed animal in my room. People would always tell me how impressive it was. But it was hard to the point of being stiff, and it was, like, practically the size of my *bed*. Its expression seemed mean and it was imposing and . . . well, scary. That tiger scared the crap out of me. But when I complained my father took my fear as an insult and accused me of being ungrateful. He and my mother had spent a lot of time looking for something special for me; it had been the most expensive stuffed animal in the store; other children would give their right arm for something like this; yada yada yada, stop being an unthankful bitch, Melody.

The upshot is that I was forced to spend years of my childhood with this horribly realistic-looking predator in my bedroom that was impossible to cuddle with.

Well, this little mammoth guy is *Mr.* Cuddly! In fact, *that's* what I'll call him, Mr. Cuddly Bubbles. Cuddly for obvious reasons, and

Bubbles in honor of the eerily slow and disturbingly beautiful bubbles that come up from the tar pools where they extract the bones.
Cuddly Bubbles.

The art museum is next, and while it's no more than ten steps
from a tar pit being excavated, the place has a totally different vibe.
There is nothing run down about the LACMA, which I guess makes
sense, since it has a different purpose, striving to show beauty rather
than scientific knowledge. Brad begins by taking me to the Japanese
art collection, telling me that it's his favorite part of the museum. It
is beautiful, but I don't know if I can completely relate to it. When I
tell Brad, he seems a little disappointed, but mostly confused, as if
the very idea that someone could see these works as anything short
of transformative is inconceivable. "What's hard to relate to?" he
asks, gesturing to a color woodblock print. "Look at the detail, the
intricacy. This is from the eighteenth century, and when you com-
pare it to the art that was being done in Europe at this time . . ." He
shakes his head, trying to find the right words. "It's more detailed,
more intricate, and the craftsmanship . . . the kind of control you
would have to have in order to create something like this is astound-
ing. It's perfect."

"Yeah," I say, hugging Cuddly Bubbles to my chest. "That's why
I can't relate."

He absorbs this. "I just think it's nice, inspiring even, to see what
human beings are capable of when they're given the opportunity to
really master their craft. That our flawed species can create something this impeccable, it's a beautiful thing."

"Okay, I can see that," I admit. But what I don't add is that everything he has just said has taken these works from being unrelatable
to being straight-up intimidating.

But it's not all like that. The sculptures of the indigenous people
of Mexico really speak to me. These works cut right through all the
facades and just get to the gritty heart of what makes us human. I
fall in love with a sculpture of the Virgin Mary that looks heartbroken, resigned, strong, and so uniquely beautiful. She conveys a

sensibility that has nothing to do with the sanitized Christianity I was fed as a child. Or this: how brilliant is this ancient sculpture of the childlike man, crouched on the pedestal like he could jump out at you at any moment? He has his tongue sticking out in a mischievous manner, and everything about him broadcasts an almost dangerous love of life.

And then there's the art piece in the courtyard titled *Penetrable*. I stand on the pavement with Brad, the wind playing with my hair, staring at a bunch of yellow plastic tubes hanging from a structured steel grid that's about fifteen feet above my head. The tubes are *just* long enough to touch the ground. "I don't get it," I say as I turn my head to the side to see if it might be prettier at a different angle. "How is this art?"

"It was created by Jesús Rafael Soto, one of the key figures of the kinetic art and op art movement from the 1950s and 1960s."

"It's plastic tubes, Brad."

"It's supposed to be a manifestation of the dematerializing effect of light."

"Why, because it's yellow? And it's not dematerializing, it's *right there*."

"Go inside."

"Seriously?" I glance at a security guard standing near the door of one of the cafés. I've never been one to shy away from doing something just because I might get in trouble for it, but . . . not today. I don't want anyone yelling at me today. "Museums are sort of look-but-don't-touch kinds of places. Maybe we should just—"

But he stops me by grabbing my hand and pulling me in. Immediately the tubes close in around me, but their rubbery composition weighs so little that each tube brushes rather than bumps against my skin. It's like walking through tall grass. With just the lightest touch of my free hand they part for me, only to come floating back. I look up and all I see are these streaks of yellow shooting up into the sky. It's like . . . like we've become part of the art, if that's even possible. When I look ahead, behind, up, or to the left, all I see are the simple streamlined details of this artist's creation.

And when I look to my right I see Brad, right here, holding my hand inside the light. His eyes are dancing with a sort of childish glee, and I guess that if he held up a mirror I'd see the same thing reflected back at me. Those streaks of yellow are between us, but they don't separate us. And when he laughingly uses his right hand to push them aside, I know what he's doing, and I don't resist. I let him kiss me, right here inside this light. And I don't feel bad about it. Not now as his lips brush against mine. This isn't a kiss of passion. This is a kiss that says, yes, we're here, and we're going to be okay.

Wouldn't that be fantastic, to be *okay*? Wouldn't it be incredible if this were real? If this could last? I know it can't, but God, do I love pretending.

We pull away at the same time, both of us grinning sheepishly, like kindergarteners who have held hands for the first time.

"Do you want to see the rest of the museum?" he asks.

"Yeah," I answer quickly, playfully batting at the tubes. "Yeah, I do."

And so we spend the whole day there. We look at the art from all different cultures and periods. Works that were inspired by war and works that were inspired by hope and love and humor and tears. *Everything.*

And when it starts to get dark he takes me to the lampposts.

How many times have I driven past this cluster of lampposts on the sidewalk, over two hundred of them pushed together in tight little rows, right in front of the LACMA? I always saw it as a piece of utilitarian art. It's even called *Urban Light.* But when you get inside of it, when the night is falling and the lights are casting their white glow and you're weaving in and out of those gray textured columns, it changes. It's classical and modern and incredibly romantic. Brad takes my hand and we zigzag through the maze. I don't remember ever having this much fun without indulging in some kind of vice.

I always thought museums were built for people more worldly and intellectual than me. But I'm okay here. I almost feel at home. But then, maybe that's because I'm with Brad.

It doesn't seem possible that last night could have been so ugly. The night I ran out of the restaurant toward oncoming traffic, that had to have been years ago, right? No, no of course not. But it's nice to forget for a little while.

And then my phone rings and without even looking at it I know.

It's reality calling. Ugly and heavily burdensome reality.

Reluctantly I peer into my purse and see Traci's number on my screen, but decide to ignore it. I just want a little more time. Another hour, or another minute, just a *little* more time before I have to face the necessary repercussions.

But when I don't pick up it's Brad's cell that rings, and just like that, it's . . . it's over. The magic is taken away, like Cinderella's carriage at midnight. It's just gone.

I lean against one of those beautiful posts as he lifts the phone to his ear. Closing my eyes, I focus on the happiness I had today. I want to remember it. I want to be able to draw upon it when things get hard.

And they're about to get hard.

"Hey, Traci," Brad says into the receiver. "Yeah . . . yeah, I'm with her now." As I open my eyes, I see him smiling at me. "I think so, I'll ask her, and if we need to reschedule, she'll give you a call . . . Yeah . . . No, she's fine, I'm sure she'll talk to you about it later . . . Yeah . . . Of course . . . Talk to you soon."

He flips his phone closed and stuffs it into his pocket. "She's worried about you," he says with a smile. "And she also wants to make sure we're still on for Saturday's rehearsal. If you want to reschedule it won't be a problem."

I take a deep breath, lower my eyes to the concrete. "Yeah, I don't think we need to rehearse on Saturday," I say, trying to keep my voice casual.

"Okay, so when do you want to rehearse? She's free on Sunday, but if that doesn't work we'd have to wait for—"

"Let's get out of this, okay?" I say, gesturing to the lamps. I don't want to soil this place, this memory, with what I have to do now. I wind through the streetlights as Brad swiftly follows me. I still have my stuffed animal in my hand and my grip is so tight I'm afraid the imprints of my fingers might be on him forever. Once we're on the outskirts of the lights I take a deep breath and continue. "I think I'm done with Resurrection."

I have my eyes cast down so I don't look up to see Brad's face, but I hear his silence, feel his shock. On Wilshire Boulevard the sound of traffic is increasing with the rush hour. Funny that I'm only noticing it now.

"You're not serious," he finally says.

I swallow hard, but then put on a lazy smile before lifting my head. "Look, the band's played out. Traci and Tonio will never take it seriously, they're not interested in improving, you're not interested in *not* improving and it's not like we're getting great gigs. I don't even remember the last time we were booked for more than four days in a month, and at least half of those gigs pay shit. Time to pack it in and move on, don't you think?"

"I . . ." He shakes his head as if trying to clear it. The shadows play on his features, exaggerating his distress. "Where is this coming from?" he asks. "Are you . . . do you want to start off on your own? Unattached to a band? If you do, I absolutely support you. You're right about Traci and Tonio, but you'll still need instrumentalists. I'm happy to be your drummer for your gigs—"

"No."

Brad's brow creases as he studies me. "What's going on, Me—" He starts to say my name but stops.

"You don't know what to call me," I say with a humorless laugh. "It's why you haven't said my name all day. I'm not Mercy to you anymore. But I'm not Melody, either, because Melody's a stranger, right?"

"No, I just wasn't sure what name you *wanted* me to use."

"And that's a problem," I say definitively. I'm overtaken by a sudden feeling of exhaustion. I turn with slumped shoulders and walk toward a cluster of empty benches. "I think we're done with this."

"Did I do something?" Brad asks, his voice edged with both concern and bewilderment.

"Sort of. I mean, you did something good." I sit down on a bench and gesture for him to do the same. "Last night, what you did for me . . . I don't mean when you stopped me from putting myself in physical danger, I mean when you listened to me . . . you'll never know how much that meant to me." I finally raise my eyes to him. "Thank you."

"You're welcome, but—"

"But," I say, gently cutting him off, "you shouldn't have done it."

"What?"

"I didn't change my name to hide from my family, Brad. They're not looking for me."

"Yes, I know why you changed your name. You told me last night," he says slowly, in a voice you would use with a confused child. But it doesn't bother me. This was never going to be easy.

"I told you that Melody is dead," I say gently. "I want her to stay that way. I don't want to ever think about my past. That history, it can't exist for me, not if I'm going to stay . . . well, maybe not sane, because that ship might have sailed. Still, I can live. I can survive. But only if I let go of Melody completely, and I can't do that with you anymore. Besides, your world can never be mine. I can visit it, but if I stay too long I'll just screw something up. It's what I do. And as for the rest of the band, if I see Traci or Tonio again they'll want an explanation for what happened at that restaurant and then they'll see me as Melody, too, and I . . . I just can't." I wipe my palms on my jeans. "I think . . . I know, that this was . . . it's the best day of my life." I need to keep myself together, steady voice, no tears. "You gave me that," I continue. "But . . . we . . . we have to keep it to a day.

We can't maintain this, *I* can't maintain it . . . I—I just need you to trust me on this, okay?"

He stares at me for a long time. And I almost reach out, give his hand one last squeeze. But then he straightens his posture and his eyes flash with anger. "You don't know what you're talking about."

"What?" I say with a shocked laugh. "I'm talking about *me*!"

"Exactly."

"Oh okay, I see where this is going," I say. "I don't need to listen to this." I start to get up, but before I'm more than an inch off the bench, Brad reaches forward and yanks me back down.

"You're *going* to listen to this," he says in a cold voice. "You don't think I see you, but I do. I watch you and I see how many times you fall into quiet contemplation. And what's causing you to scowl at the floor or shake your head when no one's talking to you, it's not what's happening in the present. You're *always* thinking about your past. You *live* there."

"Yeah, well I'm trying not to. That's what I've been telling you." A couple of teenagers walk by us as they head to the magic of the lampposts.

"Yeah, you're trying to get your mind out of the past by running away from it. But that's like running away from a mountain lion. Soon as you start to run it'll give chase."

"Oh, and what should I do?" The air has taken on the chill of night and I have to will myself not to shiver. "Should I hang around and let my past—or as you would call it, a mountain lion—devour me?"

"No, you have to face it, stand your ground. Let it know that you're stronger than it thought you were. *That's* how you survive!"

He's still holding my arm. The man is so strong. There are people around. I could make a scene, but even now I don't want to do that to him. So I suck in a breath through my gritted teeth and try to reason with him. "My past is not an animal. It's abstract."

"Not to you it isn't."

"Brad!" His name shoots out of my mouth with enough volume

to attract some looks, and I have to bite down on my lip to restrain myself again. "You have to let me do what I need to do," I say, pleading now. "We had a beautiful day. I love the museums, the park, my stuffed animal—" I stop myself before I add his name to the list. "You're a poker player. You know what it means to quit while you're ahead."

His hand doesn't leave my arm. "What about Ash?"

"What about him?" I ask wearily.

"He said that the two of you go back for some time. Does he know . . . Wait a minute." And now he finally releases his grip and his expression changes from one of frustration to one of pure shock. "Is he . . . Mercy, is he the father?"

My whole body tenses to the point of immobility. I can't even loosen my jaw enough to answer.

"He is," Brad whispers. "Jesus. Does he know?"

A couple and two families stroll past us, and the people stuck in traffic honk their horns in the deluded hope that raising a commotion will get them somewhere. Finally I shake my head no. It's the only answer I'll give.

"So let me get this straight." Brad is looking aggravated again, but now I think he might actually be within seconds of grabbing me by the shoulders and shaking me. "You say you want to erase your past," he continues, "but you're dating the father of the child you lost? Really, Mercy? How messed up *are* you? You can't even decide if you want to save yourself or punish yourself, and you clearly don't know how to do either!"

"Oh, oh I'm messed up?" I ask. I look up sharply; my left hand is in the shape of a claw. "Have you looked in the mirror recently?"

"What are you talking about?"

"Hmm, well let's see." Glaring at him I put my fist under my chin as if in deep thought. "Harvard didn't work out and you're probably not going to be president at thirty-five, so you give up on *everything* and start playing poker for a living. Is the world really that black-and-white to you? You can't have it all so you'll have nothing? Or perhaps it's option B and you're just one of those people who falls so deeply in love with their own plans that when there's a detour they fall apart. I mean, UCLA is right fucking *here*! If you want to go to law school, stop spending all your time brooding like some kind of frat boy with a James Dean complex. Go already!"

"It's not easy being a single dad," he growls. "My mother works. She can only watch June on nights and weekends. I can support her by playing poker. I pulled in six hundred on that night you watched her for me."

"Ah, so it's option C! You can't walk and chew gum at once! June's going to kindergarten next year, right? So sign her up for after-school care, go to law school, and play poker! I'm sure it's been done before! And what's the deal with you carrying a torch for a woman who came this close to accusing you of *rape*?"

"She didn't accuse me of anything—"

"Oh, whatever. Your baby mama's a mess and *I'm* a mess and that gets you off, doesn't it? You got that whole white knight thing going on, but that doesn't make you a hero. All it means is that you go around trying to save screwed-up women like me because you don't know how to save yourself."

"You don't know what you're talking about," he says again, this time with even more venom. "And while there are those who may wish it otherwise, *white knight* is not a derogatory term."

"You're right, it's not. It's an archaic one. Because let's face it, to-day's distressed damsel is more likely to reach for a White Russian than a knight of *any* color. But you're still galloping around trying to save damsels who are giving you the finger. So I guess that makes us both clueless, doesn't it?"

And now I do get up, storming away from him. I'll have to take the bus home because I just can't afford to shell out for any more cabs.

Brad doesn't follow me this time. It's what I want, of course it is. I wait until I'm sure that I'm completely out of his sight before I press Cuddly Bubbles to my chest. By the time I get to the bus stop I've done the calculations. I'll have to transfer three times to get to the street where I left my car. Traffic being what it is, it'll take me at *least* two hours.

That's two hours before it'll be safe to cry.

CHAPTER 27

❀

F OR THE NEXT few days, despite the ten to twelve messages
Traci has left for me on my answering machine, I only answer
my phone for Ash. He tells me things are going great. The director
loves him, the other actors love him, he's having a fantastic time.
He's even taken to calling me baby. That's how Hollywood he's become.

Eventually I send an e-mail to both Traci and Tonio, confirming
what they already suspect, I'm done with Resurrection. But while
Tonio doesn't respond, Traci keeps calling. Each message is a little
different. One joking that we need to set up exit interviews before
we disband (and of course she points out her painfully obvious
pun). Another is an invitation to a rave, and in yet another message
she demands to know why I lied to her about my name and why I
won't return her calls. A huge part of me wants to just disappear on
her, but I can't do that. I owe her a good-bye.

So after five days of this I stop by the medical marijuana clinic
during her shift. I find her chatting with one of the sales reps at the
back of the store where the different kinds of weed are displayed inside glass counters, like fine chocolate. When she sees me she stops
talking to the rep and beelines to me, brushing past the few customers here to grab me by both hands.

"I'm so glad you're here!" she says with a giggle, but the sound
quickly dies on her lips as she takes in my expression. "Shit," she
mutters under her breath. "This is the last time I'm going to see you,
isn't it?"

My silence gives her the answer. She sighs and pulls me through the store and then through the door that leads to a small office papered with *Reefer Madness* posters. She walks around a small bleached-wood desk, pulls a small bag of weed from the top drawer, and dangles it in front of me. "Amnesia Haze," she says. "Ranked as one of the top-five cannabis for stress relief by *High Times* magazine. Want to light up and chill for a few hours?"

"Tempting," I admit. "And I do like the name, but I'm not staying."

"Suit yourself," she says as she rolls a joint. Her tone is light but I can tell by her posture that she is stung by my refusal. "I don't care, you know."

"Care about what?" I ask cautiously.

"That you had an abortion. You did, right?" When I don't answer she puts the joint between her lips, retrieves a Marilyn Monroe lighter from her pocket, bringing the flame to the paper as she sucks in. She holds the smoke in her lungs for a few seconds before blowing it out between pursed lips. "I've had two abortions myself. It's no big deal. Certainly nothing to change your name over, *M*," she says, pronouncing my initial with an accusatory tone.

I turn slightly away, unwilling to take the bait.

She takes another long drag as the silence between us grows. "You lied to me."

"I'm sorry," I whisper.

"Hey, everybody lies, right?" Traci says, a tinge of desperation in her voice now. "One of these days you can tell me the whole story. And we can cool it on the band for a while if that's what you want. You know what? Maybe we should take some shrooms together. Remember when we did that? We could find a remote spot in the hills, or maybe the desert, and just meditate on things. Let the visions guide us, you know?"

"I got you something," I say softly, not acknowledging her offer. I search through my purse and pull out a thick envelope. "I got the pictures developed from Benji's disposable camera, remember? The one he had on New Year's Eve?"

"Yeah." She pauses a moment to take another hit before continuing. "I remember."

I hand the envelope to her. "It seems he had his camera trained on you throughout the entire performance that night. I know you guys have had your ups and downs but I think he really does love you."

"Yeah, I think he does, too," she says, her tone a little gentler now. "But . . . it's, like, the wrong kind of love. I don't know how to describe it but . . . it's the kind of love that hurts more than it heals. Does that make sense?"

I shrug. "You know best," I mutter, crossing my arms over my chest. Something about that statement makes me want to change the subject. I nod at the envelope now in her hands. "The first photo's my favorite. I made a copy for myself."

Traci raises her eyebrows and then, putting the joint down in an ashtray, pulls the picture out. It's the group shot. The one of Brad, Tonio, Traci, and me in the back of Apocalypse. She stares at it for a long time and when she looks up, there are tears in her eyes. "I loved this night."

I smile down at my shoes. "It was certainly memorable."

"Our band wasn't always perfect," Traci says. "Brad's a pain in the ass, but still, I liked it. Getting into all these clubs, being treated to drinks, being the cool kids in the room . . . I really liked it."

"I liked it, too." I bite down on my lip before adding, "But it's time for me to move on. The wind is blowing and it's . . . like it's pushing me forward. I got to go with it, you know?"

She goes quiet, her eyes back on the photo.

"Well," she says after a minute or so has passed, "if you ever need a great deal on some Amnesia Haze, you know where to find me." Then she looks up with a teasing grin. "Or if you ever decide to share your Johnny Depp, I'm game for that, too."

I laugh and shake my head. "I'm going to miss you."

"I'm going to miss you, too, M." She throws her arms around me and suddenly I realize that Traci is one other person who has hugged me, if only briefly, in the last several weeks. I *am* going to miss her. But I can't keep singing with Resurrection. Even with Brad out I would never be able to be part of that group without thinking about him, missing him. And every time Traci called me M, I'd know that it stood for Melody.

No, this is the end for our little band of merrymakers.

And it's yet another beginning for me and for Ash.

❀

CHAPTER 28

IT SHOULD BE easy to move on, if for no other reason than Brad doesn't call and Ash does . . . albeit not as often as I'd like. But still, he wants me and he's coming back to me. I'm not alone. And Brad . . . that was a bizarre little whirlwind of an almost romance. He and I were never going to end up together. It was never even a question.

But oh my God, do I miss him. How ironic that I planned that dinner at the restaurant because I thought it would *keep* me from losing him. But instead it cost me so much, more than I even realized I was willing to pay.

I've upped my phone sex hours and I've convinced Matt to let me dance at Envy every Thursday night. So while money's still tight, it is there. I can pay my rent, pay for my groceries and my alcohol.

I've actually been buying a lot of alcohol lately. I don't know why. It's never been my number-one choice for escapism. But more and more often I find myself at home, alone, in front of my TV with a bowlful of popcorn and a glassful of vodka.

And sometimes I take out that piece of broken glass. I never threw it away. I don't cut myself again, but I think about it.

I think about it a lot.

There should be an explanation for that. There's usually something that triggers these kinds of thoughts. But I don't know what that trigger is this time.

When Ash flies home I meet him right at the gate, and this time I'm the one holding the roses. He doesn't know I'm going to be here. It's a surprise. The plan is to whisk him away, take him out on the town, buy champagne I can't afford and toast his latest success. Once again I have taken extra care with my appearance. I'm wearing a long shaggy coat, a cropped top that stops just a few inches below my bra line, and straight-legged, low-rise jeans. It's a *look*—which is why I'm getting looks, not all of them approving, but I know Ash. He'll like it, and more importantly, he'll *get* it.

There's a long stream of passengers getting off the plane and I stretch my neck to the left then the right as I try to spot him. Finally, I do. He's got his duffel bag draped over his shoulder, standing a little taller than usual, his walk a little more confident. He's absorbed in a conversation with one of the other passengers as they exit. He looks straight-up gorgeous.

I start jumping up and down, the bouquet of roses stretched up in the air above my head like an Olympic torch. "Ash!" I cry. "Over here, Ash!"

He stops in his tracks, almost tripping up the people behind him. I beam at him, probably the brightest smile I've been able to manage since that day at the LACMA.

But Ash isn't smiling back. And the passenger he's talking to . . . the *woman* he's talking to with the bright pink top and chestnut hair piled up in a purposely messy bun, she's looking at me, too, and then her eyes shift back to Ash. She looks a little confused and maybe . . . a little guilty? Does she look guilty?

But then Ash just flips a switch. His stunned look is gone and he flashes me his signature impish grin and walks right up to me without so much as a look at the woman he was speaking to. He weaves his fingers into my hair, holding my head as he gives me a deep, beautiful kiss. "I can't believe you came to meet me. I love that," he says, brushing my hair from my face. "You have no idea how much I missed you."

"Yes?" I wince when I hear how insecure my voice sounds.

"Yes, of course!" He gives me another kiss, lighter this time. "Come on." He links his arm with mine and starts pulling me toward baggage claim. When I turn to glance back at the woman, Ash inadvertently stops me by giving me a rather provocative kiss on my neck, making little chills run up and down my spine.

At least, I think it was inadvertent.

"There's a party tonight," Ash says once we're at the carousel waiting for them to unload the bags. "It's going to be off the hook. Are you up for it?"

"If you're going, I'm all about it," I say, throwing my arms around his neck and leaning in to nibble on his ear. And as I do I look at the woman he was speaking to earlier. She's on the other side of the carousel, watching us. But the moment she sees I'm looking at her, she starts studying her nails.

Well, isn't that interesting.

"All about it," Ash muses. "Isn't that a cliché?"

"I think something has to be several decades old to be a cliché. Until then it's slang," I say absently as I pull back, letting my arms drop. "Were there other people from the show on this flight with you?"

"No," Ash says with a little shake of his head. "Everybody has different filming schedules so we come back at different times. But you'll meet a couple of them at the party tonight."

"Fantastic," I say, giving his hand a squeeze. "It's been an eventful few weeks."

"Tell me about it!" He laughs. "You have no idea how intense it is to be on a TV set. And this *set*! They re-created an entire world! It was crazy! I'll show you the pics. Oh look, there's my bag. I really appreciate you coming to pick me up. Normally the studio sends a car, but there was a little mix-up and . . ."

I know Ash is talking, but I find that I'm not listening anymore. For the second time I've caught that woman looking over here, and again, when I manage to catch her eye she looks away.

It doesn't mean anything, of course. So they were flirting on the plane. Maybe she had hopes that it was going to lead to more and now she's disappointed. And it's not like Ash has been looking at her since he's seen me. He hasn't even glanced in her general direction. This whole thing is most likely totally innocent.

So what is it about this situation that doesn't feel innocent?

Maybe it's the *way* Ash isn't looking at her. It reminds me a little of the way that nurse at the psych ward wouldn't look at me. It's the way you don't look at someone when you're trying really, really hard not to look.

Ash's bag gets to our part of the carousel and he grabs it and then gestures for me to lead him to my car. I give him a vague smile, suddenly feeling a lot less secure than I did when this day started out. But when we get to the car he stops me. "I did have a little free time when I was there. Not much," he says quickly, "but enough to go shopping and get you this." He opens up his duffel bag and pulls out a small jewelry box.

"Are you kidding me?" I ask as I take it from him. I open it up and gasp. "Oh my God, these are so cool!" They're earrings, skull-shaped studs dotted with onyx and attached to small white gold hoops from which little opals, sapphires, and rubies jut out in alternating round and emerald cuts.

"They reminded me of you," he says. "Edgy, different, maybe a little in your face, but feminine, too. Sweet."

I just continue to stare down at the earrings. "You know me so well," I whisper, getting dangerously close to teary. "But, Ash, they're too much." I try handing them back. "These must have cost a fortune."

"Hey, money's not going to be a problem," he says with a laugh, moving into my space, putting his hands on the small of my back. "You better get used to getting spoiled, because this fame and fortune stuff? It's *on*."

THINGS JUST GET more decadent from there. When we get back from the airport Ash insists that we have lunch at Spago. I feel totally out of place there, but he seems to enjoy it, and the food is amazing, so eventually I relax and enjoy it, too. The party that night is at some dude's house in the Hollywood Hills and Ash was completely right: it's Off. The. Hook. It has a gorgeous view of the Hollywood sign and an awesome pool with a waterfall that goes right into it. The house itself is *crazy* modern. Like ultrasleek, cosmopolitan, must-have-been-built-in-the-last-two-years modern. The suspended staircase is almost scary; it feels like you're walking through air. And the place has an honest-to-God movie theater! With red velvet seats, full-on movie-theater-style popcorn machine and everything! Of course, no one is watching a movie tonight. Offspring's "She's Got Issues" is playing on what is easily the best sound system I've ever heard in a private residence. Waiters walk around with mixed drinks and delicious hors d'oeuvres. And the people! There are so many beautiful people here! Ash introduces me to one of the actresses who is on his show and I can't decide if I should hate her or go lesbian. And more to the point, she's actually nice! She gushes over my clothes and the earrings (yes, I'm wearing them), and then she whisks me away to introduce me to a friend of hers who just happens to be the founder and lead designer of my favorite brand of jeans I can't afford. And then I'm talking to a model, and then another actor, and the drinks keep coming and everything is just fun . . .

. . . but I've lost track of Ash. I have no idea where he is at all.

"Have you met the host?" asks a wavy-haired blond guy with some kind of accent. Caleb? Cameron? Something like that. The person who introduced him said he owns a hip bar in Hollywood, but he doesn't host live musical acts so I don't have to worry about remembering him.

"No," I admit. "I feel a little like a crasher."

"Just count yourself lucky," he assures me. "The host, Jeremy, *he's* not bad. Nice guy, a producer. But his live-in gold digger is a nightmare. He got her a role on some TV show, but I hear she's horrible."

"Oh, I—" But then I stop, reaching forward and grabbing Caleb-Cameron's arm. "Who is that woman?" I whisper, my eyes glued to the brunette in the corner laughing as she chats up some guy. It's the same woman who was at the airport.

"You mean Mindy?" He raises his eyebrows. "She's a hairstylist. She's working on that same TV show. Talented, but a little too into the nose candy. Then again, we all have our indulgences, don't we?"

"Mmm," I reply. It's all I can manage. Every muscle in my body has frozen. I can't even open my mouth to scream.

"Oh dear lord, here comes the gold digger."

I look over and see another beautiful woman walking toward us, and Ash is by her side. She has her arm linked through his in a friendly, mildly flirtatious manner.

"Connor, darling," she exclaims as she gives my companion European-style kisses on each cheek. "So good to see you, and you must be the beautiful Mercy I keep hearing about!"

"That's right!" Ash says, placing his hands on my waist before moving in for a full embrace and literally lifting me up off the ground for a moment. "God, have I told you how much I missed you?" he says when he pulls back enough to see my face.

I just stare at him. I'm still feeling frozen . . . but I'm also feeling observant, and what I'm observing now is Ash's eyes. His pupils are dilated, and this time I can't blame it on lack of light.

"Mercy, this is Olivia." He gestures to the woman I have previously only known as Gold Digger. "She was filming on the pilot with me and she is fucking fantastic. Just fantastic, Olivia."

"Your boyfriend is so sweet," she says, smiling at me. Connor (maybe) has already quietly made his escape. "But I'm only in one scene. My part doesn't really take off for weeks," she explains. Even as she's talking, she's dancing. The music has just switched to Lenny Kravitz's "Fly Away." "Have you met everyone? Yes, no? Well, let me introduce you to more. Ash simply would not stop talking about you in New Mexico. This man is in love," she says, swatting him playfully as she leads us forward.

"How can anyone *not* be in love with this woman?" he asks, one arm still around my waist. He gives me a little shake. "Look at her!"

She laughs and continues to lead, introducing us to everyone who has ever been in anything, never pausing to talk to any individual for more than two minutes. I quickly learn that her producer boyfriend, Jeremy Powell, is actually one of the executive producers for the show she and Ash are on, though she assures me that has nothing to do with how she got the role.

And now, as we continue to flit from one group to another, I find that my distress has sobered me up and I begin to pick up on an undercurrent to this party that I hadn't noted before. There's a frenetic energy here, a level of giddiness and grandiosity that usually has to be bought by the gram, vial, or bottle.

And this crowd . . . I now realize that it's a very particular kind of Hollywood crowd. There are a lot of people here who are famous more for their exploits than for their work. Each introduction Olivia makes immerses me a little more into the dynamics of the room, and it all just starts feeling disturbingly familiar.

It's like the Twilight Zone. Here we have people who look so polished and together. Everything about them screams wealth and glamour. But if you just lightly scrape the surface you can see that this is the same party they throw in dirty warehouses and cribs in the hood. It's just that instead of wearing secondhand rave-wear or gangsta bandanas they're wearing Prada and Dolce & Gabbana. *But it's the same thing.* Being brought into this circle isn't an elevation at all! It's a lateral move.

I watch as Olivia continues to flutter about, tossing her hair here, batting an eyelash there, and suddenly she looks different to me. Instead of seeing her beauty, I see her details. I see the way her foundation is caked over her pimple and the shadows under her eyes that she wasn't quite able to cover with concealer. I hear how she always interrupts people when they're midsentence, feel her obvious indifference masked by a bleached white smile. I see beyond her superhip fake lashes to the red lines that squiggle through the whiteness of her eyes. The practiced quality of her air kisses. And she stops being beautiful; now she's almost grotesque.

As for Ash? Ash is having the time of his life. Sweat is beginning to bead at his brow and he's talking a mile a minute. I've felt that way before. But not in a while.

Ash leans over, whispers in my ear. "Ready to turn the volume up a notch?"

"Mmm," I say again.

"What did I hear?" Olivia whirls around with a big smile. "Are we heading to the VIP room? I think Faith and Seth are there now."

"Well then, that's where the party is," Ash says with a Cheshire cat grin.

I hate this. I hate this party, hate these people, hate everything and everyone. And yet I let Ash and Olivia lead me out of the main room, downstairs through the throngs of people, through a hallway and into a . . . a library.

On TV and in movies the super rich sometimes have actual libraries in their homes. Rooms lined with book after book after book. The books usually have dark brown leather bindings, and the room itself is always elegant and gorgeous. I didn't think anyone in real life had a library.

But here I am in this library, and it's breathtaking. The only difference is that all the books aren't bound in leather . . . Well, the ones on the south wall are, but there are also photography books, and paperbacks, and literary titles, and sci-fi. It's sort of incredible.

And on the floor, sitting around a glass coffee table, are two people doing lines. Ash leans over to me. "Olivia has the purest snow you have ever sampled. And she's only sharing with Faith, Seth, and us."

"Just my nearest and dearest." Olivia giggles and gives Ash's free hand a little squeeze. "Your man is such a doll. I just *love* him! He and I are practically besties now!" And then she twirls away before kneeling down next to Faith and Seth, who greet us with smiles and sniffs.

"Come on," Ash says, his breath tickling my ear. "We haven't been flying together since that night in Seattle. You remember that night?"

"Go on ahead," I say coolly, stepping away from him. "I want to take a look at some of these books."

Ash pulls back and gives me a funny look. "Are you upset about something?"

"No, just . . ." I sigh and wave toward the coffee table. "Please, indulge. I just want to look around for a second, okay?"

"Okay, beautiful, you're the boss." He tries to kiss me on the mouth but I look away and he only gets my cheek. He hesitates, knowing there's a problem. But then he steps away and kneels next to Olivia, waiting patiently for her to finish telling Faith and Seth some story before cutting him a few lines.

I move closer to the overflowing shelves. I used to love to read. I read all the time when I was a kid. My father would send me to my room as a punishment and I'd just get under the covers and read. When I got older I would read things like *The Vampire Lestat*, *The Clan of the Cave Bear*, *The Witches of Eastwick*, *Good Omens*, even *The Accidental Tourist*. I liked fantasy novels the best. The farther away a book could take me from my reality, the more I liked it. I would sneak slim paperbacks inside the textbooks I was supposed to be reading so I could read my novels in class unnoticed. It worked . . . most of the time. And when it didn't . . . well that hadn't stopped me from trying again.

When had I stopped reading?

"Baby, you have to try this."

I lift my hand and caress the spine of *Memoirs of a Geisha* by Arthur Golden. "I don't do coke," I say idly.

Without turning to look I can feel all the eyes in the room on me. I can sense their suspicion and paranoia as they suddenly find themselves wondering why I'm here and if I have an agenda.

"You don't do coke?" Ash repeats. "I thought you told me you did."

I don't answer. The things Melody told him have nothing to do with me.

"We met in a club in Seattle," I hear him tell the others. "That was . . . was it a year ago, baby?"

"Closer to a year and a half," I say as my fingers move over to *The Giver* by Lois Lowry.

"They had a live band," he continues. "Some indie group, not much of a following, but I could tell she was swept up in their sound. She was right at the front of the stage dancing like, like she was Isadora Duncan. Just totally free."

Girl with a Pearl Earring, The Golden Compass, Fight Club, so many I haven't read yet. It's like I've missed an entire decade of literature.

"I waited until the break to approach her and then I asked what it was about the band that moved her. And she turned to me, her eyes glassy and her smile welcoming . . . she just reached out and took my hand and said, '*You're beautiful.*'"

The group starts laughing and Faith calls out, "What were you on?"

Again I don't answer as my fingers dance over to Donna Tartt's *The Secret History*, my eyes scanning the few titles I *have* read: Stephen King's *It* and *The Hitchhiker's Guide to the Galaxy* by Douglas Adams.

But I read those when I was twelve.

"She was on E," Ash supplies. "She still had more left; she put a tablet on my tongue. That's how giving she was. And it was such an amazing high. When it kicked in . . . how do I describe it . . . it was like I was inside that music, and I *wanted* to be inside *her*."

The group laughs. Oh, the things people say when they're on cocaine.

"I'm serious," Ash says, although there's a laugh in his voice that undermines his words. "Just like how that high helped me see the music more clearly, it helped me see her, too. We stepped out into the alley and it was . . . intense. I remember thinking this was a woman I was never going to be able to get enough of. I can't get enough of you," he says softly, and I know the comment is mine. "You know that, don't you, baby?"

"Has anyone read this?" I pull out George R. R. Martin's *A Game of Thrones*, my eyes trained on the steel sword on the cover. "I hear it's good."

There's a moment of silence, then Seth blurts out, "Sweetie, are you rolling now?"

More giggles from the group. But I just keep looking at the book. I don't have to ask Olivia if she's read it. I'd bet money that she hasn't. Perhaps it's her boyfriend who's the reader. But he's not here. She is. She's in this room full of amazing books and she's hunched over a totally common-looking glass table doing lines. She doesn't understand what's around her. She can't even see it! None of these people can! And *A Game of Thrones*, I mean the sequel is already out! I think I've read about six books in the last seven years and four of them were graphic novels . . . excellent graphic novels, but still, I haven't been reading as frequently or with the same passion I did as a kid. It's as if at some point I forgot I liked to do it.

I feel Ash's hands on my shoulders before I even fully register that he's gotten back up. "You okay?"

I put the book down and turn to face him, gently place my hand on his shoulder. "Yeah, I'm okay." I go over to the Hollywood druggies on the floor and sit next to them, my legs crossed in front of me as I lean back on my hands. "Ash and I have definitely had a rather dramatic romance," I say, smiling at my new companions.

"Do tell!" Olivia exclaims, her eyes still on the powder.

"Well, like Ash said, there have been some pretty intense nights. Passionate moments in alleys, that time in the VIP room of Graffiti"—I look up at Ash—"when I was dancing on the bar, sorta for the room but really for you."

"Yeah." Ash smiles, sitting back down by my side, putting his hand on my leg. "We were the ones who got that party started. And you, you were magnificent."

I tilt my head to the side as I redirect my gaze to the ceiling. "Of course, when you have that kind of passion you're bound to have some times when things get a little heated. The way that night ended, do you remember *that*?"

Ash laughs, but there's a hint of discomfort to the sound. "That was a mess. But like you said, when you have passion, you're gonna have fights."

"Ooh, let's hear about the fight," coos Olivia. "What are you like when you get mad, Mercy? Jeremy says I go full harpy. I scream, throw things, stomp my feet, just really give in to it. Guess it's the actress in me."

I give her a vague smile. "I suppose my anger changes based on the situation." Then turning back to Ash, I ask, "Do you even remember what our fight was about?"

"We were pretty wasted," he says, pulling his hand away from me. "Who the hell knows, right?"

You do! I want to scream. I can tell he remembers everything. The way he just went off on me out of the blue. The way he insulted me and everything I was doing with my music. "It was crazy," I say to my little audience. "He called me by a nickname I don't use anymore and I stormed into a crowd of people and told them all that my boyfriend had called me by the wrong name."

"No! What happened?" Faith asks, leaning forward, her red hair dangling in her face.

"Like I said, it was crazy. Some chicks that were waiting for their rides busted out with Destiny's Child's 'Say My Name.'" Everyone in this group cracks up at that and Ash's hand is now on my leg again. I giggle, too, and start singing the song.

Getting caught up in your game
When you cannot say my name

And then I turn to Ash. "So, why *are* you calling me baby lately?"
He blinks several times, clearly taken off guard. "What?"

"I just want to know." Around me I can feel the mood shift. A new kind of curiosity, an eager anticipation of a train wreck.

"What are you going on about?" Ash says with a forced laugh.

"Is it because you're afraid you'll accidentally call me Mindy?"

Olivia lets out an excited little gasp as the rest of the room grows quiet, quieter than you would think a bunch of cokeheads could manage.

"Mercy," Ash says, pronouncing my name slowly, but before the word is completely out of his mouth I've slapped him across the face, hard. He grabs my wrist roughly, but I manage to pull it away as I stand up.

"It's okay," I assure the others, who are now all gaping at me as I turn to walk out. "I've been told I'm worth the pain."

CHAPTER 29

❈

I LET ASH GIVE me a ride home. I'm tired of finding my own way
back after storming out on the people who brought me. I even
let him walk me to the door. But when he asks to come in I simply
sit on the front steps of my building, indicating that if there's anything he wants to say, he can say it here.

"It was a 'locationship,'" he explains as he takes a seat by my side.
I give him a funny look and he continues, talking a little too fast, his
fingers tapping out an uneven beat on his knee. "That's what they
call it when you hook up with someone on the cast or crew during a location shoot. You know, we're all away from our loved ones,
thrown into this really intense shoot schedule, things get crazy, and
people, they . . . they bond over the experience and sometimes it
goes a little too far. But locationships get their name because everybody knows that things have to end when the shoot is over. They're
not meant to last. They . . . they don't mean anything."

"Of course they mean something," I say wearily. "Everything
means something."

"No, but what I mean is . . ." He hesitates, glancing back at the
door to my building. "Come on, bab—Mercy. It's getting cold. Just
let me in for ten minutes and if you don't like what I have to say—"

"No," I say simply without even a hint of anger or irritation. And
perhaps it's the evenness of my voice that makes him immediately
back down. There's no emotion for him to play on.

He rubs his hands up and down his jeans a few times, staring
down at the cracks in the concrete. "What I'm trying to say is that

I have no interest in continuing things with Mindy. And I know I screwed up. God, I know it because I . . . I can't lose you, Mercy. You're the one I want. It's *Mindy* that doesn't mean anything to me."

"I believe . . ." I begin, then pause before adding, ". . . that you don't want to continue things with Mindy."

"Well, that's a start," he says with a sigh.

"You had an impulse and you gave in to it," I say, gazing up at the overcast sky. "I get it. After all, it's what you and I do. We are slaves to our impulses."

He reaches over and squeezes my knee. "Hey, that's not such a bad thing, right? Or . . . what I'm saying is the *affair* was bad, but our being driven by emotions, that we live in the moment or . . . or that you're teaching me to live in the moment—"

I start giggling. And when Ash looks confused the giggles morph into a laugh. "Ash," I finally manage, "you were living in the moment *way* before I came around. I didn't teach you a damn thing. I can't because you know everything I know and you don't know the very things I don't know . . . and what we don't know? It's *so much*!"

"No, you've got it mixed up," he insists. "I'm always too focused on the future."

"Only because you think the future and the present are the same thing!" I throw up my hands. "You think you're going to be famous, so you live like you're famous. You think you're going to make a lot of money, so you spend it like you have it now *and you don't*. You tell people that the place you want to live in is the place you're actually living in. For you the future is now and you see the world the way you want to see it." I pause a moment before adding in a slightly more conciliatory tone, "Maybe we all do that. But . . . I don't know, Ash, maybe it's time to stop pretending and start seeing things for the way they actually are."

He nudges me playfully with his elbow as he pushes his lips into a little half smile. "Where's the fun in that?"

I press my lips together and let my eyes follow the cars as they pass my building.

"Come on, Mercy, you have to forgive me for this," he pleads, changing tack again. "You and I, we're fated to be together. We're connected. You feel that, right? Don't throw it all away over one fuckup."

"We are connected," I admit. "But not by fate. We're connected by life . . . and by death."

"What the hell does that mean?"

I inhale, deeply. The air is so crisp tonight, so unlike the polluted air I've become accustomed to. "That night in Seattle, the night that we met . . . I thought that night was one of the most beautiful nights of my life."

"It was *the* most beautiful night of mine," he says without a moment's hesitation.

"You were supposed to call," I say, unable to keep the pain out of my voice. "You promised! If you had called, you could have helped me. You could have helped *us*."

"Okay, I'm totally lost here—"

"I got pregnant that night, Ash."

He looks at me, his eyes wide, his posture suddenly stiff.

"We made a life," I whisper, "you and me . . . but then it was just . . . gone. I miscarried our little girl in the fourth month."

"I . . ." He shakes his head, finding himself at a complete loss for words.

I fall silent as I wait for the news to sink in. The concrete is uncomfortable and cold to sit on, but I won't let him inside. We'll finish this here. Ash is sitting stock-still, but I can tell that his mind is moving at a hundred miles an hour. I can almost see his thoughts, see the images and memories of the night our daughter was conceived. I can see his imaginings of what he would have done if he had known. I can see them because I've imagined them myself. "A girl . . . and she made it to the fourth month," he says slowly. "You were going to keep it."

I give a curt nod. I don't want to cry, not now.

"That's what I would have wanted . . . to keep it," he whispers, almost more to himself than to me. "I would have wanted her . . . I . . . would have stayed with you, Melody. We would have raised her."

I smile even as I continue to struggle to hold back the tears. It's the first time he's called me Melody since our last fight, but for once I'm not mad at that. "You know, I think I knew that," I say. "I've always told myself that if you had called, if you *knew*, you would have stood by me and our baby." He moves a little closer, his expression serious, his own eyes a little watery as he gently puts his hand on my back, making small caressing circles right below my neck. "You know what else, Ash?"

"What?" he whispers.

"We would have been horrible parents."

He drops his hand. "What are you talking about? We would have loved the shit out of that kid."

I laugh and the tears finally make their escape, charting little rivers down my cheeks. "God," I gasp, "we are so clueless."

"I don't know about that," Ash says irritably.

"You're thinking just the way I was when I found out," I say, sobering up a bit. "I thought that all I had to do was want her in a way my parents never seemed to want me, and somehow that would be enough."

"Love is always enough," Ash retorts.

"*No*," I insist. "Children need more than that. We *all* need more than that. And to say we're not ready to raise a kid is the understatement of the century."

"No one's ever ready for a child, Mel, you just . . . learn as you go along."

"Ash," I say, now exasperated. "We haven't even learned how to live our own lives. In so many ways we're not even walking yet, we're . . . we're stumbling and we're crawling and . . . and we're *lost*." I whisper the last word into the wind. "We're lost."

He stares at me for a long time and then turns away. I wonder if he's crying, and yet even if he is it won't change a thing.

"I would have loved our child," he says in a voice so low it doesn't even sound like him. "And I *do* love you. I'm in love with you and I know you're in love with me." He nods as if making a decision. "Our love is enough. I know that."

I'm quiet for a minute, maybe two as I keep my eyes on the pavement.

"Melody? Are you hearing me?" Ash asks, turning back to me, strands of his hair clinging to the part of his face where the tears he was hiding are not yet dry. "I just told you that I'm in love with you!"

"I know you are," I whisper, "and the feeling's mutual. But it's the wrong kind of love." A plane hums above us as it makes its descent and I pull my knees in tightly to my chest. "It's not the kind of love that heals." I take a deep breath and force myself to look him in the eye. "It's the kind that kills."

"What? What are you saying?" I can hear a note of desperation in Ash's voice. It's the desperation of an addict.

"I'm saying we're connected and that we have love. But there's nothing about us that's fated." I swallow hard and press my hands into my knees. "I'm saying it's over."

He stares at me for a long time, completely baffled, hurt, and a little teary.

And then I see his eyes narrow. Color rises to his cheeks and his hands slowly curl into fists. "Are you fucking kidding me with this bullshit?" he hisses.

"Ash, please don't—"

"You fucking bitch!" he continues, cutting me off. "You pathetic little cunt! You think you're going to do better than me?" he asks, his volume now rising to a yell. "I'm going to be a goddamned celebrity!" He leaps to his feet and glowers down at me. "*Everybody* wants me! I'm a *star*! And you're nothing! You'll never even get a song on the radio! Even your parents know you're a loser! You will *never* do better than me!"

I turn my gaze to the pavement for a moment. "I don't think that's you talking," I say as I slowly take the earrings out of each ear. "I think it's the cocaine." I get to my feet and brush off my jeans.

"But either way, you've made my point." And here, while his jaw is tight and his hands are curled into fists, I lean over, kiss him on the cheek, and place the earrings in his coat pocket. "Good-bye, Ash," I whisper. "Thank you for opening my eyes."

I let myself into the building, quickly closing and locking the door behind me. After all, Ash is a lot like me, and that means that he's dangerous and unpredictable. It means he's capable of hurting me.

As I climb the stairs I hear him cussing me out from below. I think about what I said to Brad on that night when I watched his daughter: *Those of us who are self-destructive will always love the ones who hurt us most.*

But what if I don't want to be self-destructive anymore? What if I *want* to have higher expectations for myself?

I go to my kitchen and find that one shard of glass that I've inexplicably kept. I stare at it for a very long time. Thoughts about hurt and loss cross my mind. I think about whether or not I deserve the things I want. Do I even deserve to live?

"Yes, I deserve more," I whisper to myself as I lift the glass to a different angle so I can see my reflection in it. "Yes, I *do* deserve to live. I just don't know how to do it."

And with that I drop the glass into the trash, fall to my knees on the hard kitchen floor, and cry.

✿

CHAPTER 30

I T HAS BEEN a long time since I've felt like this, like I can't get out of bed, like answering the phone or opening the mail presents a challenge similar to climbing Mount Everest. I take a vacation from phone sex. I call in sick to Envy, which is a risk, since I can so easily be replaced. But of course that thought just makes my urge to stay in bed even stronger. I am so very replaceable. Any middle-aged, hawk-nosed illiterate can make their living from phone sex. Anyone with a decent body and a sense of rhythm can dance in the cage at Envy. And the dog walking? I don't have any dogs to walk this week, or the next, which isn't surprising, because for every dog living in LA, there are probably four of us dog walkers. I'm simply not needed.

And every day I think about calling Ash. I could apologize, beg his forgiveness, accept whatever affection he's willing to offer me. Really, who cares if he sleeps with other girls? As long as I can be his number one. As long as I can be *someone's* number one. How awesome would it be to feel special again, if only intermittently? Intermittently would be better than *never*.

Of course I'm acutely aware that the self-pity I'm languishing in is disgusting and pathetic. But that doesn't mean I'm able to dismiss it.

And then I think of Brad. Brad who took me to the LACMA and the tar pits and trusted me enough to watch his daughter. Brad who *listened* to me. Brad who seemed to have been growing to really care about me and who has in turn awoken feelings in me that are both more intense and more comforting than anything I've ever experienced.

But I've burned that bridge, assuming of course there was ever a bridge to burn. And really, how could I ever let Brad, of all people, see me like this? I just can't.

And there's one more thing that keeps me from calling him. It's the unsettling and inescapable knowledge that while reaching out to Brad might help me, it would not be in the least bit helpful to him. I have nothing good to offer that man. So instead of reaching out to him, I reach out to his surrogate, Mr. Cuddly Bubbles, who accepts me unconditionally as I nuzzle up to him in bed.

And I let the days pass, wrapped in my sheets, my unwashed hair greasy and matted, the mail piling up on the floor. The room smells musty due to my unwillingness to open a window. Maybe if I had money they'd call me an eccentric. I could be, like, the punked-out female version of Howard Hughes.

But I don't have the money to buy the kindness of euphemisms. What I have is a whole lotta nothin'. And as I lie here it's almost as if I can *see* that nothingness filling up the room. Like I can feel the pressure of it against my chest making each breath a chore.

Three days go by like this, then four, then a week. Each day I find the motivation to heat up some Top Ramen and pick at it for a few minutes before pushing it aside. When you're not moving you don't need much food. By the time my phone rings on the morning of the ninth day I'm considering staying like this forever, maybe going out just long enough to adopt a few cats so I can fully realize the stereotype. The ringing phone is only jarring enough to get me to pull my worn sheet over my head, let the machine pick up, and listen to a happier version of me chirp out a recorded greeting.

"Hey, it's Mercy. Throw a little love to the machine and give it your message."

The beep jabs at the stillness of the room and then . . .

. . . then that gorgeous baritone rumbles through the speakers.

"Hi, Mercy, it's Brad."

I pull the sheet down enough to reveal one eye, which I use to peek out at the machine.

"*I . . . look . . . I know you don't want to talk to me,*" the voice continues. "*I didn't want to talk to you, either, for a while. The things you said to me . . . you pissed me off, but I shouldn't be shocked that a woman who is different from anyone else I've ever met said things to me that no one else has ever said. What is surprising is that I . . .*" He takes a moment, clears his throat. "*What's surprising is that I needed to hear it. It's funny, but you've helped me in ways only you could. I don't think I owe you an apology, but I . . . I know I owe you a thank-you. Please give me a call back so I can give it to you, all right?*" There's a long pause and then a heavy sigh through the line. "*Okay, I'll be waiting for your call.*"

There's the click of the hang-up and then the answering machine falls silent. I uncover the other eye and stare at the phone for a long minute. Then, slowly, I push back all the covers, sit up, cross the short distance to the machine, and play the message again.

"*Hi Mercy, it's Brad. I . . . look . . .*"

I listen to the whole thing and then press rewind and listen to the message again.

And then again.

And again.

And again.

I listen to it ten times. Then I stare at the machine for several more minutes and replay the message in my head, turning over each word and examining them from every possible angle.

"*You've helped me in ways only you could.*"

Has anyone ever said anything like that to me before? No, not possible.

"*. . . a woman who is different from anyone else I've ever met said things to me that no one else has ever said . . . What's surprising is that I needed to hear it.*"

It's like he's suggesting that I've done something right just by being me . . . *Is* that what he's suggesting? If so, *no one* has ever said anything like *that* before. Never, ever, ever.

"You've helped me in ways only you could."

Huh.

I finally turn away from the machine and take in the state of my studio, seeing it with a slightly different perspective than I've had in some time.

It's *disgusting*. I've totally let this place go to hell. There are old bowls of Top Ramen on the coffee table and on the kitchen counter. There's mail in a pile by the door. The wastebasket is overflowing with trash.

Almost without thinking I get a garbage bag from underneath the sink and empty the trash, collecting the overflow, and then move to the bowls, dumping the remainder of the hardening noodles in there as well. I place the dirty dishes in the kitchen sink before I turn on the water, letting it warm while I crack a window. I look out at the world for a while, that message still echoing in my head. I open the window a little wider, feel the mild chill of the air. "I think," I say to the streets in general, "I think I'd actually like to take a shower."

I look over at my bed. Cuddly Bubbles is there on my pillow, silently trumpeting his approval.

CHAPTER 31

✾

T HE NEXT FEW days are a little better. Slowly I begin to integrate my routine back into my life. I ask for one more week
off from cage dancing, and to my surprise Matt gives it to me, while
assuring me that my job will be there when I'm ready to resume. I
do start back with phone sex right away. I need the money so I take
the late-night shift, which pays better. I soon find that the horny,
lonely insomniacs are a little classier than the horny, lonely dudes
who call in the late afternoon. For one thing, most of the insomniacs have jobs. And some of them tell me about them. I coo about
my feet to a stressed-out intellectual property attorney and pretend
I want to be spanked by a manager of a tanning salon. I even get
to sex up a physicist, faking an orgasm in response to his in-depth
explanation of the multiverse theory, which I find so interesting I
end up asking him to recommend some books on the subject before
we hang up.

Oh, and that's another thing: I start reading. Three days after that
message from Brad I go to LA's central library, which is *insane*! It's a
cross between a Frank Lloyd Wright–inspired office building and a
gorgeous Renaissance castle.

I know this because I've been checking out the architecture
books. I've also been reading books on tattoos that are inspired by
the Native American tribes. And everything Ash told me about his
tattoos is totally *wrong*. The phoenix is *Greek*, not Native American, and it doesn't bring the thunder. None of the Native American
tribes saw the sun as a deity. And those arrows? Okay, yes, one arrow

pointing to the west means protection, just like he said. And yes, one pointing to the east is supposed to ward off evil. But both of those arrows together, the way Ash has it? It means war.

Dumbass.

But I don't really care too much about Ash's ignorance anymore. I'm just amazed that I was able to find a book on this subject—*several* of them, in fact! Who knew so many books even existed? Why on earth had I stopped reading? *This* is what I should have been doing when I was bedridden with depression. But now I don't have a schedule that accommodates reading all day every day. I have other things I have to do. I have to learn how to live.

And so every day I get up and take a shower, even if I have nowhere to go. I start running again, first four miles, then five, and finally six, even seven or eight if I'm feeling particularly anxious. I start surfing again, too, and hiking around Griffith Park and Runyon. And every day I listen to Brad's message . . .

And every day I decide not to return his call.

I *want* to call him back, but I'm absolutely terrified to do so. What if he tells me that I've misunderstood his message completely? Or what if I didn't misunderstand but he's changed his mind and decided I'm weird in bad ways rather than good ones?

Or it could be worse than that. It could be that he only wants to thank me. He could pick up the phone, tell me how I've helped him, and once that's off his chest he'll never call me again. We'll just be done. He could turn that thank-you into a good-bye and that goodbye into a rejection.

That would kill me. That's not a metaphor or hyperbole. It could actually end my life. I'm feeling better right now, but I'm beginning to understand myself a little better, too, and what I've come to understand is that I'm delicate. Or to be more blunt, I'm not okay. It's not difficult for me to imagine taking another shard of glass to my wrist and pushing it into the vein. No one would be or should be surprised if I were to swim out to sea in order to drown myself.

There's something inside of me, like . . . like the horrible little worm in that *X-Files* episode. It's something dangerously destructive and unpredictable, something that pushes me to do things I absolutely shouldn't do. I know that. I've *always* known that. But the difference now is that I want to kill the worm. I don't know what path I need to take in order to heal, but I'm beginning to get a feel for what paths I need to avoid.

Breaking it off with Ash was devastating, but I'm still here. And if he had broken things off with me it would have been the same . . . Well, okay, maybe a little worse, but it still wouldn't have been fatal. What would have been fatal was staying with him.

But Brad's a completely different story. Yes, I said good-bye to him. I pushed him away. The memory of that tears me apart, but I can now recognize my actions for what they were, a preemptive strike. Even then, on some level, I knew I would not be able to survive being rejected by Brad Witmer.

TWO MONTHS GO by. I'm back to dancing at Envy twice a month. My hours for 1-900-555-SEXX have decreased as well. But it's okay, it's my choice, because I have a new job. I'm the sample chick at Trader Joe's. I make up little tastes of the various things they sell at the store and give them away to customers. Everyone, practically without exception, likes the person who gives them free food. It almost doesn't matter what kind of free food I give them. Sometimes I prepare a pasta dish using a special goat cheese, extra-virgin olive oil, and fresh veggies that I've meticulously chopped into fine tasty bites. Other times I just toss a few small sugar cookies into paper cups. No matter what, people like it. Sometimes I think that if I took some plutonium, deep-fried it, and put it on a cocktail napkin, people would gobble it up and thank me for it. But rather than test the theory, I put effort into coming up with things people might actually enjoy if they were served it in a restaurant. The customers notice, my bosses notice, everyone's happy.

And the other workers at TJs are surprisingly cool. The majority of my coworkers have tattoos, alternative lifestyles, and happy dispositions. One of the checkers, Liz, is a guitarist and she and I are talking about starting a band. She already knows a keyboardist and bass player. All we need is a drummer.

A drummer like Brad.

And yes, I still have his message, and yes, I still listen to it a few times a day. And no, I still don't call.

One of these days I'll have to talk to my shrink about that.

Oh yeah, that's another great thing about Trader Joe's. Great health care. It even covers mental health costs. This is the first time I've ever talked to a shrink of my own volition. Her name is Ines Alvarez. I haven't shared everything with her yet but already she's helping me see things a little differently. It's Ines who convinced me to cut back on my drinking. Which is not the same as stopping—something Ines is constantly pointing out to me. But it's not like alcohol is cocaine. It's a perfectly legal beverage. In France they serve wine to their kids for, like, their kindergarten graduation. I've even heard that a few glasses a day can be good for your heart. Still, Ines won't let it go and I have to admit that since I've cut back I have noticed that my focus is better and it's easier to sleep through the night.

But I haven't agreed to her request that I take medication yet, although I know that's coming. I guess part of me wants to know if I can do without. If maybe I have the power within myself to take care of my own issues. Ines says it doesn't always work that way. But I don't know . . . I want to try. I want to figure out what I'm really all about, and I'm afraid that if I take meds I'll lose a little of who I am.

So yes, things are better. And yet I still think about Ash a lot and the child we lost. I wonder about his pilot and if he went back to Mindy McSlut—my pet name for her. And I think about Brad All. The. Time. I think about the time he asked the band to play the song he wrote. I think about the first dinner I had with him and June, about sharing bagels at his home and our trip to the LACMA and the tar pits, which was so perfect until I chose to completely screw it up.

And I still have Cuddly Bubbles. I sleep with him every night.

I wonder if Brad still thinks he owes me a thank-you, or if he even thinks about me at all.

I wonder what would have happened with us if I hadn't rushed out of his home that one night . . . the night I discovered the acceptance letter from Harvard. The night he touched me and kissed me in a way that made everything else disappear.

I wonder if he's kissed anyone else like that lately.

I've been thinking about all those things tonight as I lie here, sprawled out on the couch, wrapping up a call with the guy who pays me to pretend he's rescuing me from quicksand, which I stumbled into while wearing nothing but a string bikini. That's how bad it's gotten; even the revelation of a quicksand fetish isn't enough to distract me from thoughts of Brad.

I get less than a five-minute respite before the phone rings again. "This is Cherry Pop," I coo into the phone, "and I'm *so lonely*. Are you calling to keep me company?"

"No," says a man in a very familiar baritone. "I'm calling because you never returned my call."

I bolt upright. "Brad?"

"Cherry?"

"No, no, no, no, you can't call here!" I insist.

"I disagree. The ad says everyone is welcome at 555-SEXX."

I press my lips together, unwilling to laugh at his joke.

"Mercy, I just want to talk," he says with a sigh. "We left things in such an ugly way and . . . I just want a chance to tell you, you were right."

I squeeze my eyes closed. "Okay," I whisper. "I hear you, now please . . . you have to get off the phone."

"I'm applying to UCLA Law."

I open my eyes immediately. "You are?"

"I am."

"Because of me?" I squeak.

"Yes," he says with a warm laugh, "because of you."

"Oh." I fall back against the couch cushions. "Oh wow."

"Yeah, wow," he agrees. "It's too late to get in for fall, but that might be a good thing. If I'm accepted, June will already be well into kindergarten by the time I start classes. I'll be around to help her with the adjustment. And I've been playing a lot of poker. I've gotten good enough that I've been able to go to Vegas and win at a few of the tables . . . I've won a lot, Mercy."

"Wow," I say again. My eyes go from the coffee mug on my table to the surfboard leaned up against my wall. "Are you going to be, like, the first presidential candidate to fund their campaign with poker winnings?"

"Well," he says with a laugh, "I haven't won quite *that* much. And I still don't think the president thing is going to work out, but there are other things I can do."

"Other than being president?" This time it's my turn to laugh. "Yeah, just a few."

"I've missed that," he says softly.

"Missed what?"

"Your laughter."

For a long time I don't say anything. I just focus on my heart, futilely willing it to slow down. "I miss your laugh, too," I finally manage. "Look, I may have been right about UCLA and some other stuff, but . . . it's not like I don't know I was acting crazy. I did a total 180 on you that day, and I know you felt like it came out of nowhere. I . . . I do know that's fucked-up and I . . . I do know I owe you an apology, even if you did need a little kick in the ass."

I can almost hear his smile. "Apology accepted," he says. "But it's not necessary. We've both done worse things than have a sudden mood shift at a museum. It was still the best afternoon of my life."

"Of . . . of your life?" I repeat.

"Of my life."

I pause for a moment; my heart is thrumming in my ears now. "It was the best afternoon of my life, too."

And again, we share a moment of silence. I wonder what he's thinking. Where he is. "Brad," I whisper.

"Yeah?"

"You're being charged by the minute."

He laughs and then he says in his beautiful voice, "You're worth it."

I feel a slow smile spread across my face. "Well, in that case"—I lean back into the cushions—"why don't you tell me about these poker games?"

"Not much to tell. At the clubs it's usually the same players, unless you're lucky."

"What do you mean?"

"When someone sits down and says it's their first time at a poker club, it's a good day for us regulars because we know we're about to clean the guy out."

I run my finger along the fabric of my couch, curling my legs beneath me. "Sounds ruthless."

"I can be ruthless, Mercy."

I smile, move my fingers to my calf. "Call me Cherry."

His laugh is low, sensuous. I glance over at Cuddly Bubbles, who is so valiantly guarding the bed. "I've told you this before," he continues. "If there's something I want and it's within my reach, I go after it, with everything I have."

"Like poker winnings?"

"Like you."

I press my lips together. I'm beginning to understand what people mean when they say their heart explodes.

"Are you still with Ash?" His voice is even, almost a little menacing.

"No," I breathe. "That's over. But . . . but that doesn't mean I'm yours."

"No," he agrees, "it doesn't. It just means there's one less thing I'm going to have to kick out of my way to win this."

"Ash is not a thing," I say, a little more sharply. "And I am not a trophy."

"That's true," he agrees again. "You are a woman. You are *the* woman who sees the world in ways no one else sees it. You're the woman who has empathy for the people others scorn and who speaks truths to people who need to hear them. You're the woman who is a complete mess and yet in some ways is more together than anyone else I've ever met. You're the woman who has an angelic voice and devilish moves. You're the woman I've fallen in love with."

"Brad . . ."

"I want you, Mercy, mood swings be damned. And I'm not giving up on you. Not even if you start charging me by the second."

I smile, bending my neck, letting my hair fall forward. "This is crazy."

"Maybe," he agrees. "But right now I'm parked four blocks away from your apartment. And if anyone saw the state that I'm in, just from hearing your voice, they'd have me arrested for being indecent in public."

"Really?" I say with mock scorn. "Are you really calling a sex line from your parked car? Even the foot fetishists know better than that."

"Can I come over, Mercy?"

"Yeah," I whisper. "Yeah, you can come over." For another second we stay on the phone, not saying anything. And then I gently put the phone back in the cradle.

I count to three and then pick it up again and call the office of 555-SEXX to tell them I won't be able to take any more calls tonight. Quickly I go to the bathroom and fluff up my hair and apply some lip gloss. I look down at my outfit, pink-and-purple-striped yoga pants and an oversized blue boat-neck sweatshirt that says in white, cursive font, Keep It Surreal. I could *lead* Sergeant Pepper's Lonely Hearts Club Band.

I rush to my closet and sort through my things. What the hell do you wear for a romantic booty call with the future president of the United States? Do I go with a Marilyn Monroe vibe or Jackie O?

Although he did call via my 900 line; maybe I should go with cage dancer . . .

The buzzer for the front door goes off. Damn it! I whirl around, try to come up with a strategy, and then decide to just buzz him in. I open the door to my apartment and try to pose in a seductive manner . . . unfortunately there simply is no sexy posing in pink-and-purple-striped yoga pants. It can't be done.

But when I see him climbing up the stairs, all concerns about posing just go out the window. It's Brad. He's . . . he's back! And when he gets to the top of the stairs I see him take in the pants and the sweatshirt and he just smiles.

It's a nice smile.

And now he's right in front of me. He lifts his hand and gently places his palm against my cheek. "My God, I've missed you." And then slowly he leans in, brushing his mouth against mine before adding just a little more pressure, gently parting my lips with his tongue as he takes me in his arms, right here, in the hallway of my apartment building . . .

. . . he's holding me.

I lift my arms around his neck and, oh wow, I remember this, this feeling of just being lost in him. Like he's surrounding me, protecting me, *loving* me.

He bends his knees and lifts me up, cradling me in his arms, carrying me over the threshold like a groom carrying his bride, his lips never, ever leaving mine. I move one hand to the back of his head, feel the way his hair prickles between my fingers before he gently puts me down on the bed. I can't stop smiling as he stands over me, now caressing my cheek with the back of his hand. I prop myself up on my forearms, looking up into those deep-set eyes, falling in love with his chiseled features as if I'm seeing them for the very first time. With smooth, almost graceful movements he takes my sweatshirt from me. I'm not wearing a bra underneath and he reaches down, caresses my breast before sitting by my side, with one hand pushing me back while the other winds behind me, supporting me, keeping me from falling. And with my back arched against his palm he leans over, teasing my hardened nipples with his tongue, sending little shivers down my spine as I clutch his shoulders.

He pushes me farther down until my back is flat against the mattress and I'm watching him climb on top of me, feel him as he brings his face to mine and kisses me again, but this time the kiss is passionate right from the start. It's intimate and beautiful and enticing, and I feel his hands on my waist as his lips move to my neck, my shoulder. I'm running my hands against the blades of his shoulders; he's too broad for me to wrap him completely in my arms. It's impossible to touch this man without being aware of his might, and yet he's so very gentle, so sensitive to the reactions of my body, so skillful at anticipating what I crave.

My hands move to the hem of his shirt and I pull it off him, my legs wrapping around his. His scent is clean, like fresh water and sunshine. His teeth graze my ear as his fingers slip into my waistband. Slowly he pulls on the cotton and Lycra, sliding it down my skin so that it almost tickles before finally yanking it from my body.

And now I'm wearing nothing. Nothing but him.

His hand moves up the inside of my thigh as he kisses my waist, my belly, the curve of my breast. As his lips move up so does his hand, until he's kissing my mouth just as I feel him touching me right at my core.

And with that touch everything in me just lights up with a new kind of vitality. I writhe beneath him as he nibbles on my neck. His left hand is pressed between me and the firmness of my mattress; my breasts are pressed against the hard muscles of his chest as his fingers of his right hand toy with me, little movements bringing forth sensations that are so intense, so powerful, so fucking fantastic that I think there's a chance I've gone mad. I mean nothing this amazing can be real, right? It has to be a fantasy, a hallucination. And yet, these feelings are most definitely real. The denim of his jeans scratches provocatively at my skin and I begin to shake, not just tremble, *shake* as my hands begin to claw at his back. My body is no longer under my control. The whole world has become a blur. I've never been this wet before, this wanting . . .

. . . this in love.

And when the orgasm comes it's the most delicious sensation I've ever experienced. I cry out his name as he kisses my cheek, my hair, as one hand slides away and the other moves along my skin. I'm in a daze as he pulls the condom from his back pocket, pulls those jeans off his body, exposing himself to me, showing me everything.

It's doubtful that Adonis ever looked quite as hot as Brad. Every muscle is hard and perfectly sculpted. He could be a model, a world-class athlete, an Olympian.

He could be mine.

I finally allow my eyes to move down to his erection, which is reaching for me . . . well, if the lawyer and president thing doesn't work out, he could always go for porn star.

I let my fingers dance down the ridges of his cock as it strains for my attention. "I want you, Mercy," he says, his low voice vibrating against my skin.

I gently take the little gold packet from his hand, open it with my teeth. "Do you always carry around condoms in the pocket of your jeans, Brad?"

"No," he says with a little smile, "this is especially for you. This is all for you."

I feel my breath catch in my throat. And it hits me: I don't have to second-guess Brad. I don't have to wonder if the things he's saying are true. There is no mystery here, just barefaced desire . . . and genuine affection. And love. I can trust him.

I let the packet and the condom drop to the floor. "I'm on the pill now," I say. "And I want to feel all of you."

A little groan escapes his lips, and in an instant I feel him, for a moment just the tip, and then with a powerful thrust he's filling me, all of me to an extent that no other man has before. Again I find myself clinging to him, my face buried in his shoulder as he continues to move, rotating his hips against mine as I squeeze my legs together, finally lifting my hands from his body so I can brace myself, placing my flat palms against the wall behind my head. And he continues to rock against me, each movement hitting nerve endings that shoot sensations of pleasure through my body. With a start I realize I'm still trembling.

And that's when he uses the might of his thighs to open my legs wider, planting his hands on the mattress on either side of my head, lifting himself up like a cobra as he continues to ride me, now in a slow, sensuous figure-eight motion that allows me to feel not just the full length of his erection inside me, but the hardness of his pubic bone brushing against my clit.

Oh . . . oh wow!

Nope, this is definitely not possible. Not *possible* that I could be this close to coming again. That's never happened before, and yet as he continues to massage my body with his, my trembling increases. He grabs me and turns us on our sides, never breaking our connection, and I spider my legs through his, my lips inches from his face. When he looks down at me, taking me in even as he possesses me, I truly go a little crazy, my hips gyrating against him, his grinding against me, and the second orgasm comes fast and hard, totally overpowering me. I hold on for dear life as he claims my lips with his, absorbing my cries of passion.

This. Is. *Happening.*

When he finally ends our kiss, I gasp as if I need air. I look around wildly, once again taking in the broadness of his shoulders, the way the muscles in his arms bulge as he places a firm hand on the curvature of my back, making me feel delicate and feminine, feeling him, still hard inside me. He's looking at me like I'm the most beautiful woman on earth.

And this time it's me who lays my hand against his cheek as he gazes into my eyes. "My turn," I whisper. And while he's least expecting it I throw all my weight against him. He offers no resistance as I turn us over so now I'm on top. I dig my knees into the mattress, hook my feet around his legs just below his knees, almost as if giving myself little stirrups, and while grabbing fistfuls of sheet on either side of his head I start to make controlled, evenly paced little thrusts. He's looking up at me smiling, but I can see that he's now struggling for control. I start to increase the rhythm. He's all the way inside me, making us completely connected, and my movement is rubbing my clit against him again just as my sensitive aching nipples slide against him, tickled by the spattering of hair on his chest.

He wraps his arms around the small of my back, gripping me, but I still manage to increase the pace. My hair falls forward, over my shoulders, brushing against his as his hold on me tightens. Still, I pick up the speed even more, each little movement adding more friction against my clit . . .

. . . oh my God, I'm going to come again.

And as I move faster and faster—no control, only want, only need, only love—I am utterly and completely overcome. I cry out his name once more, and I hear him cry out mine. *Mercy.* And I feel him throbbing inside of me, filling me with the very essence of what makes him a man, making me his and making him mine.

It's not like anything I've ever experienced before. It's perfection, it's crazy . . .

. . . it's pure.

It's love.

CHAPTER 32

❈

H E SPENDS THE night. I don't ask him to, even though it's what I desperately want. It just happens. We fall asleep wrapped in each other's arms, cuddled up together in the way people do in the movies but so rarely do in real life. I love feeling his breath in my hair, his sweat on my body, hearing the beating of his heart.

I wake first, just as the sun begins to sneak in through the gaps in my blinds. When I realize who's with me I think I must still be in the middle of a blissful dream.

And then reality smacks me across the face and that bliss is replaced with panic.

I prop myself up and shake him by the shoulders. "Brad! Brad, wake up!"

His eyes blink open, and when he sets those sleepy eyes on me I almost give in to the temptation of just falling back down against his chest. But with herculean effort, I resist the urge. "It's *morning*!" I say. "Where's June? Is she with Maria? How long can she stay? Should we—"

"Shh," he says, and gently places his fingers against my lips. "She's not with Maria. She's well taken care of."

"Oh phew," I say with a little laugh, now willingly falling back against him. "I got a little freaked there. Is she with your mom?"

"No." There's just a hint of strain to his tone. "She's with her mom."

"*What?*" I sit up again, clutching the sheet to my chest.

Brad sighs and stares up at the ceiling. "A lot has happened in the months since I've seen you."

"I *guess*! When the hell did Mommy Dearest show up?"

"Just under six weeks ago; this is the second time June has spent the night with her." He pushes himself up to a sitting position and stretches one arm, then the other across his chest. "Do you have coffee?"

I lean back, shaking my head. "Coffee? Are you . . . your ex is back and you want to know about coffee?"

"Granted, there was a time when talking about my ex made me crave tequila," he says with a little smirk, "but things are better now. Coffee will be fine."

I shake my head, completely baffled by his calm. "Okay, I have coffee." I get up, still completely naked, quickly grabbing my over-sized sweatshirt from the floor and pulling it on, tugging it down to my thighs under his watchful gaze.

"You truly are a beautiful woman," he says softly.

I turn to reply, but stop as I now have the distance to fully take him in. The sheet is resting just below his narrow waist as he leans his broad back against the wall. For *this* man to look at me naked and then call me beautiful, it's sort of shocking.

And then my mind travels back to that photo I found in his sweater drawer and I feel an uncomfortable tightening in my chest. Keeping my head down so my hair blocks my face, I go to the kitchen and start the water boiling. "So what," I say, my back now to him. "She just dialed you up and said *Hi! How ya doin'? Mind if I reenter your life?*"

"She called to apologize," he explains as I pull the ground coffee and some half-and-half from the refrigerator. "She's older now, we're both older," he says with a slightly self-conscious laugh. I glance back at him. I've never known Brad to be self-conscious about anything. "She'll be starting in a PhD program in the fall."

"Uh-huh." I grab two mugs, one with an exhausted and grumpy-looking Tinker Bell on it and another with Rosie the Riveter. I'll be nice and give him Rosie.

"She knows how badly she handled things and, predictably, she's been thinking a lot about her daughter. In the end she just couldn't stay away anymore."

"Well gee, it only took her four and a half years."

Brad doesn't answer, and I can't bring myself to turn back to see his expression. The kettle works up to a high-pitched whistle and I take it off the burner as I put coffee cones on each cup. "She's not a bad person, Mercy," he finally says as I place the filters and scoop the coffee in. "She made a mistake. We're all guilty of that."

I take a deep breath and then blow it out through pursed lips. "What does she want, Brad? Shared custody?"

"Visitation. Just any time I'm willing to give her. She just wants the opportunity to know our daughter."

Our daughter. Dear God, do I hate the sound of that. "What about you?" I ask tersely. "Has she said anything about wanting *you*?"

Again, silence, and this one's loaded. If I could I'd crawl into a corner and cry. Instead I brace myself against the counter, staring down at the coffee as it slowly drips through the bottoms of the cones. "What about you?" I whisper. "Do you want her, too?"

I don't hear but feel Brad's approach. When he places a hand on each of my shoulders I lean back against his chest, close my eyes as he kisses the top of my head. "I want you," he says quietly. "That's why I'm here. I've chosen you."

Something about the phrasing sets off alarm bells, although I'm not sure why. "Where's she getting her PhD?" Another long pause, and this time I don't need to wait for an answer. "She's getting it at UCLA, isn't she? You fucker!" I pull away and glare at him. "She's the one who convinced you to apply there!"

"No," he says sternly. "She's going to UCLA because it's one of the few schools that has a strong genetics program. She wanted to attend Cambridge, but UCLA was always a more likely scenario. And me? I'm applying there because this is where June and I live and because of *you*. I've been afraid of not being there for June when she needs me, but you were right when you pointed out that I couldn't use that as an excuse forever. You made me see that a plan postponed is not the same thing as a plan destroyed. I can be inflexible at times, even rigid, certainly stubborn. But you shook some sense into me. I hope that Nalla will stay involved with June, and if she does, that will help, but if she doesn't, that doesn't mean I can't be the man I want to be. You helped me see that. I owe you everything, Mercy. Just you."

I swallow hard, force a smile, mumble an apology. I have no reason to doubt Brad. He's never misled me, never lied. Plus he's here with me, not Nalla, *me*. I let my eyes run over his body. He's not wearing any clothes.

"You, get rigid?" I ask, reaching between his legs, feeling him immediately grow hard against my palm. "I think I can live with that."

"Can you?" he asks as he gently moves the coffee cups farther down the counter. "I'm so glad to hear that." And with that he grabs me by the waist and lifts me up onto the counter, quickly stepping between my legs. "And now that I think about it," he says as he pulls up on my sweatshirt so that there's nothing beneath me but the hard, cool countertop, "there are ways to start the morning that don't involve coffee at all."

I stretch my arms forward, wrapping them around his neck, and tip my head to the side coyly. "Show me?" I ask with false innocence.

He yanks me forward so that now the tip of his cock is right up against me, opening me without quite entering me. "Are you ready for me, Mercy?"

I bite my lower lip and give him a slow nod, and then he pulls me forward again, entering me, thrusting inside me; I can't believe how wet I'm getting so quickly. How does he do this to me? I scrape my teeth against his skin and he rocks against me.

I bend my knees, lifting my feet up, digging my heels into the counter so I can take him in even deeper, and he responds by grabbing my ass and pulling me against him, pushing even further inside me, moving me back and doing it again. It's intense and incredible. My nails scratch against his skin and I hear him let out a little moan.

That moan speaks of victory. Knowing I can draw that out of him ignites me in a whole new way. I scratch and claw even as I kiss his skin and cry out his name. The rhythm he's set for us is ferocious and I absolutely love it. Already I'm close to coming.

But then he lifts me up, still inside me, and slams my back against the refrigerator door. As I cling to him, I put one leg down but keep the other wrapped around him as he bends his knees and now penetrates me in an upward motion. It only takes seconds before the orgasm completely overtakes me. And again he comes with me.

And here I had thought that the simultaneous orgasm was just short of a myth, something as rare and elusive as a solar eclipse.

But not with Brad. With Brad I'm in sync. As I struggle to catch my breath, my cheek against the warmth of his skin, my back against the cool of the refrigerator, I try to convince myself that this is forever. That he and I will always have this. That no obstacle will ever stand in our way. That our bond will never be broken.

But as he gently pulls away, as he kisses my forehead, I know I don't really believe it. The kind of bond I dream of takes decades to form. Brad's been my lover since yesterday.

I could lose him tomorrow.

❀

CHAPTER 33

EARLY THE NEXT evening, I go over to Brad's, TJ's bag in hand, and cook dinner for him and June. It's a wonderful night. Really wonderful. I had feared that June would be more aloof with me. After all, I haven't seen her in quite some time, and now with her mom around, any other woman by her dad's side might be seen as a threat. But June is nothing but warmth and giggles. She does tell me about her mom, whom she still calls Nalla. "She's the prettiest lady in the *world*!" she gushes. "And everybody says I look just like her."

"I'm sure you do," I say sweetly as I stab a potato chunk with my fork.

"I just wish she was more *cool*," June says contemplatively. "Like you, Mercy!"

Okay, that's enough to mollify me. "What's so cool about me?" I ask. Brad gives me a bemused look, but I just flutter my eyelashes innocently. As far as I know, there's no rule against milking a compliment.

"You have pink in your hair!" June points out. "And you sing cool songs! And you . . . you have . . ." She looks at her father for help.

"She has a certain je ne sais quoi," Brad supplies. June gives him a blank look.

I lean over and whisper conspiratorially. "That's French for 'your dad's a dork.'"

June breaks into giggles immediately. "Can you stay to watch a movie with us? We're going to watch *Toy Story 2*, right, Daddy?"

I glance at my watch. "We'd have to start it in the next twenty minutes. I have to work tonight."

"Are you going to be singing?"

"Dancing," I say automatically before I have a chance to think better of it. This time Brad shoots me a warning look. "I . . . I sing, dance, you name it, I do it."

"But where do you dance?" June asks, her mouth full of chicken.

"At a club," I say, shifting slightly in my seat.

"What kind of dancing?"

"Ballet," Brad says testily.

"Yep," I confirm as I reach for my sparkling water. "It's *Swan Lake* every night."

"Can I dance ballet, Daddy?"

"Yes," he says with a relieved sigh. "Next year we can sign you up for lessons."

"And can we be done with dinner in twenty minutes?" she presses.

"We can," he assures her, squeezing my knee under the table.

"Good! *Toy Story 2* is the best movie *ever*! And Buzz Lightyear is just like Daddy."

"She's so right!" I press my hand against my heart. "You're Buzz Lightyear!"

"All right, enough," Brad says with a little smile playing on his lips.

"No, you *are*!" I insist. "Say '*To infinity and beyond!*' Please? You gotta say it."

"Yeah, Daddy, you *have* to!" June agrees.

"No," Brad says as he reaches forward to move June's plastic cup back from the edge of the table. "I don't have to. It's most definitely a choice."

"Is it a choice for Buzz Lightyear?" she asks.

"Yes, I suspect it is."

"Mmm," I say, waving my fork in the air, "I'm not so sure about that. It might be part of Buzz's programming. He probably can't help himself."

June narrows her eyes. "But you can help yourself?" she says to Brad.

"Apparently, I can," he says as he eats his last bite.

"Do you *choose* to help yourself?"

"No." And with that he stands up, thrusting his fist in the air. "To infinity and beyond!" he bellows, and June bursts into applause as I, laughing, get to my feet and throw my arms around his neck. "I love you," I whisper in his ear. And he answers me with a light kiss and a look that says it all.

June and I finish our dinner minutes later and we clear the table as Brad gets the DVD set up. We all sit down, and he's just reaching for the remote when someone buzzes the apartment from the gate. "Expecting company?" I ask, but Brad shakes his head.

There is no intercom, so he steps into the courtyard in his bare feet. Then, glancing back at us briefly, he goes to the gate. June and I both look at each other and shrug.

Less than a minute later he reenters . . .

. . . and standing by his side is the prettiest lady in the world. She looks just like her picture.

CHAPTER 34

✺

NALLA'S HAIR IS brown and wavy with what look like natural golden highlights. Her skin is lightly tanned with an almost golden hue. She's wearing a tan-and-black patterned sundress, belted tightly at her itsy waist.

I feel like a WWF wrestler just slammed me to the mats.

She smiles at June, reaches into her dark red hobo bag, and pulls out a well-worn teddy bear. "Did you forget something?" she asks as she crouches down.

"Fuzzy!" June squeals, jumps up from the couch, and runs to the teddy bear.

To the teddy bear, but she doesn't run to Nalla. Still, June's clearly happy. She squeezes Fuzzy to her chest and rocks him back and forth. "I'm sorry, Fuzzy! I didn't mean to leave you!"

Nalla smiles warmly at Brad. "I couldn't let her go a night without Fuzzy."

Brad chuckles and nods. "I appreciate that. It would have been hell come bedtime." He gestures to me. "Nalla, this is my girlfriend, Mercy."

Brad just called me his *girlfriend*! It's almost enough to make up for Nalla's party crashing. I smile broadly and get up to shake her hand. But my smile fades a bit as she takes in my outfit. I'm wearing camouflage cargo pants and a white long-sleeved cropped top with a big ol' silver-sequin peace sign in the middle of the chest. I personally like the mixed message. But from the way she's looking at me, you'd think I was wearing a cone bra and an upside-down cross around my neck.

But the look of judgment vanishes before Brad can catch it. Now she's all smiles as she accepts my hand, shaking it weakly. "I've heard a lot about you, Mercy," she says a little too sweetly. She glances at the DVD case on the coffee table. "Oh, were you about to watch *Toy Story 2*?"

"It's my favorite movie!" June chirps as she makes her way back to the couch. "Daddy took me to see it at the theater. Remember, Daddy?"

Brad nods. "I remember. We got popcorn and licorice, but you forgot to eat any of it because you were so into the movie. That's never happened before . . . or since, come to think about it."

"That's lovely," Nalla says wistfully.

Did she just say *that's lovely*? Who under the age of fifty says *lovely* . . . Well, maybe the British, but that's *it*.

"It's so nice to see this," she continues. "You are a spectacular father and"—she gently puts her hand on Brad's arm—"we have a spectacular daughter."

I quickly look away as Brad agrees that they do. The comment shouldn't bother me but it's . . . it's just so intimate. Girlfriend or not, I'm the outsider.

"Are you all right?" Brad asks.

I turn back to reassure him only to see that he's looking at Nalla. I feel myself flush, but then, no one is paying enough attention to notice. Nalla takes a deep, shaky breath . . . *wait, why is it shaky?* She whispers in a voice that is almost, but not quite, too soft for me to hear, "I can't believe I almost stole all this from you." She gives Brad's arm a squeeze. "I'm sorry, I'm interrupting. I should have called."

"No, no," Brad reassures her. "Like I said, anytime you want to come see June the door's open to you."

Anytime? Like, in-the-middle-of-the-night kind of anytime? I don't think so!

"You treat me better than I deserve, Brad Witmer," she says rue-fully. "I do wish . . . I . . . well, I just hope you all have a lovely movie night. I didn't meant to . . . I simply . . . I'm sorry." She looks up at Brad and there are tears, actual *tears* running down her face. "I'm so, so sorry for the interruption." And then she rushes out.

"Nalla," he calls, concerned . . .

. . . and he goes after her.

Are you fucking kidding me?

I look down at June, my mouth hanging open. June seems completely unimpressed with the scene we just witnessed. She's grooming her teddy bear.

"What just happened?" I whisper to myself.

"Nalla cries a lot," June replies, assuming I had been address-ing her.

"She cries a lot . . . in front of *you*?" I ask incredulously.

"Yeah, but Daddy makes her feel better. He's good at that."

I suck in a sharp breath through my teeth. "June, can you stay right here?"

"Sure, where are you going?"

"To rescue Buzz Lightyear." I walk out and find them just outside the gate and, yep, she's still crying. She's crying on his shoulder, and while he doesn't exactly have his arms around her, he does have a hand on each of her arms as she leans against him.

"Brad," I say, trying my damnedest not to sound testy. "We promised June we'd watch this movie and as you know, I'm on a tight schedule."

Nalla looks up, a bit startled, her face streaked with tears. "Of course," she says weakly as she pulls away from Brad. "I'm so sorry, I . . . I've just been going through some things lately." She dabs her eyes with her fingertips. "I didn't realize you had time restrictions this evening. I had assumed you were spending the night." I think I hear a slight smile in her voice but that could be my imagination. "Anyway," she says with a little nod, "it was so good to meet you, Mercy."

I give her a tight-lipped smile, which she answers with a warmer one of her own before turning around and walking off, sniffling all the way.

Brad gives me a *what-can-you-do* shrug. "She wants to be here for June," he says as he opens the gate that separates us and steps back into the courtyard. "She just doesn't know how to do it. It's overwhelming at first, but she'll figure it out." He slips his arm around my waist and pulls me close to his side as we walk back to his apartment.

"She'll figure it out . . . with your help?" I ask.

Brad sighs. "She's the mother of my child," he explains. "I have an obligation."

It's not the answer I want to hear.

To be honest, what I want is to kick Nalla's butt to infinity and beyond.

BY THE TIME I get to Envy that night I am feeling edgy and just, well, *off*. Like, I-want-to-crawl-out-of-my-skin off. One of the bouncers has some strong weed and for the first time in ages I decide to light up.

But even after I smoke the joint I am still kind of pissed . . . and worried.

As the days go by that worry doesn't really subside. It's true that with Nalla around Brad's availability has improved. If there's something I want him to go to with me, she is always happy to babysit. Maybe I should be glad about that. After all, if she's agreeing to watch June while Brad dates, that must mean that she's not all that interested in him, right? But then, it also means that Brad's feelings about Nalla are becoming increasingly positive. According to Brad she has an Einstein-like brain when it comes to the sciences. That may be true, but it doesn't change the fact that she has the emotional maturity of a tadpole. In a matter of two weeks Nalla has called Brad late at night *four times* that I know of. And we're talking midnight-to-1-a.m. late. Each call is a tearful one, a few of them the result of a little drunk dialing on her part. She tells him how embarrassed she is that she fell apart in front of me. She tells him how guilty she feels about hurting him and abandoning their daughter. How she wishes she could go back and do everything differently. How she wants to be a mother but doesn't know how. How her parents still haven't fully forgiven her and how she's having a certain crisis of faith, which I think is sort of irrelevant to everything else, but Brad sees it differently.

When it comes to Nalla, Brad sees everything differently. It's a problem.

That's what I'm thinking about as I step into my apartment after a day of working at Trader Joe's. I throw my keys onto the coffee table and cross the room to the kitchen for the cranberry juice and vodka, just a little cocktail to take the edge off. Although what I really want is to just get stoned again. Medical marijuana is healthy. It's particularly healthy for Nalla, because if I get stoned I'll be too blissed out to track her down and tear her fucking hair out. I'm seriously thinking about calling up that bouncer dude for a small score when my cell rings.

"Hello?" I say once I've dug out my phone.

"Mercy?"

I pull myself up onto the kitchen counter, swinging my legs in the air. I recognize the voice but I can't quite place it. "Who is this, please?"

"It's Olivia . . . we met at a party a few months back."

I'm silent. Why am I getting a call from the gold digger?

"Are you still there?" she asks.

"Yeah." I twist my body so I can see Cuddly Bubbles on the bed. Nothing about this call feels right to me.

"I got your number from Ash's phone. I just thought you should know . . . or what I mean is . . . I found him. I found Ash."

I cock my head to the side. "Was he lost?"

She gives a startled laugh. "Well if he was, you'd know, wouldn't you? You're the one dating him."

Again I don't say anything. This woman was basically there for our breakup. What's she talking about?

"I'm sorry, that's not what I meant to say. I just don't know how to say what I *do* need to say," she continues. "After all, I know how in love you two are."

"Really," I say flatly.

"Oh yes, when Ash announced that you had forgiven him . . . well, it was so emotional for him. I don't know what he would've done if you hadn't. Personally, I think you made the right choice. After all, *every* actor has locationships. They're harmless."

I start chewing on my thumbnail. He told everyone we were back together? Why would he do that? And do I care? I'm not sure I do, but I'm not sure I don't, either. All I know for sure is that I don't want to talk to Olivia. "Is there something specific you need to tell me? Because I'm sort of in the middle of something," I lie.

"Okay . . . okay, here it goes." I can actually hear her take a deep breath through the phone. "I only found out he was fired from the show yesterday," she continues, "and I figured that since I wasn't going to be seeing him on set I should probably get back some things I had lent him, you know, like the extra printer I let him use when his broke. But when I got to his place, he was on the floor and there was an empty bottle of vodka and drugs, and I don't know if this was an accident or if he wanted to commit suicide, but—"

"Wait!" I drop to the floor so I can pace the kitchen. "Is Ash . . . are you saying . . ." I place my hand on my stomach as bile stings my throat. "Is he still alive?"

"I don't know, they took him away in an ambulance and . . . well, I figured I should call you. I'm not very good at breaking bad news. I'm sorry if I'm being clumsy, but . . . well, someone needed to *call you*, and there doesn't seem to be anyone else to pass the job off to, so I suppose it had to be me," she says with a slightly hysterical laugh.

"What hospital?" I sputter. As soon as she gives me the name I simply hang up.

Ash overdosed? Tried to commit suicide? *Did* commit suicide? I squeeze my eyes closed. God, the man is so fragile, so weak . . .

. . . so much like me.

❀

CHAPTER 35

WHEN I GET to the hospital pretty much all they'll tell me is that he's alive. That is enough to bring tears to my eyes. He's alive. Ash is alive.

I'm not family so more information is privileged. But there *is* no family here. Not even his great-aunt who he shares a yard with. Maybe that's why a nurse lets me into the hospital room once he's stabilized . . . or maybe it's because I told her I was his live-in girlfriend. A small fib for the greater good.

And when I get to the room . . . dear God, he looks awful. His skin looks almost sallow and he has an IV inserted into his arm. And while I can tell he's breathing, he's so still I find myself wondering if he's closer to the end than the nurses are letting on.

I claim a chair in the corner, pull my knees to my chest, and just . . . wait.

He doesn't wake up for another hour, and when he does he simply blinks and stares blankly at the ceiling for at least two or three minutes. Then slowly his eyes sort of slide over to the right, bringing me into view. His movements are sluggish and he turns his head gingerly in my direction.

"Melody," he whispers, his voice close to gone.

I look away, consider not answering before I finally nod. "Yes, it's me, Melody."

He continues to stare but he doesn't speak. "Were you trying to kill yourself?" I ask, my voice low, rough.

Another long pause before he whispers, "I don't know."

A sad smile plays on my lips. I've given that answer myself. "You were fired?"

"I didn't test well in the focus groups." With effort he turns his head again so he's looking away from me. "So that's it. Someone else gets my part and I'm nothing again."

"It's just one stupid show," I point out. "It's not even network."

"It's not just the show," he rasps. "It's you. I lost you."

I think about that for a moment before replying. "That's how I would feel if I were you and you were me. I'd blame you for my self-destruction," I say, enunciating the words carefully. "But, Ash, if you're standing on the very edge of a cliff, leaning forward while on tiptoe, you can't blame the wind when you lose your balance and fall."

"You're a fucking philosopher now?" he says. The words are harsh, but I hear a note of humor in them.

"I've just . . . I've given a lot of thought to what it is to die and what it is to live," I say with a shrug and a halfhearted smile.

"Oh yeah?" he asks, glancing down at his IV. "You think about death a lot?"

"Mm-hmm." I chew on my bottom lip and stare at the stark cream-colored walls. "I'm not here to save you, Ash."

Again, silence. I can make out the beeping of some medical equipment in the next room. "So why are you here?" he finally asks sullenly.

"I don't know . . . I guess . . . maybe I wanted to tell you that it's . . . it's difficult, but possible for us to save *ourselves*."

"I don't want to save myself," he growls. "Surviving isn't good enough. I need to *thrive*! I . . . I need to prove them wrong. My parents, Eva, my great-aunt . . . hell, even my ex-girlfriends and the teachers who treated me like I wouldn't amount to shit, I need to prove them all wrong. I can't do that by just *saving* myself! I have to be better than them! I have to be on top!"

"Yeah," I say as my eyes move from the IV to the dark circles under Ash's eyes and his uncharacteristically pale face. "I'm not sure that succeeding just to prove others wrong is all that much better than failing just because it's what people expect of you. Either way you're letting other people dictate the way you live your life, right? Flip sides of the same coin."

"And what exactly do you propose I do? Just get by? Be mediocre?"

"Not necessarily," I say with a sigh. "But God, Ash, there really are worse things in this world than being average. Trust me, there are days when I'd *kill* for average."

"It's not what I want," he says bitterly.

I sense he wants to say more and I also sense that talking is hard for him. Which means there's a chance I can say what I need to say without being interrupted. "Look, all I'm going to suggest is that instead of trying so hard to figure out how to be great or . . . you know, *not* average, why don't you just try to figure out who you are? I mean, do you know? Are you an actor? A singer? A biker? A family guy? Who the hell are you?"

"Don't give me that," he snaps. "Who the hell are *you*?"

I throw my hands up in the air in a beats-me gesture. "Still trying to work that one out. But I *know* that I don't know. That's the only area where I'm ahead of you. I'm actually aware of my ignorance."

"Congratulations," he says sarcastically.

"Thank you," I say sincerely.

Again we slip into silence. He's eyeing a glass of melting ice chips that's just out of his reach, so I get up to hand it to him. He takes it without comment just as a nurse comes in. "I'm afraid I'm going to have to ask you to step out for a moment," she says.

With a nod I find a place in the hall. A moment turns into well over a half hour, during which time what looks like a doctor and a social worker go in and out of the room. At a certain point I actually fall asleep sitting up, although the sleep seems to come from a place of emotional rather than physical exhaustion.

When I'm finally let back in Ash looks even more drained than he did before.

"They're keeping me here for observation."

"Yeah," I say as I reclaim my seat. "I figured."

He hesitates a moment and then whispers, "I'm sorry."

He's not looking at me directly, but I can make out the regret and guilt on his face. "What are you sorry for?" I ask cautiously.

"For being a dick. I've . . . I've never treated you well."

"Sometimes you did," I correct, but he continues as if he didn't hear me.

"I . . . had this fantasy. I would become rich and famous and . . . and I'd find you again and, okay, maybe you'd still be angry, but I'd have so many ways to make it up to you. I'd be able to take you to red carpet events and the best parties. I could help you with bills, buy you a new car. We'd send postcards to your parents made up of pictures of you and me living the high life."

I laugh despite myself. "Is that why you told people we were still together? You thought we'd reunite before they found out the truth?"

"Yeah, I guess I thought . . . if I had enough money and power I could fix things. People who talk about how money isn't important are the people who have it. Money and fame can fix problems, buy happiness—at this point it can practically buy eternal youth."

"It can't buy love," I offer.

"No," he rasps, "but it can buy some pretty interesting substitutes."

I immediately bust up and Ash cracks a smile, then he starts laughing, too, which is painful for him, so he struggles with himself, silently shaking with suppressed laughter. It's sweet, and it's incredibly sad.

When we finally settle down he turns his head to me, his hair gently spread over the pillow. "I didn't have to buy your love," he says softly. "You said I already had that."

I sigh audibly. "I also told you our love was a big fucked-up mess."

"That's what makes it interesting," Ash says hopefully. "You and I, we don't do conventional."

"No, no we don't," I agree. I lean forward, resting my forearms on my quads. "I'm not coming back to you."

He studies me for a long time and then asks again, this time in a voice that is so dejected, so weak it breaks my heart. "Why are you here, Mel? Really."

I bite down on my lower lip and stare at the floor again. "I don't want you to die," I whisper. "That would be such a *waste*! Okay, fine, you don't know who you are . . . but to die before you found out? Don't *do* that! Please, please don't do that. I guess . . ." I look up and meet his eyes. "I guess, in addition to telling you to save yourself, I'm here to tell you there's a *reason* to. I'm here to tell you that there are people on this earth, people who may be kinda pissed at you, who nonetheless love you and who want you to live. And that includes me . . . and I think it includes you. If you really wanted to die you'd be dead. But that's *not* what you want, right? You want to live. So stop fucking around and *do* it!"

He doesn't reply right away. Instead he lets the silence build up between us before he quietly breaks it.

"Fuck," he says, "your pep talks suck."

"It's not a pep talk, it's the truth," I snap. "The truth never sounds as good as a pep talk, but it usually holds up better."

He grumbles something unintelligible.

I could just strangle this man.

"You should call your parents," I say, pushing myself to my feet. "They might be mad, but from what you've told me, they do care. And call Eva, she definitely cares."

"What about you? Do you care?"

"Yeah," I say softly. "Yeah I do, but I can't stay. But . . . try to remember what I said, okay? Take it to heart?"

"You said a lot," Ash mutters, "and I'm not entirely with it right now. Maybe you could leave me the CliffsNotes?"

I stare at him for a moment, then fish out an old receipt and a pen from my purse. I hold the receipt against the wall so I have a flat surface, and across the back I write:

1. Figure out who you are.
2. Try not to die.

I hand it to him. "CliffsNotes." He doesn't even glance at them; instead he catches my eye and for a long moment we just look at each other. "Ash, you haven't always treated me poorly," I say. "There were times when you made me smile and laugh, *so* many times that you made me happy. But you never kept a promise to me."

He averts his eyes but doesn't disagree.

"If you make me a promise now, will you keep it?" I ask, my voice cracking. "Just this one time, can I trust you?"

"Yes," he croaks, and then meets my eyes again, and again, with conviction this time, says, "Yes."

"Good." I exhale a breath I didn't know I was holding. "Then promise me you'll follow the instructions on the CliffsNotes, okay? Promise me, Ash."

He finally looks at the receipt, and this time he can't suppress his smile. "Yeah," he says softly. "I can do that. I promise you, I'll follow the notes." He looks back up at me. "I do love you, Mel."

"And I love you," I say softly.

But even as I say the words, I know I'm not *in* love with him anymore. That's gone—which makes me wonder, *was* I in love with him? Or was I just in love with what he represented? Would either of us know the difference? And then I remember what I told him on my front steps the last time I saw him: . . . *you don't know the very things I don't know . . . and what we don't know? It's so much!*

Again I feel the bile rise, but I manage to hide it, and even lean over to kiss away a tear rolling down his cheek. "I'm so sorry," I whisper. "But I've gotta say good-bye."

CHAPTER 36

⚜

AFTER LEAVING ASH, I don't go home. Instead I go to the beach and sit on the sand, listening to the waves for a very long time. There are so many thoughts going through my head. As self-involved and obnoxious as it sounds, every time I picture Ash in that hospital bed I can't help but think about how that easily could have been me. What drugs had he been taking, anyway? And really, how many times have I mixed copious amounts of drugs and alcohol? How many times have I flirted with death? Sometimes weekly . . . sometimes daily. And yet I don't want to die. I *do* want to figure out who I am. But more than that, I don't want to hurt people, not like I have in the past. And . . . and to accomplish both those goals, I'm going to have to learn to live with myself . . . and . . . and maybe, for just a little while, *by* myself.

I fish my phone out of my purse and call Brad.

"Hello," he says, yawning through the line. "Mercy?"

"Yeah," I say, staring out onto the dark sea. "I was wondering if I could stop by."

"Now?" I can visualize him looking at the digital clock by his bed, noting with alarm that it's after 2 a.m. "Is everything okay?"

"Yeah, it's okay . . . but . . . can I just come over?"

And of course he says yes, because someone like Brad will always say yes to a damsel in distress. And damsels in distress are the only damsels he knows.

By the time I get there it's almost three. Brad looks like he's hovering between exhaustion and anxiety. He ushers me in, closes the door softly behind us, and leads me into his bedroom.

"What's going on?" he asks as I sit cross-legged on his bed.

"It's not fair," I say quietly as I stare down at his comforter. "It's not fair that I'm going to tell you this now, in the middle of the night . . . but it can't wait."

"Mercy, you're scaring me."

"I just . . . I want you to know that I'm in love with you," I say quietly. "I've never really been in love before. It . . . it makes me wonder if the other time was even love at all."

From the corner of my eye I can see his body relax. He closes the distance between us and sits next to me. "I'm in love with you, too, Mercy, I told you that."

"And Nalla?"

"Mercy, I promise you—"

"When you said you chose me," I say, cutting him off, "did you mean that you made a choice between her and me? Was she an option?"

He hesitates, then runs his fingers through my hair. "What does it matter?" he asks. "I chose you. That's what counts."

I smile sadly, keeping my eyes down. I'm afraid if I look up at him I'll chicken out of what I have to do. "It matters because from the little I know about Nalla, she shouldn't be a choice at all. It's great that she's going to UCLA and that she's trying to be part of June's life, but . . . calling you late at night crying because of something she's done to *you*? She expects you to comfort her because she fucked with you? Do you see the problem with that?"

"Okay, she's a little lost. She just needs an ear and she is the mother of my child."

"Oh, Brad, she's more than a little lost. And these crises of faith . . . I mean, what is that?" I pick at the comforter with my nails, my heart going a little faster than it should.

"She was . . . or she is, a religious Catholic but . . . well, there are some things about the church—"

"*What does any of that have to do with you?*" I demand, finally looking up to meet his gaze. "I mean, come on, Brad! You use Jesus' name in vain more often than that girl with the rotating head in *The Exorcist*! God, the woman is going to be getting her PhD in genetics, she should be able to figure this out!"

"Mercy—"

"And she *has* worked it out!" I say, unwilling to let him defend her. "She's manipulating you. She wants you to save her, and if I have any kind of read on this, what she wants you to save her from most of all is herself."

"Why are we talking about this?" Brad asks with a heavy sigh. "It's not important. It's not even vaguely relevant. I'm not *with* her, and no matter how many times I need to comfort her or guide her, I will still never be with her. I choose *you*."

"It's relevant," I say quietly, "because I need to know that she's not the woman you're going to run to when I'm not here."

"When you're not here," he repeats. "You mean, when you're at your place or working? You think I'm going to cheat on you?" He wraps his arm around my shoulder, kisses my hair. "I'm never going to do that."

"I'm not going to be here because I'm going to do the right thing," I say dully.

"What's that?" he asks as his kisses move down to my ear.

"I'm going to find myself," I say, laughing a bit at the cliché. I unfold my legs and stand up, putting distance between him and me. "We've had this conversation before, but . . . I want to try it without the animosity this time, okay?"

"I . . . I'm sorry, I'm just not following this."

"A few months ago I was borderline suicidal. I wasn't sure I wanted to live. I just . . . I wasn't sure."

"Mercy," he whispers, getting up and crossing to me. "I promise, I'm never going to let you get there again."

I laugh, and even I can hear that the laugh hints at encroaching hysteria. "You don't get to be in charge of my mental health." Once again I move away from him, this time finding a spot by the bookshelf. "Do you remember when I told you that those of us who are self-destructive will always love the ones who hurt us most?"

"Of course . . . wait." He grows rigid as he lifts his chin up a bit, almost defiantly. "Is this about Ash?"

"No, not really. Not at all, actually. But . . ." I pull out one of his books, turn it over in my hands. "No one ever hurt me as much as my dad, and yet . . . do you know that I still love him?" When Brad doesn't say anything I lean against the bookcase and close my eyes. "Every day I . . . I hope. I hope and I pray that my father will call me. That he'll seek me out. That he will give me his love and his approval. I still want that. The man hit me. He threw me out. He tried to have me locked up in a psych ward; he disowned me and he had me declared dead. And if he called me right now and asked me to forgive him in exchange for his love I'd do it in a heartbeat."

Brad remains silent. I know he doesn't understand. I *knew* he wouldn't. But I'm going to have to *make* him understand. It's important now. "The way I see it," I explain, "is he cared. He was completely fucked-up, and if they made a World's *Worst* Dad mug I wouldn't be out of line if I bought it for him and stuck it under the Christmas tree. But he was *not* indifferent. Furthermore, he must be going through some kind of struggle himself. I mean, I don't know exactly what's wrong with him, but emotionally healthy people don't pull the shit he pulled . . . or at least that's what I tell myself. It's so easy for me to make excuses for him. So no, I don't hate my father. You know who I *do* hate?"

I look up to see Brad's brow crease, clearly unsure of where I'm going with this.

"I hate *her*. I hate my mother. I hate the woman who never once raised a hand to me. Never once tried to lock me up in a psych ward. Never once told me I was a complete freak and a failure and who never *once* spoke *one word* in my defense."

"Ah," Brad says, comprehension finally setting in.

"She didn't protect me," I say, my voice low, resentful. "I should never have even had a chance to love my father. She should have gotten Kasie and me out of that house the minute she saw what kind of man he was. The first time he hit me she was in the kitchen. She *heard* it and she came rushing in to see what the commotion was. And then she saw me, on the floor, and my father standing over me. I saw the look of distress on her face and I just *knew* she was going to help me. I was sure she was finally going to step in. And do you know what she did?"

"I can guess," Brad says in a low voice.

"Yeah, well, if you're putting your money on her turning her back and walking out of the room, then congratulations. You win." Brad meets my eyes and then lowers his to the floor. "It was her duty to protect Kasie and me and she didn't," I continue. "I should hate him more than her. I'm not being fair. Maybe she's sick, too. Maybe she needs help, but I didn't *see* that. What I saw was weakness, and cowardice, and . . . and neglect in an area where she had the *obligation* not to be neglectful." I take a step forward and then another until I'm standing in front of him, taking his hands in mine. "You are such a wonderful father, Brad," I say softly. "But you're going to have to protect your daughter a little better. You're going to have to protect her from messed-up, self-destructive people. You need to keep your eye on Nalla because that woman is like a time bomb. Eventually she's going to blow and everyone around her is going to be hit with the shrapnel. And . . . and you're going to have to protect her from me."

Brad looks up sharply. "That's insane. You would never hurt June."

"You're right, I wouldn't," I agree. "Not intentionally. But I could hurt myself. I . . . I don't think I would do it on purpose, but our subconscious can drive us to do some pretty messed-up stuff. And until I know I *won't* do myself harm, in any way, you just can't let me be a big part of your daughter's life. I *have* to get myself together first. I have to . . . I have to figure out who I am and why I do the things that I do . . . and then . . . then I have to stop doing some of those things. Not for a few months, but for *years*. I need to just *stop*. And I don't know that I'm there yet. I'm not ready to say that . . . and that means I can't be ready for you."

Brad's jaw is tighter than I've ever seen it; he's flexing and curling his fingers as if he's fighting the urge to make a fist. And yet I know that he is no more a threat to me than I am to him or his daughter. Which is to say, he would never hurt me on purpose. But considering our issues, that's just not enough. "What you're saying is nonsense," he says between gritted teeth. "This is just like what happened at the end of our day at the LACMA. This is just your self-destructiveness manifesting itself. You're pushing me away because you don't think you deserve to be happy. But you're wrong about that, Mercy. You're wrong about everything."

I take a deep breath, force myself to meet his eyes. "Maybe," I admit. "But right now what I know is that if you broke up with me, I might end up in the hospital. Seriously, it could get that bad. And you don't deserve that responsibility. You can't *take* that responsibility. You have a kid."

Brad stares at me for a long, long time, and then something happens: he just crumbles. The pain just rolls over his features like an avalanche and he reaches for me, pulling me to him, and in this moment I find I can't resist him. My desire to be in his arms is just too strong. "You can't walk away from me," he whispers. "Please, Mercy. Let me . . . let me help you."

There is no place in this world that is better than here, right here, in Brad's arms, my head pressed up against his chest. This place where I feel so warm, so safe and cared for, so *loved*. And oh God, do I want to stay here, forever and ever. And when he lowers his head to mine and I open my lips for him, when I feel that kiss so powerful and needing and exquisite . . . how on earth can I give this up?

Because I have to. Because it's the right thing to do.

"I wish I could do this," I say, the tears now freely streaming down my face. "But the problem is you don't want to help me, you want to save me. And only I can do that." And with strength I didn't know I had, I pull away.

The love this man feels for me. The way he *wants* me . . . I see it in his eyes and in the way he stands as if it's everything he can do to keep from rushing to me, taking me back into his arms, laying me down on the bed, finding some way to make this better.

But he doesn't, because he knows that wouldn't be right. So we stand there, faced off in his bedroom. Both of us wanting the same thing, and both of us awash in the pain of our own resistance.

"Figure out how to be happy without saving people like me," I say quietly. "Figure out how to make your dreams come true . . . And if you can't do that"—I give a meek little shrug—"figure out how to find new dreams."

"But this doesn't need to be forever," he says hopefully. "You . . . I . . . we might still have a chance, sometime down the line. Tell me this doesn't have to be forever."

I let out a staccato breath and look up at the ceiling as I struggle to keep it together. "I don't know what forever means! So . . . so I guess maybe, someday . . . but not now, and I can't . . . I can't ask you to wait for me." And again I meet his gaze, and then in a split second we are in each other's arms, and this time the kisses are even more passionate and so . . . so perfect. I feel his tears mixed up with mine. I feel the fast beating of his heart. I feel everything. And for a moment, he rests his forehead against mine. "I love you," he says. "And I don't care what name you use or how long you stay away, that will never change. I love you."

"And I love you," I whisper. And with one more kiss I pull away again . . . and this time I run out the door.

CHAPTER 37

❈

November 2006

S TANDING HERE AT the front of the stage as the last instrumental notes of the song are played out behind me, it's impossible not to be impressed by this crowd. The club's almost filled to
capacity. There must be close to three hundred people here!

And they're all here for *us*!

Impulsively I wrap my hand around the mic and pull it to my
mouth as I scream, "I love this country!"

And I swear to God, it feels like all of Belgium screams back at
me. They don't even care that I'm speaking English; in fact maybe
they love me a little more for it. They know I can get by in French,
I've lived here for over two years now. But when you're moved by
passion only your native tongue will do. I whirl around to see my
Spanish guitarist, Rubén, grinning at me like a madman. Only my
drummer and bass player are local. I met our Dutch keyboardist when she signed up for one of the pole dancing classes I teach
downtown. We're a truly international group and yet Brussels has
become a home to all of us. And what an amazing home it's been.

I hold up my hand and start snapping my fingers in a resolute
rhythm, which my drummer quickly imitates. I turn back to the
crowd just as Rubén adds his strings to the beat.

And the room goes wild. They know *my* song! A song I wrote as
a wry tribute to my father. It's one of the biggest highs I've ever had,
and that's saying something.

I snatch the microphone from the stand and run to the other
side of the stage and launch into the lyrics:

I died for your sins
And came back for my own
I rebuilt my heart
I revived my soul

I will never disappear (never disappear)
I will never disappear (never disappear)

I will never disappear

And the room is singing with me. Words that might not have meant a thing to them if spoken mean everything to them when put to music. That girl standing on the table waving her arms in the air in an expression of grace and freedom, that boy who's jumping up and down by the stage, crying out the lyrics as if they're coming straight from his heart. My lyrics coming from his heart! This isn't just love, this is understanding! This is my world! And when I launch into the next stanza they're all with me:

I'm of the kind
You don't understand
We see the world
In ways you never can

We will never disappear (never disappear)
We will never disappear (never disappear)

And the energy keeps building, even as we move into the instrumentals. Now it's not just the girl who has her hands in the air, almost all of the audience does. I glance toward the bar and see my boyfriend, Logan, hold up his bottle of Belgian beer in a salute, a sweet grin on his face. I've never tasted any of the beer here. I haven't tasted *any* alcohol since 2002.

I bring my lips to the mic again:

We here are human
And sometimes a mess
We have a beauty
You'll never possess

We will never disappear

And as the music comes to a stop the voices of the crowd only grow louder, this time joined in a cheer that quickly morphs into a roar. I. Love. *This*!

"We are Tar!" I cry out and the cheers spike again at the sound of my band's name. I was the one who chose it. Many take it as a heroin reference.

Brad would know the truth.

It's surreal that after more than five years of absence the thought of him can still make me smile . . . or cry. In the time since I last spoke to him I've gone on the wagon, fallen off the wagon, and then gotten back on. In those years I started taking a prescribed medication, nothing too heavy, but enough to help me resist some of my more destructive impulses. In that time I met Logan, a Belgian documentarian with a quiet disposition and a love of books that rivals my own. In those years my country was attacked, wars have been launched, elections have been contested. I've switched continents, given up phone sex, traded dancing in a cage for teaching pole dancing classes to self-deprecating Belgians, I've moved in with Logan, I've learned French. Everything has changed!

And yet I still miss the man I walked away from all those years ago.

But tonight is not about pain. It's about the life I've made for myself. And so we launch into another song and then another and another. I'll be twenty-nine years old tomorrow. I've gone from one of the least accomplished members of my peer group to . . . well, not being the most accomplished, but I'm up there. I mean *look at this*! Tar *owns* the indie scene in this country and we're getting gigs in other European cities, too! Lyon, Liverpool, Barcelona, Florence, it's crazy! An LA-based producer who I've dreamed of working with has approached me but he *only* wanted to work with me, not the rest of the band, so I turned him down. Just like that. Because while I want to work with him, I don't need to. It's a distinction I've come to appreciate more and more with each passing year.

Of course there are record labels that've expressed interest in working with Tar, but we continue to put out our albums independently. We have total control. Just like we're controlling this crowd, this room, this *energy*!

When we finally wrap I throw my arms out to either side as if trying to embrace the night itself. People are chanting my name while others chant the name of the band. Still others cry out words of love, lyrics from my songs, so many wonderful things! No, tonight isn't about pain at all.

Tonight is about triumph.

When we move from the spotlight to backstage everyone in the band breaks into laughter. Hugging one another, ruffling one another's hair—yes, this is what success is supposed to feel like.

It only takes Logan a few minutes to work his way to where we are and then he, too, is taking me into his arms, kissing my cheek, and gazing down at me with those dark blue eyes, his blond hair as messy as ever. "You were fantastic," he says.

"Thank you," I say meekly. "And thank you for coming."

He nods magnanimously. Logan hates crowds. In his ideal world I'd be singing in dusty little coffeehouses with a lone guitar and a beret on my head. But since tomorrow's my birthday he has agreed to spend about thirty hours doing all the things I love to do regardless of his own preferences. That starts tonight with this concert. Then tomorrow he's accompanying me and some friends to a soccer . . . er . . . football match, and tomorrow night we'll be meeting more friends at a different club to go dancing.

In other words, it'll be a day of hell for him but he's willing to walk through that hell for me. If that's not love, I don't know what is.

I give each of my bandmates one last hug good-bye before Logan and I head out through the back door. Last week the city was covered in snow but tonight the cobblestone streets are merely a little icy, making them both beautiful and precarious.

"It's after one in the morning," Logan says in French as we walk past a few fans who are hoping I'll stop to sign their CDs. Sometimes I do, but rarely when I'm with Logan . . . or when it's exceptionally cold like tonight. "You played for three hours straight," he continues. "You must be exhausted!"

I shrug and give his hand a squeeze. I'm actually not tired at all. The adrenaline is still pumping through me. But I have no doubt that in an hour or so I'll be ready to crash. "Did you really like the performance?" I ask, also in French, once we get to his car. He holds the passenger door open for me as I slip inside.

"You were amazing," he says in response before closing the door.

I smile and rest my head against the leather seat as he gets behind the wheel and directs us toward home.

I STARTED DATING Logan in 2004, while he was studying to be a documentarian at USC. And now here we are, living in Brussels, the city he grew up in, which is perfect because in this case what he sees as *his* comfort zone is *my* adventure.

"Home," he says, yawning as we pull into the small parking lot for our building. I know the yawn is his subtle way of telling me he might be too tired for sex tonight. I don't mind. It's not that our sex life isn't good—it is. But something about turning twenty-nine, the very last year of my twenties, has gotten me thinking about everything that's happened in this last decade. In nine years I went from being a cokehead, to being pregnant, to being an alcoholic, to heading my first band, to being with Ash, the unwitting father of my child, to being with . . . with . . .

I squeeze my eyes closed, trying to force the memories of Brad out of my head. Brad is gone. Eventually my heart will figure that out, right? It has to. This simply cannot go on forever.

We take the elevator up to our flat and I slip into our bedroom as Logan slips into the shower. I should change into my nightshirt and start preparing for sleep. But instead I go into our closet and dig out a box I've hidden in the back. Inside is Mr. Cuddly Bubbles and the picture taken at the back of Apocalypse. The picture is folded over. I don't have the strength to look at it. But I do allow myself to hold Mr. Cuddly Bubbles. Part of me feels guilty for keeping my plush little friend. But then, Logan knows all about Mr. Cuddly Bubbles. I even told him a little about Brad, albeit not much. I just told him that a man had taken me to the La Brea Tar Pits and that I found magic there. Logan had questioned my use of the word *magic*, pointing out that the phenomenon of the constantly bubbling-up tar and the finding of fossils were things that should be classified under science because we knew how things were done. But I had just smiled and quoted a Terry Pratchett book I had recently read: *"That time it had been magic. And it didn't stop being magic just because you found out how it was done."*

Still, there's a lot Logan doesn't know. For instance, I haven't told him about the last time I saw Brad, only six months before Logan and I started dating.

After I had managed my first full year without a single drink, joint, or line, I had started thinking about trying to reconnect with Brad. Maybe the best way to handle that would have been to call him up. But instead I started stalking him. Yes, yes, I know, but it's not like we had Facebook then, so I had to resort to going old-school stalker in order to figure out what was up with him. I drove by his place when I didn't need to, sometimes parking kitty-corner to it in hopes that maybe he would come out, that I would see him.

And then one day . . . he did. I was just sitting in my car and he walked outside.

And he looked beautiful.

Just utterly perfect. He was wearing jeans and a sport coat. His white button-down had the first few buttons undone, and even though it was getting dark and the distance made it impossible for me to see too many details, I still imagined that light spattering of chest hair that I had once run my hands over, feeling its coarseness between my fingers as he gently kissed my neck. Yes, this was my Brad. He walked right up to the edge of the sidewalk and then looked up at the full moon that was still low in the sky. It was draped in golden tones and looked massive. For a moment it took my attention, too, and I thought, Here we are, gazing at the moon together . . .

. . . and he doesn't even know it.

Slowly, hesitantly, I got out of the car and stood there on the street, right in plain view. But Brad didn't see me. His eyes were on the moon. And so I took the opportunity to study him, now without the impediment of my car window being between us. There was just the slightest breeze and it ran through my hair and through his. Even sharing that felt unbelievably intimate. When he closed his eyes against the breeze, when he took what appeared to be a deep cleansing breath, I stepped forward . . .

. . . And she came out. Nalla, wearing a sophisticated and sexy little black dress. And she was holding June's hand.

In an instant I retreated, ducking behind the bumper of my car as I peeked out at them. June was taller. So much taller it took me aback. But she was definitely still June, wearing a long pink skirt that she held out to the side like she was a Disney princess. She was skipping by her mother's side.

When Nalla put her hand on Brad's shoulder, he turned to her, and though I was too far away to see his smile, it was easy to remember the way he used to smile at me. It always made me feel so beautiful, so happy, and . . . and now he was smiling at Nalla.

I stayed hidden as the three of them got into Brad's car and drove away. Just one happy family going out for an evening of fun.

After that I stopped stalking him.

That was the last time I saw Brad. I sigh and lean my head against the doorframe of the closet, staring at my clothes crammed in with Logan's while holding Mr. Cuddly Bubbles to my heart. There have been times when I considered contacting Brad. Like when Logan asked if I'd move to Brussels with him once his student visa ran out. We had been dating for about four months at the time and I knew I'd miss him if he were gone. After all, Logan is nothing short of wonderful. He's hot and he's smart, funny, creative, giving . . . I could go on and on. Any woman would be happy to have him. *I'm* happy to have him.

He's just not Brad.

But then, no one ever will be.

So yes, I considered tracking Brad down at the time, but by then I wasn't sure how to do it. I didn't even know if he was in LA anymore. The building he used to live in had been demolished, sacrificed to the housing boom and the dreams of ambitious developers. And June, she would have been eight years old by that point! *Eight!*

Undoubtedly she forgot my name shortly after I left Brad. She may not even remember I exist. And Brad probably wishes I never had. Judging from what I saw during my last stalking trip it's likely he's with Nalla now. And if he isn't (*dear God, I hope he's not!*) he still might not want to see me. How many times did I pull that man close only to push him away? It must have been crazy making.

Perhaps I broke his heart.

So no, I didn't scratch at that wound. I chose to move on.

"Are you all right?" Logan asks in French. We've agreed to speak French in the house until I'm fluent, unless I'm particularly emotional, busy, or overly tired. In other words, we occasionally speak French in the house.

I turn my head to see Logan by the bed wearing navy pin-striped pajamas. He's the only man I've ever known who actually has pajamas. Not sweats or boxers, not pajama bottoms with a T-shirt, oh no. For Logan it's straight-up pajamas. He's adorable.

I discreetly tuck Mr. Cuddly Bubbles between some sweaters on a shelf and then close the closet door as I step out to meet Logan. "Just trying to figure out what to wear tomorrow," I lie smoothly in his language as I give him a light kiss. He laughs and makes some teasing comment about my obsession with style and fashion and then he crawls into bed. By the time I've brushed my teeth and washed my face he's dead to the world. So I get in next to him, as quietly as possible, remind myself how lucky I am to have such a good life despite all my previous fuckups, and then send up a silent prayer that I don't dream of Brad.

It's a prayer that's rarely answered.

CHAPTER 38

❁

THE NEXT MORNING is perfect. Logan makes us brunch, which consists of fresh-squeezed orange juice, bacon, eggs, toast, and *rice pudding*. Yes, really. I've become a pretty good cook but Logan is a friggin' gourmet. I tap my fork against the plate and smile across the table at him. "This," I say in French, "is why I moved here."

"Really?" Logan deadpans as he switches to English. "I thought it was for my amazing wiener dog."

I laugh even though the joke doesn't quite work. No one calls hot dogs wiener dogs and even if they did, someone who cooked them would be known for their wiener *dogs*. Plural. But you gotta respect a guy who attempts wordplay in a foreign language. "It's your day," he says as he reaches for his orange juice, "so we speak your language."

I nod, accepting this reasoning but no longer willing to sacrifice eating for talking in *any* language.

"I forgot to tell you," he says as he watches me shovel in more pudding, "I was able to set up another meeting with a prospective financier. He seems very enthusiastic."

"Logan, that's fantastic!" I manage. Since he moved back here Logan has created a series of very well-received shorts. He even did a little rockumentary for Tar that he posted on YouTube, delving into everything from our music to our eating habits. He interviews the band, too.

Now he's working on a bigger documentary about the integration of Muslim immigrants into Belgian society. I know it's going to be great but he needs more people to invest in order to get it off the ground. "Who's the investor?"

Logan launches into explaining how he attracted this man's attention, what he hopes the meeting will lead to, how much he needs. I try to pay attention, but these are the kind of details I have a hard time getting amped about. "It seems things are going well for both our careers," he says, once he's completely filled me in. He lifts his OJ as if making a toast. "Here's to living the American Dream . . . in Belgium."

"Where else?" I counter, clinking my glass against his. I stare down at my plate. "Almost all my food is gone," I point out. "How did that happen?"

Logan laughs. "You'll work it off during one of your pole dancing classes." I roll my eyes. Pole dancing is a point of contention between us. I say it's an amazing workout. He says it's silly and not real exercise. One of these days I'll insist that he watch me work a pole like an athlete, but until then we'll agree to disagree.

Just then the buzzer for our flat sounds and Logan checks his phone to see the time. "They're early," he says, referring to our friends who are meeting us here before going to the stadium. He excuses himself as he goes down to greet them and lead them back up here while I busy myself with licking my plate.

But when he comes back up it's not with friends, it's with a small package. "It was a delivery," he says with a smile, handing me the box. "Seems someone sent you a birthday present from America."

"I bet it's from Olivia," I say eagerly as I get up to take it. But then I stop.

The return address is a latitude and a longitude.

And just like that, the world changes.

"Let me do the dishes before everyone arrives," Logan says, not noticing my shift in mood. "You just relax. It's your day!"

I don't answer. I can't. I can hardly even breathe. As Logan deals with the plates, I take the package into the living room, drop down onto the couch, and tear it open, using my fingernails in lieu of scissors or a knife. Inside is a small box and a card . . . a postcard featuring a bunch of yellow tubes hanging delicately from a grid. It's the LACMA.

Before I even turn the card over to see the note, my hands are shaking.

Happy Birthday, Mercy.
    Thank you for giving me some of the most beautiful moments of my life.

                                        Brad

I open the box and find that it contains two sterling silver earrings shaped like little mammoths.

My heart is pounding so hard now I think it might actually be damaging my rib cage. I should probably be wondering how he found me. Here, all the way in Belgium. But . . . but, oh my God, he *wanted* to find me. He went to the effort, and the earrings . . .

Six years, one month, five days. That's how long it's been since I've spoken to this man. Since I've held his hand. Even longer since he took me into those yellow tubes and touched his lips to mine. Six years, one month, and five days ago I laid my head against his chest and told him good-bye.

And now he's given me this gift, letting me know he still thinks of me.

My eyes move from the card to the earrings, the earrings to the card. Carefully, I take off the earrings I put on this morning and replace them with the little mammoth studs.

"Mercy?"

I turn to see Logan standing behind me. "Is everything okay?"

"Yeah," I say quietly. "Yeah, of course it is. Just a gift from an old friend." I discreetly slip the card into my purse before crossing to him, kissing him on his cheek as I take one of the glasses. "Thank you for this. And for coming to the concert last night and for taking me to this match and for the night we're going to have. It means so much to me . . . you know that, right? You know how much this means to me?"

"It means a lot to me, too, to celebrate your twenty-ninth birthday with you." He studies me for a moment and gestures toward my ears. "New earrings?"

"A gift."

"Mammoths," he says thoughtfully. He walks over to the coffee table, where I left the earrings I had been wearing earlier. "Different from these," he notes as he holds up the two dangling white tear-shaped earrings I had been wearing earlier.

It's only in that moment that I remember that Logan had bought me those, from a street vendor after an overly indulgent lunch. My stomach knots as the realization hits me. "Logan, I . . . I was just trying these on, that's all."

"No, it is good," he says, waving away my concern. "The new ones, they are whimsical, unique, they suit you," he says, his eyes still on the earrings in his hand. "These are nice, just not quite as exciting."

"They're just earrings, Logan."

He doesn't say anything for a moment, and then he looks up. He's wearing his uniform of dark jeans and a T-shirt, his blazer draped over the back of his chair in the kitchen. He's a poster boy for casual sophistication. But he seems to have gotten something on his jeans while doing the dishes. A small stain that I know he won't be able to overlook. "This is your day," he finally says. "And it will be wonderful, but I think I must change clothes before we begin."

"Right," I say, relieved. I start to take off the earrings, but he stops me before I can.

"No, keep them on," he requests. "As I said, they suit you." And now it's his turn to give me a kiss before he slips past me, heading into the bedroom where he can change.

Everything is about to change.

❀

SETTLING MYSELF INTO the guest room Logan and I share as a home office, I spend the bulk of the next day on Google. It's been almost two years since the last time I did a search for Brad. I had found virtually nothing, and then . . . well, Logan had walked in, and while he never figured out what I was searching for, the guilt combined with the futility of the exercise had made me resolve not to try again.

But now I can't help myself. I mean, how can I *not* search for him after that letter? Dear God, what if he's in Europe?

But when I figure out the coordinates, it becomes clear that he's in San Francisco, or maybe Daly City? Marin? He's near San Francisco. I sit back in my chair as I absorb this, then glance up at the wall where Logan has hung his photo of the Golden Gate Bridge. My fingers automatically lift to my earlobes and touch the silver studs. I haven't taken them off.

Turning back to the computer, I refocus on the digital map in front of me. "I have a life here," I explain to my Mac. "A real life. I have friends and a boyfriend and a job and a band that's beginning to really take off. My life's in Brussels now."

Not surprisingly, my Mac doesn't answer. I start searching again, this time plugging *"Brad Witmer"* into the search. That's when I realize, Brad has a life, too. He's a lawyer. That alone is enough to bring a big smile to my face. He did it! He's a lawyer! The Secret Service better be ready, 'cause he'll be strutting into that Oval Office in no time.

And here, right here, is the name of the law firm he works for. I quickly go to the firm's website and immediately click on the tab that says Attorneys. There's his name, and it's connected to a link. If I press the link there will be a profile.

There may be a picture.

My fingers hover over the mouse. Am I ready for this? For three and a half years, the only images I've had of him have been in my head. But if I click this, that changes.

I probably shouldn't; I'm only asking for trouble. Big, big trouble. But then, *come on*! Of *course* I click the link.

And then . . . oh wow. My stomach does a little flip-flop. The man in the picture is clearly recognizable as the man I remember. Deep-set eyes, strong jaw, chiseled features. Short, well-groomed brown hair. But there are distinctions between the picture and my memory. The faint lines in his forehead, the very beginnings of crow's-feet around his eyes. Even in his suit and tie he looks a little more rugged than he did in his twenties. A little more worldly. I swear, men don't really start hitting it until they're thirty. That's when the *real* hotness starts to set in.

My eyes go down to the text of his profile. It lists his degrees at both Stanford and UCLA (yay!). He's part of a few professional associations, his areas of practice are . . . Oh, this is good. His specialty is sexual harassment and discrimination suits, and apparently he's had some success bringing civil suits against sex offenders.

In other words, he's still saving women in distress. Ha! Except of course these are women who *want* a little saving. That's gotta make things easier.

The last lines of his profile are about his hobbies. According to this, he enjoys reading, rowing (really?), going to museums, and spending time with family and friends.

Spending time with family and friends. What family are we talking about here? His daughter? His mom? Does he have a wife? A married man sending a girl mammoth earrings . . . that's some messed-up shit. The SOB better *not* be married.

But then, it's probably messed-up to spend this much time Googling a man if you're living with another man. *Googling*—even the word sounds vaguely perverse. *What were you doing all day, sweetie? Oh, I was just Googling my ex.*

Can I even call him my ex? We only officially went out for, like, three weeks. We knew each other for just over half a year. And yet . . . how is it possible that a love that built up over mere months and ended years ago can still be stronger than a love that has built up over years and continues to be nurtured today? I will never understand time.

But the physics of time isn't really important here, is it? It's the physics of love that matters. If numbers are the language of the universe, then what are the numbers that will explain this undying feeling I have for Brad? Like that tar that bubbles up through the earth at La Brea, it's irrepressible.

But I have a life here in Brussels. And he has a life in San Francisco.

I let the cursor hover over the ominous little X that will close the tab. "Press it," I whisper to myself when my finger refuses to move. "Press it, press it, press it!"

"Mercy!" sings Logan as I hear the front door open and slam closed.

My previously rebellious finger immediately leaps into action and clicks the tab closed, and I slam the computer shut. "*Je suis ici, chéri!*" I call out.

A moment later he's at the door. I get up and give him a warm hug and quick kiss, but then withdraw before he can pull me in for something more passionate. "I've been home all day, wasting time online," I say in French. "So glad you're here to finally get me away from it."

"Home," he repeats. His gaze moves from me to the closed computer. He's dressed in black jeans, a black T-shirt, and a black tweed blazer. His hair is as lovably mussed as ever. But there's something . . . severe about his countenance today. "Home," he says again, "it can be many different things, yes? Most of us have more than one."

"Oh?" I shift uncomfortably in my chair. "How's that?"

"Okay, there is this," he says, gesturing to our flat as a whole. "There is the home our parents raised us in and cared for us in . . . oh, I did not mean . . ." His voice fades off and he makes an apologetic gesture as the possible insensitivity of that statement dawns on him. These days other people seem more sensitive about my childhood than I am.

"It's okay," I rush to reassure him. "For most people, where they grew up is home. I'm an exception. What else is home?"

He sighs and leans against the frame of the door, crossing his legs at the ankle and his arms across his chest. "It is as you Americans always say, no?" he asks as he locks me in his gaze. "Home is where the heart is."

My lips part slightly as I let that sink in, for the first time seeing the full implication of the cliché. His tone, the words, it all hovers between a question and an accusation. How much has he figured out? I have not let the postcard out of my sight since it arrived, so I know Logan hasn't stumbled upon it. Of course the mammoth earrings . . . but really, they're just earrings.

Sure, a little voice in my head says, *and Lady Liberty is just a statue, a statue that represents hopes and dreams and, well,* everything. I swallow hard and look at my hands. "You have my heart," I mumble. "You know that."

He doesn't answer right away, and the silence is so loaded I'm surprised neither of us is completely flattened by it.

"Well," he finally says with a sad little smile playing on his lips, "at least I know there is a little room in it for me." He steps forward and musses my hair. "Shall we go out to dinner tonight?"

IT GOES ON like that for about a week. A week of my reading and rereading Brad's card, his professional profile, gazing at his picture. A week of giving myself virtual smacks upside the head and trying to force myself to see the futility of it all. Forcing myself to recall all the truly great times I've had with Logan. How much I love the little dimples that appear when he smiles. There is absolutely nothing wrong with Logan, and so much that is very right.

Last night we made love. Sex with Logan is always fun. He's playful, apt to use pillow fights and spirited wrestling matches as foreplay, which is surprisingly effective. And yet last night, as he held me in his arms, I felt *guilty* about it. It's ridiculous. This is the man I live with . . . but . . . when he touched me, I didn't see him. I saw Brad. I imagined *Brad*. It's not the first time that's happened, but this time the image was more vivid, and the line between fantasy and reality is dissipating at an alarming rate, making my imaginings far from innocent.

I try to compensate for my mental infidelity by putting the earrings away, tucking them deep inside my jewelry drawer . . . which only means that my jewelry drawer is now a mess because I'm constantly digging through all the stuff in the front so I can gaze at the earrings in the back. And I'm positively bending over backward for Logan these days. I've been making his favorite meals every night and have them waiting for him when he gets home, even on the nights when I have a gig. I do his laundry, iron his clothes (and I *hate* ironing), and I'm as attentive as I can manage . . . which is not as attentive as I should be because, well, I'm distracted. There's simply no way around that.

And then one day I take my BlackBerry to a café and write an e-mail to Brad. I know what I'm doing is wrong. But I do it anyway. I only include two words of text:

Thank you.

Pressing send is absolutely terrifying. I sit there sipping my coffee, thinking, wondering, hoping, fearing . . . and fifteen minutes later I get a response:

You're welcome.

**How are you? I've read about Tar (love the name) and
seen some performances on YouTube. You continue to be
amazing.**

Are you well?

I stare at the words, at the automated signature. His name, his law firm, his contact info, everything that was on the website, but now it's in a private e-mail . . . to me.

I have to still my shaking hands before I e-mail back.

**Thank you, and yes, I'm doing well. It looks like you are as
well, Mr. Lawyer. Is that your full-time gig, or are you still
raking it in at poker? And what about the drums? Do you still
play? Do you write songs?**

This time it only takes a minute for him to respond:

**Yes, I'm a lawyer, and I'm one of the few who actually enjoys
my work. I have a weekly poker night with some friends, but
that's it. As for the drums, well, I try to keep in practice. Every
once in a while a performer here will need a drummer for a
one-time gig and sometimes I'll do that. But it's rare. I have
written a handful of songs, all of them with you in mind, but to
be honest, they're not as good as the ones you've been playing.**

I miss you. Would love to get together to catch up.

I stare at the words. Is he kidding? He's been writing songs for me? I look up as if maybe the woman serving coffee behind the counter can explain what's happening here. But no one seems to notice me. I look back down at my phone and type:

I miss you, too, but we can't. I'm in Belgium.

I press send and then start refreshing like crazy. And in no time at all, there's a reply:

I know that, it's where I sent your gift ;-). Maybe it's time for me to take a European vacation?

He'd come to Belgium, for *me*? At the next table two girls are laughing; at another a couple appears to be quietly arguing. And I'm just sitting here silently freaking out. It's been *so long* and I have a life here, and he has a life there. This just can't work. I e-mail back:

I can't see you. I'm sorry.

God, how can I be so cold? But to respond any other way . . . I mean, I'm living with another man! I press send and then start jabbing my finger against the little circular arrow again. And then the reply comes:

Can I at least call you?

Don't do this, Mercy. Just don't. I prepare my fingers to say no.

Yes.

And I give him my number. *Why did I do that?* What the fuck am I thinking? I can't—

My phone rings, and swear to God, I nearly pass out. I'm seriously shaking now. It's a minor miracle that I'm even able to pick up. But I do and I bring the phone to my ear without saying a word.

"Mercy?"

Oh that baritone! Everything inside me just *melts*. I didn't even know I was missing him this much! It's like all these emotions that I had practically forgotten about were just hanging out, crouched in a corner somewhere deep inside me, and now they just pounce, completely flooring me. "Yes," I say weakly, "it's me."

A long pause, and then a large shaky exhale on his side of the line. "I didn't think you'd contact me. I hoped, but . . ." His voice trails off and then he adds, "How are you?"

"I'm . . . I'm good," I manage. "I'm . . . well, I've been singing a lot."

"Yeah," he says softly, "I know."

I glance around at the few other people here who are completely preoccupied with their laptops and whatnot. "So, you saw some things online?"

He laughs ruefully. "I have spent hours on Google image search. You . . . you look great, Mercy. You look . . . beautiful. More beautiful than you even did before."

"Brad—"

"You're going to tell me that I shouldn't be calling you," he says, cutting me off.

"Yes," I agree. "I'm going to tell you that."

"All right," he breathes. "I just wanted to wish you a happy birthday. I have been reading up, and I'm just so happy for you."

"Thank you," I say, trying to sound cool, and completely failing.

"Okay, well then I'll—"

"Wait!" I say, stopping him. A few of the other patrons look up, startled by the urgency in my voice. I sink a little lower in my chair. "Tell me," I say, softer this time, "how's June?"

"She's wonderful." I can hear the smile in his voice. "She's already getting excited about middle school next year."

"*Middle school?*" I exclaim. "How the hell did she get old enough to be in middle school next year?"

Brad chuckles. "Beats me. I tell you, this aging business is pretty disconcerting."

I laugh, run my finger around the edge of my cup. "I guess we all have to do it. Is she happy? Does she like school?"

"Yes and yes," he replies.

Okay, so she's already way ahead of where I was at her age. "Is . . . is she still close with her mom?" Do I want to hear the answer to this?

There's a long pause on the other end of the line, and then Brad says, "Nalla isn't really in the picture anymore. She has a job in Massachusetts, but . . . she's just not cut out to be a mom."

"Oh?" I say, trying to sound surprised.

Again Brad chuckles. "It's okay, you can say I told you so. For well over a year I tried to find a way to save Nalla from herself, just as you predicted . . . And then at a certain point I couldn't ignore your words of wisdom anymore, not when I was seeing so much evidence that you were right. I finally wised up."

I don't say anything. I really shouldn't even be on this call.

"The whole white knight thing, it blinded me to a lot. I made some huge mistakes and, I'm just lucky I figured it out before I ended up doing serious damage to my daughter. Mercy, I don't think I would have figured it out if you hadn't said the things that you said. When I finally stopped . . . well, I suppose the right word is enabling. When I stopped enabling Nalla, it was because I couldn't stop thinking about your warnings. You saved me. Again."

"Brad . . . I . . ." I take a moment to swallow those emotions that are threatening to overflow. ". . . I really have to go."

"Okay," he says quietly. "I just wanted to say that and . . . to say happy birthday. It really is wonderful to see you doing so well. You really are doing well, right?"

"Yeah, I actually got myself together," I say with a little laugh. "I don't even drink anymore. I don't drink in *Belgium*, a place where drinking the local beer is a point of national pride. And I . . . I like myself. I usually like myself a lot, actually," I say with another laugh. "I'm okay."

"I . . . I can't tell you how much it means to me to hear you say that. You deserve so much. Before, I don't think you ever realized how truly extraordinary you are."

"Like no one you've ever met," I say softly, remembering his oft-repeated phrase.

"Yeah," he agrees. "Like no one I've ever met."

This is going to kill me. "I—I really have to go," I say for the umpteenth time. "It was so good to talk to you, Brad. I'm, I'm just so happy to hear things are going well."

"Ditto, Mercy."

"Okay, okay, um." I squeeze my eyes closed. "Okay, good-bye Brad. Take care of yourself."

"Good-bye, Mercy."

I hang up quickly before he can add anything else. The café is still buzzing around me, and for a moment I think I'm going to cry . . . but then my BlackBerry rings again.

"Hello?" I squeak.

"Listen," Brad says quickly, "I promise this will be the last call. I'm not going to force this, not if you're really happy with the life you have there with . . . with him. But you contacted me and now I'm talking to you—I'm *finally* talking to you—and I have to use this opportunity to tell you something."

The other patrons are drinking espresso, nibbling on pastries, hanging out, laughing, debating; it's all so very normal, and yet here I am in the middle of it having the most extraordinary moment of my life. "What do you need to tell me?" I ask.

"I'm still in love with you. More than that, you're the love of my life."

"Brad," I whisper. I lean forward and put my forehead against the table in front of me. *Now* I can sense other patrons looking over here, but it's okay, they'll just chalk it up to another American eccentricity. "It's been six years."

"Exactly," he agrees. "Six years since I first fell in love with you, and so now I get it. I get the purity and the permanence of the love I have for you. This isn't about infatuation or lust. It isn't just a lingering crush from my younger days."

So I *am* crying now. I don't know what to say, what to do!

"Do you think about me, Mercy?"

Don't answer, don't answer . . . "Yes."

"I think about you every day and I dream about you almost every night. You've been haunting me for six damn years and now I have you on the phone and I—I have to at least tell you. You have to *know* that." He pauses and then adds, "Do you remember that night when we had dinner, you, me, and June? And I jumped up and rattled off that Buzz Lightyear line?"

"To infinity and beyond," I say meekly.

"Yes, to infinity and beyond." Once again I can hear the smile. "And you stood up and you wrapped your arms around my neck and you whispered, *I love you.*"

I close my eyes. "Yes, I remember that."

"What those words did to me, the sincerity of them . . ." Brad pauses, then adds, "I don't know how you feel about me now, but I know you loved me once."

"Yes," I say. *I still do.* "It was a great evening until—"

"Until I let Nalla screw it up. I know, and I want to say this again, you were right about her. And you were right about how I used to try to save everyone regardless of whether or not they wanted saving. And . . . and you were right to leave. I know that. I see what you've done with your life and I . . . I know you're in a good place now. I can see it in your smile. God, the photos of you . . . I just can't stop looking at them! And I know you're okay and I know you needed space to *become* okay. And I know I needed to get my shit together, too."

"Well, not as much as I did," I say with a little laugh, "but yeah, you kinda did."

"I know," he says warmly. "My mistake is that . . . I gave you *too much* time. I know now is probably too late. I know that . . . six years, it's ridiculous. But I want you to know that all that time . . . it didn't change things for me. I want you to know that, Mercy."

"Why?" I sob, almost pleading. "*Why* do you want me to know that?"

"Because I can't handle keeping it to myself anymore," he says simply. "I can't handle the burden of my silence, not now that I'm talking to you. I'm selfish that way. But you know that."

"Oh my God," I say, laughing, "you and your declarations of self-ishness. You are the least selfish person I've ever met in my life. You're unselfish to a fault."

"I'm selfish in that I don't want to give up on you, even if you're happy with the life you have with this other man," he says solemnly. "I'm selfish because if I knew there was a way for me to just win you away from him, I'd do it, damn the consequences. But I don't know if there's a way. *You* know. And . . . if you're happy with him, Mercy, then . . . I'll *really* try to be happy for you. I'll try hard. But I'm not going to stop loving you or wanting you. That's simply not something I'm capable of."

The tears are streaming down my face. The other patrons are now looking legitimately alarmed. "I gotta go."

"I love you, Mercy."

Don't say it, don't say it, don't say it . . . "I love you, too."

And I hang up.

CHAPTER 40

❀

W HEN LOGAN GETS home, I have lamb loin chops with
rosemary warm and ready to serve. I'm trying to shake off
the afternoon, although . . . *how do I do that?*

And poor Logan, he's spent the day coaxing bigwigs to invest in
his documentary. He looks exhausted and a little lost. I rush to take
his coat and give him a gentle kiss before leading him into the dining room. I've used about a bottle of Visine to get the red out from
all my crying. "Long day?" I ask in French with the most upbeat
tone I can manage.

"Complicated," he replies with a sigh. "A complicated and confusing day." His head turns toward the kitchen. "You do not have to
make dinner every night. But . . . it does smell fantastic."

"I spent years, *years* at Trader Joe's learning all these recipes. The
very least you can do is let me put them into practice," I tease as I
go into the kitchen to arrange the food pleasingly on the plates. I
take the opportunity to do a few deep-breathing exercises. A deep
breath, and then another, and then I plaster on a smile, grab our
dinner plates, managing to also carry a beer for him and a Perrier
for me, and reenter the dining room. "So tell me," I say as I take my
seat and give him his meal, "what made it so crazy?"

He hesitates, tapping his fork against the lamb chop as if to test
the solidity of it. "I think I have an investor. A big one."

I put down my Perrier before I can even get it to my mouth.
"How big?"

He's still staring down at his plate, contemplating. When he finally answers he says, "He will invest three million."

"Logan!" I squeal and start to jump up from my chair ready to throw my arms around him in celebration. But he stops me with a look.

"He wants me to expand the project," he continues. "He wants to take it beyond Belgium. He thinks it would be better if I look at how Belgium is handling its influx of immigrants compared to how Germany is handling it and the UK, France, or Sweden. It will be a much bigger project."

"Is . . . that something you want to do?" I ask warily as I settle back into my seat.

"It's not a bad idea," he muses. "Follow a few different immigrant families, look at their experiences in their respective new home countries. Look at the issues. Maybe it is not a single documentary after all. Maybe it is a BBC miniseries or, I don't know, something for France Télévisions. It is something to think of . . ." His voice trails off and he takes a long sip of his beer, his food still untouched. "We should switch to your language," he says, switching to English.

"Okay." This is not a good sign.

"There would be a lot of travel," he continues. "We would be apart much more."

"Logan, if this is an opportunity you want, you have to take it. I—"

"We will not survive it," he says simply. "If we spend more time apart than we do now, what we have together will end. Our . . ." He takes a moment as he searches for the right English word. "Our bond is . . . fraying. I am using the right words, yes?"

I press my fingertips into the solid wood of the table. "Yes," I whisper. "Those are the right words."

"Where is your home, Mercy?" he asks, looking up at me, and for the first time I see his eyes are red, too. "Where does your heart live? Not here, not since your birthday. Is it still with him? The one who showed you magic at a tar pit? The one who gave you the earrings?"

I look away, my lips pressed tightly together. "Logan," I eventually say, "what you and I have . . . it's beautiful."

"It is," he agrees in a whisper.

"It's the healthiest relationship I've ever been in," I continue, talking a little faster now. "I don't want to just walk away from that!"

"But you are thinking of walking away," he says quietly. "No?"

I shake my head even though both of us know the gesture is a lie. "I learn from you!" I say desperately. "I've learned what it is to be supportive without . . . oh, I don't know . . . without needing to be enabling."

"Enabling," he repeats, clearly not grasping my meaning.

"You don't take drugs," I say plainly with a little smile. "You're not self-destructive or self-sacrificing to a fault. With you I've learned how I can be part of a two and still be a one. Does that make sense?"

"Yes." He puts his beer down without letting it out of his hand.

"What we have . . . it's *good*!" I choke out, my voice finally breaking. "And you're . . . you're good to me and I . . . I want so badly to be good to *you*." I abruptly get to my feet and turn toward the wall as I wrap my arms around myself. "I'm so sorry. God I'm such a bitch. I'm so, *so* sorry."

After a moment I hear him get up from his seat, and then he places a hand on each of my arms. "So you are honest," he says softly. "Or as honest as anyone can ever be with a lover." But then he releases me, steps back. "But I wish you would answer my question. Because . . ." He grows silent for a moment before saying, "Because I believe I have lost your heart. Even if I stay, you will leave."

I close my eyes. I've walked away from a lot of things before, but never from something this comfortable. Logan isn't just my lover. He's my friend.

And as a friend he deserves to know the truth. I take a deep, shaky breath and force myself to face him. "You mean so much to me. I love what we have, but . . ." I look away. I can't say this.

His smile quivers slightly as he continues to hold my gaze. "But even though I used to be right for you, that is not true anymore, is it?"

The end of that last sentence was not just a reflection of his native tongue. I hear the note of hope that lingers around the question mark. Faint, vulnerable hope. He wants me to tell him he's wrong. He wants me to tell him we're still meant to be together.

And I can't do it.

"No," I whisper, "it isn't. And I . . . I want to change that. Maybe I can try to change that."

"Ah," he says with a heavy sigh, and I can see now that he's swallowing tears. Again that horrible silence as he averts his eyes, takes a small step back. I can't breathe in this silence. I can't move. "It won't work," he says quietly. "You can't change it. I wish to God you could, but no." He squeezes his eyes closed for a moment. "It won't work."

"We're going to end it? Just like that?" I ask through tears. "Years thrown away because I had one conversation with a man I haven't been with in over half a decade?"

"You spoke to him?" he asks dully, and I look away. "You *are* honest," he says, almost more to himself than to me. Then he looks up with a weak attempt at a smile. "I have known this was coming. I hoped it would not, but . . ." He scratches at his cheek, hiding a tear. "I knew. Maybe some flowers are only meant to last a season." He steps forward, pulls me to him again, and gives me a long, lingering kiss. "Good-bye, Mercy Raye."

It's our last kiss.

Some flowers are only meant to last a season.

❀

CHAPTER 41

WITHIN DAYS I'VE moved my stuff into my girlfriend's garage on the other side of Brussels. But I don't call Brad. I have to give myself time to grieve this most recent loss. I may never have felt as strongly about Logan as I've felt about Brad, but . . . that doesn't mean that he wasn't important to me. And now I have another decision to make. I need to decide if I'm going to stay in Belgium, where I've begun to build a career for myself, or if I'm going to leave my band, my new home, and . . . and what? Go back to where I was six years ago?

And so I call that producer again. He still wants to work with me. He is even willing to pay for a flight to LA. It's a big deal. When I talk to my band, most of them are pissed that I'm even considering it . . . everyone except for Rubén, my Spanish guitarist. He graciously takes me aside after everyone is done chewing me out.

"Is it just the producer?" he asks.

I stare sullenly at the ground in lieu of answering.

"I know you moved out of Logan's . . ." he begins.

"I'm in love," I snap, my nerves now totally fried. "I'm in love with a man in San Francisco. And I don't know if we have a snowball's chance in hell. It's been over half a decade since I've seen the guy, but I love him. So, you know, there it is." I wipe angrily at a tear. "I don't want to disappoint everyone—"

"Fuck everyone," he says. "If you are in love you have to go."

"You and your Latin-lover sensibilities," I grumble, but I do it with a smile. "Everyone here is right. Things are going well. Giving it all up just when we're beginning to build a real name for ourselves . . ."

"*You* write the songs!" Rubén points out. "You lead us. When they write about us, they only write about you. And there's a reason why everyone wants a Latin lover," he says. "It's not just that we are the best in bed, it's that we know about the ways of the heart. You love him, you go."

I look up into his eyes. "Really?" I ask. "The *best*?"

He smirks and puts his hand on my shoulder. "Sadly, you'll never know. You're in love with an American."

THE NEXT DAY I quit the band, and a week later I'm flying off to Los Angeles to meet with the producer.

And I *still* haven't called Brad. The truth is, I'm scared. Not scared in the same way I was when I was a twenty-two-year-old girl. I don't worry that I'm going to hurt myself if I end up disappointed. But that doesn't mean this fear is easily dismissed. I don't care how stable you think you are, when the heart is involved, the fear of rejection is always overwhelming and intense. But perhaps being distracted by matters of the heart is exactly what I need to keep myself from being too freaked out about this matter of my career. I mean, what am I thinking? I was getting good-paying gigs, and *now* I decide to start from scratch again? Really?

But . . . but my heart isn't in Belgium. And Logan's right, I can't change that.

And when I do meet with the producer, well, we just gel. It's the first time in forever that I've talked to someone who understands my style, but has suggestions that can improve my work without taking me in a totally different direction. I've never been a solo act before. But . . . maybe at age twenty-nine I need to be trying new things. If I'm going to change things, maybe I change *everything*.

As soon as I get back to the hotel I call Rubén and tell him all about it. "This is fantastic!" he exclaims. "And what about your American man, have you called him?"

"No," I admit softly. "It's been six years and I've . . . God, I've already given up so much. What if I meet him and it doesn't work? What if he sees me and realizes he doesn't want me after all? What if—"

"Mercy?"

"Yes?"

"Shut up," he says simply. "Stop thinking, stop letting your fear guide you. Find courage in your love and get your butt to San Francisco."

"Is that how the Latin lovers do it?" I ask.

"Yes," he says definitively. "And remember, we are the *best*. Go find him. Now."

"Now?"

"*Now!*"

And so I postpone my flight back to Belgium, rent a car, and get my butt up to San Francisco.

BY THE TIME I make it to The City by the Bay it's almost four o'clock. Hopefully that's a good thing. I drive straight to the financial district and park my car in a ridiculously expensive parking lot on the outskirts of Jackson Square. I walk past the beautiful brick buildings that miraculously have survived both the 1906 and 1989 earthquakes that terrorized so much of this city. I peer up at the TransAmerica pyramid pointing audaciously at the sky, demanding acknowledgment and respect. But it's Brad's office building that interests me. It's a skyscraper, obviously not as grand as the pyramid or as tall as the Bank of America Tower, but still impressive. People in suits brush past me, and beneath my feet the sidewalk is suspiciously clean. Almost Brussels-clean.

It's cool but not cold. The sun shines warmer on these industrial types than it does on the artists who tend to live closer to the ocean. And here I am, across the street from it, standing around like an idiot, chewing on my thumb as I try to figure out what to do. Do I go in? Ask to see him? Should I wait here and hope this is the exit he takes? What if he isn't in the office today? What if I've gotten this all wrong?

I start pacing. I'm wearing a lightly frayed pink gingham wool trench and dark jeans tucked into brown heeled ankle boots. My hair is touched with pink again, maybe even more pink than it was when I was twenty-two, but the highlights aren't streaks, they're underneath, and a softer shade that sort of melts into my light blond hair. I currently have it all piled up on top of my head. Will he like the way I look? Do I look different? The morning of my twenty-ninth birthday I had been so excited about my age. I figured I looked just as good as I did in the beginning of my twenties, but was *so* much smarter. But maybe I *don't* look as good as I used to? Or even more likely, what if I don't look as good as I do in Brad's memories? Memories altered by time and lost love? What if he sees me and runs in the opposite direction?

Or . . . oh God, what if Brad needs to feel like he's rescuing a woman in order to be enamored of her? And now that I finally don't need to be rescued, will that change everything? Maybe he started dating someone since our last conversation. He's a gorgeous single lawyer, he's got to have women lined up, right?

And then I just . . . stop. I feel someone looking at me. I *feel* it.

Slowly I pivot and . . . oh my God.

My thoughts are all tangled up in an indecipherable heap. I'm looking at *Brad*. He's right across the crowded street of Montgomery. Cars are passing between us, and yet in the midst of all this, without knowing I'd be here, he's spotted me. And he's standing stock-still. The messenger bag he used to have has been replaced with a briefcase that looks like a messenger bag. He's standing next to a male colleague who is looking at him and then me in utter confusion.

Brad. I mouth the word without making a sound. People are moving in front of me, behind me, and he's just . . . he's there. And then he hands his briefcase to his colleague without even looking at him and starts to walk down the sidewalk. Is he walking away from me? I look to my left and right, unsure what I should do. Oh God, he can't walk away from me, not now after I've broken it off with Logan and I can't even drown my sorrows at a bar. That just can't happen.

But then . . . wait . . . he's going to the crosswalk. He's not walking away from me at all.

I start to walk, then stride, then run to the crosswalk to meet him, and he's increasing his pace right along with me. When we reach the corner, the light turns green as if it was waiting just for us, and I run, not into traffic this time, but to him. *I run to him!*

And then, after pushing past the throngs of workers and their clients and shoppers, we meet, halfway through the crosswalk, and we both just stop, inches from each other. I take in his eyes, the line of his mouth, the broad shoulders that I have never stopped fantasizing about. His eyes move to my hair, my nose, my body . . .

. . . and then we just flip a switch and in an instant we are in each other's arms, right here in the middle of the street with all these people moving this way and that. His lips, *Brad's* lips, are on mine, his hands on the small of my back as he crushes me to him and I wrap my arms around his neck, standing on tiptoe until he simply picks me up, cradling me in his arms, the kiss never really breaking.

I'm vaguely aware of people applauding.

As the light turns red he carries me to his side of the street. This is crazy; I haven't seen or spoken to this man in six fucking years!

It's one of those days when I'm just so happy to be crazy.

He's walking at full stride again, just short of running. His colleague is still standing there, gaping at us, Brad's briefcase in his hand. "Max, this is Mercy," Brad says, his beautiful and so fabulously familiar baritone moving his words along at a rapid, clipped pace. "Briefcase, please," he continues.

Max lifts the briefcase, offering it to Brad as if in a daze. "Nice to meet you, Mer—"

But I never hear him fully pronounce my name, because Brad has already grabbed the briefcase and is rushing me through the lobby of his building. He puts me down only so I can sign in at the security desk, and then he pulls me to a crowded elevator. He holds my hand so tightly it almost hurts as his eyes stay glued to the floor numbers. The damn thing stops on almost every floor. "Jesus, why does my office have to be on the top floor?" he growls.

That's when I start giggling. It just comes out. I'm standing here with pink hair and thrift-shop-chic clothes holding hands with a man wearing a two-thousand-dollar suit and a designer haircut on his way up to his top-floor law office . . . and it's *Brad*!

I peek up at him, the giggles still spilling from my lips, and I see his mouth twitch, which turns my giggles into a laugh. And then he's laughing, and everyone here thinks we're nuts, and he turns to me, once again pulling me to him, placing his laughing lips on mine, and now we're laughing and kissing and crying in a crowded elevator while people awkwardly maneuver around us to get on and off. When we finally get to his floor he pulls me past the receptionist, making his introduction so fast that I don't catch any of it, through a hall filled with people heading out for the day, and then he pulls me into his office. I step into the middle of the room and see he has a view of the city and the expanse of the bay. And when I turn to the walls, I see the poster of the tightrope walker. For a moment my eyes fall on the Twin Towers. We had all thought those would be there forever. Was that an age of innocence? Ignorance? Naïveté? I pull my eyes away. "It's lovely," I say quietly.

"And you're stunning," he says, matching my low tone.

"Are you sure you still know me?" I ask meekly. "Six years, Brad."

"You live in Belgium," he says, putting his briefcase on a chair in the corner before turning back to me. "You're in a band called Tar, which was inspired by your trip to the La Brea Tar Pits with me. You teach pole dancing classes in your limited free time . . .

which, by the way, is one of the tamer jobs you've ever had." I laugh and look down at my feet. "You love Brussels, but miss the surf in LA." I look back up and he nods, taking a step forward. "I've seen the YouTube interview," he confirms. He takes another step. "You've become a big fan of Liège waffles served by street vendors, but try to keep the rest of your diet organic and healthy." He takes another step. "You see magic in ordinary things. You're comfort-able in your own skin. And . . ." He hesitates a moment and then takes another step so that now we're only a foot and a half apart. "You live with another man, the man who filmed that interview." He reaches forward and tilts my head back. "But you don't love him," he says, his voice now hoarse. "Please . . . please tell me you don't love him. Because it's been six years. And I've been with other women, women you've never met and never will. And yet you have ruined every one of those relationships because I simply couldn't stop thinking that not one of those women touched me the way you did. And they all know about you, and I'm pretty sure they all hate you." I start giggling again but don't look away. He smiles, his fingers now caressing the underside of my chin. "Your presence was always there. Six years, Mercy. And it's always been you." He takes a deep breath. "Please . . . please tell me you're not in love with him."

"I'm not in love with him. I've never loved him the way I love you," I whisper. "It's why he and I broke up just a week after I got your let—" But I don't get the rest of the sentence out, because he's kissing me again, and now the passion and joy is at a whole new level. I won't ever let him go. Never, ever, ever! He's my Brad, my walking, talking, rebellious Ken doll. My frat boy with a James Dean complex. My white knight, my love.

He's my love.

And so I unbutton that ridiculously expensive jacket of his and pull it off as he works on my pink gingham coat. And then he's lifting me up in the air again and I'm wrapping my legs around his waist. As he presses me up against the wall, my hair falls free and around my shoulders. I feel his hands going up the fitted heather-gray T-shirt I'm wearing as his lips find my neck. I reach down, making quick work of his tie. And then my fingers are woven into his perfectly groomed hair, messing it up as I try to pull him closer than is even possible, because I don't just want to feel him against me. I want him inside me. I want that now. And when my shirt comes off I make sure the buttons of his are undone, all the way to his waist.

Good God, did he *always* look like this? How does anyone make their body look like this without spending their whole life working out?

And it's *Brad*.

He slowly lets me down to my feet as he runs his fingers through my hair, kissing me again and again, his fingers moving to the back of my bra. And . . . oh, he's crying, and so am I.

When my bra falls away he can see that my nipples are already hard and reaching out to him, calling to him. He bends his knees and kisses them while I run my hands along the length of his shoulders; my head falls back, basking in this feeling. "I love you," I whisper even as my body shudders. "I love you." And he rises and again his lips are on mine. My skin is pressed against his and I can hear his heartbeat even as my own thunders in my ears.

"Don't leave me again," he whispers.

"Never."

He searches my face, sees the truth of it, and then lifts me up *again*, this time placing me on his desk as he gets down on one knee and pulls off each one of my boots and then, unable to contain himself, stands and moves between my legs, pressing me hard against him, his tongue opening my lips, skin to skin, tears mingled with tears.

Oh, this isn't just Brad. This is *everything*.

I start working on the button of his pants and he works on mine. And we're giggling again as we wriggle out of the things that separate us, only slowed down by our inability to stop kissing each other. Now he's wearing nothing but his Calvin Kleins. He hooks his fingers into the waistband of my tiger-print panties and slowly, oh so slowly pulls them off me, letting the silk caress my skin, making me shudder. And when I'm wearing nothing he takes a step back, his eyes caressing me with every bit as much intimacy as his hands had. "Look at you," he says, shaking his head. "Here with the entire city at your back . . . how can anyone be this beautiful?"

"Don't just look," I say quietly with a playful smile. I reach my hand out to him. "Feel."

And again he's moved against me, another kiss, more heartbeats, his breath against my skin, I pull down those boxer briefs . . .

Oh wow, my memory hasn't been exaggerating.

I run my fingers up and down over the length of him. He's looking in my eyes, breathing hard. I lean back, slowly, controlling my movements until I'm propped up on my forearms. "Now," I whisper.

He leans over, an arm on either side of me, his palms pressed against the desk, and then, with a single thrust he's inside me, filling me, and—oh, to be connected to this man again! He moves inside me with force and need, and my head falls back again. I'm looking at the upside-down city, loving the beautiful chaos of it all. And then he's straightening as he lays my back flat against the wood surface of the desk and lifts my hips, keeping our connection, until my back is lifted and it's now only my shoulders and neck on the desk, both my legs over his shoulders. And he rotates his hips, grinding himself into me, touching me differently now, driving me absolutely insane. I'm not just trembling—I'm shaking. He's using his strength to support me, holding me up with no effort at all as he gazes down at me, moves against me, I can't contain myself for much longer . . .

And the orgasm is so strong it tears me apart . . . but in the most wonderful way. I bite down hard on my lower lip. I don't want to alert the whole office to our passion . . . but then, part of me just doesn't care. As long as I'm here, as long as I'm with him.

And then, almost magically, he has me against the wall again.

His legs are bent as he thrusts up into me again and again, and I'm biting his shoulder. I want to taste him, I want to possess him, I want to be possessed. I want *all* of it!

I lower my right leg, touching my foot to the ground as I keep the left wrapped around him and then, as he eases his rhythm, I further lift my left leg, placing the flat of my foot on his shoulder, his hands now firmly supporting my lower back. Wrapping my arms around his neck, I slowly slide my foot over his shoulder so I'm in a vertical split.

He blinks, clearly shocked and impressed.

"It's all the pole dancing," I say.

His smile turns to a grin and he slowly moves inside me, his eyes on mine, his hand keeping me in place. I can see he's barely able to hold back his own explosion now, and when his lips touch mine, it's all I need to be brought to the brink again.

"I love you, Mercy."

And that's when my second orgasm comes as I quickly lower my leg, wrapping it around his waist once more, pulling him as far in as possible as he buries his head in my shoulder to muffle the sound of his cry and I bite down on my lip once more, this time so hard that it bleeds. He lifts his head, pressing his cheek to mine, keeping our connection so I can feel him throbbing inside me, giving me everything, making me feel that love.

"I want this to be forever," he whispers against my skin.

I know it's crazy. We haven't so much as gone out to coffee in six years. I'm going to have to get reacquainted with his daughter. I'm going to have to move back to this country, and even then I'll be at the other end of the state for a while. It's totally insane to agree to forever right now, in this moment.

Sometimes I just love being crazy.

CHAPTER 42

❁

I SUPPOSE IN A normal relationship this is when the challenges would begin. We'd get to know each other, realize that we had grown in different directions, June would have a hard time accepting me, he'd tell me that my pink hair and pole dancing won't go over well at the firm's Christmas party, whatever. But for the most part that's not how it works at all. I *know* Brad and I have grown in different directions, but our differences are complementary. As for June, God, the first time I see her I don't recognize her! Brad reintroduces us at a restaurant, and on her tiptoes she's almost as tall as me. She has her mother's hair, and her almond-shaped eyes and delightful smile have stayed the same.

"Hi, Mercy," she says, offering me her hand in a formal handshake.

And I stand there, trying not to gawk. "Hi, June, I guess you probably don't remember me," I say.

"Of course I remember you!" She laughs. "I remember your hair."

I laugh, too, and then restrain myself from hugging her. She leans forward and in a soft voice asks, "Are you really in a rock band?"

And right then and there I know we're going to be just fine. Although if I'm going to be completely honest, as the weeks and months go on, we do have some touch-and-go moments. Having her mother disappear on her, well, it was hard, and now she's wary of the possibility that I might disappear the way Nalla did. But we make progress, and thanks to Brad, she actually remembers quite a bit about me and our brief time together. Apparently he's talked about me over the years . . . a lot.

As for what his firm will think of his dating a rocking, pink-haired pole dancer, it never really becomes a problem. Everyone he works with is actually pretty cool.

And every once in a while Brad and I jam together, him on his drums, me on the mic. He's not as good as he used to be, a little out of practice and all. But even so, he's still pretty great, probably the best drumming lawyer around.

Of course, I'm living in LA for the first six months of the relationship while I record the album. Then I'm playing in as many of LA's hot spots as possible, getting my name out there before the release. In a way, that just adds to the excitement of everything. When your boyfriend meets you for lunch, that's cool. But when your boyfriend takes an hour-long commuter flight just to have lunch with you and you end up sneaking into the restaurant's bathroom for a quickie before he has to fly back . . . that's hot.

Toward the end of my stint in LA I manage to book a San Francisco gig on a Saturday night and fly up on Friday to spend the whole weekend with Brad and June. On Saturday afternoon the two of us hike through Land's End, holding hands and looking at the pure awesomeness that is the San Francisco Bay. The hike treats us to views of the boats sailing under the Golden Gate Bridge and the sloping lines of the hills as they rise from the choppy waters of the bay. Brad spends the first ten minutes of the hike trying to talk me out of getting a nose ring, but by the time we're out of sight of the golf course we've slipped into an easy silence.

We eventually stop to watch the waves crash into the ragged rocks that pepper the coastline, feeling the wind in our faces, holding hands, and just . . . breathing. "It's incredible, isn't it?" I ask, breaking the silence.

"The view?" he asks.

"No," I say, tossing my hair behind my shoulders and pulling my camouflage jacket around me a little tighter. "I mean us. Did you ever really believe we'd get back together, after all that time?"

"I didn't believe it," Brad says quietly, wrapping his arm around my waist. "I *knew* it."

"How?" I ask, peering up at him, studying the way the light plays in his eyes.

"Physics," he says simply before turning me to him so we're now facing each other. "When I met you all those years ago, I felt a force, something invisible that was just pulling me to you. And now I know what that force is: *gravity*. We are each other's gravity. We will always fall back together. So you see, it's simple physics."

"Good God, are you a lawyer or a poet?"

He puts his forehead against mine. "I'm a man in love."

I giggle and wrap my hands around his neck. "We're gross. Like, sappy cliché gross."

"You have a problem with that?" he asks.

"None whatsoever." I turn in his arms so my back is pressed into his chest, both of us now looking at the view again. "Can I tell you something?" I ask.

"Anything," he assures me.

I hesitate a moment before blurting the words out. "I'm scared."

He shifts his upper body to the side so he can see my profile. "Of what?"

"I was a mess when you first got to know me. A total mess. And you didn't see me heal. I wouldn't let you. I pushed you away and went through this whole process on my own. Now we've had this whirlwind romance while living almost four hundred miles apart, and if I move here . . . if I move in with you the way you want me to . . . that's when you'll really get to see who I am today. To know someone, really know them . . . you can't do that while rocking out at their concert in an LA club or dining out at some new restaurant. To know someone you have to go grocery shopping with them. You have to see how they handle it when their computer freezes right before they need to send out an important e-mail, or their car breaks down on a day they have a bunch of plans. You haven't seen those things. And what if, when you do, you decide that I'm not the person you or June need me to be? Because Brad?" I twist my head a bit so I can see him. "I can't be anyone other than who I am. If I could, I'd be my father's golden child, not Kasie."

Brad studies me for a moment, then looks out at the sea, his arms tightening around me. "I once told you that you were the most messed-up and the most together woman I've ever met," he says. "Do you remember that?"

I give a small nod as I watch a pelican dive into the water.

"I meant that. You walked away from me because you knew that wasn't our time. You knew that you had a process to go through and you gave yourself room to go through it. I'm not sure if you're aware of this, but people don't *do* that."

"I'm not sure I'm following," I say slowly.

"When people are going through hell, especially when that hell involves emotional issues and a degree of self-destruction, they don't usually have the clarity to see what they need. They only see what they want. They want comfort, they want to feel better, they want someone else to shoulder some of their burdens. But you, you saw what you needed, which was to carry your own burden and find a way to whittle it down to something manageable. You did this while you were drinking like a fish, faking orgasms for a 900-number, and dealing with the occasional urge to run into traffic."

I shrug, my shoulders moving up and down against the hardness of his pecs. "Maybe I just really absorbed the life lessons of that Rolling Stones song. You can't always get what you want, but—"

"Okay." Brad laughs, cutting me off. "Trust me when I tell you that you have always been much more together than Keith Richards. No one is like you, Mercy. And I know you're together because you wouldn't be here if you weren't. You wouldn't have come back to me. You have always been stronger than me in that regard."

"Stronger than *you*?" I ask, incredulous.

"You were right about my white knight complex, just like you were right about Nalla," he says. "And like I said, I'm not unselfish. I would have stayed with you even if it wasn't good for you and . . ." He pauses and then takes a deep breath; I think I feel a slight tremor in his hands. "I would have stayed with you even if it wasn't good for my own daughter. I wouldn't have been able to see it."

"Oh, Brad, you don't know that."

"Yes, I do. I even let Nalla mess with her head, and I never felt half as strongly about her as I do you."

"That's totally different," I counter. "She's her mother."

"She's not really," Brad argues. "Not in the ways that count. And I couldn't see that because I wanted June to have a mom, and to be honest, I wanted help. I wanted to share the load with someone other than my own mother. And I was arrogant enough to think that I could *fix* Nalla. You are the first person who basically told me that my urge to fix people isn't healthy. It took me a while to get what you were saying, but now that I do, I'm so grateful that you said it."

I'm quiet for a moment as I let that sink in. "Brad?"

"Yes?" he says as he places a kiss on the top of my head.

I smile and put my hands over his. "Do you think you and I are fated to be together?"

"No," he says simply.

"*No?*" I crack up and then he laughs a little, too. "Then what the fuck is this?"

"Destiny," he replies. "Fate is out of our control. Destiny is something you can work toward. *We worked toward this.* We've controlled our own destiny."

"Brad?" I say again.

"Yes, Mercy?"

"Will you feel me up?"

He laughs, and this time the laugh is rich and full. I love the way it rumbles in his chest, vibrating against me. One of his hands moves up, under my jacket, under my shirt, over the thin fabric of my bra, where he toys with me until my nipples are hard and rough against his palm. I reach up, putting my arms around his neck, arching my back, pressing my butt up against his groin as I feel his desire growing for me. I close my eyes and give in to the sensations. The clean air, the seduction, the love . . .

This is what it's supposed to feel like to breathe.

CHAPTER 43

✿

Six years later

BRAD GAVE ME a ring, and it might just be the coolest ring ever. A cluster of diamonds cut and set to look like a blooming flower. And I do mean *blooming*: the little leaves wind up the side to where the flower is placed in its white gold setting as if opening up to the world for the first time. It's an engagement ring. I'm engaged to Brad Witmer . . .

We've been engaged for four and a half years.

That's my fault. I'm not really in a hurry. I don't care about a piece of paper. Not when I have Brad. But he definitely wants to get married. So we will.

Soon.

Pretty soon.

Eventually.

Honestly, it's not that big a deal. It's just that if we're going to have an actual ceremony, I want to do it right, and as pathetic as it is, I'm not sure what "right" is for us. But what I do know is we're both swamped. For one thing, we're getting June ready for the college application process. *College.* She's putting together a portfolio so she can get into the CalArts character animation program. She's seven-friggin'-teen, and in a year she'll be leaving us! I cried on her birthday. I made her a big round ice cream cake and then I cried all over it. Fortunately she just laughed and gave me a hug, told me she loved me, and assured me that she likes a little salt on her frosting.

She said she loves me. And I love her, too. I know she's not mine, but there are days when that's easy to forget. She calls me M, which initially brought back bittersweet memories of Traci. Traci with her wild party-girl ways, her unconditional acceptance of me, and her well-meaning but misguided advice. I really did care about her.

Traci died of an overdose while I was in Belgium. She's buried at Forest Lawn. I visit her sometimes when I'm in LA, although not as much anymore. I wish I could say that when I stand in front of her grave I only think about how much I miss her. But really? When I stand there, I'm thinking, *This could have been me*. Maybe that's wrong, but I can't help it. And sometimes I think, *This could have been Ash*.

Last time I saw Ash was on TV two years ago. June and I had been watching a Grey's Anatomy *rerun while doing our nails and then, out of nowhere, I heard a very familiar voice say, "Glad to be of service."*

I jerked my head up and there he was. Ash. He was wearing a bright orange vest, playing a clerk in a Home Depot commercial. He was still attractive but not in a way that could really turn heads. He smiled a little too broadly at the camera and I think I saw a tiny flicker of desperation in his eyes, but perhaps I imagined it. And then the camera moved on to the younger, perkier clerks demonstrating their customer service skills.

"Wow," June had said while giving me a sidelong glance. "I didn't know you found Home Depot commercials so captivating."

"I don't." I forced a little laugh and went back to doing my nails. "I'm not interested in Home Depot at all."

I have no doubt that Ash is unsatisfied with the state of his acting career, but at least he has a pulse. Most people in their thirties and forties will occasionally find themselves wondering what the friends they've lost contact with are doing today. But when you spend your youth partying the way I did, you mostly wonder if those long-lost friends are still alive. So many of them become fatalities of a war they didn't even know they were fighting.

But not me. I'm a deserter. I get to live. And *what a life*. For all intents and purposes, I'm a stepmom to a truly wonderful girl and my partner is the love of my life. How many people can say that?

Speaking of which, things are getting kind of crazy for Brad, too. He's now the right-hand man for San Francisco's DA, and while this DA was just reelected six months ago, there's some talk that he may not run again, in which case . . . well, Brad might run. I'm a little nervous about that. I mean, finding dirt on me would sort of be like finding sand on the beach. It's hard to miss. Plus I'm not exactly your prototypical political wife. Granted, my hair is no longer pink. It's still blond . . . with lavender highlights at the tips. Brad seems to think that my free-spirited style choices and rocker sensibility will be helpful to him, that if the voters saw he was married to me they would know he was not only hip, but also open-minded.

I'm not sure if that's a compliment.

Anyway, Brad says that if San Francisco can't handle having a DA who's married to a former phone sex worker with purple hair, we'll just move to Berkeley. And he keeps reminding me we have at least three and a half years to figure it all out.

And me? I am touring All. The. Time. It's *crazy*. If you're into indie music you probably know my name. And if you aren't, you won't . . . or at least that was true until about three months ago. I'm not sure how it happened, but I seem to have stumbled onto a hit. This song I wrote, "Try Again," is getting serious airplay, and all of a sudden *everybody* knows me. My incredibly low-budget music video currently stands at just over thirteen million hits two months after its release.

Can I say that one more time? *Thirteen million friggin' hits!*

Oh, and in case you're wondering, I do still swear, I'm just more selective about when I do it. But I'm getting off topic.

Thirteen million hits!

My manager thinks this could be the start of something huge. My music is being gobbled up on iTunes and added to everybody's Spotify playlist. Even my older songs are enjoying a resurgence. I would have been totally happy just being the "it" indie girl, queen of underground music and whatnot. That world was fine with me and I did pretty well. But this hit . . . well, it's like I'm realizing dreams

I had given up on years ago. I'm getting requests for interviews all the time. *Spin, Pitchfork,* and this morning I talked to *Rolling Stone*! That was *amazing* . . .

Until it wasn't.

Now, as June is off on a road trip with her girlfriends, Brad and I sit in the living room of our small but very expensive home in San Francisco's Sunset District listening to Brett Dennen sing "Only Want You" as we try to chart a path through the disaster zone that lies ahead.

"This was bound to happen, Mercy," he points out. He's only half out of his work clothes. Tie and shoes off, shirt on but open, belt and pants firmly in place. He sits next to me on our soft gray couch, ankle crossed over his knee, arm draped over the back of the sofa. His tone is casual, but I can see the concern in his eyes. And me? I'm huddled in the corner of the sofa, one knee drawn up to my chest while the other is stretched out so my toes can weave into the softness of the shaggy floor rug. Our Yorkshire terrier, Mammoth, is napping peacefully under the coffee table.

"No one has ever asked me about my name change before," I say quietly.

"It's an official document; when you became big inevitably someone was going to ask."

"When I became big?" I look up at him. Even after all these years, I'm a little in awe of how beautiful he is, how incredibly powerful. And yet all that beauty and power won't protect me from what's coming. "Brad, singers don't become big at my age! I can see forty from where I'm sitting!"

"You have years before forty, and you still look like you're in your twenties—"

"Yeah, well I'm old enough to know that years go by in seconds, and looking twenty-something is hardly impressive in this industry. I swear, I look at the new 'it' girls of pop and they all look like they're twelve! There was no way to predict that all of this would happen to my career!"

"*I* predicted it," Brad reminds me. "You're too good to go unnoticed forever. Anyway, it will definitely be up for public consumption if I ever get around to running for office." He sighs and runs his hand through his short hair as he contemplates the situation. "You know, Mercy," he says slowly, "I don't know that this is a big deal."

"Excuse me?" I ask loud enough to wake Mammoth, who pops up and trots over to me.

"You didn't do anything wrong," Brad continues. "Your father did. So what if that gets out. After what he did he deserves a little shaming."

I press my lips together as I pick up Mammoth, holding her against my shoulder. "It's not that simple," I mutter.

"Why not?" Brad asks, almost exasperated.

"Because I have a sister, that's why not!" I snap. "Because I've made a . . . a peace treaty with my past, and part of the deal is the past agrees not to haunt me as long as I agree to leave it the fuck alone!" Mammoth begins to squirm in my hands and I put her down and let her run.

Brad studies me for a long moment and then turns his eyes to the picture windows with a view of an overcast sky. "The other day I was talking to Mayor Donovan—"

"I swear to God, if you gave more money to his campaign fund—"

"When he was fifteen," he continues, refusing to let me get to him, "a group of boys dumped the entire contents of his backpack into a dumpster filled with rotting food and maggots."

"Oh God." I put my hand against my heart, wincing at the very idea of it. Even Mammoth looks a little grossed out.

"He had to crawl in just to get his things while the boys watched and laughed as he tried to keep the maggots off his skin."

"Seriously?" I curl into myself. "Where did he go to school, Nazi Germany?"

"You could say he got the last laugh," Brad says, his eyes now trained on me even as Mammoth tramples his foot. "He graduated from Yale, married a beautiful woman who loves him. And now he's the mayor of a major city. People say he has a political future. His life is good, great even, and yet he still told me this story. You know why he told me this story, Mercy?"

I bow my head, unsure if I want to hear the answer.

"Because that incident that happened forty years ago still shows up in his nightmares today," he says gently. "Because he still harbors fantasies of revenge on the boys who did that to him, boys who are no longer boys. There's something about the things that happen to us as children . . . they affect us differently and the memories don't go away even when we do our damnedest to ignore them. You can't tell your past not to haunt you, Mercy. You know that. The best you can do is decide not to be afraid of ghosts."

I continue to stare at the ground. "I can't do this, Brad," I whisper.

"You can," he says, reaching forward and taking my hand as he picks up Mammoth with the other. "You can, because this time you *are* going to let me help you."

"And what about Kasie?" I whisper. "She doesn't even know this ghost exists. Her entire childhood is going to be exposed as a lie and the whole thing is going to be hung out there for public consumption."

"We'll warn her," Brad assures me. "We'll do everything we can to prepare her. I'll find out where she is and . . . and you can talk to her."

I wince. I have no idea how this is gonna go down. How do you tell your sister that you're not dead after she's spent over fifteen years thinking you were? I mean, this is some *Days of Our Lives* shit! "Did I ever tell you that I crashed her college graduation?"

"You may have mentioned it."

"I was already living in Belgium at the time but I arranged a visit back to the States," I say, keeping my eyes on the ground. "I hid in the back row, wearing big sunglasses and baggy clothes to make sure no one recognized me. She graduated summa cum laude at *twenty*! She started college at *sixteen*!"

"She must have been very academic," Brad says impassively.

"It's so weird. I mean, I remember teaching her how to Vogue when she was three. She sucked at it, which made it more fun. Oh, and there was the time I taught her the lyrics to Right Said Fred's 'I'm Too Sexy.' That one didn't go over too well with Dad."

Brad laughs. "I bet not."

"I considered approaching her at the graduation but she was clearly doing so well without me and I . . . I chickened out." I lift my shoulders in an embarrassed little shrug. "I got scared." I finally pull my gaze away from the floor and look up at Brad and . . . oh, he's sitting there with his open shirt, our little terrier pressed up against his muscular chest, and he's looking at me with such love and such concern . . . If I saw this image on a poster I'd buy it and masturbate to it every night.

But he's not a poster.

And I'm going to let him help me this time. This man cradling our little puppy, he's going to help me, and oh my God am I going to need it. "I'm still scared," I say.

"I know," he says, still holding my hand. "And I'm here." He puts our dog down on the ground, and now I'm the one pulled to his chest as his arms encircle me. I curl up in his lap, the soles of my feet pressed into the sofa cushions as I bury my head in the nook of his neck, taking comfort in the way his hands move up and down my back. The music switches to Florence + the Machine's "Never Let Me Go." And when I lift my face to him he kisses me just as the music begins to soar. When he pulls away it's only by inches, and he glances to the speaker before giving me his eyes again. "Don't worry," he says, "I will never let you go."

I smile and kiss him again as his hand moves up my side, bunching my tank a little in his hand. His lips move to my neck, sucking lightly at the skin as his hand finds my breast and I press myself into him. *No matter what happens, I'm safe. He'll never let me go.*

I let one of my hands wander down, moving into his shirt as he gently pinches my nipple through the lace fabric. And then he pulls the tank off completely, supporting me as I lean back, letting his teeth graze the lace as his free hand moves to my inner thigh and then up between my legs, adding just the perfect amount of pressure, moving just so, and I let out a little moan as I let this feeling drown out everything else. The anxiety, the doubt, the traces of anger that still taint every childhood memory. And when he unbuttons my jeans and unzips them, touching me, finding me wet for him, I shudder, gently scraping my nails against the muscular swell of his pecs, down to his abs as I begin to writhe. He's using his teeth to pull down the lace bra, and now I feel the tip of his tongue against my skin as his fingers penetrate me.

I fumble with his belt, but my hands are clumsy and the feelings he's eliciting too intense for me to manage such an intricate task. As his thumb moves up to toy with that most sensitive little button, I cry out his name and he lifts his head from my breast so he can watch me, and I'm his to watch, to touch, to provoke with his ministrations of lust and love. It's all it takes to bring forth this first orgasm. Just his touching me, looking at me, loving me, all with his unique mix of ferocity and tenderness. Again I say his name as his fingers continue to stroke me, toy with me, drawing out my ecstasy.

And after this first wave of pleasure begins to calm, I make quick work of his belt. I straddle him, my knees pressing into the couch as I rip his shirt from him, buttons flying, before I lean down to kiss his chest, then rise just enough to drag my tongue along that tender bit of skin that sinks behind the collarbone as I pull the shirt off him entirely. He unhooks my bra with one hand.

Is it possible that he's really getting better looking every year, or has my vision been altered by my own growing love?

I get down on the ground, almost crushing our poor Yorkie, who is getting seriously freaked out. I pull off Brad's pants, then his boxer briefs, and oh, there he is, his erection reaching for me, wanting me . . . Brad will always want me. I take him in my hand and then slowly let my tongue trace the contours of him, feeling the little ridge of the tip before taking him fully in my mouth. His head falls back and he grips the back of the couch so that his arms are outstretched to either side, making himself completely open to me as I continue to slide my mouth up and down, one hand gripping his thigh, the other cupping him, feeling him, tasting him. He groans and it sounds both rough and musical, like a Joe Cocker love song.

And when he reaches down, touches my hair, I know it's time. Slowly I stand between his legs as he pulls down my jeans and panties, his fingers continuing their journey, touching each inch of skin as it's exposed to him. And I stand before him naked as his hands explore me, the small of my back, my waist, my thighs, touching, toying with my core as his other hand slides over my chest. And I slowly straddle him again, gripping his shoulders. But I don't lower myself onto him right away. For a moment I just look into his eyes as he gazes into mine, and then slowly I lower myself, until he's pressing against me, teasing my lips. "I love you," I whisper, and then I take him, pressing down onto him so that he enters me completely and then I'm so close to him, my hair falling over my shoulders so that the lavender tips touch his cheeks, blinding him to everything but me. Slowly I ride him as he grips my waist and adds his own power to my movements, pulling me into him with even greater ferocity every time I thrust against him. Then he reaches up with one hand, moving my hair behind my ear, and whispers, "Mercy."

And then with one swift movement he lifts me, and without losing our connection turns me on my back so he's on top. He holds my calf, bending my leg so he can go as deep as he likes and . . . oh, he does go deep. I'm clawing his back now, losing control as he kisses my hair, my neck, my shoulder, never letting up on his intense rhythm. Until I cry out again, my whole body shaking, and we roll, crashing down to the floor (once again missing the dog, thank you God). Now I'm on top again, but he lifts himself, leaning back on his hands as I press my breasts against his chest, grinding against him, taking control once again as I kiss him passionately, connecting myself to him in every way.

I tease him by pulling back just a little, so only the tip of his cock is inside me. Seeing the need in his eyes thrills me. And I continue to tease, thrusting shallow then deep, then moving in circular motions against him, stimulating new nerve endings until his bulging arms are trembling, overcome with *my* power, *my* love. That's when I take him in entirely, every inch, and the sensation is so intense he explodes inside of me, and as I feel him throbbing, pulsing inside my walls, that's enough to bring on one more orgasm for me, too. I collapse against him so he falls back and we lie on the floor, drenched in sweat and affection. I close my eyes, savoring this perfect moment.

And we do savor it for at least a minute or two, hearing nothing but our mingled breath and Moby singing on the stereo about what love should do. Neither of us moves . . . until the dog starts licking the bottom of my foot. I squeal and start giggling and Brad starts laughing . . .

. . . and then it really is perfect.

I'm safe. I'm with him. I can face these demons. I can face my sister. I just have to remember I have strength.

The strength of happiness. The strength of just being okay.

CHAPTER 44

❧

I T TAKES LESS than two days to find Kasie. She has her own
company now, some business consulting thing. Brad says that
from what he's found out it looks like a promising start-up, in business for less than a year. She used to work at the top global consulting firm in the country.

How different can the two of us *be*?

And that's one of the many reasons I can't get myself to just call
her up. I don't *know* Kasie. Not anymore. And everything that we've
found through Google . . . I don't relate to it. She graduated from
Harvard Business School. I didn't go to college. She used to be a
player in a major firm and now runs her own company in LA. I'm
a former pole dance instructor who sings in nightclubs for hipsters.
In every picture I can find of her she looks like she's ready to go on
a power lunch. I have purple hair. The only thing we have in common is that we both have been with our boyfriends for a significant
amount of time.

So I start there. I decide to contact her boyfriend first. Let him
tell me how best to broach the news. After all, he's someone who
must care about her and who *does* know her, someone who won't
feel beholden to our parents and will put Kasie's needs first. And
he'll be ready to support her when the shit hits the fan, just as Brad
is supporting me.

At least, I hope that's the deal. What if he's abusive or something?
What am I talking about, if he's abusive I'll just kill him. Surely one

murder will make up for all the years I've been negligent in my big-sister duties.

The man she's seeing is named Robert Dade, and he's one intimi-dating dude. Very attractive, fit, salt-and-pepper hair, founder and CEO of Maned Wolf, a company that provides security, Internet and otherwise, for some of the biggest corporations in the world. There are a slew of articles about him, in *Businessweek*, *Forbes*, the *Wall Street Journal*, and so on. He's a self-made billionaire who appears to be highly respected but not necessarily well loved. Even in his photos he looks . . . intense. But what's nice is that in his recent inter-views he never misses an opportunity to mention and praise Kasie.

I don't want to be the one to call. If I do I might be asked to ex-plain in detail why I want to see him, and I really don't want to do this over the phone. So I get my manager to call for me, hoping my newfound celebrity might be enough to get me in the door. And fortunately for me it is. Mr. Dade's assistant is a fan and she gets me in for the following week.

The wait is excruciating. I play and replay what I'm going to say. And then I pray to every God that has ever been worshipped ask-ing that the blogosphere doesn't blow up with this before I have a chance to tell Kasie in person. I go from chewing my nails, to cry-ing, to jumping up and down with excitement. Brad is a saint for putting up with my hysterics. He makes arrangements for June and his work so he can come down to LA with me. June is easy, she's seventeen and responsible. She can pretty much take care of herself. But work? The amount of juggling he has to do to get this time off is mind-boggling, and if possible it makes me love him even more. He doesn't have to come, after all. He won't be able to go to the meeting with Robert Dade, and I have no idea if he'll be able to meet Kasie. He's just going so he can hold my hand as much as possible. It's both excessive and totally necessary.

And then . . . it's time. We fly to LA the morning before the meeting, get an early check-in at The London, and get settled in our hotel room. I could have easily left Mammoth with June, who loves her, but what's the point of having a small dog if you don't drag her along with you? Anyway, she's perfectly happy toddling around the room as I have my nervous breakdown.

It's the kind of morning that makes me wish I still drank. I consider going out and buying some business attire for the meeting, but then decide against it. They should know what they're getting with me. I'll be myself. Well, I'll be myself on a low volume setting. I'm wearing dark skinny jeans and a loose gray top with a superwide boat neckline that slips around this way and that. It's longer in the back and has a sheer triangle inset that reveals the center of my back through dark gray gauze. That way if I get a little shaky he'll still be able to see that I do indeed have a spine. For accessories I settle for a few silver chains of various lengths and my mammoth earrings for luck.

"Keep your phone with you," Brad reminds me for the umpteenth time as we prepare to leave the room. "I'll just be in the café across the street. One call from you and I'm there in a heartbeat."

"Don't use clichés," I say absently as I put on my shoes; I've changed my mind about what shoes to wear about a thousand times now. Mammoth yips in agreement.

Brad laughs and kisses me on top of my head. "You're going to be just fine."

We take a cab there and then Brad goes to the café and I walk into the lion's den . . . or in this case, the wolf's den.

It's a dark mirrored building and the office is on the top floor. I'm escorted to Mr. Dade's reception area, where I'm presented to his receptionist. It's clearly not the same woman my manager set up the appointment with, because she doesn't have a clue as to who I am. In a way that's a relief. I don't know if I'm up for signing autographs right now. And yes, lately people have been asking for my autograph all the time. When my income catches up with my growing fame, I'll be great.

"Mr. Dade is ready for you," the receptionist says.

"Great." Finally I stand and wipe my now sweaty palms on my jeans. "What's your name again?"

"Sonya," the woman says with a cool smile. I get the feeling I'm being sized up. She reaches forward and opens the door to the office. I close my eyes for a moment, take a deep breath, and step in.

It's a *gorgeous* office. The view is almost better than the view from the roof deck of The London. Well appointed, stylish in a classic kind of way, although not exactly warm. And the man behind the desk is . . . um . . . quite the specimen.

He stands up, revealing about six feet of height and a physique that is actually more impressive in person than it was in pictures. Of course he's not bulked up and broad like Brad. He's got more of a lean-mean-killing-machine thing going on. He's wearing a suit that probably cost more than my car, and it's tailored to perfection. He's scary hot.

And I mean that literally. I'm scared to death of this guy. If I could go running from this room I would.

"Miss Raye," he says as he maneuvers around his mahogany desk and offers me his hand.

"Mr. Dade," I say in a surprisingly steady voice. Thank God I wiped the sweat off my palms before walking in here.

"I'm afraid there's been a mix-up," he says as he leads me to one of the chairs in front of his desk and then goes back to his seat. "Cheryl, the temporary employee who set up this appointment, should have informed you that I don't actually handle the accounts. I can make sure that one of our top executives takes on whatever security needs you may have."

It takes me a second or two to figure out what he's talking about. "Oh," I finally say once I get that he thinks I'm here for some sort of security bullshit. "Yeah, I'm not here for that," I correct him as I shift uncomfortably in my seat. I let my eyes wander around the room, taking in the leather sofa, the art on the wall, anything other than the man in front of me. And yet I have to do this thing. I take another deep breath. "I'm here for personal reasons."

"I see," he says coolly. "What personal matters could you have with a complete stranger? We haven't met before, have we?"

"Oh no," I say, shaking my head. *Say it, just say it!*

"If we haven't met, and you don't want to talk to me about business, what do you want to talk to me about?" he says. His irritation is showing now. His voice has gotten lower, his words just a little more clipped. He reminds me a little of a sexy Bond villain. I wonder if he'll shoot me.

I press my lips together, shift my position again, and then force myself to meet his eyes. "I'm here because . . . because . . ." *Come on, you can do this! Just one more deep breath and then spit it out!* He's looking more impatient and more menacing by the second. I exhale through pursed lips. "Sorry," I say weakly. "This is hard for me." *Oh my God, oh my God, oh my God how do I say this? I can't do this!*

Yes you can, says a little voice in my head that's slightly more reasonable. *You can because you are comfortable with who you are and you have the strength of Brad's love behind you. It's all you need.*

I straighten my posture and offer Mr. Dade a small, determined smile. "Okay, here it goes . . . I'mHereBecauseIHearYou'reDating-MySister."

I hold my breath and give him a second to divide the one long word I blurted out into nine separate ones. If anything, he looks more irritated than he did before. He is definitely going to shoot me.

"I'm afraid you heard wrong," he finally says as he makes a show of looking at the clock on the wall. "The woman I'm involved with only has one sister and she passed away some time ago."

"No she didn't," I say softly. I think the beating of my heart might actually be louder than my words.

His eyes sharply turn back to me. "Excuse me?"

"Melody didn't die," I say, forcing myself to speak slowly, clearly, and with the appropriate conviction. I roll my shoulders back, lift my chin, and give him a small, shaky smile. "I'm right here."

He stares at me for a long time. But this time he doesn't look irritated. I can tell he's taking me in, feature by feature, that he's thinking, perhaps calculating the age Melody should be, going over what he knows and what he doesn't. Whatever's going through his head, it must give my story some credence, because now the look on his face is one that can only be described as shocked.

"Maybe we should start again," I say. *You can do this!* "I was born Melody Fitzgerald, and I've been very much alive all my life." It's the first time in years that I've spoken my full birth name. It does not roll easily off the tongue. *Be professional about this! Speak his language so he understands.* "Now," I say in what I believe is the nasal diction of the 1 percent, "I'm hoping you can reacquaint me with my sister, Kasie. Will you do that, Mr. Dade?"

Again he just stares at me. I don't know this guy, but he doesn't seem like the type to ever be at a loss for words. Under other circumstances I'd be proud of myself for getting someone like him off balance. But the circumstances aren't different and I don't know what I'm supposed to do now. Should I keep talking? Should I wait for it all to sink in? If this were a soap we'd stare at each other meaningfully for another few seconds and then they'd cut to commercial. But I don't think Procter & Gamble is going to save me from this.

Slowly he rises from his seat, and I almost duck just in case this does go into Bond territory. But instead he crosses the room, stops in front of a lovely dark wooden cabinet, and opens it, pulling out what looks like a very expensive bottle of Scotch and a glass. He leans down, and I realize that the bottom part of the cabinet holds a minifridge, or maybe it's a freezer, because he has ice in there, and it's one of those big round ice cubes that people use for their Scotch these days.

"Would you like to join me?" he asks as he pours himself a glass.

"I don't drink."

He turns to me, bottle still in his hand. "You can't be Melody."

"Oh, so she *has* talked about me," I say with a wry smile. "I used to drink. I did lines, chased the dragon, candy flipped, et cetera, et cetera, yada yada yada. Okay? I did it all. But I don't anymore; that's probably why I'm *not* dead. But please," I say, waving toward his drink, "don't let me stop you, because if there was ever a situation that called for alcohol it's this one. So I'm counting on you to tie one on for both of us."

He stands there glaring at me, his drink tightly gripped in his hand. "Why did you do it?" he asks in a low voice.

"Do what?"

"Fake your own death," he growls. "Do you have any idea what you have done to Kasie? Or are you too selfish to care?"

"I . . . I didn't fake anything," I say, holding up my hands as if to block the accusations. "I didn't *do* anything other than ask my father for help when I needed it. But he decided he was tired of helping me, so he wrote up my obituary and had some loser working at a second-rate local rag print it for everyone in his backward little town to see. Yeah, I've had to lug the weight of that little deception around for my entire adult life, but it's not actually *my* lie."

He's still staring at me. He hasn't touched his drink, but he hasn't put it down, either. "You expect me to believe that your parents declared their oldest daughter dead out of, what, spite? And then they have spent a lifetime lying to their youngest daughter about it? Letting her grieve?"

I swallow hard and glance away. "Look, I'm sure that when you see my parents through Kasie's eyes, my claims seem ridiculous. She had a totally different relationship with them than I did. Kasie was the child they wanted me to be and, I don't know, I guess they've been good to her, because she seems to be doing well enough. They probably didn't have to try to control her the way they did me. I mean with Kasie, the hole was round, she was round, and so everything just fit. *I*, on the other hand, was the fucked-up peg, you know, the square one that doesn't fit into the motherfucking hole." Mr. Dade doesn't say anything, but he appears to be thinking as I hunch down in my chair. "Sorry," I mutter. "Sometimes I swear." He still doesn't say anything, and his silence is completely unnerving. I rush on. "Look, it may not seem like it from the outside, but my parents are controlling. Particularly my father. I didn't fit into the picture that he wanted his family life to be, and he couldn't handle

it, so he just sort of bumped me out of the picture, and I guess killing me in print seemed like the easiest way to do that."

More silence. This time I look down at my hands, wondering at
what point I should just get up and leave.

"Why now?" he finally asks.

"Hmm? Oh, you mean why am I coming to tell her about all this
now?" I bite down on my lower lip and shrug. "I'm a singer, and one
of my songs is sort of blowing up right now. I'm doing interviews,
journalists are beginning to dig . . ." I shake my head. "I can't keep
this under wraps for much longer. One way or another, the story's
gonna get out there."

And *again* he doesn't respond! God, I have never known anyone
who can use *not talking* as effectively as this. He could bring men to
their knees with his silence.

I let out an audible sigh. This was obviously a mistake. I should
have gone to Kasie directly. In fact, I will go to Kasie directly. This
man is not going to help me.

"I think it would be best if you met her at my home," he says out
of the blue.

I look up, surprised. "You . . . you mean . . ."

"If at any point during this meeting she tells you to leave or I tell
you to leave, I strongly suggest you do it, and swiftly," he continues.

"When is this meeting?" I whisper.

"Tonight. Seven o'clock. Sonya will give you the directions on
your way out. Do not be late."

CHAPTER 45

✿

I MANAGE TO WALK out of there and across the street to Brad, but as soon as I reach him my legs go out beneath me and he literally has to catch me before I crumple. I think I notice at least one person snapping a picture of me with their cell, as he helps me into a chair at his table. Great, so I'll probably be seeing that on Perez Hilton in the next twenty-four hours. But I push the thought out of my mind as I tell Brad everything about my meeting with Robert Dade, from what was said to the whole Bond villain vibe.

"Wow," Brad says, pausing only to stop a waitress so he can order me a cup of coffee. "Does that mean your sister is going to be a bad Bond girl? Like Pussy Galore or Xenia Onatopp?"

"Okay, let's stop with the Bond talk before you start having sexual fantasies about my sister."

Brad chuckles and shakes his head. "She couldn't hold a candle to you. No one could."

"No clichés," I tease with a smile. I press my hands flat against the blond wood of the table to keep them from shaking. There's a pleasant buzz of voices in this room that calms me. The place is pretty full, bustling even, just the way a café should be.

"Are you excited at all?" Brad asks, leaning forward. "You're about to meet your sister for the first time in, what has it been, sixteen years? No, it's been over twenty, right? Because by the time that asshole declared you dead, you hadn't seen her in about five years."

Brad never refers to my father as, well, my father. *Asshole* is his go-to term. *SOB* is a distant second. *Scumbag*, *dirtbag*, and *prick* all tie for third. I actually like that he's angry on my behalf. I don't know that anyone ever really has been before.

"So tell me," Brad presses, "are you excited to see her?"

My smile wavers and I shrug.

"Mercy?" he asks carefully as my coffee is placed in front of me. "What's going on?"

"It's just . . ." I hesitate, and then find the words to forge forward. "Okay, I've always loved Kasie," I say. "I've loved her almost as much as I've hated her."

"Ah." He sits back in his seat and waits for me to continue.

"She was *perfect*," I whisper. "She was sleeping through the night by, like, day *two*, while I apparently kept the whole neighborhood up with my screaming for the first two years of my life. And as she grew older, she just got *more* perfect. She was pretty, soft-spoken, studious, and well behaved. She never colored outside the lines, literally or figuratively. I'm serious, her coloring books were like friggin' art portfolios! And . . . and the more perfect she became, the worse things got between my father and me, because now he had proof. It wasn't him, it was *me*. All *me*."

Brad folds his hands on the table as he considers this. "You told me Kasie never saw your father hit you. That he was able to hide a lot of the abuse from her, both physical and emotional."

"Yeah, so?" I mutter bitterly as I glare at the table.

"Maybe," Brad says carefully, "there were things you weren't seeing, too."

It's an incredibly simple and obvious statement, and yet for a brief second, it's like the whole world slams to a screeching halt. *Is it possible . . . wait, how has this never occurred to me before?*

Because I was just so wrapped up in my own chaos, that's how. I never imagined there might be a whole other mountain of chaos under the same roof as me, one that was being hidden in a different room.

"It was a long time ago," Brad goes on as my mind frantically whirls through the possibilities. "You were a kid; part of the time you were on drugs, and even in the best of circumstances memory is notoriously unreliable. Trust me, as someone who works in the district attorney's office and has to deal with eyewitness testimony all the time, I know all about the weak and deceptive nature of memory. Talk to your sister. See what she has to say. Give her the benefit of the doubt. Hopefully she'll do the same."

"And if she doesn't?" I ask meekly. "What if she doesn't even hear me out?"

Now it's Brad who shrugs. "Pick up the phone," he suggests. "Call a reporter. Let her read the truth in *Rolling Stone*."

I glance toward the table where that girl took my picture. She's with her friend and they keep glancing over here and whispering despite the fact that she's clear across the room. I couldn't hear her if I tried. I look around and I note another table, a couple this time, and they, too, are trying—and failing—to discreetly look over at me.

My privacy is tottering on the edge of a cliff. I need to wrap up my loose ends now before that privacy falls and is swallowed up by the sea of tabloid fodder.

AS IT TURNS out, Robert Dade lives very close to The London. He's a little up in the hills, but honestly, I could walk. I don't, of course. I take a town car provided by the hotel and Brad promises to keep his phone in his hand, ready to run to my rescue.

The house looks nice. It's at the end of a cul-de-sac with a reasonably impressive driveway. The gates have been left open to me. I get out of the town car and take a deep breath before ringing the doorbell.

Mr. Dade greets me, and as soon as he opens the door I realize that the front of the house is deceptive. This place is built on a hill, so what looks nice on the outside looks fucking amazing once you step inside. It's all done in dark wood and feels a little masculine to me.

He looks me over with just a touch of disdain. "You brought your dog," he notes, making it clear he doesn't approve of the decision.

"She's an emotional support Yorkie," I explain as I clutch Mammoth to my chest. When he doesn't reply I say, "Would you have preferred it if I brought my emotional support boyfriend? Because I can make that happen with one phone call. Totally up to you."

I think I see Mr. Dade's mouth twitch, like he might have been about to, God forbid, smile. But of course he manages to suppress the urge as he finally leads me in.

Mammoth wriggles in my grip, perhaps disturbed by the unusually loud beating of my heart. "She's in here," he says, and then leads me into the living room.

And yes, there she is. She's wearing a black slim-cut pantsuit, her blazer perfectly tailored and cinched at the waist with a black belt with sleek gold metal detailing in the front. I *think* she's wearing a camisole under the blazer, but it's hard to tell, because all I see is a diving neckline and a fair amount of skin. Her long, wavy dark hair is loose around her shoulders. It's a sexy look, and every bit as intimidating as the look of her partner.

As she stands there, her hands are covering her stomach, as if protecting herself from an oncoming blow to the gut, and her eyes are wide with confusion and fear. She must have been prepped for the meeting and yet, really, how do you prepare for *this*?

So we just stand there, about ten feet apart, sizing each other up. I try to steady my breathing, petting Mammoth with a rapid urgency that she is clearly not enjoying.

"Is it really you?" she finally says, her voice strained.

I nod and bite down on my lower lip. *What do I say?* I look around the room, desperately hoping for some clue as to how to proceed. Finally I turn my eyes back to her and I see it. She's shaking. She's shaking just as I am. She's my sister, and she's scared.

"I'm sorry," I whisper. "Oh my God, I'm so sorry."

A small sob escapes her lips, and immediately I put Mammoth down and in seconds we have our arms wrapped around each other,

her tears on my neck and mine on hers. I'm vaguely aware of Mr. Dade quietly leaving the room.

We stay this way for a minute or two, and then she abruptly yanks herself away. "How could they do this?" she hisses, still trembling. "How could they be this *evil*?"

I look away for a moment. I have to admit, I've never really seen this in terms of good and evil. Rather, I've seen it as something that falls in the realm of really fucked-up. "I was," I say after a deep breath, "a difficult child."

"So they decided to have you declared dead?" Kasie asks with both incredulity and venom. "I wasn't even allowed to mourn you. They just told me you had . . ." Her voice fades off and she lifts her fingers to her mouth before turning around and walking to the window. A window that has one of the most impressive views I have ever seen. The whole city sparkles beneath us, and I sense that if it were daytime I would be able to see the ocean. Mammoth is weaving around and under antique furniture and over rugs that probably cost upward of ten thousand dollars.

Dear God, Mammoth, please don't pee on the ten-thousand-dollar rug.

But most of my focus is on Kasie. I sense that she is about to say something that she thinks will hurt my feelings. "Kasie," I say as I step up behind her. "Whatever it is they said, if you want to say it, say it. I mean, they already declared me dead, it doesn't really get worse than that."

"They said you overdosed," she says, her eyes still on the view.

"Oh, that," I say with a nod. "Yeah, I read that in the obituary."

Kasie turns to face me. "You read the obituary?"

I give her a wry smile. "He sent it to me, wanted to make sure I got the point."

She stares at me in horror. "How could they do it?" she asks quietly again.

"I don't know, Kasie, maybe . . ." I hesitate, and then decide to blurt it out. "Maybe they were trying to protect you."

"Protect *me*?" Kasie snaps. "Please tell me that's a joke."

"Look, you were a good kid. You were doing all the things you were supposed to do. And I . . . wasn't a good influence, let's leave it at that. So yeah, maybe this was a way of making sure you never tried to seek me out so I couldn't screw you up. Maybe they thought they were doing something good."

Kasie lets out a humorless laugh. "Our parents never had the slightest interest in protecting me," she says in a low voice. "They loved me like people love their Rolexes. I was some type of status symbol for them. It was always, *always* about their image. They used your death to control me. If I ever did anything they didn't fully approve of, I was accused of turning into you. They convinced me that your problem was lack of self-control and that if I didn't practice perfect discipline in my own life I would spin out of control, too. That I would suffer your fate and they would . . ." She gasps as something new dawns on her. "They would erase me," she whispers. "After they told me you died, they never spoke of you. Not once. It never really did feel like you were dead, just that you were erased. They erased you."

"Um, yeah, no." I cross my arms across my chest. "They may have erased me from *you* and from their lives, but I'm right here living loud, with purple hair and a microphone. They did not erase *me*."

"I'm sorry, I didn't mean to insult you—"

"Why would I be insulted? Just because apparently your worst nightmare was turning into me? No really, I'll take that as a compliment."

"Melody—"

"Mercy," I correct, holding up my hand to stop her. And then I wince at my own defensiveness. Mammoth comes up and tramples my toes, and with a sigh I bend down to pick her up. "I'm not insulted," I say quietly. "Not by you, anyway. I'm just . . . this brings up a lot of feelings for me."

She nods, regarding me carefully now.

"Really," I assure her. When she doesn't answer I gesture toward the window. "It's a gorgeous view."

She smiles, appreciating the change in topic. "The lights look like sparkling jewels, don't they?" she asks as she turns back to the window.

"Like diamonds," I say softly. "Do you remember when I told you I was going to be a jewel thief?"

She lets out a light laugh. "You said you would steal the highest-quality stones, stones that sparkled without even the benefit of light. And you said you wouldn't even sell the jewels you stole, you'd just hide them in the attic."

"And eventually I would have so many that when I went up into the dark ol' attic it would be sparkling like the night sky. Like the ground was covered with stars."

"Yes," Kasie says quietly. "I remember that." We stand there in silence for a moment or two as Mammoth nestles against my chest, soothed by the now normal pace of my internal drumbeat. "I've missed you," Kasie whispers.

Another tear slides down my cheek. "I've missed you, too."

She turns, gestures to the leather sofa. "Come, let's sit down. Let's get to know each other."

❧

CHAPTER 46

AND WE DO get to know each other. We talk for hours that night, days later we talk on the phone, and we just keep it up. I find out that I actually really like her. She's smart, stylish, and she doesn't take shit from anybody . . . although apparently she used to. As it turns out, our parents did a number on her, too, but that's her story to tell, not mine. Oh, and how do I know we're *really* related? We're both exhibitionists. Seriously. I mean, okay, she hasn't danced in a cage or anything, and she hasn't danced on a bar, but she has done things on a bar that would make *me* blush! Totally crazy shit.

I even get to know Robert, who, as it turns out, isn't so scary once you get to know him . . . unless you get on his bad side, in which case he's *terrifying*. He's planning on proposing to Kasie. He has a ring and everything although she doesn't know it. He's just holding off until she has more time to digest the shock of . . . well, me. Also he's apparently putting a lot of thought into how to stage the proposal. He hasn't shared any details with me but now that I'm beginning to understand how Robert operates, I'm assuming he'll hire Yo-Yo Ma to give them a private performance on Air Force One while the president of the United States is serving them champagne.

What's really interesting is that Brad and Robert actually grow close. As it turns out, they're both gamblers—yes, I still call poker gambling, although Robert plays blackjack, too. In fact, Robert is a high roller. When he goes to Vegas he gets the best suite, tickets to the best shows, and the kind of VIP treatment that even I don't have access to, and that's saying something, because as my music continues to take off I'm finding that I'm getting more and more perks and privileges. My video is now up to over ninety-eight million hits.

I even take June to the premiere of the latest Channing Tatum movie. She's had a huge crush on him since *Magic Mike*—girlfriend has *taste*. And yes, she gets to meet him. Brad tells me that if I let her hook up with a single actor while we're in LA he will leave me. He's joking . . . sort of.

I consider changing my name back to Melody but at this point it seems silly. Everyone on earth, including all of my fans, knows me as Mercy. And as I once told a former boyfriend, a name is just the first gift your parents give you.

I really don't want *anything* from my parents.

For a while Kasie wanted us to confront our parents together, but here's the thing: I don't need to. Those feelings of wanting, needing my father's approval? They're finally gone. Just gone. I'm now old enough and wise enough to know that the approval of a fucked-up jackass doesn't mean a lot. And really, that's the nice thing about having your parents declare you dead. After that, you have the perfect excuse to avoid dealing with them for the rest of time. Of course, if Kasie had insisted, I would have gone with her for emotional support, but she decided she doesn't need it. So no, I didn't confront my parents. But I did send them the issue of *Rolling Stone* in which I was interviewed and revealed the full details of what they did. I attached a note to it saying:

> *Not quite as attention grabbing as an obituary, but I like it.*
>   *Cheers!*
>
>   *Your Most-Definitely-Alive Daughter,*
>   *Melody*

Maybe that was petty, but oh my God, did I love sending that.
And now, just a few months later, we're all here in Vegas together,

at the Venetian. Robert booked us all amazing suites. He also found us a beautiful space in one of the courtyards of the hotel for my wedding to Brad.

I'm standing here now, under the domed roof of a glass gazebo. Rose petals line the aisle, Kasie and June are by my side, and Robert and one of Brad's poker buddies are at his. The sky is blue, just like the highlights in my hair. I hold Brad's hands as he looks into my eyes. June holds Mammoth in her arms—I carried her in lieu of a bouquet, and no, I won't be throwing her. I'm wearing a tea-length strapless gown with a full tulle skirt and an ivory silk sash around my waist, and major floral embroidery all around the bustier, because if you're gonna do it, do it right. And as the minister asks Brad if he will take this woman, for better or worse, in sickness and in health, regardless of hair color, until death do us part, he says *I do*.

There is nothing more amazing than the realization of a perfect moment.

ACKNOWLEDGMENTS

THANKS TO MY EDITOR, Adam Wilson, for being so patient with me as I continued to dramatically change, add, and delete scenes after turning in this manuscript. Seriously. I am so incredibly lucky to continue to have you on my team after all these years!

And thanks to my truly amazing agent, MacKenzie Fraser-Bub, who always provides wonderful guidance, advice, and assistance whenever I need it.

Special thanks to my sister-in-law, Shona Sullivan, for catching so many of my typos and spelling errors—you saved me!

Huge thank-you to my husband, Rod. Although this book is a complete work of fiction, it's true that some of the things Brad says to Mercy when he calls to tell her she's the love of his life are things my husband said to me. Rod, you continue to be my inspiration, and I'm so very thankful that we found our way back to one another.

Last but absolutely not least, I want to thank Brad Witmer, who won the honor of having his name used as the male lead in this book after he placed a winning bid in a charity auction that benefited my son's school. Brad, if I did my job well, when women hear the name Brad Witmer, they will think of a man smart enough to be president, loving enough to be an amazing parent, and well equipped enough to make it as a porn star. Use your new fame wisely.